MW01644265

In dedication to my children,

may you always find your way

Table of Contents

1. The Dream 1
2. Rogue Vampire Hunter 27
3. Smoke and Mirrors 79
4. The Owl 101
5. Silver and Wolfsbane 137
6. Change 177
7. The Uktena 203
8. The Wendigo 237
9. La Lechuza 251
10. Taken 279
11. War 319
12. The Medicine Wheel 373

Chapter 1

The Dream

Mags

The desert night was a canvas of heat and rebellion, a barren expanse where the air shimmered with anticipation. Cacti stood as silent sentinels under the bruised sky. The last sliver of the sun dipped below the horizon.

It was time.

The primal energy built around me as I laced up my black leather moccasins. The soft material hugged my feet with familiar comfort. My friends were nearby, a ragtag group of misfits and dreamers, all drawn together by the siren call of anarchy in the form of hard punk rock music.

The makeshift stage was nothing more than a battered pickup truck, its bed piled with speakers that crackled with promise. The first chords screamed into the night, electrifying the atmosphere.

My heart pounded in sync with the thundering bass, a wild rhythm that urged me forward. I plunged into the mosh pit, a writhing sea of bodies that collided and surged with unrestrained abandon.

The desert air was a furnace, every breath a searing gust that burned my lungs. Yet, in this cauldron of chaos, I felt alive, every nerve ending sparking with raw exhilaration. I pushed against the bodies around me, a primal dance of aggression and camaraderie.

The music was a living entity that filled me with an uncontainable energy.

A shove from the girl behind me brought me face-to-face with a guy whose shoulder was bleeding. The crimson streak was narrow and straight as if someone had put it there with the fine bristles of a paintbrush. I stumbled, and the metallic tang of blood brushed my lips. For a heartbeat, time froze. The taste was electric—a jolt that shot through me like lightning.

My senses sharpened. I could feel his heartbeat, a steady drum that matched the pulsing music. An inexplicable hunger unfurled within me—the urge to bite was all-consuming. I could hear the river of blood beneath his skin. My vision narrowed, focusing on the pulse at his neck, every instinct screaming at me to give in.

Then, cutting through the delirious haze, a piercing screech split the night. My head snapped up, and I saw it—a giant white barn owl, ghostly against the dark sky. Its wings spread wide as it hovered above the mosh pit, eyes glowing with otherworldly light.

The owl's call resonated deep within my soul. The primal hunger ebbed, replaced by a profound sense of awe.

As it swooped low, its feathers brushed against my cheek, cool and soft like a whisper. The supernatural encounter grounded me, pulling me back from the brink of something I could not fully comprehend. The music still roared around me, but now it felt different—less like a call to chaos and more like a celebration of life's fierce, unyielding beauty.

Suddenly, I was alone in a dark cave. My ears started ringing tremulously as the last remnants of the punk song ebbed down. Silence filled the air around me and all I had were my thoughts to remind me that I was even alive.

Then, I woke up.

I hurriedly scribbled down the fragments of my dream before I woke up too much and lost it. The details were already slipping away, but I knew this one was important. I had only meant to take a short nap before heading out to a party, but this dream . . . it was different. It was vivid, surreal even. The kind that clung to the edges of your mind long after waking.

I finished writing it out, transforming it into an essay that I had forgotten I needed to complete for school. Creative Writing—my favorite class. The assignment had been to focus on imagery, and this dream gave me more than enough material to work with. The scenes, the sounds, the emotions—they were all so intense. But then again, I was no stranger to intensity. Since being diagnosed with bipolar disorder years ago, my life has been a constant swing between extremes. It seemed almost cruel that even in my sleep, I couldn't escape it. My soul screamed in vivid colors, whether awake or asleep.

Still, I have a finished essay now. Mrs. C would probably love it. I could already imagine her reading through it, looking for the adjectives and metaphors I'd packed in like ammunition. She always told us to focus on description, on making our writing feel like our words were alive. Well,

I'd given her everything I had. If she didn't give me a good grade, I wasn't sure I had any more synonyms to throw at her.

I yanked the paper from my old Brother typewriter and placed it neatly in my binder. It felt satisfying to have something completed, even if it was just a school assignment. Then, with that out of the way, I stepped back into the real world.

The night was still young, and there was energy in the air. I could feel it buzzing as I hopped on my bike and pedaled toward the outskirts of town. The Freaks, a local punk band, had already finished their set, and though I had missed them, it didn't really matter. What mattered was catching up with my friends. A large group of us had planned to escape the dusty streets of our town and head to the Pit, our spot in the desert where no one could bother us. No parents, no rules—just us, the stars, and the open sky.

I rode my bike down the familiar back roads, the wind rushing past me. The Pit was a secret, a place that only we knew how to find. It was wild and free, much like the people I hung out with.

"Yo!" Called out the baddest looking punk girl named Cell. She pulled up next to me in her fathers old beater truck. Manda was with her smoking a clove. The smell of cloves was always a delight but I didn't care about smoking.

"Get in girl before you mess up that pretty skirt of yours." Muttered Manda with no emotion, she was a blond version of Wednesday Addams. I threw my bike in the back and squeezed in.

"I thought you were getting a ride with Raybans?" asked

Cell.

I just sighed and stared out the window.

"Trouble in paradise aye?" She asked as she took off down the dirt road causing a bellow of dust to fly behind us.

"I wouldn't call it trouble." I said finally. "I'm just bored."

"Boys are boring!" Manda spat out. And we laughed, as we blasted music on the way there.

The Pit was always at the same designated area out in the desert near our small town. There was only one dirt road that led back into town from there. It was ugly, barren, flat and in between two large farm plots but it was our paradise. We didn't need much—just some drinks, the desert, and each other.

The moon hung high in the sky, full and luminous, reigning like a queen over the night. She cast her silver glow over everything, making the world look softer, almost magical. A few dark, brooding clouds drifted across the sky, wrapping around her like swirling robes.

Tonight, something felt different—a strange pang settled in my gut as I gazed up at the moon. Tonight felt sharp and restless as if the air itself was vibrating with tension. Was this going to be one of those *sharp note* nights? The kind where everything inside me buzzed with untamed energy, where I hungered for release, for something wild. Images flooded my mind—raw, primal fantasies of a time when humans were closer to beasts, when they hunted with their hands and tore into raw meat. Out of nowhere, I craved a steak, which was odd for me. Red meat wasn't something I usually ate, thanks to my foster mom's affinity for cheap cuts. But tonight, everything felt heightened, different.

I felt hyper and uncontrolled—my own type of wild card.

I started to headbag in the car as if I were in some mosh pit. As we neared the gang we saw Moniker's car, the other blond Wednesday Addams goth and we started to holler at her to squeeze into the truck with us.

"I got some shrooms!" Giggled Moniker as she sat down and opened her little coffin purse and started handing them out. I refused as always. Something about constantly feeling on the verge of a mania made me fear myself. I felt I only had only so much control over my emotions. But I did drink.

"You're not gonna have any?" Moniker said as if I just insulted her.

"You know I only prefer the drink." I answered back in a deeper than usual voice.

"Yeah yeah Dracula, more for us then." She giggled as she took another mouthful.

It was definitely a sharp note night. My emotions were jagged, electric, and on edge. That's how I always described my feelings: as musical notes. When I was on a flat note, I was calm and serene but also a bit too lethargic. I could sit for hours, reading, painting, sewing—content to ignore the world around me. My lows weren't depression; they were just a kind of numb peace. A middle C was just about normal. This is when I was favorably medicated. But the sharp notes, those were dangerous. They were on the verge of something more, something manic and out of control.

I've only been truly manic a few times in my life. The first was when I was thirteen. I didn't sleep for four days, hallucinating until a faint, mumbled voice started speaking in my head. I ended up in the hospital after that, diagnosed and medicated. Lithium became my new companion.

The second time came a few years later, during my sophomore year of high school. That time was more of a blur, not as terrifying, but still intense enough to have my dose adjusted. I've been fine since. Until tonight.

This was different, though. This sharp note didn't build up slowly like the others. It hit me the second I stepped outside, like waking a monster that had been caged for too long. A wild, brutal urge surged through me, a call to the untamed. And for once, I didn't want to stop it. I wanted to let it out.

I wanted to run through the canyons, dance like Kokopelli to my own rhythm, and feel the earth beneath my feet. I wanted to scream into the wind like a banshee, free and unrestrained. I wanted to be *me*—the real me, unfiltered and raw.

"Light it, fuckface!" Romel yelled, snapping me out of my thoughts. He was directing his usual venom at Ralph, who was standing lazily by the bonfire pile. The others had been tossing wood onto the growing heap, getting ready for our desert ritual.

"Fine, damn it," Ralph grumbled, pulling out a lighter from his worn leather jacket. He crouched down and set the bonfire ablaze.

"Raaaaaaalphhhh!" Romel teased, pretending to vomit as he mimicked the sound of Ralph's name. Ralph, of course, just rolled his eyes, accustomed to the teasing. That nickname had stuck with him ever since he'd puked at one of our past bonfires.

A smile tugged at my lips. This was my crew—feral teenagers, as wild and untamed as the desert around us. Skater punks, goth kids, metalheads, grunge girls, all of us outcasts. We didn't belong anywhere except with each other, and no one could fuck with one of us without fucking with us all.

Even when I was in my middle C note state, I loved their chaotic energy. They were anarchists in the best way, and even when I pretended to be annoyed by their antics, I knew I couldn't live without them. Most of them saw me as a serious, quiet girl—thanks to the Lithium that kept me in check. But inside, I was a force of nature held back by a dam. And tonight, that dam was about to break.

The fire roared to life, massive and hungry. The flames licked the sky, dancing wildly as we howled and cheered. Someone turned on a radio and The Exploited blasted through the night, their raw punk energy fueling us. We moshed like we always did, jumping and slamming into each other without a care. Guys and girls together, it didn't matter. I was too drunk on cheap Strawberry Hill and adrenaline to feel the jabs and shoves.

The ground felt soft under my feet as I pounded my new black knee-high moccasins into the earth. One of my friends had gifted them to me, and this was the first time I'd worn them. At first, I felt naked without my usual Doc Martens—those boots were like armor. But the moccasins made me feel like I could dance in ways I never had before. I stomped and spun, mimicking the Native American dances I'd seen at local powwows, feeling more alive than I had in ages.

But beneath the dancing, the drinking, and the fire, there was something deeper. That wild, primal urge still tugged at me. The moon's call wasn't peaceful tonight—it was fierce, demanding. And the sharp note inside me screamed for release.

I didn't know what the dances were called or what they meant. I only knew that it felt good to move like that, to let the rhythm take over my body. Growing up, I never learned much about my mother's culture. She died when I was too young to remember, and all I knew was that I was half Native, from a tribe near New Mexico. I had never visited her reservation and never learned the language. After she was gone, I was swallowed up by the foster system, bouncing from home to home.

Now, I told myself, I was my own person. My identity didn't need to fit neatly into anyone's box. Mixed, not mixed—it didn't matter. I didn't need to prove my roots to anyone, least of all myself. So, if I danced in a strange way, that was just what I did. A few of my Native friends told me I was "doing it wrong," that my dancing was "too angry" or "too masculine," whatever that meant. It didn't bother me. I've always done what I wanted. Breaking taboos? It seemed like the one thing I was truly good at.

As I stomped and spun around the fire, I felt the ground beneath me soften, almost like it was bending to the weight of my movement. The fire cracked and popped, sending sparks up into the night, and I happened to look up again, drawn once more to the moon. But this time, instead of the round, glowing satellite I expected to see, there was a large white night bird.

I froze mid-dance, my heart thudding in my chest. A powerful sense of déjà vu washed over me. High above, a giant white owl circled in a slow, deliberate pattern. It was mesmerizing; I couldn't tear my eyes away. Its screech sent shockwaves through my bones, rattling me to my core. It was the same as in my dream.

I exhaled slowly, unable to look away. Just then, I felt a push from behind—one of my drunk friends had stumbled into me, sending me stumbling toward the fire.

Time seemed to stretch out then, with everything slowing down to a crawl. The heat of the flames licked at my skin, and for a second, it felt like I was about to become some kind of gothic sacrifice to that owl spirit above. But my mind clicked into a strange clarity, and I moved without thinking, without hesitation. I twisted my body to the left, spinning in a perfect 360 over the flames as if I'd been training for this moment my entire life. It was instinctual, almost inhuman. I landed on my feet, my breath ragged.

Then, out of nowhere, a howl erupted from my throat. A raw, guttural sound that I had never made before, something wild and primal, like it had come from a place deep inside me I didn't even know existed. The howl tore through the empty desert, echoing against the night sky, dissipating as fast as it had come—like shadows fleeing from light. I could feel its vibrations, slow and deliberate as if I were giving birth to some kind of ethereal monster from the depths of my soul. When the sound finally faded, I was left with a strange pang of sadness, a deep emptiness that settled in my chest like a hollow weight.

I stood there, frozen, waiting for something—anything—to answer. I had half-expected to hear a howl in return, as if what I had let out had been a call—a call to *what* or *who*, I didn't know. But there was only silence, and the feeling left me hollow. Lonely.

And then, just like that, the dam inside me didn't break—in fact, it snapped shut. That sharp note that had been building inside me, the wild energy that had been brewing all night, flattened in an instant, like a guitar string snapping mid-song. My mind went quiet, eerily calm, as if the storm had passed without warning.

The sounds of laughter and music slowly came back into focus. My friends were still there, throwing back drinks and shouting into the night. It was like I had been yanked out of the twilight zone and pulled back into reality so fast it left me dizzy. I stood there, feeling the cool desert air on my skin.

"Mags!" Raybans yelled from across the bonfire, waving me over. He was perched on one of the haystacks from the nearby farm, leaning back like a king surveying his kingdom. Haystacks were everywhere in this place. Even though we lived in the desert, the farms around here grew alfalfa for the animals and many other things. The desert sun blessed this land with two growing seasons for that stuff. Because of it, my hometown always smelled like burnt hay and cow patties. A real delight if you ask me.

Raybans had tossed his studded leather jacket over the bale, probably to keep the straw from poking through the holes in his ripped jeans. I wondered if he had heard me howl.

Did I actually howl? I couldn't tell if it had been real or just something in my head.

The fire crackled behind me, an ignored backup singer to the chaos around it. My friends were still laughing and messing around as if nothing had happened. But I couldn't stop thinking about that giant owl. It had disappeared, and I half-wondered if I had imagined it. It was too big to be a normal owl, and the screech was still ringing in my ears. It hadn't been an ordinary sound; it had felt like a wake-up call, but for what? I didn't know.

I made my way over to Raybans, sitting down next to him to try to clear my head. I had so many questions swimming through my mind but no answers. And the more I tried to push those thoughts away, the more they burrowed into me, making it harder to enjoy the party. I wasn't feeling it anymore. The thrill of the night had dulled.

As I sat there, I realized I was starting to sober up. It was one of my personal rules—never touch drugs, not with my bipolar disorder, but occasionally, I would drink when my friends could sneak alcohol for me. Tonight, I'd had my fill, thanks to the friendly neighborhood transient folks who were always willing to buy booze for some extra cash. But now, as the buzz faded, I was left wondering if any of what I had experienced had actually happened.

No one seemed to notice me jumping over the fire, no one heard me howl, and no one saw the giant owl. Everyone was too lost in their drunken haze, but it was odd. *How could no one have seen that?*

I looked around. Everything seemed normal. Shae was making out with Joe, some randos were fighting over the last beer they owned, and a few other couples were sneaking off to make out behind the haystacks. No one seemed to care or even notice that I had performed some kind of freak show.

Maybe it didn't really happen, I thought. Lately, I'd been hearing and seeing strange things, and I couldn't shake the feeling that something was off. Maybe it was time to adjust my meds. Or maybe I was drinking too much? Either way, I could write a book about all the weird things that had been happening to me recently.

Then, out of nowhere, Raybans leaned over and kissed me. It wasn't unusual—we've made out before—but tonight, I wasn't in the mood. I pulled back, looking at him, his drunk smile plastered across his face, and felt nothing. He wasn't my boyfriend, and I didn't owe him anything. The attraction that had been there just . . . wasn't anymore.

Without a word, I stood up, grabbed my bike from the back of Cells' truck, and walked away.

"Ah, come on!" he yelled after me.

"I gotta go!" I yelled back.

"I thought we were gonna hang out afterward." He said trying to catch up to me on my bike.

"I think we're done!" I stated as I looked back at him with a serious look. Raybans just threw his hands in the air and had a mini conniption.

He was supposed to give me a ride home, his home where we usually made out at, but I needed to be alone. I started pedaling down the dirt road, away from the music, the fire, and our break up. The sound of the party, once so loud and full of adrenaline, was now just an annoyance, and I pedaled faster to escape it.

My metabolism had always been fast, and alcohol never stayed in my system long. I was usually sober within an hour, which made drinking almost pointless. I remembered one night, riding my bike home after curfew, when a cop stopped me. He breathalyzed me at random, but by then, I was already clean. So tonight, as I pedaled down the dirt road, I knew the alcohol was already gone from my body.

"What the hell is going on?" I muttered to myself as I turned a corner. I laughed bitterly, shaking my head. My mind was playing tricks on me again, blending reality with dreams.

I can't move like that, I thought. *I've never been in gymnastics, and I sure as hell am not a cheerleader.*

Standing up on the pedals, I pushed myself harder, the dirt road turning into pavement as I flew down the empty street. The wind whipped through my hair, and for a moment, I felt like I could fly. My long, dark hair trailed behind me like a cape, and for the first time that night, without a high note, I felt weightless. Free.

I sat back down on my bike, gripping the handlebars tightly, and pulled back, lifting the front tire off the road. At that moment, it wasn't just a bike beneath me—it was a powerful black stallion rearing up on its hind legs, a wild creature ready to charge into battle. I imagined myself riding bareback, a Native warrior on the verge of war. Yeah, I know—I'm kind of weird. Most of my friends were skaters, but I was different. I loved my BMX. I'd spent countless hours babysitting rowdy kids just to save enough money for this bike. It was mine in a way nothing else was.

I was protective of my things; as a foster child who bounced from house to house when I was little, you tend to appreciate getting to keep some familiarity around you.

But to call me a tomboy would be wrong—at least on the inside. What I loved most was being unpredictable, breaking the rules, and doing things people thought I couldn't and wouldn't do. One of those things was riding my bike in long skirts.

Tonight was no exception. The skirt I wore was one I'd made myself: a black ribbon skirt I'd crafted from a thrift store sari. I'd sewn three red ribbons around the bottom in a Native ribbon fashion, using leftover Christmas decorations my foster mom had too much of. Red was my favorite color, a sign of strength, of rebellion. I called it my "enigma" skirt—a nod to the fact that Columbus couldn't tell the difference between Natives and Indians from Asia. The irony wasn't lost on me.

My hair whipped behind me as I pedaled, the length a quiet tribute to my Native heritage. Though I never grew up with my mother's culture, I still felt more Native than European. It was a bigger part of my soul.

I never knew my father. The social worker told me he was European and that had gotten my pale skin from him, but that was all I knew. He had fled back to Europe when my mother passed, leaving me in the care of the State, my life handed over to the foster system. The Bureau of Indian Affairs had stepped in, giving me access to certain benefits, but I had always been a mystery, a mix of two worlds I didn't fully belong to.

At night, I would braid my hair into two thick braids so it would be wavy the next day. During the day, I let it fall loose, but by the end of the day, it was straight as a rod, a simple nod to the past I had never fully known.

Was my father still alive? Who knew? He was "unreachable," they said, and I had stopped wondering about him a long time ago. My life had been shaped by the desert, by the town that smelled of burnt hay and cow patties, and by the solitude I found riding my bike through the streets late at night.

As I pedaled, I let the music from my headphones take over. My portable CD player was bulky, but I didn't care. I had burned my favorite songs onto a disc—tracks from Requiem in White and Dead Can Dance. They were completely different styles of music, but both held the same haunting, dark energy that I craved. I was a Goth to my core, though no one in this dusty little town seemed to understand what Goth was. It was 1994, but here, it felt people were stuck in the 1950s.

Tonight, I wore a long-sleeved, black silk blouse—sheer, with a tank underneath to cover what I didn't want exposed. The shirt looked like something a hippie would wear, but because it was black, it was mine and, therefore, Goth. My makeup was pale, almost ghostly, with dark red lipstick that bordered on black. A smudge of red eyeshadow curved like a half-moon over the creases of my eyelids.

The eerie, ethereal voices from my headphones wrapped around my thoughts, calling out to something deep inside me. I swerved slightly, moving my body in rhythm with the music as I coasted down the empty streets of my sleeping town. For a moment, everything felt right. Then I felt it—a strange sensation, like eyes watching me. I stopped abruptly, my heart skipping a beat as a shiver ran down my spine. I pulled my headphones off and scanned my surroundings.

The street was empty, but there was something—*someone*—nearby. I could feel it. And then, faintly, I smelled it. Rot. Something dead, decaying. The scent drifted toward me from behind, and a wave of unease washed over me.

My instincts kicked in. This town might have been small, but it was dangerous, especially at night. Living so close to the border, I had seen enough crimes during my nocturnal bike rides to know when to get out of Dodge. I peddled hard to escape the smell, my pulse racing as I pushed myself toward home. I wasn't far now.

Home. A place I had never considered safe. But right now, it was safer than these streets.

I cut through Bucklin Park, hoping to shave off a few minutes from my ride. That's when I heard it.

Something—*someone*—following me howled.

The sound made me stop dead in my tracks, my breath catching as I perked my ear toward it. The howl—deep, menacing, like the one I had summoned earlier, but darker, more dangerous. It wasn't a mournful or lonely cry, but if danger had a sound, this would be it. A siren call of something far more threatening than anything I had ever known.

I whipped my head around, scanning the park. Nothing. No dog, no coyote. Just scattered trees standing on their small grassy man-made mounds—poor attempts by the city to fool the people of El Centro into thinking this desert wasn't a barren wasteland that stank of manure and sunburnt hay. Normally, I felt safe here at the park, but something about this moment made the air feel thin, suffocating. Yet when you start to question your own sanity, maybe nowhere is safe.

"Hello?" I whispered, my voice trembling. The park felt unnaturally quiet. I could still hear the faint thrum of music leaking from my headphones, so I quickly turned it off, wanting to hear everything—anything—that might clue me into what was happening. Usually, there'd be desert owls hooting or the restless honking of geese by the pond as I sped past on my bike. Now, not even the wind moved through the trees. It was like the entire world had stopped breathing.

Then, I heard it again—but this time, it wasn't a howl. It was a voice.

"Hello, Little Red," a deep, almost guttural voice said, cutting through the silence like a knife. The words came from above and to my right. I spun around, heart racing.

There he was.

He leaped down from a tree, crashing to the ground with a thunderous snap, bringing a thick branch with him. The crack of wood echoed, sending shockwaves through me and making my skin crawl. I couldn't move. My feet were frozen as my mind struggled to catch up with what was happening.

As he stood before me, his form came into focus. My legs started moving toward him as if on autopilot while my mind screamed at me to stop. Everything slowed down. The scene around me burned itself into my memory—his tall, looming figure, the shattered branch at his feet, his sharp, predatory smile.

He grinned at me, his fangs glinting in the dim light. Long, exposed fangs. Not human. He couldn't be. But what terrified me most wasn't the fangs or his unnerving presence—it was how calm I felt. My fear wasn't directed at him. It was directed at this entire surreal moment.

He stood tall, much taller than anyone I had ever seen around here, with striking red eyes that gleamed like a demon's. Was he a Vampire? *Dracula?* The thought would've made me laugh if it weren't for the icy dread settling in my stomach. All goths fantasized about Vampires, sure, but I had never truly believed in them. Not until now.

He wore a large, worn black hat that looked somewhere between a cowboy hat and a top hat, its brim casting shadows over half his face. He tilted his head, as if studying me—or allowing me to study him. His long, dark brown hair framed his angular face like curtains, and he was brawny, his chin strong and clean-shaven. He was cloaked in a long black coat, his jeans worn and faded. But then that smell hit me—the same rotting stench from earlier, creeping into the air around us. It was suffocating, like the aftermath of a forest fire, where everything is charred and dead.

I realized, with a sudden jolt of panic, that my feet were still moving—carrying me closer to him, away from the path, toward the tree and the shattered branch at his feet. Was I going to end up like that tree, broken and discarded?

I blinked, forcing myself to stop. Three feet away from him,

I stood, my last step landing on the crushed leaves from the fallen branch. The scent of eucalyptus filled the air as the oils bled through my moccasins, mixing with the stench of decay.

For a moment, we stood in silence. I could hear the slow, steady rhythm of my breathing and the thudding of my heart in my chest. His glowing red eyes bored into me, and I felt the weight of his presence pressing down on me like a heavy, invisible force.

He didn't move. Neither did I.

The wind picked up, rustling the leaves around us, but the park remained eerily quiet. It was as if the world was holding its breath, waiting for something to happen. My heart raced, and yet there was a strange calm settling over me, an acceptance of whatever this was. It felt like the moment before the storm, the brief pause before everything changed.

A strange strength surged up from deep inside me then, like a power I didn't know I had. Adrenaline, stupidity—who knew? But I held his gaze, unflinching, and watched as his grin quickly turned into a look of disapproval. Whatever spell he'd cast over me was slipping, and he didn't like it.

"What do you want?" I asked, my voice flat, emotionless, robotic.

I noticed him sniffing the air, slowly at first. Then I realized—he hadn't been breathing at all until I stopped in front of him. Now, he was taking in deep, slow breaths, tasting the air around us like a predator testing its prey.

Suddenly, his movements stopped, and those red, piercing eyes locked onto mine again. His voice boomed when he spoke, even though it was no more than a whisper. "What *are* you?" he asked, his tone both bewildered and commanding.

The question caught me off guard because it was exactly what I wanted to know about *him*. Why would he ask such a silly question?

"You smell like a wolf . . . or the undead . . . like both?!" he hissed at me, his words dripping with confusion. I could hear a slight accent, but I couldn't place it. Then, just as quickly as his anger had surfaced, his face softened, and those red eyes shifted into a warm, human amber brown. For a moment, I saw the man beneath the monster. He was beautiful in that instant, startlingly so.

"MATE!" he suddenly declared, the word slicing through the silence like a blade.

And just like that, the strange bravery I had summoned vanished. My knees felt weak, and my heart thudded in my chest. Suddenly, I was just a lost teenager from a forgotten desert town, someone who didn't know where she was going, didn't know what would happen after high school and didn't know what to do if her foster mom kicked her out, like she'd threatened so many times since turning eighteen. I felt vulnerable, exposed—like dinner.

Something about his words stirred an ache deep inside me, a feeling I didn't understand. But I didn't move. If there was one thing my past had taught me—through abusive foster homes and run-ins with the law—it was how to keep my emotions hidden. No matter how scared or confused I was, I knew how to stay stoic, calm, and unbothered. My face remained a mask, my breathing steady, as if nothing unusual was happening. It was a learned instinctive reaction to stress.

But then, he surprised me. He smiled softly and made a slight motion to inch closer but stopped himself. I couldn't stop staring at his lips—full, inviting, and impossibly close. Some part of me wanted to reach out, to touch them, to kiss them. But I didn't move.

What was *wrong* with me? Shoot, is this how seduction works for Vampires?

He bowed suddenly, tipping his hat over his chest, revealing his full face and hair. He looked nervous, a stark contrast from earlier.

"Excuse me, m'lady . . . Good evening. My name is Andy." he said, his voice gentler now. His whole demeanor had shifted, and he looked less . . . dangerous. More human. Like someone else entirely.

He paused, waiting for me to offer my name. But I couldn't speak. My mind was racing, my thoughts spinning in circles. I just stared at him, unable to form a single word.

After a long silence, he spoke again, his voice cautious.

"You are a hybrid. Excuse me, but I've never seen one who has lived to adulthood," he said, pausing. "You're half Werewolf, half Vampire," he continued, speaking slowly, as if he couldn't quite believe it himself. "A Vaewolf."

His eyes scanned me, waiting for a response, but I still couldn't speak. All I could do was blink, my shoulders relaxing slightly under his gaze.

"And the last time I saw one like you . . . was a few hundred years ago," he said with a sly smile. But then something changed. Panic flashed across his face, and he quickly looked away. What had spooked *him*?

Before I could react, he stepped behind the tree he had jumped from, and just like that—he was gone. Vanished.

I didn't need to look behind the tree to know he had disappeared. The stench, the eerie feeling, everything that had accompanied his presence was gone. The park came back to life. Ducks quacked, geese honked, and the frogs in the nearby pond croaked in unison. The wind picked up, rustling the leaves, and the world returned to normal. But I wasn't quite normal.

I fell to my knees, gasping for air, realizing I had been holding my breath for what felt like an eternity. My body was trembling, adrenaline still coursing through me. Goosebumps covered my skin, and sweat pooled under my arms. I wanted to cry, to scream, to release everything I was feeling—but I didn't.

I grabbed my bike and rode home in a daze, barely noticing the streets as they blurred past me. When I reached the house, I snuck in through the back door, the one I always left unlocked. This time, I made sure to lock it behind me. I stumbled into the bathroom and awkwardly got into the shower, fully clothed.

The hot water rushed over me, washing away the grime but not the confusion. I peeled off my layers and dumped them unceremoniously into the hamper.

After drying off, I stood in front of the foggy bathroom mirror, a towel wrapped around my head, ready to start my nightly routine. I surmised that this night was just a small manic night and decided best to just forget about it.

I wiped away the steam to the mirror, revealing my face—but what stared back at me wasn't my image.

Two glowing red eyes, bright as fire, looked out from my reflection.

I jumped back, my heart pounding in my chest. I almost slammed into the wall, but the towel around my head cushioned the blow. I couldn't tear my gaze from the mirror. I blinked, hoping the eyes would vanish, but they didn't.

They glowed, even in the fully lit bathroom, burning into me like the eyes of a banshee.

What the hell was happening to me?

I yanked the towel from my head and frantically wiped the mirror, hoping—praying—that there was some stupid red smudge or trick of the light causing the reflection. Then I rubbed my face with the towel, thinking it was left-over red eyeshadow.

But there was nothing. The glass was clean, and my reflection stared back at me with wide, bewildered eyes. My damp black hair clung to my heart-shaped face, sticking to my skin like cold fingers. I suddenly felt exposed. My arms reflexively pulled the towel tighter around my body, covering myself. When I dared to look up again, the glowing red eyes were gone. Just my own face, pale and shaken, looked back at me.

"What in the fucking fuck?" I muttered, the words tasting bitter as they left my lips. My voice sounded foreign in the small, steamy bathroom. I stared at myself a while longer, scanning every inch of my reflection, trying to convince myself that I wasn't losing my mind.

Once I was somewhat satisfied that I wasn't seeing things, I hastily applied my night creams, my fingers trembling as they moved across my skin. The usual ritual—so calming on any other night—did nothing to soothe me now. After braiding my hair, I slipped into bed, my mind still racing in all directions.

I couldn't stop thinking about the man from the park. His face, his voice, the way he had appeared out of nowhere. No matter how hard I tried to push the memory away, it kept creeping back like a shadow.

And the worst part? I wanted to see him again. As much as I wanted to deny it, I needed to find him. I needed answers. If he was real and not some hallucination or trick of my overworked mind, I needed him to return the peace he had stolen from me.

I needed him.

I cringed at the thought, disgusted with myself. *What is wrong with me?* I felt like some needy, lovesick girl—a far cry from the independent rebel I prided myself on being.

How could I be so drawn to him? The pull. The need.

Whatever it was, I hated myself for it.

What had he called me? A hybrid—half Werewolf, half Vampire? The words echoed in my mind, twisting and turning, refusing to let go. Andy. His name rolled around in my head like an unanswered question. The name was such a common name. Nothing I pictured a monster having.

What was *he*? A Vampire? A Werewolf? Or was he both, just like he claimed I was? I remembered the howl—the way it mirrored mine but was somehow deeper, darker. Could he be like me? No, wait. *I'm not like that.* I'm not any of those things, I reminded myself, trying to push the absurd thoughts away. This was crazy—*I* was crazy. Had to be.

I sighed, sinking deeper into my bed, letting the mattress cradle my weary body. "Well, this is it, Mags," I muttered aloud to myself, my voice barely above a whisper. "You're officially looney tunes."

I rolled onto my side, making sure my damp braids were pulled away from my head so they wouldn't break as I slept. I closed my eyes, determined to leave the madness of the night behind me, to bury the strangeness in the silence of sleep.

But just as I began to drift off, a voice pierced through the darkness—a voice clear and strong, as if it was right beside me.

No, Magdalena. You are definitely not crazy. I am your wolf, Luz. I'm so glad you're finally able to hear me.

I shot up in bed, my body shaking with shock as a scream tore from my throat. The sound rang through the house like an emergency siren. Suddenly, any resolve that I had succumbed to my anxieties.

Luz? My wolf?

My heart pounded against my ribcage, my breath coming in ragged gasps as I frantically looked around the room, expecting to see someone—*something*—there. But there was nothing. Just the quiet hum of the house, the soft rustle of the curtains in the breeze.

I clutched my chest, trying to steady myself. "What . . . the . . . hell," I whispered, my voice barely audible.

But deep down, something clicked into place. Something ancient, something primal. *Luz.* The name echoed in my mind, and though I wanted to reject it, part of me knew—deep down—that it was true. This wasn't just in my head. Something had changed tonight, and there was no going back.

I wasn't alone anymore.

Chapter 2

Rogue Vampire Hunter

Andy

I can't believe you just let her get away! Growled Ash in anguish at me.

"Relax!" I replied out loud. "It's not that simple." Since becoming a rogue, I had wandered this world searching only for a way to regain my alpha status. Ways to become stronger so that I could one day return to the motherland, regain my father's stolen throne, and rid myself of this rogue life for good.

It was a lonely and silent road, but I succumbed to it because I had no choice. I had no desire for a mate either. Well, at least I had thought so, until tonight.

Ash made me follow our mate from a safe distance. He wanted to see where she lived and thus "protect" her from all the ghouls and goblins of this world, even if we ourselves were one of those monsters.

I was thankful for my wolf, for Ash. He kept my mind sharp when so many rogues grew insane after a time. Some rogues have even been known to remain trapped in wolf form for so long when cast out of their pack that they could no longer shift back—losing their humanity altogether because they could not deal with the pain of being a lone wolf or rogue. It made them insane.

I, for the most part, am able to partially control when I shift. Being born with alpha blood made this so. Normally, it was as if two souls lived inside a rogue, and because they were packless, they were disconnected. Sometimes, the disconnect would be so severe that the man and wolf could not even speak to each other.

I could control when I shifted, hear his thoughts, and picture him in my brain, but once I did shift, my mind usually went to sleep. My wolf had full control, and I was at his mercy to allow me access again to my body. He's always returned me unharmed.

On rare occasions, he could partially take control if I allowed it, and he could look through my eyes like he did tonight while getting a good look at our mate, but I am always able to hold him back if we were not fully shifted. Likewise, I could see through his eyes as a wolf, but the amount of energy that was required always took a toll on us afterwards. So I rarely did so.

I trusted him, and he trusted me, but I did not give him full access unless I truly needed him. I would not allow myself to give up control like that. Rogues were the cryptic monsters of the old and new worlds.

They became myths, labeled as fairytales and monsters of the night. They were usually completely feral and dangerous. I never failed to take one out when our paths crossed, but only if they initiated contact, which was not very often.

So, for self-preservation and to deal with the loneliness of being rogue, I always replied to Ash out loud. I look crazy talking to myself, but then again, no eyes ever see me. I have become a master at being invisible, at being alone. I held onto my humanity like an anchor, never wanting to join the rogue rank of monster.

No feral rogue could ever claim the title of alpha. Blood alone wasn't enough. Without a pack, alpha powers are meaningless—just an empty title. I had alpha blood, sure, but I needed more than that. I had to be strong in both worlds—human and wolf—to reclaim what was rightfully mine. My father's pack was mine to lead, but first, I had to take it back from my uncle, Regis. And that was going to require some cunning.

Werebreeds functioned in a patriarchal society and with a royalty-type lineage, unlike our allies, the Skin Shifters. Skin shifters did not have royal customs and were a matriarchal society, but we were allies just the same.

As for my pack, it had been usurped by my uncle, Regis. He had gone mad, driven by ambition and jealousy. He killed my parents with poison during the sacred harvest meal. As they enjoyed the fruits of their labor, savoring the warmth and camaraderie of the evening, the undetectable poison had struck.

The poison seeped into their veins, a silent, deadly betrayer. How he managed to conceal its scent is beyond me. I was barely thirteen years old at the time, and it had happened almost two hundred years ago, but the memory is still sharp in my mind.

From my perch on the rafters of the Great Hall, I could see the entire room, the flickering torchlight casting long shadows on the faces of the adults below. I had watched them conduct business, dreaming of the day I would join them, receive my wolf, and become an alpha like my father. Children were not allowed at these functions in those days. I already had his alpha genes; it was just a matter of time before my wolf would come and my birthright could be claimed. So I did what any curious child would do: I spied on them from a hidden spot intermingled with the leather drapes and wooden rafters in the ceiling.

Suddenly, one by one, I saw the distorted faces of my father's betas and gammas begin to grope for air. They stood up from their feast, gasping, coughing, and casting their eyes wide with terror. Foam bubbled at their mouths and their bodies convulsed as the poison took hold.

My parents stood and watched in horror, their regal bearing crumbling in the face of such a sudden and cruel death. Their elaborate white winter furs, adorned with jewels from the sacred mountains, seemed grotesquely out of place amidst the chaos. The room, once filled with the warmth of laughter and light, was now overshadowed by darkness and dread.

Just then, my coward of an uncle rose from his seat. He looked to be the only one around not suffering from the same attack. His eyes gleamed with twisted triumph as he approached my parents, who, too, had suddenly started to feel the sting of whatever poison was in their food.

"It's over Bayan!" Regis yelled out at my father. "The Thunderwolves are mine now!"

Before I could jump down from the rafter to help them, Regis pulled out a silver-laced sword. In one swift, brutal motion, he sliced both their heads off. Blood sprayed across the tent, a macabre display that seemed to hang in the air, freezing time in a tableau of horror.

My mother's horrified expression still shone on her face from her detached head as it fell and rolled then came to a stop in front of me. Her eyes, once so full of life and love, were now frozen in a mask of terror. I couldn't move. I was shaking violently.

It was at that moment I knew that my wolf had come, forced early from its sleeping den to rise and protect my family.

I could feel the energy vortex rising from the ground. It slammed right into my gut and forced me to hunch over in pain.

The full moon hung low in the sky. It peeked at the scene through the open, vented leathers that acted as a window. In my pain and rush of adrenaline, I pictured the moon calling to me as if it were a person. The light cast an eerie silver glow over the chaotic scene. She was an active witness to this horror and seemed to beckon my wolf forward.

I stood there, paralyzed by the sight of my parents' lifeless bodies, their faces contorted in agony. The smell of fear mixed with the metallic scent of blood lingered in the air. Then, as if a veil had been lifted, I could suddenly smell the poison.

Wolfsbane, but there was also something else I was not familiar with. My heart pounded in my chest, a drumbeat of terror, and suddenly, a rage consumed me, overtaking the fear I once felt. Then, all I could see was red.

My uncle Regis, his eyes cold and triumphant, loomed over my parents bodies, his sword dripping with blood. The royal furs he wore were splattered with crimson, a grotesque parody of the power he had stolen.

As Regis turned his gaze towards me, a sinister smile curled his lips.

"You're next," he sneered, his voice dripping with malice. The fury froze me in place. I could feel my body respond as if the fury itself fed it, but it was only starting to transform.

He had awoken my wolf's appetite for destruction.

I felt a surge of adrenaline, the primal instinct to survive, explode within me. My vision blurred, the world tilting as my body began to tremble uncontrollably. A type of low rumble escaped through my mouth and I knew I was bearing elongated fangs at him.

Another searing pain shot through me, starting in my gut and spreading outward. It was as if a volcano had erupted within and molten lava was flowing through my veins. The sudden change from ice to fire caused me to double over. I clutched my stomach, the agony twisting and contorting my body. My bones began to shift, the sound of cracking and popping echoing in my ears like the sound of a thousand fir trees being brought down.

My skin was on fire—the heat radiating from every pore. I fell to my knees, gasping for breath, my mind a whirlwind of pain coupled with an overwhelming desire for destruction. I was going to rip him limb from limb. The monster in me was yearning to taste his heart.

"No...not if I could help it." I managed to growl at him. He simply looked down at me in disdain. He seemed to be enjoying my pain and yet disgusted by it at the same time.

I had seen first shifts before and they were not usually this fierce, not for a royal. But coupled with impending death, my wolf seemed hell-bent on shifting quickly, and he didn't care if it went "smoothly" for me. He was protecting my life.

The energy vortex that had been dormant within me until now surged upward, slamming into my core once again with a force that stole my breath away. I could feel it, the wild, untamed power of the wolf rising from its slumber. My vision sharpened, colors became more vibrant, every detail etched in stark clarity. My senses heightened. The scent of blood and poison was overpowering, but the sound of my uncle's laughter was a cruel symphony. It made my wolf hate him even more.

I growled a low, menacing sound that rumbled deep in my chest. I could feel the new presence within me; his consciousness born within, just like the moon from moments before who had become a real entity in mind. My wolf was now true and also had a soul. And though separate from me, he was a part of me, I was also a new creature.

I bared my teeth, sharp and gleaming, ready to fight for my life, for my parents, for my pack, even though I was still in transition. Only moments away from being so.

Regis stood there, looking at me with looming eyes. His dark blond hair, plaited back in braids away from his coarsely chiseled face, exposed all his emotions. He stood there with hate in his gleaming blue eyes but did not move, only watched.

This is not how our pack settled claims for the throne. There had to be a ceremony and a public spar that usually lasted days. He was taking it by cheating! He was a coward, but I sensed he didn't think so. He did not want to honor our ways.

As I was close to feeling the change complete, something hit me hard on the back of my head. I heard faint laughter coming from Regis and his helper, who had hit me from behind as I lay there next to my beautiful mother's black curls.

My vision faded to black and I slowly succumbed to the darkness as all the pain from the transition expired. I could feel myself sink back into my human form. My wolf, never having had a chance to fully emerge, was now locked in an eternal battle to keep me alert and alive from a dark place inside my mind.

Stay alive.

He beckoned from the recesses with a deep and rough voice both primal and commanding. Then, as if a candle was extinguished, the whole world went black.

When I awoke, I was being carried by unknown arms and deposited like trash on the permafrost outside with many other bodies of wolves next to me. I was naked from having torn my clothes as I shifted but still so numb that I didn't feel the cold. I was barely a teen. I had never known betrayal or distrust. So, part of me wanted to beg this man for help, while the wolf in me wanted to tear his head off.

My eyes unintentionally fluttered at the man who had carried me out. Though my vision was blurred, I strained to examine his face. He knew I was still alive. He wasn't from our pack. That much, I could tell. From what I could smell, he was a Skin Shifter, not a wolf.

He had a bald head and earrings made from human incisors, root and all, that pierced his ears like daggers. In his nose hung a bone from a human finger, but on his head were feathers of birds with vibrant colors worn like a crown—red, orange, and green birds that were not native to my land. He had large, piercing black eyes and sharp teeth. His face was smudged with white and black ash that made his cockeyed smile look even more sinister. His image will forever be tattooed on my mind.

Witch.

He sneered as if he could sense my thoughts. He placed one large, thin hand over my heart and chanted something in a language I was not familiar with. It, too, was covered with soot and ash markings.

Then the pain came again, an intense headache that felt like my head was about to explode. I tried to wiggle out of his arms, but I had no strength. My nose must have started bleeding because he reached up towards my face and wiped at the blood; he then used the same two fingers to spread my blood over his forehead and over his eyes, downward, in two linear strokes.

I have no words for what he did, but somehow, through magic, he cast me out of my tribe before I was awake enough to attempt to mind-link the rest of my pack that was still alive.

He had managed to banish me, and he was not my father, the alpha, nor was he even a wolf! Only alphas could cast out a member from the pack. He banished me from my own father's tribe using a foreign language and then threw me on the ground to suffer the pain alone, in the ghastly cold in a wolfless, fragile young human body.

I felt my wolf leave me then. The banishment hurt me more than any final blow he could have used to end me. I knew that my newborn wolf had borne the majority of the pain from it, for I felt his spirit dissipate like a smoke from a candle being blown out. I didn't know at the time if he would ever return. So, for a second, I thought that whatever that man did, whatever magic that Witch cast on me, had killed him.

He left me there, on the bank of what is now called the Volga River in Siberia. That is where my clan, the Thunderwolves, are from, having wandered away from Turtle Island many years ago during the great migration and settling there. They had lived and breathed there for centuries. But now, within one single night, my rightful legacy was stolen.

I called out to my nameless wolf several times once that man had left me for dead. But there was no sound, nothing from him. And I could not shift. Though he remained silent, a glimmer of hope sparked in me as I noticed my senses had remained heightened and started to heal from the blow on the back of my head.

"Wolf! Come back!" I tried to yell, though it was barely a whisper. "Come back!" I kept muttering.

He must have gone into hibernation to heal, I thought. I could barely feel him but he was there! He had protected me from the brunt of the blow to the head and the rejection! I just prayed that I was right and that the Witch did not kill him. Being cast out, I knew then that I was a rogue, but I didn't realize the disconnect would be so sudden.

With this slight bit of hope, I pushed on, alone without his warmth or companionship, without my pack or mind-linking ability to reach out to the rest of my family. I thought for a second that the man might change his mind and return to finish what he had started, so I hurried as fast as my little frame could in the permafrost.

I ran until I found a little fishing boat. I climbed in and rowed south with the current until I was far from my home. I used an old fishing net and a tattered piece of leather from an old sail to piece together a makeshift loincloth and cloak to keep me somewhat covered.

A storm started to brew the moment I got on the boat, and I could hear horrific thunder drumming up in the sky, followed by the largest and most frightening lightning hitting the ground in the direction of my pack house. Dark clouds sprouted above the skies as if born from the wings of the Thunderbird himself. But these were not life-giving clouds; it was as if a curse was being cast down from the heavens. I could smell ozone in the air, but it did not rain.

I was thankful for the wind that carried my little boat further and further away.

Whatever magic that Witch was up to, I knew I had to escape so I could come back and avenge my family once I was strong enough to do so.

Witches should know better than to go against the natural order of things, Ash replied in response to my memories.

For my people, a Witch is anyone who uses bad medicine. A part of me secretly hoped that Regis didn't do what he did willingly but was under some kind of spell or curse. The truth is, I feel that he had bewitched himself with power and greed. The attack seemed too personal.

"Something tells me we will be seeing that Witch again soon," I replied to Ash. This strange desert, the mountains, and the air seemed to hold memories of this Witch. But why and how, I did not know.

I sense some of his dark energy too. I agree we will most likely see him again. Best be ready. Ash responded in a serious manner. He is and will always be a warrior first.

"What about our mate?" I asked, almost teasing him. I couldn't imagine my wolf leaving his new obsession to train for combat of a new kind. And if he could smack me he would. I sensed his annoyance and it made me smirk.

She and our pack are the reasons why I am the way I am. To protect and defend. What good is a warrior if there is nothing to fight for? He said, appearing stoic in my head.

"And what about love? Is it worth giving up your life's mission?" I asked poking the bear further. My mission, of course, was reclaiming my throne. But I was met with stubborn silence.

Once out of my territory, I narrowly escaped rogues and rogue hunters traveling down that icy river. The gravity of the situation suddenly dawned on me: Because I was now a rogue, I had the reek of death on me—the curse of rejection. As long as I stayed on the boat over the water, my scent was untraceable. I kept my head down throughout most of that journey. I didn't stop for anything until I was far enough away.

Days passed without food or water, and when the river ended, I traveled West, stealing horses from sleepy meadows and only traveling at night. I didn't dare hunt or light a fire for fear of being caught. The lingering remnant of my hibernating wolf kept me strong. I didn't see many rogues here. But there were other things. Things whose scent was just as bad as a rogue's and more intense.

Catching another boat in the Black Sea, I traveled even further west until I finally stopped on land once again. The scent of these new creatures on this land became even more intense than my own.

Vampires.

So many Vampires. I had entered Romania—their den. This was where I chose to stop running.

My survival instinct kicked in again. It was kill or be killed in this land. But this time, I had no wolf to transform into, nor a pack. I was a rogue, and my wolf was still in hibernation. I needed to find a way to arm myself. I needed silver.

It was no longer safe to travel at night. During the day, I hunted venison for sustenance and Vampires for their weapons and clothing.

Feeling nostalgic?

"Yes, actually," I replied. "Something about this Vaewolf is taking me back. I hadn't thought about these years since we

left."

Well, this Vaewolf is our mate. Nothing like those memories.

Nonetheless, she had awakened my Vampire-hunting memories. Wolves didn't like to reflect. Not unless it was about a kill or something of that nature. It was this tactic that had brought me out of depression for my lost family and pack. Ash kept me facing forward, even during his hibernation. The initial shift had already bonded him to me, strengthened my resolve, and kept me going.

As the night slowly came to a close and Ash was content on ruminating whether or not to steal our mate away, I let myself wander again to the memories of my past. I had not thought about Vampires for quite some time, and though I'd come across a few in these new lands, they seemed somewhat different from the ones I encountered back then. Weaker—more diluted and frail. I was looking for clues to help me understand her.

With that, I regressed once again in the long past.

Romania.

It was dawn, and the shadowy wraiths and thirsty Vampires had descended into their crypts. I walked uninterrupted into the largest mausoleum in the center of a large cemetery. I broke the rusty lock, armed with only some small wooden stakes that I had hand-carved myself with a little piece of flint rock, and walked right into the dusty tomb.

This was to be my first kill, and my wolf of today would not approve. Vampires were defenseless during the day, succumbing to a deathlike sleep in coffins. Today, Ash was a master hunter who only fought when necessary and certainly not a foe who could not fight back. I did not want to be a coward like my uncle, but Ash was not with me then. He was just a nameless shadow of a ghost. And I needed supplies, fast.

The plan seemed easy enough: kill the Vampire, steal the sword. And maybe his clothes. I had seen him, hours before, walking right into this mausoleum right before dawn. It had rained that day, and I was covered in mud to hide my scent.

He had no idea I was watching him from afar.

I was thin, young, and wolfless, yet the fear of Vampires never touched me. It couldn't, not after everything. My father had taught me how to track and hunt reindeer in the frozen wilderness of our homeland with nothing but a knife—how to move silently and strike swiftly. His lessons had etched confidence into my bones, even though I had never faced anything like this before. A Vampire. Sleeping. Vulnerable. It should be easy enough for a wolfless rogue.

What could go wrong?

I told myself it was just another hunt, that the creature's pale, still form was no different from the reindeer I had brought down as a child. My hands should not have trembled, but they did. Maybe I was still in shock from everything that had happened—the chaos, the blood, the loss. Maybe that's why I thought I could handle this. The plan seemed so simple in my head: get in, strike fast, and get out before it ever stirred.

But nothing went as planned. The moment I stepped closer, everything went wrong—terribly wrong. Maybe I was careless. Maybe it was the lingering grief or the adrenaline still surging in my veins, giving me a false sense of security.

I hadn't expected the fear to hit me then, cold and paralyzing, my heart trying its best to climb out of my throat. I forced my hands to steady.

The mausoleum was cold, damp, and reeked of decay, but I didn't hesitate. I shoved the casket lid open with one quick, desperate push, exposing the Vampire's lifeless body. His pale face sickened me, but I had no time to flinch. I raised the stake high and slammed it down into his heart with all the force I could muster.

The sound was horrific—a wet, grotesque suction noise that made my stomach turn as if the wood had plunged into something unnatural. Then came the scream. It wasn't human. It was a gurgling shriek that tore through the air, a high-pitched wail that burrowed into my skull and rattled every bone in my body. I staggered back, my hands flying to cover my ears, but it was no use. The scream pierced through my mind like shards of glass, amplified by the cursed gift of supernatural hearing.

I barely had a moment to catch my breath when I heard it—other screams, smaller, shrill, and growing closer. My blood turned cold as I realized what was happening. The sound of footsteps—small, fast, and many—echoed from outside the mausoleum, and I turned just in time to see them.

Children. Dozens of them, all younger than me, their eyes hollow, their movements unnervingly stiff as they rushed toward me. Are these the ghouls I had heard of?

And then, from behind, came the voice I wasn't prepared to hear.

"You missed . . ." the Vampire hacked weakly, "my heart." And for a moment, I froze.

The Vampire's voice was wet, gurgling with blood, but filled with a twisted satisfaction. His laughter—a snarling, guttural sound—sent a fresh wave of terror through me. I spun around, eyes wide with disbelief as I watched him rise from his tomb, the stake uselessly sticking out of his chest. His death had been a lie.

He was still alive, and hungry. His fangs were fully exposed. The ghouls had now gathered behind me, their doll-like faces twisted in hunger, blocking the exit. Panic clawed at my throat, and I had no choice but to push through them, their little hands grasping at me, their teeth snapping at my skin. I felt the sting of their bites, their nails tearing at me, but I kept moving, shoving them aside with desperate strength.

I burst out of the mausoleum, stumbling into the bright, blinding sunlight. My chest heaved as I stood there, the warmth of the sun a barrier between me and the nightmare lurking inside. I knew the bloodsucker couldn't follow me here. The ghouls stopped at the threshold, their dead eyes watching me with a hunger that would never fade.

They laughed at me then fluttered out of the mausoleum into the sun. I had half expected them to burn up, but to my surprise, they did not. So it was true: Ghouls really were part Vampire but immune to the sun's rays.

My heart squeezed inside my chest, choking my air. I hadn't expected this fight to be so messy.

There had to be at least ten, maybe twelve of them—children, but not children anymore. They moved with unnerving speed, darting around me like twisted little hobgoblins, circling me as if I were the center of some grotesque dance. Their small fists rained down on me like pinches, nothing I couldn't handle. They yanked at my hair with the same playful cruelty of fairies, but their eyes betrayed something far more sinister. I couldn't understand why he had made children his ghouls. What kind of monster would turn innocents into these vile creatures? But I knew, physically, I could easily overpower them.

It wasn't their attacks that overwhelmed me, though. It was their voices. Their screams and wails tore at my heart in ways I hadn't expected. They spoke in their native tongue, a language I was beginning to understand in fragments—enough to feel the weight of their words.

Some begged me, their faces streaked with what looked like tears, pleading for mercy, for me not to kill them. Others cursed me, their eyes wild, their mouths spitting venomous insults and hatred. My grip on the stakes tightened as I faltered, my breath hitching.

How could I fight children, even if they were ghouls? They sounded so much like the living. For a split second, I hesitated, stepping back and lowering the stakes I held in each hand. My mind raced to make sense of it all, to grasp the horror of what I was doing.

But then, in unison, they all hissed as if under the command of some unseen conductor. It was a sickening sound that sent a jolt of icy fear through me. Their eyes flashed with a hunger that couldn't be reasoned with, and at that moment, I knew these weren't children anymore. They were something else entirely. They lunged at me as one, their tiny bodies moving faster than any human could.

Instinct took over. I jumped, spinning as I kicked one of them in the head. His skull cracked with a sickening snap, and his body crumpled like a rag doll. His head, soft and fragile like rotted fruit, separated from his body.

They weren't normal children. That much was clear. And I didn't realize just how strong I had become since receiving my wolf. Even though he hibernated inside of me, not only did I have his senses and healing, but his strength, too it seemed.

Something suddenly took over inside of me, and I stopped thinking. I just acted. The next one came at me, and I stabbed it through the heart, the stake splintering as I withdrew it. I beheaded another with a sharp swipe of my right hand, the force breaking the stake in half. Their skin was soft, almost too soft, but their speed—oh, their speed was the real danger.

A few carried small silver daggers, and if one of those daggers stabbed me deep enough, well, the wound may never heal, so I had to be careful. But their screams were also a type of weapon, one that deadened my senses.

I dispatched the next few with brutal efficiency. One I stabbed with a wooden stake, another I dismembered with my bare hands, tearing its head from its neck as easily as ripping paper. The last few I took down by slamming their heads together until they were nothing but mush. Using their frantic momentum against them, I hurled them into the ground head first. The final thud of a small body hitting the earth left a cold silence in the air.

I stood there, breath ragged, adrenaline pulsing through my veins, my hands coated in blood—black, thick, and un-oxygenated...dead. I turned toward the mausoleum, fury coursing through me like wildfire as I locked eyes with the Vampire. He had been watching the whole time, slinking in the shadows like a wounded lion hiding in its den. How dare he create these ghoul children! How dare he make me fight them!

My lip curled, and I growled through clenched teeth, my rage boiling over.

"Wait, wolf!" The Vampire's voice was weak, rasping through the blood that clogged his throat. He was still sitting on the floor, half-dead—or undead, whatever he was—leaning against the mausoleum wall. He knew what I was.

"Let me offer you a chance at eternal life!" his voice cracked with desperation, his words pathetic and hollow. He tried to sound enticing, but there was no power left in him, only the gurgling sound of blood as he gasped for air.

"There is nothing you can give me that I want," I said loudly.

"You're wolfless!" he screamed. "I can make you strong!"

My eyes flinched at his words. What a terrible blow those words were to me. Part of me did worry my wolf would never return, but it was not a problem for the undead to remind me about!

"I carry the strength of the sun in my blood, undead. I am already strong!" I growled at him. He laughed back at me. "But you are the moon's child," he said. "You get your strength from the moon. Just like me. I can help you." His eyes pleaded with me.

"The moon is my mother, but the sun is my father!" I said, tired of hearing this Vampire speak.

My eyes darted around the ground, searching for anything I could use to finish him. But there was nothing. The stakes I had brought with me lay shattered in pieces, broken from the battle. My heart raced as I faced the bloodsucker with only my bare hands, the sun my only remaining weapon.

In a single motion, I leaped up to the nearest tree, my hands gripping a thick branch as I swung my body around it. I yanked it down with every ounce of strength I had, feeling the weight of it, solid and heavy in my grip.

The Vampire's eyes widened with palpable fear, the raw terror of a creature with nowhere to run and nowhere to hide. He knew what was coming.

The branch was larger than me, taller and more gnarled than I expected, but at that moment, it felt light. My blood surged through my veins, pulsing with a power I hadn't known I possessed.

In my ears, I could hear the steady rhythm of a drum, the sound of my ancestors. I felt their presence, my dead family members and pack surrounding me, their sacred chants forming a circle of energy around me. I was no longer alone.

They were with me. I could feel them.

"You have no wolf! I can still help you get strong!" The Vampire's voice was desperate, his words slithering through the air.

I paused. I wanted strength, yes. I wanted to kill Regis, to tear him apart for everything he had done. But I needed more than just strength—I needed to be powerful enough to face the wolf army he now controlled. I could not run the pack as a vampire and I wouldn't want to.

"No more words," I roared back, my voice resonating with the power of my ancestors, their strength surging through me like wildfire.

The chant of my people grew louder, filling me with purpose. With supernatural speed, I raised the branch high above my head and swung it like a spear. It flew straight and true, plunging deep into the Vampire's chest, crushing his heart entirely. This time, I didn't miss.

The chanting ceased, leaving an eerie silence in its wake. I stood there, alone once more, just an orphaned boy in a foreign land. There was a sense of peace in this quietness I did not expect.

Quickly, I scavenged what I could from the Vampire's remains. His clothes and shoes were all too big for me, but I took his sword, the one thing that felt useful in my hands.

My heart raced as I ran, my body trembling with the leftover adrenaline, haunted by the images of undead child ghouls circling in my mind. I wanted to howl, to release the beast inside me, but my wolf . . . my wolf was still gone.

The Vampire's words echoed in my mind: *wolfless*. The insult burned deep. It was the worst thing you could call someone like me, a Werewolf without his wolf.

I gulped down air, my chest heaving as I climbed back up the same tree that had helped me end the Vampire. From high above, I pressed my hand against its sturdy trunk, murmuring a quiet thank you, just as my mother had taught me when I was small. My people believed in the cycle of life, in the deep connection between all living things. Right now this tree was like a big brother who lent me his arrows and comfort.

When a reindeer gave its body to feed us, we offered our thanks in return. One day, when my time came, my body, too, would feed the earth, nourishing new life to rise in my place.

I curled up in a ball on the branch, the weight of everything crashing down on me all at once. And for the first time since I left my homeland, I cried. I cried for my family, for my pack, for the journey that had led me so far from everything I knew. The tears came in heavy, wracking sobs that I couldn't hold back.

My first kill. My parents and my tribe weren't here to see it, to witness this moment. And yet, in some way, they *were* here. They had been with me when it mattered most, even if I didn't fully understand how.

Back home, there would have been a ceremony, a celebration to mark this event—my first kill after receiving my wolf. The shamans would have blessed me with a relic, something to carry with me as a symbol of my new strength.

But here, there was only silence and death. And the question gnawed at me: was killing something undead even considered a true kill? Was a hibernating wolf still a wolf?

Just then, my eyes caught sight of a small gleaming dagger lying near one of the dead children's bodies, and I didn't hesitate. I climbed down the tree and rushed to it, gripping the cold steel in my hands. I hadn't noticed it before. How could I have forgotten about the daggers?

I didn't want to take anything from the children. They were innocent in my eyes, and it seemed too dark to wear their clothes . . . but this one dagger. Just this one, I'll take.

Its weight felt foreign in my hands; it was very light. It was probably all silver, not just silver-lined. A surge of determination coursed through me, driving me forward. The drumming and echoes of my ancestors started coursing through my ears again, and I could feel the tears prickle at my eyes. I wanted the tears to stop. I wanted the pain to quiet. With a fierce resolve, I moved the dagger quickly behind me, the blade slicing cleanly through my hair, severing the strands that fell to the ground like an amputation.

The motion was final and sharp. With the swing, I said goodbye—not just to my hair but to the boy I had been, to the life I had lived, to my ancestors. In that moment, the constant drumming that had echoed in my ears, the sacred chanting of my ancestors, fell silent. The weight of their presence lifted, and I was alone again. But this time, the quiet felt different. It wasn't crushing or even peaceful. It was . . . stillness. I was numb.

The tears evaporated like forgotten memories. I glanced down at the scattered locks of hair at my feet, symbols of the person I had been, and felt the finality of it all. I made a small fire and disposed of my hair appropriately, as I had been taught. I also burned the bodies, leaving no trace of them behind.

There was no going back. The road ahead was dark and uncertain, but I was not afraid of it.

I walked back to the tree that had offered me refuge, the bark familiar beneath my fingertips as I began to climb. Higher and higher I went, each branch I grasped pulling me away from the ground, from the bloodshed, from everything that had just happened. I climbed until I couldn't climb any farther, until I was perched at the highest point, gazing out at the world that now stretched before me, endless and unknown.

I stayed up the tree fasting and occasionally napping until night had returned.

The night air was cold against my skin, but I welcomed it. I breathed it in, feeling it fill my lungs, steadying me. I didn't have my wolf yet. I wasn't complete. But I had something else—a new start, no matter how dark and dreary the road ahead might be.

I clutched the sword tightly in my hand, the blade a reminder of the battle that had just passed, of the strength I had found within myself. A new resolve burned in my chest, filling the hollow space where my grief had once been.

I am a man now, I thought to myself. Even if I didn't have my wolf, even if I hadn't yet fully become what I was meant to be, I knew this was just the beginning. I survived today. I had survived the Vampire, the ghouls, the doubts that had clouded my mind.

I wish I had been with you then, Andrei, teemed Ash with a protective staunch.

"Don't worry, you were there," I said, glaring off into space with his eyes. "You're always with me, wolf."

Yes, just like our mate, she is young and defenseless until her wolf fully emerges. Her wolf is almost here, though; I can smell her. She needs us right now.

"Yes, she might need us, but I'm not sure if she wants us," I said, recalling the way she recoiled at our scent when she first sniffed it. "We aren't exactly a prime bachelor."

Don't sell yourself short. Besides, we will fix that. We have a big job to do.

Ash was right; we did have a job to do. And a destiny to fulfill. He reminded me how having a true mate would only make my wolf stronger. My only question is, what to do about her Vampire side? Would she pollute my bloodline? Is she suitable as a Luna, or will the pack reject her?

Ash just laughed at me.

You can't even get her to tell you her name, Romeo. Worry about the bloodline and pack we don't have yet, later. Right now, just make her yours!

"Honestly, I don't even know why I keep trying to get deep in my thoughts with you around," I replied.

Too many thoughts! Just go get her already! Ash rebuked. This time, it was my turn to laugh. Damn wolf is relentless.

"You know I never rush into decisions! Not until we see who is protecting her," I said defiantly.

So we sat, watching her window and I couldn't help but let fear once again enter my mind. I cannot have a mate right now. As a rogue, how could I give her a home when I don't have one myself? What do I have to offer? I don't really feel ready.

You had two hundred years to get ready! You will never be ready enough, exclaimed Ash. I huffed.

"Yes, you're right," I responded. I had never been so ready and yet not ready for anything in my entire life. I didn't need her and she definitely didn't need me, not the way I am now. Yet I wanted her, I cannot lie. If I didn't truly want to be here I would have dragged Ash away. And he knew this.

The pull of the mate bond between us wolves was just too strong to resist—all rational thought flew out the window. It was enough to drive Ash and me wild.

Not even in the darkest days of my exile did I feel this torn. Back then, I had no choice. Every decision I made was driven by necessity, by the raw, brutal instinct to survive. I did what I had to do because there was no other option. It was survival—simple, clear, without room for doubt. But this . . . this was different.

A mate. The word itself felt heavy, binding in a way that survival never had been. Technically, I could walk away right now. Turn my back, push forward, and keep hunting for relics, just like I've always done. And I would survive. I would be fine.

And she? She'd be fine, too, since she's got a protector.

That's what you're telling yourself? Ash muttered as if he thought I was an idiot.

I ignored him. Yet his words rung true. Somehow, that thought doesn't bring the comfort it should. Something inside me twists at the idea of leaving her, of walking away from the connection that now tugs at me. It feels wrong, like abandoning something sacred.

But then again, it would be easier. Safer.

Liar, muttered Ash. *And those relics are useless to us!*

I sighed to myself. Maybe he's right; I do think too much.

Well . . . she did resist us somewhat, so maybe, just maybe, your plan to scope things out a bit isn't entirely wrong, as much as I hate to admit, Ash said.

I looked down at the ground, pondering his words but not wanting to remember. I had proclaimed myself as her mate, but she hadn't said anything. It was as if she had no idea what the word even meant!

To be a fated mate was more than destiny—it was a blessing from the Creator himself, a divine bond that transcended everything. It was deeper than any oath, more sacred than any promise. No other connection in the world could come close to the power of marking your mate. The moment the mark is made, you become one with them, body, soul, and spirit. Your wolf and theirs, bound together in an unbreakable union.

It wasn't just a commitment but a merging of two beings into something greater, something eternal. Stronger than any marriage certificate or human vow, it was a primal connection, written in the stars and in your very blood. To have a fated mate was to know a love that was infinite, a bond that could never be broken, no matter the trials or distance. It was a force that would shape you, change you, and complete you in ways you never imagined.

After two hundred or so years I had started to wonder if fated mates were really true. Or maybe if I had one, she was long dead. So I had not given the thought of finding her any attention until now.

Having a fated mate also made you stronger, Ash instructed in the back of my head in soft rumbling whispers. Because your other half made up for whatever you were lacking. If she was weak, I could make her strong. If I was slow, she could make me fast. It was the perfect balance of strengths and weaknesses.

Yet she did not seem to care. She resisted me. Was it because I was a rogue?

Honestly, anyone would resist you after scaring them like that. What were you thinking, jumping out of a tree and breaking that branch?! Jeez man! Did you think you were going to win her over with acrobatics? You're not applying to the Olympics! Ash scolded.

"I didn't know she was my mate at first, Ash, and neither did you! I still cannot smell her wolf, only her wolf blood," I said.

She's a hybrid, Ash responded. *And I knew she was our mate, was just confused because her wolf is very repressed. And I'm not going to lie, she's very beautiful. She probably has guys doing cartwheels in front of her all the time. You need to do better.*

"Me?! You're the one who wants to kidnap her. You think that'll make her love us?" I snapped back. But he was right so I reset my fury and calmed my mind with a long exhale.

"Okay, yeah, I do need to do better," I replied, my voice barely more than a whisper. The weight of everything pressed down on me, my chest tightening with the familiar ache of conflict. Ash's words weren't going to ease my anxieties, and I could tell from the way she looked at me that she didn't really understand the mate bond.

She was a hybrid—half Vampire, half wolf—a creature born of two worlds. And me? I was a rejected rogue alpha Werewolf turned Vampire hunter. Nothing could change that.

I had to laugh at myself for a second there. We were surely an odd couple. And yet no matter how I tried to twist it or what feelings had grown between us in that short meeting because of the mate bond, the fact that we are fated mates is as unshakable as the ground beneath my feet.

The tension between us was suffocating. I can feel it. It won't be easy. But I'm used to things not being easy in my life. If I could make her mine. Perhaps I could find a tiny piece of happiness.

How could I forget the mission I'd been carrying my whole life, though? To kill her kind. To end the very bloodline that ran through her veins. Every time I looked at her, I was torn between who I was supposed to be and what I felt.

But love doesn't erase fate. And fate doesn't care about love.

I sat back in the moody darkness, allowing Ash almost full control to watch over her again as I scoured my memories for anything that could help me understand her better.

Romania . . . the motherland of the Undead. The year was 1807 in their calendar when I first set foot on its soil, a land steeped in shadows and ancient, forgotten evils. The air felt different there, thick with the scent of death and decay, and the sky always seemed to hover under a perpetual shroud of darkness. I had spent more years in that cursed place than I had ever spent in my own country. It had become my battlefield, my graveyard. My home away from home.

After that one lonely night, the night of my first kill, something inside me shifted. I no longer felt human, not entirely. The weight of what I had done bore down on me, but I couldn't stop. I didn't feel fear or doubt, just a numb determination that carried me forward. From that night on, I ran on autopilot, moving from one kill to the next, my hands stained with the blood of the Undead.

Armed with my new weapon—a silver-laced iron sword—I cut through Vampire after Vampire, decapitating as many of those creatures as I could. The weight of the blade became as familiar as my own heartbeat, a constant companion in a land that offered nothing but enemies. I met a few locals along the way, villagers haunted by the Vampires who stalked their nights.

They paid me in coin, sometimes with a warm meal, grateful for the protection I offered. But I never stayed long. I couldn't afford to get comfortable. I couldn't risk anyone learning who I truly was or what I was after. Word of a young Vampire slayer with my description would spread like wildfire, and I needed Regis and his Witch to think I was long dead.

Once I had rid an area of its monster, I set out on the hunt for the next one. Paid or not, it didn't matter. This was my purpose now.

I learned more about Vampires in those years than the sacred tomes back home had ever taught me. I learned that the older Vampires were the strongest, and their power was growing with every century. And I learned that some, like my first kill, kept ghouls as servants, mindless creatures who existed only to protect their masters. The ghouls were always the first to come at me, throwing themselves between their masters and my blade, but they were no match for me—not even with my wolf still slumbering inside me, barely conscious of its own existence.

Yet, I never encountered ghouls like those children again. For that, I was grateful. Those children were different, twisted in a way that chilled me to my core. They didn't come out to protect their master, not at first. It was almost as if *he* was protecting *them*. They only emerged after they heard his scream, like frightened animals. It was a scene that haunted me long after I left that town.

Slowly, methodically, I amassed a vast collection of weapons—so much so that even my horse began to struggle under the weight: silver daggers, iron stakes, holy water, and crucifixes. The only thing useful to me was silver, but if the crucifixes had silver, I used them. What I couldn't carry, I buried and hid away.

I probably would have emerged sooner if you hadn't carried all that silver! Ash interjected. I just rolled my eyes.

True, silver did weaken werewolves. Just being in the presence of it, but like I said, my wolf was hibernating then. At the time, silver did nothing to my strength.

I gathered them all, always preparing for the next fight, for the next Vampire that would try to end me. But it wasn't just weapons. I had become a thief, raiding the homes of the Vampires I killed, taking their clothes, their relics, and anything that might serve me in the battles to come.

The clothes weren't for fashion. No, they were a disguise. I needed to blend in, to slip through the shadows unnoticed. I could have bought clothes from the villagers I helped, but that wasn't enough. I needed to cover my scent, to mask the stench of humanity that clung to me. I soaked my hat and cloak in the blood of the Vampires I killed, letting the blood congeal in the daylight.

It turned the clothing black under the sun, the stain a strange, inky substance that never failed to surprise me. I half-expected it to catch fire in the light of day, but it never did. Instead, it hardened and became a type of armor.

With this new "armor", I became someone else—someone who could walk unnoticed and blend in with the land of the Undead.

Each kill, each stolen relic, each disguise, brought me closer to my ultimate goal—Regis. But with every step, the path grew darker, and the child I once was faded further into the past. I was becoming something else. Something cold.

Something relentless.

The years were dragging by and I didn't know if I would ever get my wolf, but I knew one thing: I was hunting something much worse than Vampires. I was hunting the part of me that still felt anything at all.

I started leaving caches of old weapons, spare clothes, and even coins buried all across Romania—hidden in the forests, tucked away in the hollow of trees, or beneath rocks. It was a habit ingrained in me as a Werewolf. When we shifted, we were left naked and vulnerable, as natural as the wolves we became. So, we stash supplies wherever we roam, hidden from the elements to keep them from deteriorating, ready for the next time we might need them. Wolves travel light because we have to. There was no room for carrying extra weight when survival was always on the line.

With my wolf dormant, it dulled my rogue Werewolf scent, but truthfully, old Romania stank of death back in those days. The putrid air hung thick with decay, and I was certain my rogue scent blended right in with the rot. They never suspected me, not until it was too late—until I was close enough to end them. That's when the alpha hunter in me would surface, striking swiftly and without mercy.

After mastering the art of hunting Vampires during the day, I began to push my limits and take risks. I started hunting at night, creeping into their world. It was dangerous, reckless even, but I craved the thrill of it, the satisfaction of becoming their nightmare.

I developed a method. I would position myself high above them—on the branches of trees, atop cliffs, anywhere I could gain the advantage. I'd leap down without warning, crashing through the air deliberately to create a cacophony of noise. The sound would jolt them, shocking their senses for just a split second, and in that moment of confusion, I'd strike. They never saw it coming.

Vampires had an incredible sense of smell, but it wasn't like a wolf's. Their noses weren't attuned to the subtleties of scent the way ours were. Instead, they were bloodhounds—drawn to the smell of blood like sharks to the scent of the ocean's wounded. It was almost more of a taste than a scent to them. They could detect it from miles away, and it made them reckless.

But their hearing—that was something else entirely. It was like sonar, sharp and precise. I learned to adapt, to move with the kind of silence that could rival even the most skilled of hunters. The rough leather of the clothes I wore often betrayed me with the slightest rustle, so I taught myself the art of stillness. I'd freeze, blending into the night like a corpse, waiting for them to come to me.

They would follow the scent of death on my stolen, blood-soaked clothes, thinking they were approaching one of their own, only to be blinded by the sudden glint of my blade catching the moonlight. That split second was all I needed—just enough to send my sword slicing through their necks, the silver-laced iron separating the head from the body before they could even react.

I had no rules back then. No teacher. No battle buddy. It was just me, a rogue Werewolf without his wolf, relying on nothing but instinct and the will to live. I killed them all, male and female, young and old. There was no hesitation, no mercy. They were simply obstacles in my path, each one a step closer to reclaiming what was rightfully mine—the Thunderwolves pack. Romania was my training grounds on the hunt for peak physical performance before returning to fight my uncle.

I stayed in Romania for so long because of the few werewolves it had. Apparently, Vampires loved to drink from wolves because of our vitality, so most wolves steered clear. I stayed here because it allowed me to train away from the prying eyes of my uncle's spies. This was the last place he would think to search for me.

I only stayed as long as I needed, until Ash returned. I had never ventured beyond the borders of my pack's land before.

The Thunderwolf territory, vast as it was, had always been my world. It stretched endlessly, an expanse of untamed wilderness, but the land was harsh and unforgiving. Winters were brutal, the cold biting and relentless, with permafrost that clung to the earth year-round. Farming was near impossible, and the terrain itself was wild, raw, and uncultivated. It was a place that demanded respect and submission, a place that could never be tamed. Because of that, few humans ever dared settle near us. Even now, centuries later, the area remains untouched by human hands, save for a few nomadic tribes brave enough to roam its desolate expanse.

In my younger years, I assumed the rest of the world was much like Thunderwolf—vast stretches of land filled with wolves, packs like ours, thriving in remote isolation. I believed we were the norm. But I was wrong.

For thousands of years, we had that land all to ourselves. No rival packs came to challenge us; no other wolves pushed us out or forced us to compete for resources. We were self-sufficient, content in our secluded corner of the world, cut off from the chaos that lay beyond. There was never a need to explore, never a desire to travel or expand our reach. We had no reason to leave, no knowledge of what waited outside our borders. It was a quiet existence, but one filled with strength and pride.

I had heard tales of Vampires—whispers passed down through old stories and scrolls—but I had never laid eyes on one. Not until fate forced me to travel, to leave the only home I had ever known. When that time came, the lessons from my youth, those long hours spent studying with tutors in preparation for my role as the alpha's heir, finally proved useful.

I had been taught the ways of warfare, the art of strategy, and the value of understanding one's enemies. My tutors drilled into me the importance of studying an opponent so thoroughly that, if necessary, I could mimic them, become them. The scrolls, etches made from thin animal skins and ancient cave carvings and drawings, were filled with knowledge of the world outside our territory. Vampires, Witches, even the elusive Fae—I learned about them all, especially the shapeshifters, the Skin Shifters and all the were-breeds.

But for all that I had studied, I never expected to need that knowledge. There was not a whole lot of information on the half-breeds like my mate—not really. Looking back, I wished I had paid more attention.

My father had told me the same when I was young. To study the scrolls. I remember him sitting with me, those old scrolls spread out before us, the flickering firelight casting shadows on his face.

"You'll probably never need to use this information, my son," he said, his voice calm, reassuring. He looked down at me, his only son, his heir, with a softness that I rarely saw. "But still, you must learn it. You must memorize these words, for they are sacred to our people. These scrolls were handed down to us from our ancestors. Some of the caves and stones from which they were copied do not even exist anymore. Protect them, guard them with your life, and keep their teachings in your heart."

I remember the warmth in his eyes, the pride he felt as he watched me study. Back then, I couldn't imagine a world where I would need to use that knowledge. The

Thunderwolf pack was safe, eternal in its isolation. But now, as I looked out over the foreign lands I found myself in, far from home and faced with enemies I had never thought I'd encounter, my father's words echoed in my mind.

Ash squirmed in my mind. *You're spiraling. Get it together. Why are you thinking of this? Our mate is not like these Vampires. She is a Vaewolf.*

I could feel his patience wearing thin.

"Because . . ." I replied, not wanting to say it out loud because the thought was too dark.

Because what if she has to die first to reach her full form? I responded for the first time in many years via mind link. Was life as a Vampire hunter training me for this day?

Ash was silent.

Vampires were once alive, died, and then were reborn into something else—something that straddled the line between life and death. It was a transformation unlike anything in the world of shapeshifters. No other creature had to die first to become what they were. That idea alone fascinated me. Every other shifter—Werewolves, Skinwalkers, Fae—had their powers awakened within them, but Vampires had to pass through death to claim their new form. It was both a curse and a rebirth, a cycle I had never truly understood until I came across it.

I had only encountered one other Vaewolf in my life before our mate. That much was true.

He was a Vaewolf in Romania—a half-breed caught in the limbo between Vampire and wolf. He wasn't old, far younger than I imagined someone trapped in such torment should be. He was still struggling with his transformation, caught between worlds, neither fully wolf nor fully Vampire. His eyes held a kind of suffering that spoke to the battle raging inside him. At the time, I didn't think much about learning from him and didn't consider that his condition might hold answers I would one day need. I saw only his torment, his suffering from being stuck in transition, and I ended his life, thinking it was mercy.

But now, with my mate, the question gnaws at me. How did she survive it? How did she manage to exist as a Vaewolf without being forced into that painful, permanent shift? Without becoming trapped between forms, a tortured soul like the one I had ended in Romania? Has her protector managed to keep her wolf from emerging like the Witch had done to me?

She is older and stronger than the Vaewolf I met, but that only deepens the mystery. What allowed her to remain in control, to stay whole when so many others have lost themselves to the madness of that transformation? There had to be something—or someone—who protected her.

Someone or something that kept her from slipping into that irreversible state of being stuck between worlds.

My mind went to the Witch. Was she a trap set for me by that long-ancient enemy? Had I been found out? Was my identity finally revealed and she was my lure for his trap? I shook my head. It couldn't be.

The thought of her having endured such a fragile existence made my chest tighten. How many times had she come close to losing herself, to being forced into that shift, and never finding her way back? How many close calls had she faced without me ever knowing?

It was hard to fathom. In my dealings with the undead, I realized that I, too, had become reborn in a way. A hundred years had passed, and my wolf had finally returned while I was in Romania. Risen from the dead, from the ashes of yesterday.

I learned one thing from the Vampires. Sometimes, things come back.

And that is why you call me Ash, my wolf stated.

"Yes," I said. "You rose from the ashes like a Phoenix."

And so, with that, I became Andy, a name that felt simpler, smaller—an echo of who I once was. It was short for Andrei, the name my mother used to call me. Andrei, the last of my four royal names, a name that had once carried the weight of lineage and power. But those days felt distant now, as though they belonged to someone else. I was fairly certain my uncle had already scratched my name from the totem back home, erasing me from the family's heritage.

We left Romania together, my wolf and I, when he resurfaced. By then, my wolf scent had returned, stronger and more potent than before, along with the stronger rogue scent. With the wolf inside me fully awake, it was no longer safe tolinger in those lands. Romania had changed—everything had. The old world was shifting, and it wasn't just the supernatural creatures that felt it.

Humans were evolving, building larger, more powerful machines that could carry them across great distances. They called them steam horses—trains and they could take you almost anywhere. I welcomed the change. It gave me the opportunity to slip away from the ghosts of my past and into the unknown.

Ash had me bury or hide all the silver and leave it behind in Romania. Yes, even my dagger, which had become somewhat sacred to me since cutting my hair. But the clothes I kept, they helped to hide my scent.

That is when I met my first real love interest—a Fae woman who was also a druid.

*Ahem . . .*Ash interrupted. *Okay, I am officially stopping this useless nostalgia. Are you forgetting that we are supposed to be protecting our mate? Why are you thinking of her at this time? Hello! Earth to Andy, are you there?*

I grinned. Ash was getting protective and did not like me bringing up our past lover. But he was right. I was thinking of everything else in my life except our mate. But it wasn't because I didn't want to; we had barely met, yet her hold over me was so strong. The idea of being close to our mate, hiding close to her bedroom, made my heart skip a beat. I was trying to keep myself from ruminating over her like Ash was.

How baffling it was to me that the urges I felt for this stranger were much stronger than anything I felt for that other woman whom I had known for at least a year.

"I'm here, aren't I?" I replied, more determined than ever to protect her. Yes, I've made up my mind. I'm staying for her. Whoever she is. And I'm going to figure out who's protecting her and why.

Humph! he snubbed. *Barely. Lost in the past!*

I sighed deeply. I only thought of our ex now because, up until meeting our mate, Saoirse had been my one and only love interest. And yet, things were so different. Looking back, I knew I hadn't loved her.

"And you didn't love her seal either, did you?" I asked Ash. Saoirse was a Selkie. A water Fae. I knew instantly that Ash never liked her, but she didn't mind my rogue self. And for a while, she occupied my time.

Nope! Ash butted in. *Not at all! Ugh, will you stop with all this thinking? I can't concentrate!*

"Well, it's your memory," I said, referring to the time Ash and her seal Aine met for the first time when I had let him have control one night. Aine had spit water at him from the ocean, and it took all of Ash's power not to kill her. Ash always thought of Aine as prey, and that was when Saoirse sent us away. She told me what had happened and Ash did not deny it. Looking back, I was more sad to leave Ireland and the other druids than I was to leave her.

So here I am now, sitting like a fool, pining for a Vaewolf I knew nothing about. How could I have been so quick to leave her? If I'd lingered a moment longer, I could've asked her name, could've at least known something about her beyond this aching connection brewing in my bones. I only left because I didn't want her protector to catch onto me.

You didn't want her to reject you. Stop lying to yourself, Ash interjected.

This wolf, I swear! "That's not the only reason!"

This pull toward her—it was more than just attraction. It was something deeper. I couldn't walk away from this

Vaewolf if I tried.

I can feel it in the marrow of my bones, this raw, untamed desire to claim her, to make her mine. One day, I know I will. I'll take her as my mate, bind us together in a way that cannot be undone.

Well, then, why didn't you claim her? Ash sneers in my mind, his voice dripping with impatience. *You could've taken her away, made her ours, and we'd be happy. Instead, you're sitting on this roof like some creepy pervert, staring at her through a window!*

I scoff, shaking my head. "You think taking her without her consent isn't perverted?!" I snap. "She doesn't even know what she is. She doesn't know what *I* am."

You told her what she was! Ash retorts, his frustration bubbling over.

"Yes, but . . . oh, forget it!" I mutter, cutting off the argument before it spirals further. There was no point in arguing with him now, not when he was so fixated on her.

But what Ash doesn't know—what I can't admit even to myself—is how close I was to doing exactly what he wanted. There was a moment, within a heartbeat, where I would've been more than willing to take her, to claim her as mine, consequences be damned. But something stopped me. Her Vampire side. It's the one thing that made me hesitate, that pulled me back from the brink.

Maybe that's why I instinctively broke that tree branch when we first met. Deep down, I must've sensed the Vampire blood coursing through her veins. It was like my body reacted before my mind had the chance to catch up.

"Ash," I ask, my voice quieter now, "you sensed her

Vampire nature, didn't you?"

Of course I did, he replies smugly, as if the question itself was absurd, like I should never have doubted his ability to sniff out what she was.

But I would never have hurt her. I know that now. Not like the others. Not like the countless Vampires I've butchered without a second thought. She's different—innocent, important in a way that I can't yet explain. She's too much to lose now.

"Something, or someone, is protecting her, Ash. Can't you feel it?" I muttered, letting Ash take control of my senses for a moment. My vision sharpened, my eyes glowing a deep red as I peered through the darkness toward my young mate's window. From the rooftop of a neighboring building, I could make out her shadow moving about her room, unaware of my presence.

I had perfected the art of remaining completely still, a trick I had learned in Romania from all the mimics there that hide from the undead. If a human happened to glance in my direction, they wouldn't see me—not really. I would be just another shadow, blending into the night. Their eyesight was weak compared to ours, and I had mastered the ability to disappear in plain sight.

Yeah, I know it was creepy. I probably resembled a Vampire more than a wolf with the way I lurked in the dark, watching her. Romania had shaped me in ways I couldn't deny, molding my habits into something more vampiric than lupine. But make no mistake—I am all wolf. And right now, every instinct within me screamed to protect her, to care for her. She stirred something primal inside me, something that made me want to claim her as my own even though part of her was undead. I couldn't just walk away because of that. No, I had to understand what was happening here.

I had to be careful. Would I end up being her rescuer or something far darker—her kidnapper? I wasn't sure yet. I just needed to know more about her before I made my move. There was no going back once I acted.

For a brief second, guilt flickered through me—guilt for all the Vampires I had slaughtered over the years and for the desire in my head to even kill her Vampire father, who was most likely protecting her from the shift in some unknown way.

If he was keeping himself hidden, they probably weren't close. Otherwise, she would know what she was. But he was still her father. The idea of ending him, of taking away her blood connection, felt too much like the act of betrayal my uncle had committed when he erased me from our pack's history. I had to be better, for her.

Oh, developing a conscience now, are we? Ash teased, his voice dripping with amusement. *That's what mates do to us. They get into our hearts, and suddenly they become our everything.*

"I guess," I muttered, still trying to shake the stubbornness from my thoughts. But he was right.

I had to be smart about this. I needed to find a way to slowly draw her away from her father's protection or even the Witch's protection if need be. I have to teach her about who and what we are to guide her into accepting the bond between us. Maybe, just maybe, if I marked her, she could break free from the Vampire's compulsion and choose to come with me. But that decision had to be hers. It wasn't something I could force. I knew the mate bond would help her see, even if it was just a physical attraction at first.

Are you blushing? Ash asked slyly.

"Not now," I growled, irritated.

Oh, okay. We can remain creeps traveling on rooftops and watching her from afar, he said sarcastically.

"You know why we travel over the rooftops," I said, not liking how he called us creeps.

Ash didn't respond, too focused on watching our mate through her window, but I knew he understood. The rooftops were safer, faster. Ever since the invention of electricity, the nights have become too bright, the city lights illuminating the streets more than the sun. Up here, it was darker, stealthier. I had become nocturnal again since leaving Europe, and the desert heat made daytime travel unbearable for an old Arctic wolf like myself. The coolness of the night was a welcome reprieve.

When I arrived in this small, sleepy town, I hadn't planned on staying long. I was just passing through, searching for relics that could strengthen my wolf. These desolate deserts were filled with ancient history and supernatural knowledge. The relics I collected, some from rogues I had put down, were hidden away for safekeeping. They hadn't worked on me yet, but I knew that I'd unlock their power in time, or with the help of a shaman. The real challenge was finding someone willing to help a rogue. Shamans didn't exactly line up to offer their services to outcasts.

But you did find an even better treasure, didn't you, Andrei? Ash hinted, his voice filled with smug satisfaction.

"My mate," I said softly, a smile creeping onto my lips. For a moment, I allowed myself to savor the thought of her.

Well, I'll be damned . . . I am actually blushing.

But she is a hybrid, Ash reminded me. *Will she even like us?*

I rolled my eyes. Now, who's the one who sounds insecure? Just when I was starting to accept the idea of a mate he comes and ruins it!

"Yes, she is. A Vaewolf. The rarest of treasures. And that is why we have to wait and see what blood-sucking animal is protecting her. When we take her away, we can explain what being a wolf and hybrid is all about.

Where are we going to take her? We don't have a pack, Ash replied.

"I don't know!" I said, exasperated with him right now.

"You tell me you're the one bringing up the idea!" He simply whined in my head.

"Why is her Vampire scent so died down?" I asked Ash. The Vaewolf boy that I had put out of his misery had both scents coming out very strongly. He smelled of mint and ocean underneath the faint rogue smell I had grown accustomed to. I could barely sniff her undead blood in her until she was three feet away. I could smell her wolf genes from far away but not her wolf.

"And does she or doesn't she have her wolf?" I asked Ash. Most wolves from my clan received them at puberty, around the age of thirteen. I did hear her howl and that is what pulled me to hunt her down in the first place. Her wolf had to be out for me to recognize the mate scent.

Or near, Ash added. *Her wolf is very near. I don't know why her Vampire scent is so low. But I also smell something else on her. I don't recognize the scent. You don't smell it?*

"No," I said, frowning. "Your nose is stronger than mine, but if it's something you've never smelled before, I can't help you."

It doesn't smell right. He said, curling up his nose, exposing his fangs in my mind's eye. *It's not a rogue curse I smell on her. She's not a rogue like us. It's just something off in her chemistry.*

"Not a rogue?" I wondered. "You're right she did not smell like a rogue, so her werewolf mother must still be in the picture. They both have to be the ones protecting her." This new information was very surprising. Her mother survived her Vaewolf daughter's birth. It would be interesting to know what pack she was from. I did not sense a pack here in this particular desert.

I remembered the moment it happened. She stopped right before us, and I was annoyed that my alpha presence had stopped intimidating her.

MATE!!

Ash had called out from within my mind and I panicked! I sniffed the air to verify, and though the scent was very light, I could smell something. But I wasn't sure. I wanted to touch her and see if I could feel the electric tingles I heard happen when you touch your mate, but something was protecting her. Something like an invisible shield that repelled me. Perhaps a protection emblem of some sort. To protect her from the incredible number of rogue skin shifters I can feel surrounding this place.

Yes, the smell of her wolf was light, he replied, *but it's getting much stronger now.*

I looked up at the sky and I could see the stars slowly fading from the approaching sun in the East. I tried to sniff and was starting to catch the scent of jasmine and . . . something else. I was becoming a nervous wreck at the thought of losing control over my mate's scent.

I thought it was best to get going before the sun was up and before I lost myself with her developing a new scent of her wolf.

"Well, it's almost morning, and I think we better—" My words were cut short by a sound that ripped through my chest like a blade. It was her. Our mate. She was screaming, a sound so raw and terrified it shook me to my core. Something was wrong. The commotion from her room was sudden and violent, and the lights flicked on, almost blinding Ash as he struggled to focus.

"You little bitch!" a woman's voice screamed, venom dripping from every word. "What the hell are you yelling about? Are you on drugs?! What did I tell you about causing problems in this house? You think I need the little fucking checks I get for keeping you here?" The crack of a slap echoed through the room, and it took everything in me to keep Ash from tearing that woman's head clean off her shoulders.

"Shut up! Shut up! Shut up!" our mate's voice followed, but there was something different in her tone. The vibrations in her voice were shooting downward, sinking into the ground. I realized she wasn't talking to that woman anymore—she was talking to herself. Ash thrashed inside me, threatening to break free, and I had to force myself to scream at him inside my head.

"You shut up, Magdalena!" screamed the older woman. "Don't you dare talk to me that way!"

Magdalena is her name. Like honey on my lips. Ash and I recoiled at the realization that hit us with ardent longing.

"We have to wait and see what happens. She can't harm her. Little Red is too strong," I whispered through gritted teeth, hoping my words would calm him. Ash had affectionately called her Little Red ever since we met her. He loved her red lipstick, and I couldn't deny it—it made me want to kiss her, too, those soft, pouty lips. I hoped the thought of her lips softened Ash's rage, but it only dulled the edges.

It wasn't that I didn't want to jump in, to rip that human woman apart for daring to lay a hand on our mate, but I knew her father—or the Vampire protecting her—would soon intervene. He had to. And when he did, I'd be ready.

I carried no sword with me these days, but I had something far more lethal: Ash. If it came down to a fight, I wouldn't hesitate to defend her. He would come when her wolf stirred. He would have to, to prevent her from shifting.

My eyes caught a glimpse of a figure down the street—a young woman, pale and thin, walking hurriedly in her pajamas. Something was off. She didn't move like a Vampire. Her steps were clumsy and uncoordinated but fast. Vampires moved with grace, even when they were in a hurry. I felt the hairs on the back of my neck rise. *Of course,* I thought, *he's sending ghouls to do his dirty work.*

Ash shuddered in disgust. *Ugh, I hate ghouls. Too easy.*

Ghouls were barely more than errand runners, daywalkers for their Vampire masters. They had no real power except for a brief burst of speed or strength after feeding on their maker's blood. After that, they became desperate addicts, scavenging for anything that might mimic the high—blood from rodents or even insects, anything they could find. It didn't take long for them to waste away, reduced to skeletal figures that eventually died off within a few short years.

But then, something I had never seen before happened. The waif-like ghoul suddenly crawled up the wall like a spider, her limbs moving in a grotesque dance as she slithered through the window. And then, silence. My heart pounded in my ears, panic rising like bile in my throat. I was about to leap down from the roof when Ash stopped me.

Wait, he whispered, cautious for the first time.

"For what?! That thing is going to eat her!" I hissed back, remembering how hybrids were often hunted by others. But then, as I looked again, the ghoul emerged from the window, and I caught sight of our mate's face. She wasn't terrified. She stood there, staring out at nothing. Her expression was blank, her eyes unfocused.

Hypnotized, Ash finished my thought. I blinked, trying to process what I was seeing. Could ghouls really do that?

Yes, I suppose so, Ash answered darkly, *if they serve a very strong, very ancient Vampire with powerful blood.*

"How do you know that?" I asked, my voice barely more than a growl.

I can smell better than you, Ash teased. *And I think I know why she screamed.*

"What are you talking about?" I demanded.

She got her wolf! Ash practically howled in my mind, his excitement radiating through me.

"What?!" I bellowed.

My heart raced as I scanned the area for any sign of the ghoul. She was long gone, and I didn't think she had heard me. But before the sun rose and I risked being spotted, I leaped from the roof and sprinted toward the temporary home I had made for myself near the mountains—an old, abandoned gold mine. I was no longer afraid to leave her alone—her father was clearly invested in protecting her with high-level ghouls. I had to get out of there before my restraint left me.

It was going to take a plan and much more information to claim our Magdalena.

"Damn that bloodsucking weasel!" I growled loudly in my wolf voice as I tore through the desert faster than even a Vampire. "I need to find him and kill him. It's the only way to make her MINE!" The words echoed through the canyon as I reached its edge, and I let out a primal howl, letting the night birds hear my cry.

I knew they could hear me, the owls. A pair—a male and a female—had been watching me since I entered this desert. I had felt their presence several times, but they never came close. Still, they were there, lingering in the shadows.

Each note of my howl carried the same loneliness I had sensed in my mate's scream. Ash had won. I was no longer on the fence about her. She was the one. She was mine, and I would do whatever it took to claim her.

They might know a way, Andrei, Ash hinted, his voice tinged with something mischievous.

"I know," I muttered. He was talking about the owls. I had felt it too, that they held some kind of knowledge, some way to help. The shadows around here seemed to call them to my attention.

"But first," I said, a plan forming in my mind, "we need a gift, something to lure them out, something to make them trust us."

Their missing skin, Ash replied, the idea settling between us like a shared secret.

"Yes, Ash. Their missing skin," I repeated, a sly grin spreading across my face. I closed my eyes and let my mind drift, imagining my mate near me, her scent wrapping around me like a soft embrace.

Jasmine and rose, Ash added, his voice soft now, almost reverent.

A low growl escaped my lips as I settled down in full wolf form after binding Ash to a promise not to go after her yet. It was the only way I could find peace and quiet my mind long enough to sleep.

Chapter 3

Smoke and Mirrors

Mags

"Magdalena!" Carmen's voice rang out from outside my door, sounding uncharacteristically chipper. It was strange, really. Carmen was never this . . . cheery. Groggily, I blinked at the clock on my nightstand—it was almost noon. Great, I had slept in again.

"Yes?" I called back, my voice thick with sleep, struggling to shake off the fog clouding my mind.

"Mrs. Galindo is here to speak with you. Please get dressed and come down, mija!" Carmen's use of the word "mija" made me cringe. It meant "daughter" in Spanish, her native language, but I was anything *but* her daughter. Hell, I wasn't even one of her favorite foster kids.

"Okay," I replied, flat and emotionless.

Mrs. Galindo was my social worker. She'd been in my life for as long as I could remember, a constant figure through all the bouncing around between foster homes. She was nice enough—sweet, even—but strict. She oversaw everything: my health appointments, my therapy, the mess with the law after I'd been caught tagging old buildings. It was her who had made sure I went to therapy, and it was there that they labeled me *bipolar.* Just another thing to deal with, right?

She took care of it all, managing my prescriptions like a warden. Since I was thirteen, she'd personally pick them up and hand them to Carmen to make sure I took them daily. And I did, even though I never felt like they actually did anything. I was still the same rebellious girl, just better at hiding it. Damn adults.

I sighed and rolled out of bed, throwing on my favorite old pair of jeans and a red Motley Crüe t-shirt I'd had since I was twelve. I didn't even listen to them anymore, but the shirt fit snug in all the right places. Good enough.

I clomped downstairs, my feet heavy with dread. Carmen and Mrs. Galindo were sitting together on the couch, Carmen smiling in a way that made my stomach turn. Why was she so happy? She usually hated seeing me. The memory of last night's slap resurfaced, hot and sharp, and my face twisted into a scowl. Carmen ignored it, of course. That was her way.

"Sit down, mija," Carmen said, motioning to the chair next to her. I hesitated, glancing warily at Mrs. Galindo. Something was off. Was this about another home? My mind raced back to last night, struggling to piece together the blurred fragments of hearing a voice and losing control. I barely remembered the details after that. I recalled the slap, but then . . . nothing. Had Carmen called her? Was this it? Was I being shipped off again?

"Magdalena! How are you feeling?" Mrs. Galindo's voice snapped me back. *Feeling?* What kind of question was that? What did she think I was? Pregnant?

"Are you still taking your medication?" she asked, barely waiting for me to process the first question.

"Yes, yes she is, Mrs. Galindo. I—" Carmen jumped in eagerly, her voice saccharine.

"If you don't mind, Carmen," interrupted Mrs. Galindo, her voice calm but firm, "I need to hear it from Magdalena herself."

"Oh, of course," Carmen muttered, throwing me a disappointed smirk. *There she is,* I thought bitterly.

I shrugged. "Yeah, I'm taking them. I feel fine."I muttered, my voice casual, masking the lie beneath it.

"The reason I'm here is that your labs from last month came back with substantially low Lithium levels, and I'm concerned for your mental health." Mrs. Galindo's words were careful, but they hit like a stone dropping into my stomach.

"My Lithium levels?" I repeated, my mind scrambling. *Low?* They'd always been perfect according to my doctor. "I've been taking them normally, and I feel fine." Another lie. The truth was, I'd been suspecting my mind was unraveling lately. The voice from last night . . . the feelings of mania creeping in. I fidgeted with a small hole in the knee of my jeans, trying to hold it together. I mean, I did take my medicine, when I remembered to.

"No manic phases? Hallucinations?" Her gaze sharpened, cutting through my attempts to downplay it.

I stopped fiddling and folded my hands in my lap, the memories of last night creeping back—the voice, the howl, the Vampire in the park.

Was it all in my head? Had I imagined everything? Was *Luz*, the voice I'd heard, just a figment of my fractured mind?

"Well . . ." I hesitated. "I've had trouble sleeping." Another lie, but safer than confessing the truth. Lately all I ever wanna do is sleep in. If I admitted what was happening, would they send me to a mental hospital?

"Well!" Mrs. Galindo clapped her hands together, startling me. "It's a good thing I'm here. I've made an appointment with Dr. Shru, and we'll probably have to adjust your dosage." She exchanged a smile with Carmen, and I could practically feel the tension between them, a silent agreement passed in front of me like I wasn't even there.

"Oh . . . okay," I mumbled, the weight of it all sinking in. I hated the medication, hated how it felt like chains holding me down. I don't feel like it does anything to my mind but physically, it felt like I was carrying bags of bricks everywhere I went. Even if it didn't seem to change anything, it was still a constant reminder that something was wrong with me.

"And don't worry," Mrs. Galindo turned back to Carmen, "as I said, this will all be covered by State funds. Because of the change in medication, your foster care rate will go up substantially due to the level of care she requires." She paused, then looked at me. "And, Magdalena, this means you'll be able to stay with Mrs. Cruz until the age of twenty-one, at which point another evaluation will take place. Mrs. Cruz has already agreed. Do you?"

Stay here? Until twenty-one? Carmen was grouchy, sure, but she mostly left me alone as long as I kept the kitchen clean and stayed out of trouble. I glanced at the three other foster kids she had who were watching cartoons in the adjacent living room. All younger than me, kids I considered my brothers. It wasn't like I had anywhere else to go.

"Sure," I muttered, feeling detached from the entire conversation. Agreeing was easier than fighting, and self-preservation was the name of the game until I could figure out how to break free.

"Oh, yay!" Carmen exclaimed, her cheerfulness now making perfect sense. The extra money had her giddy. Of course. That's all she ever really cared about. I shot her a sidelong glance, watching the greed flicker in her eyes. It would've been nice if I could get a slice of that State money, I thought bitterly.

We left for Dr. Shru's office in Mrs. Galindo's old '70s Impala. The chipped paint and sun-bleached roof gave it an air of neglect, but the inside was surprisingly well-kept. I found myself imagining what it'd be like to drive a car someday—only mine would be all black, of course.

As we pulled into the tiny office parking lot and entered the lab, I situated myself in the same old, familiar plastic seat where I always got my blood drawn. Then the voice returned.

Be careful with her.

I jolted in my seat, nearly jumping out of my skin before the tech came at me with the needle to draw blood. I forced a laugh to cover my shock. "Oh, I'm just . . . afraid of needles," I lied, watching her stick me. I was suddenly feeling ashamed of all the lies I'd told recently. It's not like me. I usually don't care what people think, but these days, secrecy seems a better tactic until I figure out what's going on.

"Mags, since when?" she giggled, knowing I'd been coming here for years.

The voice—Luz, the same one from last night—pulsed in my mind again and I needed answers. *Be careful with who?* I thought to myself. The tech?

With Mrs. Galindo, Luz whispered, her presence like a warning bell ringing faintly in the distance.

Bipolar or not, something wasn't right. And for the first time in a long while, I wondered if it was the meds, the diagnosis, or maybe something much bigger than I had ever considered.

I jumped again as the voice repeated itself, though it was softer this time, more like a whisper sliding through my mind: *Just watch her.* My heart thudded against my ribs, the tension in my body coiling tighter. I didn't want to hear it. I didn't want this strange voice in my head, especially not in public. I hummed under my breath, hoping to drown it out—anything to make it stop.

But then, the voice was gone. I exhaled slowly, trying to concentrate on my breathing. My body instinctively tensed, and before I knew it, a low, guttural growl slipped out from deep inside me.

"Oh shit!" Gabby, the lab tech, exclaimed, nearly dropping the needle she had just drawn blood with. Her eyes widened in surprise. "Oh, I'm sorry! You just scared me!"

I blinked, startled by her reaction. "Oh, it was just my stomach growling. I'm starving," I said quickly, my voice softer than usual, trying to make myself seem harmless to not arouse suspicion—and less like the stick of dynamite I felt like inside, ready to explode at the slightest provocation. It was an involuntary reaction, this growl.

Gabby seemed to buy it, though her hands still trembled slightly as she cleaned up. "Well, I'm done anyway. You can go back to the waiting room," she muttered hastily before she hurried out.

As she left, I noticed a faint musk lingering in the air, the smell of sweat and fear. Did I really scare her that much? And since when were smells so tangible? I waved my arm in the air as if I could move it out of the way before I passed through it on the way to the lobby.

My mind buzzed with the thought of why I growled, but before I could dwell on it, I stepped out of the small lab and headed back to where Mrs. Galindo waited for me.

I wasn't feeling well. My skin felt too hot, my body weak, and my nerves frayed like a live wire. Maybe I'm just tired, I thought. Maybe it's all in my head. The rest of the doctor's appointment passed in a blur. Dr. Shru adjusted my Lithium dose, gave me a hefty loading dose on the spot, and sent me on my way.

"You don't look too well," Mrs. Galindo said once they'd returned to the car. "Have you eaten?"

"No, I had just woke up," I said.

"Well, let's pass through and get you something to eat, " she said, pulling out her wallet and handing me a black card. I looked at her cautiously.

"What's this?" I asked.

"The State is also giving you some spending money to help you along while you adjust into adulthood," she said nonchalantly. Confused, I just sat there looking at her.

"It's not really safe to be babysitting on this much Lithium, especially if it's not therapeutic yet. It's not safe to be out working irregardless. The State can get in trouble if anything goes . . . awry. It's not much. Just a thousand a month to pay for necessities," she said, putting her wallet away. "It's a type of disability. And no more working until cleared! You got that?"

I gasped. I would have been insulted by the term disability if she hadn't followed with the numbers. "A thousand dollars?!" I asked, looking at the card in my hands with my name pressed into it. I had no idea I was worth this much from the State. Did she mean my tribe? Was this tribal money? I am eighteen now. What tribe did I belong to? I really wanted to know, but the card was blank. Well, I didn't question it. I didn't even have a wallet to put it in, but quickly, I placed it in my purse pocket, safely tucked away.

"Thanks," I said, still wondering if the money was coming from the State or my tribe. Why would she keep this a secret? Was she afraid that I'd run away to meet them? Well, hell yes, I would.

"I didn't wanna tell you in front of Carmen. I suspect that she might ask for money from you if she knew you had that card. Keep this card and money to yourself. So many bad people out here want to exploit our youth. There is backpay on there from when you turned eighteen, so it's nice and full." She said as she pulled away from the drive-through of a Jack in the Box with four Jumbo Jacks inside. Which, to my surprise, I wolfed down rather quickly.

"Yes, until you're twenty-one years old. I'd try not to lose that card if I were you, kiddo," she said with a smile.

"Oh, I won't!" I said, shaking my head. "So tell me Carmen, is this tribal money and what is my tribe?"

She just eye rolled at me. "I have nothing to do with your tribe. Like I've said a million times. Just be happy with this." She said looking into my eyes. And I didn't push it further.

"The extra dose of Lithium might make you a bit sleepy. Go home and get some rest," Mrs. Galindo muttered but I hardly heard her words. I was still too fazed and excited to finally have some income. I stood in Carmen's driveway and waved as she drove off.

But despite all my excitement, I must have dozed off as soon as I got to my bed because the next thing I knew, I was waking up to a dark room. I blinked groggily, trying to make sense of my surroundings. The clock read past midnight. My stomach growled loudly, a sharp pang of hunger twisting through me.

Starving.

Still? "You had four jumbo jacks, Mags!" I said to myself. I slipped out of bed, careful to avoid the third step on the stairs, the one that always squeaked, and made my way to the kitchen. I threw together a sandwich and devoured it in seconds, but the hunger didn't subside. I made another, gobbling it down just as quickly. Still hungry. Desperate, I gulped down two large glasses of milk, hoping that would fill the void gnawing at me.

Sitting at the dinette table, I finally caught a glimpse of my reflection in the sliding glass door. I froze. The pale face staring back at me wasn't mine—or at least, it didn't look like me. My skin was practically translucent, much lighter than usual. *Am I sick?* I wondered, my stomach knotting with unease.

But I couldn't sit still. I needed to clear my head. Maybe some fresh air would help. Grabbing my bike from the garage, I slipped out the house and into the cool night, the quiet streets illuminated by the soft glow of the swollen moon.

The stars twinkled brightly above, and as I rode down the familiar streets, I started to feel the tension ebb away. The heat that had weighed me down earlier lifted, replaced by a sense of clarity. My nerves, once on edge, settled into a strange kind of numbness and then—contentment.

Everything felt . . . clear. More vivid than usual. The moon wasn't full like it had been the night before, but it was still bright, casting a soft cascade of light over everything. Usually, I never had a plan when I snuck out for a late-night joyride. But tonight, I knew exactly where I was going.

Bucklin Park.

I pedaled down the trail, the peaceful night wrapping around me like a comforting blanket. The eerie silence and strange smells from the night before were gone. The park felt almost serene, normal. But as I approached the tree—*his tree*—my heart began to race again.

To my amazement, the broken tree branch was still there, lying on the ground, just as it had been. Slightly wilted by the heat of the sun that day but otherwise unchanged.

I got off my bike and cautiously walked toward it. I knelt, daring myself to touch it, to see if it was really there—if this wasn't just some leftover hallucination. After a few moments of hesitation, I reached out and plucked a few eucalyptus leaves from the branch. I crushed them between my fingers and brought them to my nose. The sharp, familiar scent hit me. They were real.

I stuffed a few more leaves into my pocket. I had always collected flowers and leaves, pressing them between the pages of old school books under my bed. Later, I'd incorporate them into my watercolor paintings to add texture. I wasn't great at painting, but it was something that had stuck with me from art class, a small creative outlet.

These leaves, though . . . they were different. Special. I might not use them in a painting. I just wanted to hold onto them, to remember. In a weird way, the scent reminded me of him— the specter with the glowing red eyes. Although there was a blanket of death and decay around him, something about these leaves reminded me of the faint scent I would occasionally pick up surrounding his essence.

Don't forget him. He is important. Part of me could not tell if these were my thoughts or the soft whispers of the voice that lingered on despite the heavy dose of Lithium in my system.

I stood and looked around one last time, hoping—against all logic—that I might see him again. But the park was empty, quiet. Maybe the tree was real, but he wasn't. Or maybe none of this is.

With a sigh, I got back on my bike and pedaled home.

The next few weeks passed in a strange sort of normalcy. Everything seemed fine—except for the occasional sharp pang of hunger that hit me out of nowhere and a growing discomfort with the sun. I'd never minded the desert heat before, but now it felt oppressive, suffocating. And still, there was no sign of Luz or the man from the park. It was as if they had vanished, leaving me to wonder if I had imagined it all.

Strangely, I was missing those two and didn't know why.

In the meantime, Mrs. Galindo started taking me to various appointments—the dentist first, then the eye doctor. I hadn't been to the dentist since I was thirteen, when I finally had my braces removed. I remembered having some kind of oral surgery for two extra teeth, but then I never went back except yearly for new retainers.

Apparently, people on Lithium are at a higher risk for cavities, so she insisted on a check-up. I didn't have any issues with my teeth, though; not even a cavity, and after a thorough cleaning, I was given a clean bill of health. I came out with a new metal retainer they said to continue wearing every night. You'd think after five years I'd be able to stop with the retainer.

The eye doctor was next, but there was no explanation for why. I didn't need glasses, so the appointment felt unnecessary, but I went along with it.

"You have astigmatism," said the hyper eye doctor with coffee breath. "That's why you've been seeing glares at night and why the light bothers you. I'll prescribe some glasses for you to cure that."

"Great," I said. "Can they be black?"

He laughed. "They can be whatever color you like."

Because there was no prescription except for astigmatism, they gave me the seventies-style black cat eyeglasses I picked out. I have to admit, they did keep me from straining.

"These will also help cut out the red eye effect," The ophthalmologist said.

"The what?" I asked, looking at him almost suspiciously, remembering how I had seen myself with glowing red eyes not too long ago.

"Oh, you know that glare that humans get in front of a bright light that turns their eyes red? It's normal. It's not good for your eyes to have all that light, though, with astigmatism that is, so I'd wear them even at night," he said.

I couldn't help but suspect him knowing something, but I left his office quietly regardless. Why was everyone suddenly so concerned for me?

Surprisingly though, I found myself growing more comfortable around Mrs. Galindo. Since I had entered school late as a child in foster care and was older than most seniors, now almost nineteen in August, she even took me to the DMV to get me tested for a driver's license. I didn't have a car yet, but I had a new shiny black card that would help me with that after I received my new license in the mail. Mrs. Galindo had happily lent me her car to take the driver's test.

Seeing her so often made me feel like I could open up to her. I hadn't told anyone about the hallucinations, the voice, or the strange encounter with the man. My friends would never understand—they'd either laugh or think I was crazy—but maybe . . . maybe she would.

Yet, every time I thought about confessing, every time the words were on the tip of my tongue, something stopped me. A faint whisper—more of a memory than an actual voice—would echo in my mind:

Don't trust her.

The memory of the voice echoed in my mind with a subtle but undeniable weight. And no matter how hard I tried to brush it off, a part of me clung to that warning, trusting it in a way that felt instinctual, primal. I couldn't shake the feeling that the voice knew something I didn't. Still, I had to keep up appearances. I told Mrs. Galindo about how sensitive I'd become to lights, sounds, and the sun lately, hoping she would have an answer.

And of course, she blamed the Lithium. "It's a common side effect," she said, with that familiar mix of clinical detachment and concern. "Just try to stay out of the sun as much as possible and drink plenty of water."

"Maybe I should move out of the desert," I said

half-jokingly. "I am eighteen."

She didn't laugh. Instead, her expression hardened. "You could," she replied, "but if you move out of this county, you'll lose your medical benefits, your Lithium, and access to your monthly stipend."

I stared at her, feeling a knot tighten in my stomach. I knew I needed the medication—at least, that's what everyone told me. Without it, I risked spiraling into mania, losing control again. But I hated this town, hated the dry, relentless heat of the desert. My throat tightened with frustration, but I just sighed, knowing I'd have to come up with a plan to leave before I turned twenty-one.

Graduation was looming closer, just a week away. I had already bought my prom gown, a sleek black number, thanks to my new shiny black card. Most of the guys I might've wanted to go with had already left school, so my friends and I decided to go as a group instead. A girls' night out—punk rock, goth vibes, and mischief.

Prom was as boring as I'd imagined it would be. We posed for the obligatory photos, plastering on fake smiles as we stood under the tacky decorations in the school gym. But as soon as the chance came, we snuck out early and piled into Cell's midnight blue sedan, ready to blow off some steam. Cell's dad had gifted her the car, and it had quickly become our escape vehicle—perfect for spontaneous trips to San Diego, our favorite retreat.

"Lets get out of here!" Cell proclaimed as we pretended to go to the little girls room but instead she held the back door open for us. None of us had to be told twice before crawling into her car.

We headed to PB, or Pacific Beach for a bonfire, leaving the desert far behind. The hour-and-a-half drive up the mountains was a blur of music and laughter. The four of us—Cell, Moniker, Manda, and me—were like a small tribe, bonded by our mutual love of punk rock, goth music, and the shared struggles of navigating high school. I didn't drink that night, not wanting to risk any hallucinations, but my friends were all planning on getting completely wasted. I volunteered to be the DD. I was eager to drive anyway since having just received my license.

"Turn off that awful shite music, Cell-utt!" Manda yelled from the backseat, her voice playful but insistent. She sat beside Moniker, our quiet, dark-humored Wednesday Addams, who smiled faintly at Manda's outburst.

Nicknames were our thing—loving insults that only made sense between us. I sat up front with Cell, who rolled her eyes dramatically but complied, switching out the CD.

London After Midnight's "Sacrifice" flooded the car with its haunting melodies, the kind of gothic love song that always seemed to stir something deep inside me. The singer's voice was full of longing and ache, and with each bellowing note, I felt my heart tighten in response as if pining for a love I had never known but desperately craved.

As the music played, I leaned my head back, watching the mountain landscape slide past in the dark. The lyrics wrapped around me, comforting the anxiety that always seemed to linger just beneath the surface. My thoughts began to drift, and I felt a strange, invisible howl reverberate through my body. It wasn't the same as the one I'd let out at the bonfire weeks ago—this one was silent, contained, but I could feel it deep within my soul.

And then I saw them—*eyes.*

Glowing red eyes pierced the darkness ahead like twin flames. I stiffened in my seat as a bolt of lightning struck the sky behind the eyes, illuminating a massive form—a wolf. Not just any wolf, but a huge, terrifying creature with a broad snout and fur that bristled in the flickering light. The wolf reared its head back and howled, the sound echoing through my mind even though I couldn't hear it aloud. Just as quickly as it appeared, the road curved, and the creature vanished behind the mountain.

My heart pounded in my chest, and I turned to look over my shoulder, desperate to see the wolf again, but it was gone. The shadows swallowed everything. I shook my head, confusion swirling in my mind. Was I seeing things again? There wasn't a single cloud in the sky, and it definitely wasn't raining. But I was certain—*absolutely certain*—that I had seen a bolt of lightning and a huge, giant black wolf with gleaming red eyes.

"What is it?" Cell asked, her brow furrowing as she glanced over at me.

"Nothing," I muttered, trying to sound casual. "I thought I saw lightning."

Cell shrugged, but before she could respond, Moniker's soft voice piped up from behind me. "It's the song, Mags." Her tone was eerie, and she gave me a deadpan look that could only be described as a perfect misguided youth impression-void but with angst.

I smirked, crossing my eyes at her in jest. "That's thunder, not lightning."

"Well, turn it up and stop yapping!" Manda groaned from the backseat, her annoyance clear. We all laughed, the tension easing for a moment. But inside, I couldn't shake the feeling that I had really *seen* something.

I started to tremble slightly, adrenaline coursing through my veins, but I forced myself to stay calm, to breathe slowly. My mind raced as I replayed the image of the wolf and the lightning over and over. I could feel it in my bones—this wasn't just a hallucination. It was something else, something more.

By the time we reached the beach, I had managed to calm myself down. The ocean air was cool and refreshing, and we quickly ditched the festival crowd for a more private spot by another pier. We stripped down to our underwear and waded into the surf, splashing each other as we laughed like kids. The world felt lighter here, the weight of everything melting away with the sound of the waves.

Then I noticed him—a man standing on the pier above us, staring at us. He was far enough away that it wasn't immediately alarming, but something about his presence unnerved me. He had medium-length thick blonde hair, neatly parted, and wore a black long-sleeved shirt tucked into black slacks—completely out of place for the beach.

My friends had noticed him, too, but ignored him. I couldn't look away. He wasn't giving off any pervy vibes, despite what my friends might've thought. His gaze felt . . . different. It was almost as if he was watching us with purpose, like he was waiting for something.

Who was he?

There was something strange about him, something that felt familiar but not in a comforting way. I wanted to shake the feeling off, to tell myself it was just some guy wandering around, but I couldn't. Deep down, I knew something was coming, something that would change everything. I swam quietly in the deep part of the water, letting the waves and undulation of the water comfort my nerves.

And for the first time since that one night of meeting that strange guy in the park, I felt the chill of the unknown wrap itself around me again, refusing to let go.

"Fuck off and leave us alone, perv!" Cell yelled from the water, her voice cutting through the night air like a blade. She was defiant, her eyes blazing with anger, but Manda, in her usual rebellious fashion, did the exact opposite. With a gleeful laugh, she flashed her boobs at the man standing on the pier. Moniker just laughed as she went over beside Manda and splashed her calling her a "wench".

I didn't react like either of them. I just stared. He wasn't like the guys we'd encountered before—there was something unsettling about him, something dark and dangerous that made my skin prickle. His eyes met mine with a look of quiet disapproval, like he was judging me for the company I kept or because I was practically naked in the water. No, it wasn't Cell's anger or Manda's wild abandon that bothered him. It was *me.* His gaze felt personal; the longer I stared, the stranger it felt.

I couldn't shake the feeling that I knew him. Not just a passing familiarity but something deeper. His name lingered on the tip of my tongue, teasing my memory as if we had spoken before—been friends, or maybe something more. He turned his whole body toward me as if he could hear my thoughts.

My heart raced, and a sudden rush of vulnerability washed over me. I looked down at the water, feeling naked in a way I'd never felt before. I normally didn't care about being exposed—nudity had always felt natural to me, even freeing—but in his gaze, it was different. I felt small. Exposed. Like prey under the watchful gaze of a predator.

Without thinking, I swam towards the beach, stood up and grabbed my towel, wrapping it around myself as I hurried toward the car. My feet pounded against the sand as I made my way to the boardwalk bringing about small gusts of sand around to cling to my wet body. My mind buzzing with confusion and unease. When I finally dared to glance back at the pier, he was gone.

"Good evening," came a deep, familiar voice. My breath caught in my throat as I turned to see him standing just inches away from me. Up close, I knew immediately—he wasn't just some man. There was something otherworldly about him, something ancient.

I stared into his eyes, searching for an answer. "Where do I know you from?" I asked, my voice barely above a whisper, my heart pounding in my chest.

He looked down at me with a softness that contrasted the danger I felt radiating from him. There was something almost . . . loving in his eyes, like he had been waiting for this moment, waiting to meet me. He had the same eerie, ageless quality as the other Vampire or Werewolf I'd met—the same unnatural red glowing eyes, the same unsettling perfection—but there was something different about him. His presence didn't fill me with fear but with a strange, calm intoxication. He felt like a puzzle piece I hadn't known was missing.

His hair was slightly wavy, framing his face, which was fully visible, unlike the other man who hid under a hat. This man—*Sebastian*, I realized suddenly—wait how did I know that name?

He was slender but strong, his broad shoulders hinting at power beneath his composed exterior. His eyes were a bright, piercing blue, and they glimmered with the same supernatural red intensity when the moonlight hit him right that I had seen in the other man's, but they held something else: patience, and maybe . . .

The voice in my head—Luz—whispered as if afraid to speak. *That is your dad, Mags. I see him in your locked memories. You are right, his name is Sebastian.* She ended with a gasp as if she had suddenly become exhausted by merely speaking to me.

"Dad?" I breathed, the word spilling from my lips like it had been hiding there all along.

A smile curved at the corners of his mouth, his sharp, faintly visible fangs catching the moonlight. "Forgive me," he said gently, his voice deep and soothing, "I didn't mean to surprise you while you were . . . indecent. But it's been so many years. I had to see you again." His eyes flickered toward mine, then lower as if searching for something beneath the surface. "To meet you . . . and your new friend."

At the mention of my "new friend," his eyes crinkled at the edges, betraying an age far older than his youthful appearance suggested. As he spoke, a single drop of blood slid from his left eye. He wiped it away with a handkerchief, his movements so graceful, almost otherworldly, as if even this gesture was steeped in centuries of refinement.

I was too entranced to react, to ask about the blood, the fangs, or the pale perfection of his skin. His face was smooth, unblemished by time—no freckles, no moles—just a ghostly white, like a statue carved from the purest marble. Even his hands, as he dabbed his eye, were flawless, free from any imperfection. I couldn't stop staring.

Something made me reach up and touch his cheek. I couldn't help myself. His skin felt strange. Cold but smooth like a dolphin who swims in cold water. Or perhaps in his case, a shark.

"It is imperative that you come with me, Magdalena—my daughter," he said, his voice soft but commanding as he reached up to hold my hold to his face. He then motioned toward a sleek black Cadillac parked nearby. His words echoed in my mind, and I felt an irresistible pull, as though my body were no longer my own.

I was calm—too calm. I wasn't afraid. I wasn't nervous. I felt . . . *safe* in his presence, even though every logical part of me knew I shouldn't. I was drunk on him, on the way he looked at me, the way he said "daughter" like it meant something more than just a word.

"But my friends . . ." I muttered weakly, glancing back toward the water where the girls were still laughing and splashing.

"They will be fine," he assured me, his voice like velvet. "I've already compelled them. They won't remember you were ever with them, and they won't remember me."

I blinked, barely comprehending his words. Compelled them? What did that mean? But before I could ask, he took my hand, lifting it to his lips with a gentlemanly grace that felt as though it belonged in another century. His lips were cool against my skin, and I couldn't help but shiver.

The next thing I knew, I was slipping into his car, still wrapped in nothing but my towel. I didn't protest, didn't fight. I simply followed him as if I had no choice, as if every part of me was drawn to him in a way that defied explanation. My natural inclination to resist, to fight, was buried deep under the spell of his presence. I was entranced, compliant, and completely vulnerable.

Chapter 9

The Owl

Andy

The night was young, and the air hummed with a raw energy that tugged at the edges of my mind. I felt the familiar itch, the undeniable urge to let my wolf free. Ash, my ever-present companion, was restless. His need vibrated through me, his spirit pacing, ready to explode into the wilderness. I couldn't ignore him anymore. My body tingled with anticipation as I leaped down from the rocky cliff I had wandered to almost accidentally, feeling the cool night wind against my skin as it whipped past.

Below me stretched the barren desert—a wasteland to most, but not to me. I had met many strange creatures in this seemingly lifeless place, and they had hinted that there was more to this desert than met the eye ever since my arrival.

"The Guardian . . ." came the whispers. Voices in the dark, almost too faint to hear, yet unmistakable. "Seek out the Guardian rogue!" The words curled around my thoughts like smoke, and I stopped in my tracks, a chill slithering down my spine. It was at that moment, with the night pressing in around me, that I realized this desolate place was far from empty. Beneath the silence, life teemed—supernatural creatures that had never crossed my path before. Creatures that didn't even exist in the ancient tomes back home.

I had spent time among the Fae, temporarily finding refuge on a Celtic island, and for a moment, I thought these beings might be similar. Some were untouchable—flickering shadows that danced on the edges of my vision, slipping away before I could draw near. They were neither human nor beast but something in between, mingling with the darkness itself. I wondered if I was finally losing it, my mind splintering under the weight of my rogue existence.

But then, one of them finally made sense when they spoke. "Go find the Owl," it whispered, a thick, raspy voice like winds through an ancient cave. A giant black Werewolf that was more human-shaped than a wolf glared at me. I saw his gleaming red eyes pass me, and though I was accustomed to seeing well in the dark, I saw that he appeared mostly shadowed like an apparition.

That's when I heard the shriek. I looked up and over the darkened sky. A bright white gigantic owl graced the sky above me, silently and serenely.

I had encountered Skin Shifters before in my travels across the States, but none like this. None willing to communicate. None that made me feel safe to befriend either. But the owl—this massive, otherworldly barn owl—didn't feel like a threat. He perched there in the moonlight, his feathers glowing ghostly white, and though he did not speak in words, he spoke with his spirit. A single, piercing screech cut through the stillness, and I understood. He would not harm me. His presence was peaceful, unlike the others I had met before.

Ash stirred impatiently. He was ready for a run, his energy barely contained. The crisp desert air called to us, and above, the stars glittered like scattered diamonds, casting pale light over the sharp ridges of Kuuchamaa mountain. The night felt alive, and so did I.

We caught their scent—the couple I had crossed paths with before, the night I met Mags. Ash's excitement surged, his instincts firing, his need to hunt overwhelming.

Not hunt, meet. Ash mindlinked me. I nodded in approval.

I shed my clothes, folding them neatly and tucking them beneath a rock. In these moments, it was necessary to trust Ash completely. I gave him careful instructions, whispering through the bond we shared. Shifting wasn't always easy, and sometimes, it was more than just a loss of control. I hated when I felt disconnected from him, when our bond faded into the background and left me adrift in the void.

As a rogue, shifting was unpredictable. Sometimes, I'd black out entirely, losing hours or even days to the void, waking in strange places with blood on my hands and no memory of what I'd done. Other times, it was like watching through his eyes—a film reel of his hunt playing before me, leaving me as nothing more than a passive observer. And on rare nights when the stars aligned just right, I could feel him—truly feel his emotions, his drive, his hunger—and even speak to him when he was in control. But those moments were fleeting, like chasing a ghost through the fog.

As I allowed the shift to take hold, I felt that familiar crackle of energy ripple through me. Ash pushed forward, and with a flick of a switch, my body transformed, fur replacing skin, muscles stretching and twisting. Relief flooded through me as I found myself still tethered to his mind, my consciousness riding alongside his. Tonight, I would not disappear into the void.

Through his eyes, the world came alive in ways it never did in my human form. The scents, the sounds, the pulse of life beating all around us were intoxicating. We were one, a predator on the prowl, guided by instincts older than time. The trail of the two owls was fresh, and Ash's determination surged through me, a hunter ready to chase down whatever lay ahead.

Ash's powerful, muscled legs tore through the rough mountain path, his massive paws trampling over the tracks left behind by coyotes or mountain lions. Up and up he climbed, undeterred by the rugged terrain. The jagged agave plants and sleeping boulders stood no chance as he barreled through the canyons with supernatural speed. His movements were so fast they blurred my vision, turning the landscape into a trail of streaking lights and shadows. The stronger the scent of the owls became, the more Ash accelerated, his singular focus on finding them overriding his primal urge to hunt the rabbits and hares that darted in the corners of our shared vision.

"Find the owl," echoed in our mind, and Ash obeyed without hesitation.

The climb was relentless. For miles, he pushed onward up the steep mountain face without rest, without tiring. He didn't need to. His wolf was a force of nature, and tonight, he was unstoppable. When we finally reached the top, the air felt thinner and colder, and stretched before us was the breathtaking sight of the valleys of Mexico and California blending together like an ocean of shadows and moonlight.

And there, standing at the edge of the cliff, were two enormous white owls—towering nearly six feet tall, their forms almost otherworldly against the star-filled sky.

Ash stopped suddenly, his glowing eyes locking onto the owls. They stared back, unblinking, their black eyes deep and as ancient as onyx.

Without warning, Ash moved. He knew what he had to do.

His large canines reached back toward his hackles, and with a swift, brutal bite, he tore into his own flesh. The sound of the skin ripping was sickening, but I didn't feel the pain—Ash bore that burden. Still, I knew the moment I surfaced in my human form, the agony would hit me full force. He howled, a primal, bestial roar that echoed through the canyon, but already his wound was healing, knitting itself back together even as he laid the torn piece of skin at his feet.

Our vision flickered, and in a blink, I shifted back.

I emerged like a newborn, crying out in a sharp, involuntary roar from the wound at my back, but I stifled it the moment

I saw one of the owls approaching. My heart pounded in my chest, and I forced myself to remain still, to be ready. If my offering was rejected, I had to be prepared for a fight.

The male owl moved closer, his massive form looming over me, and I couldn't help but peer up into his big, obsidian eyes. He was magnificent, a creature of legend, but there was something off—something I hadn't noticed before. His left leg was crippled, bent at strange angles, his talons twisted awkwardly to the side. And his mate, who had begun to step forward as well, cradled a broken wing, holding it against her body as though it were a child. She couldn't fly; that much was clear.

My chest tightened. I had known there was something different about them the moment I first saw them, but I never expected injuries this severe. I realized now, with a sudden clarity, what had happened. The first night I encountered them, the male owl had been circling above me while his mate perched on a rock. I had sensed the decay and smelled the rot of their rogue nature, like mine, but different—Skin Shifters.

"You were protecting her from me," I whispered aloud, the memory hitting me like a weight. That night, he had flown circles around me, talons outstretched, keeping me at bay while his injured mate sat defenseless on the cliff. They were rogue, yes, but their bond was unmistakable, primal in its intensity.

I had known instinctively that they would be important to me, that they could help me in ways I hadn't yet understood. But before I could seek them out again, my mate's howl had called me away.

Now, as I stood before them, I sighed, feeling a quiet hope settle in my chest. They were still sane. They hadn't succumbed to madness. And with my pain beginning to dull as my own wound healed, I bent down and picked up the torn piece of skin, offering it to the male owl.

He took it carefully, splitting the skin in two with his good talon and beak. With the smaller half, he draped it over his twisted talon. I watched, eyes wide in awe, as my skin dissolved into him, disappearing into his body like it was made of smoke. His talon straightened before my eyes, the twisted bones aligning, becoming whole once more.

He turned to his mate and tossed the remaining half of the skin over her broken wing. The transformation was instantaneous. Her wing stretched out, the bones knitting together as she let out a sharp, joyous shriek. With a single, powerful beat of her wings, she took to the sky, soaring into the night with a grace she hadn't had before.

The male owl and I stood in silence, watching her silhouette disappear against the stars. It felt like a miracle—a glimpse into the true power of skin-shifter magic. I had heard the rumors and whispered stories of other shifters who could heal and transform using the skins of others, similar to the shamans back home. The tales were never told in a positive light on this continent like they are in my homelands; they were more like cautionary fables. But here, now, I have seen it with my own eyes and know there was a familiar kinship between us.

I looked up at the male owl again, and for a moment, we existed in the stillness of the night, two rogues bound by something far older than either of us.

They were unlike the Fae shifters I had known—those who were born into their skins, born as animals, able to shed them only once they were old enough to consciously will it. The Fae shifters could never craft new skins; if they lost theirs, they were condemned to a life of permanent humanity—a fate worse than death for some.

But the Skin Shifters from this continent . . . they were different. Again, they reminded me more of the shamans allied with my pack, yet there was something wild about them, something untamed. Unlike the shamans, who worked closely with the werewolves of my homeland, these beings were rogue-like, half-mad from isolation. They didn't belong to packs, nor did they seek alliances with any creature. Or at least none of the ones I'd met.

They lived on the fringes of sanity, and when they crossed the line and attacked, I or supernatural hunters ended them without hesitation.

But those who kept their madness at bay, those who didn't lunge at me with teeth bared, I let them be. They did the same. Most allowed me to pass through their territories with barely a growl. It was only the truly lost ones, the ones driven by pure, savage instinct, that dared challenge me.

Rogues carried the scent of rot, like something decaying from within. It was how I always knew when one was near. They were dangerous—not just to others, but to themselves. Ash's nose never scented fear from the more lucid ones, though. No, it was something else. A deep, primal recognition. It wasn't fear that kept them from attacking me. It was respect. From one predator to another, they knew I was not prey. And that was all it took for them to leave me alone.

These owls—there was that same scent of rot, that rogue pungency, but it was faint. They didn't seem lost, not like the others. They were calm and collected, as if they had fought the madness and, like me, had won.

I'd encountered many Skin Shifters in my time—coyotes, wolves or bears mostly, and an occasional wolf. I had even seen deer and mountain lions, but never before had I seen an owl. And now, here in this desert, I was face-to-face with two of them.

The air felt thick, too quiet, so I decided to speak. But could they understand me? I wasn't sure. Still, I spoke in English, the language of this wild country.

"I had no idea it would work," I said, my voice filled with astonishment as I gazed up at the female owl now soaring above us. "I assumed, but never . . . never in my wildest dreams did I think . . ."

Movement caught the corner of my eye, interrupting my thoughts. The male owl, the one who had stayed on the ground, was changing. His wings shortened, his talons retracted, and his face morphed until, before me, stood a man. Surprisingly, he wasn't naked like I was. But his clothes were ragged, worn leathers, and around his neck hung bone jewelry, though time and the elements had eroded most of its detail.

His face was striking—ancient and androgynous, reminding me of the people from Siberia. But his skin was sun-touched and rough, the look of someone who had battled both nature and time but still managed to retain his looks and the youthful luster of his hair and skin. His long, straight black hair cascaded past his waist, wild and untamed, with large white owl feathers tangled at the crown of his head, framing his face.

His mate descended from the sky, shifting mid-flight, her wings becoming arms and her feet turning back into legs. She landed gracefully beside him, dressed similarly in leathers and worn hides. A single, large owl feather was tied to her head with a thin string of leather, and a pouch hung around her neck. Her hide top was old, yellowed with age, missing a sleeve and barely covering her chest, but she stood confidently, unbothered. There was no shame in her stance—only strength.

Both bore the marks of their animal forms—my skin, or rather Ash's, had magically sewn itself into their leathers. Ash's black fur, rare for an arctic wolf, now covered the woman's left arm sleeve and the man's left foot boot, where before there had been only scars. They were whole again, and yet ancient, as though time itself had tried and failed to break them.

I couldn't help but admire their beauty. There was a timelessness to them, a wisdom etched into every line of their weathered faces. They were definitely my elders, but exactly how much was unknown? Trust was hard-earned, and I wasn't about to give it freely just because they appeared wise. I kept a careful distance, never turning my back to them, my senses still on high alert.

They both gazed up at the sky, their faces bathed in the pale light of the moon. They were smiling now, holding each other, speaking in a language I didn't recognize. It was soft, melodic, and ancient. I could sense their joy, their gratitude. They were caught in the moment, and I gave them their space, turning away to take in the breathtaking view over the cliff. The horizon stretched out before me, vast and open, the Pacific Ocean shimmering in the distance like a sea of stars. The scent of salt water was faint but clean and refreshing. I sat down on a nearby rock, waiting for them to come back down to earth from their moment of jubilation.

I found myself wondering about them. Had they kept all that jewelry and leathers on while in their owl forms? Shifters like me usually shifted naked, our bodies and clothes left behind when we transformed. Nudity was never a concern—it was natural for us—but I couldn't help but marvel at how seamlessly they had shifted, fully dressed, without a hint of discomfort. I shifted in my position on the rock so I could hide my manliness from them. I don't feel ashamed but I didn't want to offend them, being clothed and all.

After some time, the female owl turned to me, her eyes soft. She extended a hand, gesturing for me to come closer. "Cousin," she said, her voice smooth and warm. "We thank you."

I blinked, surprised to hear her speak my language but relieved. She and her mate both reached for my hands, their touch gentle was full of gratitude. "Thank you," they repeated, their voices filled with emotion.

For the first time in a long while, I felt something stir within me—something beyond survival. I had done more than just help them. I had given them a second chance; in return, they had given me hope. Perhaps

I could learn from them. Could they show me how to master being a rogue?

"You're welcome?" I muttered, uncertainty clouding my voice. Though I could see their crippled bodies had been healed, I still couldn't shake the doubts gnawing at me. Stories of Skin Shifters in these lands often came with dark warnings, tales of Witches who dabbled in black magic and the arts of death. There was no telling how much of it was true.

They seemed to sense my hesitation. The man lifted a hand, gesturing for me to wait. With surprising ease, he moved back toward a large boulder—twice his size at least—and, with a deep grunt, rolled it aside, uncovering a hidden hole in the ground. My eyes widened in disbelief. These Skin Shifters had more strength than I expected—strength akin to ours, the wolves. Their laughter echoed through the quiet night, full of glee. It dawned on me that they hadn't been able to move that stone until now, not while they were crippled. And I wondered, how long had they been waiting for this moment? Why couldn't the other rogues had helped them? What had caused their injuries in the first place?

"Thank you for adding to our strength, cousin!" said the tall owl man, glee plastered to his face like a child in a candy shop.

Ash? I called out mentally, feeling the faint pulse of his presence in the back of my mind.

You can trust these ones, Ash replied calmly. *It was my skin that gave them strength like us. It is new for them.*

"I see," I said out loud, forgetting that I was not alone.

The male owl paid my words no mind and motioned for me to follow him into the hole that the large boulder had kept hidden. Peering below,

I could see a makeshift ladder of tree branches and leather straps leading us down into the earth. I peered into the darkness but remained where I stood, still unsure if I wanted to go.

It was pitch black down there, but the air smelled of herbs, tobacco, and something ancient. There was nothing rancid or foul about the scent—just rich, preserved aromas, as though the boulder had sealed everything inside like a time capsule.

For a moment, a strange sense of déjà vu came flooding over me. I felt Ash running in circles in my mind, his howls reverberating deep within my soul, unsettling me.

Ash? I called again, unsettled by the intensity of his emotions.

I'm just excited, he said, his voice bright with anticipation. *Don't mind me.*

There was something else, though—something lingering at the edge of my senses. I could smell blood, but I couldn't tell whether it was coming from inside the hole or outside. The woman owl descended the ladder first, her movements fluid and calm, followed by her mate. He glanced back at me and made a 'come here' motion with his hand.

"Come," he said, his voice gentle and without malice. "We have much to talk about."

The déjà vu surged again, stronger this time, but then it vanished as quickly as it had come, leaving me no choice but to push it aside. I took a deep breath and followed them down.

As soon as my feet touched the ground, my eyes began to adjust to the darkness. The air was cooler here, a welcome relief from the dry heat outside, and the floor beneath my feet was solid rock. The echoes of my footsteps bounced off stone walls, giving me the sense that the room was vast—much larger than I had anticipated. The coolness wrapped around me like a soothing balm, and Ash practically purred in my mind at the comfort of it.

The man's voice broke the silence, laughter bubbling from his throat. "Finally," he said, the word filled with relief, like a weight had been lifted from his shoulders. He giggled, his voice echoing through the cavern as though we stood in a grand hall. The sheer joy in his tone made the room feel alive, and I realized how long he must have waited for this moment. But what exactly is down here causing him so much giddiness?

Something soft was placed in my hands. Clothing. I looked down and saw that it was a loincloth made of buffalo skins—simple but clean, despite how long they must have been stored down here. I dressed quickly, slipping on the loincloth and a sleeveless breast covering laced with a thin leather strap. The skins were a blank canvas, devoid of any markings or embellishments. They were meant to be worn without identity.

Once I was dressed, the woman sparked flint, and suddenly, the entire room was illuminated. I flinched, instinctively guarding my eyes from the sudden brightness. It was like someone had flipped a modern-day light switch, and for a few moments, I struggled to adjust. When I could finally take it in, my breath caught in my throat.

The room was immense—far larger than any human construction could have been. It was round, with four enormous square pillars, thick and ancient, standing like petrified trees in the center. Each pillar supported the weight of the structure, and between them was a fire pit carved into the rock itself, with an indentation that created a step where one could sit around the flames. The walls were adorned with bones, hides, feathers, and the remains of ancient life. This place felt old—older than any structure I'd ever seen.

"Wow . . ." I whispered, my voice barely more than a breath, but the room's acoustics carried it far, making it sound louder than I intended.

The man left for a brief moment and returned with a large caribou buck. Its antlers scraped the sides of the entrance as he lowered the massive animal into the room. I stared in awe. How had he brought such a creature here? This was the desert. There were no caribou in this wasteland.

The buck was still alive, bleeding from its neck, a large bite wound visible. It didn't struggle, though—it seemed dazed, lost in shock. He laid it gently near the fire between two of the pillars.

"Where did that buck come from?" I asked, bewildered.

"There are no bucks like that in this desert."

The woman smiled, her hand resting on my shoulder in a gesture of comfort. "You will soon see," she said softly. She lifted my arm, and I gasped when I saw the dried blood on my skin—the same blood that was flowing from the wounded animal. I blinked in confusion, then tasted the familiar metallic tang on my lips. The truth hit me like a blow.

I brought that buck here.

No, *Ash* did. But how? When did it happen? Ah, the déjà vu . . . the missing piece of time, that's when.

The male owl sat down, facing the fire in the direction of the north. His mate took her place across from him, facing south. He motioned for me to sit to his left, facing east—toward my homeland. The buck lay still between us, its head angled west.

As my eyes adjusted further, I noticed more details—bones lining the walls, feathers woven into intricate headdresses, and handwoven baskets filled with dried herbs: sage, tobacco, mint, and even fungi. Everything had been preserved by the stone walls, the airtight seal of the boulder keeping it all untouched by time.

This wasn't just a cave. This was a *kiva*—a place of sacred power. I had seen a few of these earth dwellings when passing through other Native lands during ceremony time but this one was different. Larger and embedded into the mountain.

The man had quickly changed into fresher, but equally ancient, hides, pulling them from a wooden stand against the wall. His old, tattered skins were tossed into the fire without a second thought. Except for the pieces of Ash's black fur that had been sewn into his clothing—those he kept. He carefully placed the fur under a large barn owl headdress, reverent as he handled the gift.

I realized then that the rotting smell hadn't come from them but from the old, matted skins that had barely held them together. Now, freed from the decay, their true scents filled the room. The woman smelled of vanilla and sweet maize, a warm, comforting scent. The man carried the smell of marigolds with a sharp metallic undertone that was almost like zinc.

That's about right, Ash remarked in my head, a note of satisfaction in his voice.

What had ravaged their skins so deeply that they couldn't shift back to humans? I wondered, staring at them. They had been trapped in their owl forms for so long, and yet, they had managed to hold onto so much of their humanity. It was rare. And left me wanting to know that power.

The male owl looked magnificent in his full Native shaman regalia, each piece of his attire a testament to tradition and survival. His mate had dressed up as well, but she was even more striking. Her dress was adorned with beads made of owl bones—painted red with what I could only assume was blood. *And adobe*, interjected Ash in my mind, the distinctive smell of iron curling through my senses, though even the blood from the caribou beside me couldn't compare. Their skins were bleached white, likely the product of many owl sacrifices to craft their garments. How anyone could make leather from something so delicate and small as an owl was beyond me.

To a normal human, their outfits would appear as beautifully crafted ceremonial clothing. Perhaps clay jewelry and buffalo hides. No one would guess the sheer number of bones, blood, and flesh that had gone into their regalia. Despite the morbid reality, they were both undeniably beautiful, regal in a way that reminded me again of the ancient shamans from my homeland—otherworldly and dangerous. I could not escape from comparing them, my mind just kept returning to my past.

One thing set them apart from the other Natives of this land: they lacked the silver and turquoise that most wore in the Southwest. Not a trace of metal was found in their attire. Their decorations were purely natural—bones, feather quills, talons, and owl beaks intricately woven into their leather.

A strange tremor shook me. My heart began to race, an uneasy thrum beneath my skin.

You feel it now, too? Ash's voice was quiet but firm in my mind.

I feel something . . . powerful coming, I replied, unable to pinpoint what exactly it was. *I just wish I knew what.*

Though Ash and I shared this body, our senses were not entirely the same. His nose was sharper, his vision clearer, his instincts more primal. I often had to half-shift when my body felt up to it to utilize his senses—his eyes, larger and more attuned to darkness, his claws, his teeth. I could pull him forward just enough to use those parts of him when needed. But tonight was different. Tonight, he had taken control without asking, without allowing me to watch the world through his eyes. I was none the wiser. Perhaps, I thought to myself, I was losing my senses and becoming a true rogue.

Or perhaps it was out of necessity. He senses something I can't even begin to grasp. And though I feel something in my gut is near, I cannot put a name to it. I always trusted his instincts, even when I couldn't understand them. Ash was rarely wrong.

"It is time, Andrei," the owl man said suddenly, breaking the silence. He threw a handful of powder into the fire, causing it to flare up and sending glowing embers spiraling into the air like tiny fireworks.

"We must cleanse ourselves and this sacred space before we can speak," he continued. "We don't want any wandering spirits carrying word of what we are about to do tonight." He tossed a pinch of sage into the fire from a basket stained with the same mixture of red earth and blood.

My heart skipped a beat at the sound of him using my full name. How long had he known who I was? Had he known from the beginning? For a second, I almost got up and ran, having feared my identity being revealed for many years, but I stayed put, almost by an invisible tether to this kiva.

The basket, I realized, had no handles, and it had been dipped in blood—the caribou's blood. The owl man's fingers were stained red, but he didn't seem to mind. The buck beside the fire grunted softly but remained still, its eyes wide and glassy, reflecting the flickering flames as if they were trapped within its gaze. The owl woman let out a soft, high-pitched screech, and the buck fell silent, dazed once again.

That sound . . . it was like a dog whistle, Ash said, his ears pricking up in my mind.

I heard it too, I responded through our mental link, careful not to let the owls hear. The pitch was faint, barely audible to human ears, but it hadn't affected us. The buck, however, had fallen under its spell.

I need to learn that trick, I muttered to Ash in my mind.

The owl woman suddenly turned to me and hissed, "Shush!" Her sharpness caught me off guard. "Your cousin will now tell you the history of our people."

Ash blinked inside my mind, startled. Could they hear our thoughts? My conversation with Ash?

The owl man brought out a scepter adorned with the feathers of predatory birds. The Eagle, both bald and golden. Wrapped around its handle was a small strip of fur, the color suggesting reindeer or caribou. But it didn't smell like either—it smelled human. He held the scepter as he spoke, occasionally fanning the flames with its feathers.

He rose to his feet, his movements fluid, and threw another combination of herbs into the fire. Smoke began to fill the kiva, thick and aromatic. He chanted in a language I didn't understand, but the cadence felt familiar, like the prayers and chants of the shaman allies from my tribe. When he finished, he bowed his head to the fire and sat back down.

"I am a medicine man. Similar to your shamans back home yes, but we have slightly different customs." He announced. "My name, for all intents and purposes is Tecos. That is what you can call me. And my lovely wife here," he said motioning to the female owl, "is the lovely Santana."

Having no words, I simply nodded at them both.

"There is something you need to know about our people, Andrei, rightful alpha of the Thunderwolf Pack and ally to the Great Caribou nation of Skin Shifters," he said, pausing to let the weight of his words settle over me. He did know who I was. He knew my true identity. The full name of my pack—the alliance between the wolves and the shamans of my homeland.

My breath caught in my throat. I had been prepared for anything but this. The skin on my arms started to shiver and I could feel the tiny hairs standing erect as if electrified by this sudden realization. I had finally, after many, many moons, been found out.

Santana began chanting, a series of soft owl calls and melodic birdlike sounds, weaving together a song that evoked the wild places of my youth. The rhythm of her voice transported me back to the deep forests and windswept plains, and I couldn't help but feel a tug in my chest. Her throat and face twisted in ways that seemed impossible for a human, shaping her mouth into something like a horn as she shifted effortlessly from mimicking the calls of birds to the growls of bears, even down to the low hum of burrowing creatures. Each sound felt alive, wild, and ancient as if she wasn't merely imitating the animals but channeling them through her very spirit.

I was entranced until the owl man who called himself Tecos, joined in her song with a deep, steady voice that carried a story—one they had likely told together countless times. The way they moved in harmony felt sacred as if their souls had danced this dance for generations.

"Long ago," he began, "there were once two twin men who fell in love with two beautiful sisters. Each twin was similar in their strength and powers, but the older twin was wise and spiritual, while the second twin boy was a lover of nature and the hunt. They were both reared and taught the ancient ways and soon, each son raised up his own tribe. The twins separated, leaving their homeland to join their wives and wander the earth. One shaman hailed the spirit of the Caribou, the other the spirit of the Wolf. They were two utterly different forces—one embodying life and rebirth, the other death and chaos."

His voice seemed to pulse with the very breath of the earth, and I hung onto his every word.

"When the twins bore children, some inherited the ability to shift into their fathers' animal spirits. Yet, the two clans were always at odds, constantly warring, the children torn between their fathers' beast and their mothers' human soul. The land knew no peace, and neither did their hearts."

The tension between the words cut at me, old wounds I had forgotten starting to burn again. I had known that war had felt it in my bones while hearing the old story during ceremonies when I was a child. But being a youth kept me from learning the details.

"War after war raged," he continued, "until the Creator above grew weary of their fighting. He sent the mighty Thunderbird to show them how to live in harmony."

As he spoke, I could almost hear the rumble of thunder in the distance, as though the Thunderbird's presence still lingered in the world. I saw a storm in my mind—a storm that had come to swallow the two clans whole.

"One night," the owl man said, his voice low, "the Thunderbird unleashed a tempest upon the warring clans, forcing them to flee. They sought shelter on the highest ground, the sacred mountain, where the Thunderbird descended upon them. Those who didn't climb to higher ground . . . drowned."

The weight of his words crushed the air from my lungs. I could see them as in a vision—those who hadn't made it, swallowed by the storm, their bodies lost to the floods.

"Thunderbird," he said, voice lifting, "gave each clan leader a feather, a symbol of unity. He warned them that they must abandon their fighting and embrace one another as brothers and sisters. For the twins, born of two sisters and two brothers, were one and the same."

His words painted a new image in my mind—a unity I had never understood even with my people and their shamans.

"The Thunderbird commanded them to change their ways, to become a matriarchal society," he continued, his eyes intense. "Not to forsake their fathers, but to honor their humanity through the women who had borne them. And so, the men followed the women to their homelands, living in peace as adopted brothers and sisters when they had only once been cousins."

As he spoke, a sense of loss settled deep in my gut. I had been denied this story, this truth, for far too long. Why?

"From that moment," he said, "the Caribou Clan and the Wolf Clan were bound by an unbreakable oath. The Thunderbird's feather altered the spirits of the Caribou clans, granting them the ability to shift into other animals, but only if they sought permission and offered a pilgrimage of sacrifice."

He paused, letting the words sink in. "But you, cousin, your Wolf is different. Thunderbird also gave you grace with your wolf, tethering the wolf closer to your humanity, granting the beast a place of refuge. He is tied deeply to death and destruction, unable to accept another spirit. Yet, this makes your bond stronger. Your Wolf is always with you, one with you. Unless, of course, you have not been ceremonially joined and become what you call a rogue."

It hit me all at once—why I couldn't wield the relics of other shifters. Why I had watched others do what I could not. The relics, the skins, bones, feathers—they were more than tools. They were extensions of the spirits of the beasts they belonged to.

"Your people," the owl man said, "swore an oath long ago to live in peace with the Caribou Clan. When you gave us your skin, you fulfilled that oath to another shifter clan. You helped your cousin and that is why we are helping you now. Without that oath, our ancestors minds would have descended into madness, just as so many rogues have laid witness to." He shuddered. "I am surprised your Wolf has lasted this long," he said, eyeing me with a kind resolve.

His words were like a hammer to my chest, yet his tone remained calm and inviting. "You do not need a pack to accept this promise. But not every rogue can make this oath. I saw in you the potential from the moment we met. You just needed to ask."

His laughter echoed in the still night air, deep and warm, melting away some of the tension in my chest. He was not like the others I had known—so unlike the creatures of darkness I had encountered. He was real, grounded, and kind.

Then, the owl woman fell silent, her song fading. For a moment, I thought she might be upset, but then the owl man spoke softly to her, his hands pressed to his chest in a gesture of apology. They both burst into laughter and though I felt left out of their quiet exchange, I couldn't help but smile. Hearing their laughter warmed my heart.

"As allies," the owl man continued, "we will form a bond, a shared connection. We will remove the rogue curse, and you will gain what you have sought your whole life—the strength of your Wolf without the need to shift. And perhaps even more . . . your right to the alpha status of your father's clan. There are no more shamans that belonged to your ancient pack alliance."

The weight of his words was too much to bear all at once. Anger boiled inside me for the secrets that had been kept from me, for the years lost to my uncle's greed. Why had this been hidden from me? What happened to shamans allied to my pack. A part of me knew what must have happened. My uncle and that Witch is what happened.

I was happy, yes, to hear Tecos' words to hear I no longer had to be a rogue; a mixture of emotions took hold of me, yet the depth of this sacred oath had been kept from me for too long and the destruction of my allied clan kindled a fire inside of me.

Ash, my Wolf, stirred within me. His vision sharpened the world around us. I held him back. There was more to hear, more wisdom to absorb before action could be taken.

"My, what big eyes you have," the owl woman said softly, her voice cutting through the haze. Her mouth opened to sing again, but this time, no sound came. Yet, I felt a calm settle over me, a peace so deep it was like I had fallen into a dream. She had worked her magic on me and I didn't care. I welcomed the reset of my mind.

The owl man pulled out a large pipe, filling it with tobacco before passing it to the woman, who then passed it to me. I hesitated but took a puff. The tobacco tasted clean, the smoke sinking into my lungs like a calming balm, pushing me into an even deeper state of relaxation.

I closed my eyes, letting the world fall away. The fire crackled softly in the background, and the weight of everything I had learned settled on my shoulders.

As the smoke made its way into my lungs I succumbed to the feeling. I no longer felt shaky or nervous or angry. I was in a state of complete peace. Everything this man said to me made sense and though I was a boy when I was forced out of my lands some of the traditions and ceremonies I had witnessed started to make sense in my head.

It was customary in my land not to be coached in the ways of the spirit until undergoing the rite of passage into adulthood. Now I understood why. The ceremony was too sacred, too deep for a young boy to fully understand and appreciate without having his wolf.

My ceremony was never held as my uncle killed my mother and father and then banished me. Why the Witch did not kill me had always baffled me.

Maybe he thought he did when I went into hibernation, replied Ash.

Maybe, I thought to myself while still sucking on the pipe.

Then the man began chanting, at first in a whisper, but then the sounds grew louder and longer and more pronounced. The woman now had a small drum in between her crossed legs and she caused a slow rumble of vibrations to quicken my heart with the tap of each drum. Ash was content as well. His ears perked up, hungry to hear the music like I had never seen him. He was lulled and enchanted with each note being sung and with each beat of the drum. Soon, he was as content as a drunk child on breast milk.

I heard the woman break into another melody and join the owl man in singing. Two melodies, completely different from each other, commingled every now and again on the same note before going off again in separate directions in tone and octave. The two melodies painted a picture in my mind of two large white owls flying in the sky in a back-and-forth gesture like a mating dance. Each of them different, but in perfect harmony with each other.

They both cried out in an old instinctual language every now and then, pausing their human singing into the cry and sound of an animal. At first, it was the mourning dove, then the hawk. Then it was reindeer bleats and grunting, then the growl of the polar bear. All memories of my past life on the tundra. Even the growl of a mountain lion was there, an animal not from my lands and soon again, came the beautiful bird calls. They both mimicked the sounds perfectly and in harmony. Many more animal sounds reverberated in the air, like echoing down in a cavernous basin, but I could not even distinguish or recognize them.

He then started to chant again. I could not understand the language of his voice but the intonations and subtle changes of pitch colliding with her miraculous imitations of animals was a welcoming vibration into my heart. His voice was booming like a drum. Calm and soothing, then suddenly sharp and commanding like thunder. Each syllable they sang waxed and waned between notes and octaves with grace and beauty that I could swear in the ceiling, where the shadows from the fire met the light, were images that danced before me, danced the vibrations of life.

I closed my eyes, and suddenly, I felt connected to their own spirit. I was flying. The night sky opened up to me and I could see everything with such clarity. My flight was silent and I hung over the earth like a giant ghost sweeping across the desert.

The chirping crickets echoed near a small lake, their legs like violins crying out for their mates in a charming serenade. A stray dog howls and barks in alarm to my presence, but no one in the nearby neighborhood cares for his alarm. They want to sleep, their discontentment heard via grumbles and gripes, their bodies encased in their beds like cocoons. Two lovers in a car, groaning with passion and an ache in their loins to become one. They offer up hollow promises to each other in the dead of night, not realizing that neither of them meant any of those promises.

Owls hear everything, even secrets. And they can sing about this; their screech is both an outward and inward expression of psychic ability, I soon learned as I shrieked into the night. The vibrations of their screech returned to them like sonar. And like the moon's reflection of the sun's rays, even whispers, secrets, and emotions are carried by these images.

It was then that I felt called to open my beak and scream out an even louder and more pronounced preternatural sound that came from my very soul. It was the most magical thing I had ever experienced.

I felt my eyes twitch and I was no longer the owl. I felt myself go back to a very old memory of when I was a child in my homeland. There was snow everywhere, and everything was bright and white; it caused my eyes to squint. I was around eight years old and wore the traditional reindeer skins my people would make for our human forms in the winter. I could feel the cold seeping up through my leathered and padded feet from the permafrost, though I had mostly grown used to it.

The shamans were there, performing a rite of passage for one of my older cousins. He had just gotten his wolf and the shamans were blessing him. There were singers from their tribe there as well. Grunting and snarling with their throat, singing in a primitive and ancient style I had not heard again until now. Like the owl, they too wore a headdress, but theirs were of reindeer. The antlers of the staff are ornamented with thin strings of leather and animal bone relics, giving off the appearance of a spider web in their antlers. The antlers cascaded around the crowns of their head like a halo, lending authority and a majestic ambiance to the wearer.

Jepte, my distant cousin, had killed a reindeer with his wolf and was eating the entrails. His muzzle was a blast of fiery red, which mirrored the look of the Blood Moon overhead. His snow-white coat was washed red, and his amber eyes glowed with a type of fire inside them. I remember feeling proud and happy for Jepte. I remember that night as if it was yesterday, though I had not remembered it until now. The ceremony was one of the few that had been made public because he was not royalty. Only royal wolves held smaller ceremonies, from what I remembered.

In the background, I could hear another splash of something, causing the present fire in the kiva to roar up again. Tears formed in my eyes from the smoke and blur my vision into a new one. I saw a figure of a woman come to focus from within my mind.

She wore a blood-red leather dress, much like the dress the female owl wore now. It was laced in the front like a man's shirt by a leather string, leaving nothing to the imagination. I could feel myself wanting her. Aching for her luscious and full breasts. Her hair was black, long and flowing as she ran around in the forest as I chased her, nipping playfully at her hair. In my vision, she looked back at me, smiling, as she reached out for my hand, and I surprised myself by declaring loud and clear in my native tongue, "MATE!" Her scent of jasmine and rose devoured me. I whispered her name out loud: "Magdalena." Her name was like a silent yearning prayer on my lips as I called out to her.

Then her eyes suddenly flashed at my voice, and like a deer in headlights, she panicked. She was afraid of me. I scared her. My love, no! My other half was afraid of me. I felt like destiny was rejecting me.

Suddenly, there were shadows in front of her, and she sprinted towards them but didn't get far. My large snout reached out and closed in onto her ribs possessively as if she were prey. I was in wolf form. I saw the life drain from her eyes while she lay splayed on the ground in front of me. My wolf and I bit into my Little Red as she lay covered in blood. I bit into her entrails like my cousin did to the reindeer and ate them. There was so much blood. But my wolf was desperate to make her mine, even if it was against her will. He was desperate to join her to us, one way or another, and I could not stop him. My wolf was pitch black in color and though Jepte's image had blood all over his white coat, you could only see the proof of my actions on my fangs. They were stained red, dripping in her blood. She managed to stay alive despite all this until the very end when she looked at my wolf once more in the eye and I could see her spirit leave her.

An innate and primal howl of pain shot through my lips and I could feel Ash pushing to take control of my body as I was returned to the present. I let him. Only I didn't shift. I saw him. He was real, outside of myself, staring at me. He was standing on all fours right in front of me and though I was tall, his wolf form rivaled my height. I trembled at this sight, for I thought for a second I might lose him too. Like his spirit would leave me. I had never been apart from him like this before, not even for the years when he was hibernating and healing.

He stood there, an entirely different entity from myself, and we stared at each other in bewilderment for who knows how long. I wanted to reach out and pull him back into me, but my arms were numb and couldn't cooperate. He looked fearsome, the perfect alpha wolf who could intimate anyone and anything with just a snarl, but he looked scared, too. His teeth were larger than I expected and miraculously not drenched in the blood of my mate but instead were white as snow.

I heard the owl mutter something in his language, a type of order. Then suddenly I was awake and my eyes opened. Ash was no longer right in front of me but inside me once again, for I could hear him howling in my mind. I stood up quickly, jumping back and away from the fire, gasping for breath.

"What did you do to me?" I demanded of the owl, both terrified and angry, leaning onto one of the pillars to steady myself. I had to keep from shifting and tearing everyone limb from limb. Was this witchcraft? Maybe the local Natives were right.

He stood and blessed the fire and air around us. The woman was standing, too.

"I showed you what you came here for," he said calmly.

"You wanted answers, did you not?" the female owl asked. "We are not Witches. We are Skin Shifters, while Witches take without asking; we receive only what is freely given by the Manitou—a power bestowed to us by the Thunderbird. You must accept your fate as well! There are those who, yes, use magic for evil; they are rogues who refuse to honor the Thunderbird's oath. We are not those disgusting creatures who walk in rebellion down a dark path," she pleaded with me to understand, and I think I did.

I slowed my breathing down and coughed a few times to get some smoke out of my lungs.

I then looked at the owl man again, in shock. He was a true shaman, much like the ones I knew of in my homeland. Or a medicine man as he called himself. So similar but so different. I had felt our shamans magic in the air before, during ceremonies and festivities, but never directly focused on me. There was definitely a similarity between the two people. The owl spirit had chosen him. And from what I experienced from flying with the owl, he knew many things, many secrets and that is how he knew who I was.

I did trust them. And Ash trusted them, too.

"Medicine Man," I called out pleadingly. "What is your name? Your real name."

The owl smiled. Then he reached up and spread the caribou's blood over my face, highlighting my eye area red. Down my chin, he made two red lines. It was then that I noticed that the caribou was dead. Ripped open by its guts. I got the hunch that I was the one who had done that.

"I believe you already know my name. I have many ceremonial names, but I choose to go by Tecos, Guardian Owl of the Shadowlands. You and your wolf are now one. You have received your coming-of-age ceremony and also received a blessing." He paused. "The Creator has given you a vision of the future. It is up to you to interpret it and bring its wisdom to life. But be forewarned! It is up to you to interpret it correctly! I cannot help you with that." He reached behind his head and plucked a white feather from his crown.

"And because you showed so much bravery and sacrifice for your mate that you were willing to literally give us the skin off your back to help both of you, I give you a feather off my back. This is your first sacred relic after the Thunderbird gene activation." He reached out with two hands and passed me the feather.

"May it give you vision, protection and wisdom for your coming journey." I took the feather with both my hands, just as I had seen my homeland shamans do to my cousin.

"But will I kill her?" I asked, a lingering feeling of fear still lingering about from my vision. I knew he could not answer for me. It was more of a rhetorical question.

"Do you accept this feather and the alliance of two warring brothers? Do you swear by your honor and father's blood to protect, love and respect your cousin's clan as a brother and sister?" he said as he motioned for me to take the feather. His eyes were black like the night.

"Yes," I said wholeheartedly.

When I took the feather, it was slowly absorbed into my skin—just like my skin had been absorbed into his. It was a tickling and warm sensation at first. I felt the ripple effect transpire throughout my body. It traveled through my arms, and the last ebb and flow surrounded my heart, where it finally dissipated and hid inside, past my body and into my soul, where it touched Ash. The feather now hung from his fur near his right ear. His first relic. I could see him in my mind's eye, sitting up and looking proud. He had waited a long time for his due.

I heard a slight shuffle of feathers and looked at the two owls standing beside me. Both had transformed into beautiful nighttime birds of prey. I found it odd that I could now hear their movements, even if ever so slightly.

Safe travels, Andrei, said the owl man with a mindlink. *We will meet again soon. Remember, this is a sacred neutral ground. No killing of anything here unless cleared by me. Even Vampires or ghouls!* Then, as quick as a viper strike, he jumped out of the kiva hole and flew off into the night.

The owl woman stood back and watched me for a second before she, too, spoke to me via mind link.

You are now an allied member of our tribe. Tecos is short for drunk—a Spanish name we recently adopted when I joined Tecos. My tribe also spoke Spanish at the time when I met him. It's more of a cute joke between us two, but he's adopted it, said the woman owl as she ascended and flew through the air. I could see the skies through her eyes while connected. The sun was just starting to break the horizon.

Owls are solitary and do not require a large tribe, only each other and their children. For this reason, we are the only shifter pack that can stand with only two members. We are allied with many rogues around here. They are all your brothers now as well. I'm only telling this to you now so you will understand that though our tribe is small, we are owls, and our knowledge and understanding of life are unsurpassed.

Of course, I said. It felt strange mindlinking to someone besides my wolf. *Thank you both again.*

Take the diamond. The owl woman, Santana, was giving me a mission. Her name was of Spanish origin, but she was not European. She was also younger than Tecos. Hundreds of years younger. She was probably about as old as I was.

Suddenly, an image came to mind of a spiteful serpent hiding in a cave. It had a jewel on its head that lit up the cave like a giant light. Its fangs were unsheathed, and it appeared to see me. Right before it struck towards me, the vision went away.

Take the diamond, she mindlinked again. And just like that, the link was disconnected. They had blocked me out, probably wanting their privacy.

It was almost daylight now, so I knew the owls were off to their sleeping nest, but I could not sleep. I had lots of work to do. After cleaning up my mess and burying the caribou in the mountains outside, I made my way back to make sure the fire was completely out. I wanted to leave their sacred meeting place clean like I had found it.

I leaped up with one jump out of the kiva and secured the large boulder over the hole, making sure to secure it the way it laid for years to ensure a good seal. The boulder was twice as tall as me and about the width of the length of a car. It was very heavy. I felt stronger now, though; moving the rock was a cinch. I was gaining the full advantage of my supernatural wolf's strength. He was right; we were one now. Truly one.

I felt a sense of pride, having already aided my brothers and sisters as my oath had warranted me to do.

The oath did change me. The stories and the ceremonies were real. I felt stronger, quicker and more alive than ever before. Different, but the same. How did I ever get by without this?

Yessss, stated Ash. *So this is what being in a pack feels like.*

"Yes, my dear feathered wolf," I exclaimed joyfully. "It is entirely . . . *invigorating*."

Once the kiva was thoroughly secured, I shifted. I was not prepared for the feeling of power inside Ash's wolf. I let out a howl. Images of Ash's memories flooded my mind. I remembered searching for and taking the caribou. Ash had moved too fast for any humans to notice anything but a blur, but I saw everything.

I saw him run and jump through the mountains, past state lines and into Canada until he reached the northern US state of Alaska. The caribou had presented itself, smelling musty like dew, and Ash took him down in no time.

He returned using the same route with the reindeer in his muzzle. He was fast, like lightning. And when he made it back to the owls, they were patiently waiting for him.

Despite my renewed physical strength, I retreated to the safety of my burrow, exhaustion weighing heavily on my soul. I craved rest, but even more than that, I sought refuge from the storm that raged in my mind. For all the strength I had gained, for all the life burning inside me, I couldn't outrun the crushing weight of memories and emotions pressing down on me. This time, though, sleep came quickly, and with it, vivid, powerful dreams that felt more like journeys than mere visions.

I found myself unlocking more and more of Ash's memories, feeling them bleed into my soul until they became inseparable from my own. I dreamt of soaring high above the world, free like an eagle, the wind beneath my wings carrying me higher and higher into the endless sky. Tecos' voice echoed through the air, joined by Santana's, their songs wrapping around me like a comforting blanket. The melodies of their ancient wisdom calmed my restless spirit, filling me with a sense of belonging and purpose.

It was the kind of sleep that didn't just heal the body, but the soul—deep, rewarding, and long overdue. And in that sacred rest, Tecos' words came back to me with undeniable clarity.

He was right. It was time. And in the morning I would be off to find my other hidden relics I hid in the grand canyon. Only I will return. Stronger, faster, better for my future bride.

Chapter 5

Silver and Wolfsbane

Mags

The next morning, I awoke still wearing the red and black dress from prom, the fabric crumpled and clinging to my skin. My head throbbed with confusion and exhaustion. The last thing I remembered was being at the beach, the cool ocean waves lapping at my bare skin as I laughed with my friends under the moonlight. We had left prom early, chasing the thrill of the night, but now here I was, back in my dress, as if nothing had happened.

I hadn't slept; I knew that much. My body felt heavy, drained of all energy, yet my mind buzzed with fragments of memories that didn't quite fit together.

Mags . . . the voice of my wolf, Luz, echoed faintly in my mind, so distant that I almost didn't catch it.

Mags . . . she called again, but this time from even farther away, like she was slipping from me, fading into the shadows. Panic gripped my heart, squeezing it tight. Luz wasn't real, or at least that's what I told myself. She was a hallucination, a figment of my imagination brought on by exhaustion or whatever chemicals were still lingering in my system from the night before. But the fear coursing through me was real, as real as the tremble in my hands.

Something was wrong. Luz was in trouble, and I felt it deep in my bones, a gnawing dread that wouldn't let go. My hand instinctively reached up to my hair, a nervous habit I'd developed over the years, but instead of the soft strands, my fingers brushed against something hard and cold.

I looked down and saw it: a large silver bracelet wrapped around my wrist, its surface adorned with intricate carvings and a gleaming piece of turquoise embedded in the center. It was beautiful, a piece of art that looked like it belonged in a museum or on the arm of one of the local Natives at school. But where had it come from? I had no memory of putting it on, and now that it was there, it refused to budge. I twisted it, but it wouldn't give. The metal was unyielding, as if it had been forged specifically for me and me alone.

A surge of panic washed over me. This bracelet wasn't just a piece of jewelry—it felt wrong, dangerous. And somehow, I knew it wasn't good for Luz. I rushed to the bathroom, nearly tripping over my own feet in my haste. I grabbed the nearest bottle of lotion, slathering it on my wrist in a desperate attempt to slip the bracelet off. But it was no use. The metal clung to my skin like a curse, refusing to let go. I stifled a disappointed grunt of panic.

I jumped into the shower, hoping the water and soap would help, but nothing worked. I stood there, letting the warm water cascade over me, trying to piece together the fragments of the night before. But all I could see was his face—blond hair, blue eyes, a smile that hid something sinister. He had looked rich, with a nice car that I had inexplicably climbed into. His house, his voice—it all started coming back in disjointed flashes.

And then, the most chilling memory surfaced. *He was a Vampire.* Not just any Vampire, but one who had claimed to be my father. Luz had whispered it to me in the darkness, her voice trembling with something I couldn't understand at the time. He wasn't the same creature I had encountered in the park, the one who had sent chills down my spine, but something much worse. He had compelled my friends—used some kind of power to make them forget. He had lured me into his world with nothing more than a word, and now I was wearing his shackle, a twisted symbol of whatever hold he thought he had over me.

Quickly I grabbed my phone, I wanted to test my theory and called Cell. She didn't answer. I called Moniker then Manda. Manda's aunt answered.

"Hello? Ryan residence!" said a hyper voice.

"This is Mags, is Manda there?" I asked, trying not to sound so alarmed.

"Mags?" Oh no honey they are still in San Diego. They got a room for the night. Oh hey! How come you didn't go? Manda told me you couldn't make it when she called me last night." Said the hyper aunt.

I sat there quietly hugging the handle to the phone a little too tightly. It's true, he did make them forget I was there!

"I..." I tried to speak but didn't know what to say. I was sick of lying. "I have to go! Bye!" Then hung up.

Well, I definitely was not a bitch to be collared. Nor one to be messed with! I felt a surge of anger rise in my chest. What kind of father would do this? What kind of monster would curse his own blood? I had to get this bracelet off and free myself from whatever spell he had placed on me. But no matter how much I pulled, twisted, or cursed; it stayed firmly in place.

There was only one person I could think of who might help—Munks. She was my fellow Native friend, one of the few people I trusted, and she knew more about silver jewelry than anyone I knew. She owned tons of the stuff. Maybe she could get it off or at least tell me who can. I quickly dried myself off and threw on a black Metallica concert shirt and jeans, not caring about the damp strands of hair sticking to my neck. I just needed to get out of the house, away from the panic that felt like it was closing in on me.

The house was empty when I made my way downstairs. Carmen and the kids must have gone out, leaving me alone with my racing thoughts. I grabbed a piece of raisin toast, barely tasting it as I shoved it into my mouth, and headed out the door. The morning air was still cool, a brief reprieve before the heat of the day set in, and I was grateful for it as I pedaled my bike down the familiar streets. I had my license but hadn't managed to find a car I wanted yet.

Munks lived on the other side of town in a small house that always smelled like sage and cedar. Her dad answered the door when I knocked, his eyes bleary with sleep. He let me in without a word, already knowing I was there to see his daughter. Munks was still asleep, her room dark except for the faint glow of string lights wrapped around a white parachute that hung from the ceiling, making her space feel like a cloud. She had told me once that the parachute had belonged to her father, a vet who had brought it back from his time in the service. I had always thought it was cool, a piece of history with a personal connection. I wished I had something like that from my parents—anything but this cursed bracelet.

"Munks! Wake up!" I called out, letting myself into her room. She stirred under the covers, groaning in protest as I shook her shoulder.

"Wuuut," she mumbled, clearly not ready to start the day.

"I woke up with this fucking bracelet, and I don't know how to take it off," I said, my voice tinged with desperation. I held up my arm, the bracelet gleaming ominously in the dim light.

She squinted at it, tilting her head to the side like she was trying to figure out a puzzle.

"It's not mine," she finally said, her voice still thick with sleep.

"I know it's not yours! I don't know where it came from, but I can't take it off. And I need it off!" I was practically pleading now, my hands shaking as I tugged at the unyielding metal.

Munks sat up in bed, her expression growing more serious as she took my arm and examined the bracelet. She tried to slip it off herself, but it wouldn't budge.

"Hm. You just woke up with it on you?" she asked, looking at me with a mix of curiosity and concern.

"Yes," I replied, my voice barely above a whisper. I felt so lost, so helpless.

"It's nice, at least. And very expensive looking," she commented, completely missing the point.

"Munks!" I practically yelled, exasperation bubbling over. "Do you know anyone who can take it off?"

"Oh, yeah. Torito makes jewelry; he can probably do it. I'm sure he's got the tools," she said, finally understanding the urgency in my voice.

"Can we go now? Please?" I asked, my heart pounding in my chest.

"We'll have to have my dad drive us. He lives out in the boondocks," she said, sliding out of bed and pulling on a pair of shorts.

The ride to Torito's house felt like it took an eternity. Munks' dad drove slowly, the kind of careful driving that usually didn't bother me, but today it was unbearable. I was close to tears, the exhaustion weighing me down, but I didn't dare let myself fall asleep. Not with this thing on my wrist, not with the memory of that Vampire still fresh in my mind.

When we finally arrived, I was practically vibrating with anxiety. Torito's house was in a remote area, surrounded by open fields and a few scattered trees. His dad stayed outside, chatting with an older man, while Munks and I headed inside. The air was cool, a stark contrast to the rising heat outside, and for a moment, I felt a flicker of relief.

Munks led me to the back, where Torito had converted a shed into his workshop. The moment we stepped into his backyard, all hell broke loose. The dogs started barking, a wild, frantic sound that made my skin crawl. One of them peed and ran away, tail between its legs. The chickens and rabbits, normally so calm, scattered in fear, hiding in their coops and hutches as if they had seen a ghost. It was like the entire animal kingdom was reacting to something—something they sensed in me I felt.

I couldn't shake the feeling that the bracelet was more than just a piece of jewelry. It was something darker, something dangerous, and it was affecting everything around me. I needed it off. Now.

Torito stepped out from the shed, his lanky frame moving with a kind of nervous energy that I couldn't quite place. His long, light brown hair was neatly braided, falling over his shoulder as he eyed me cautiously like I was a threat. His reaction sent a fresh wave of unease crawling up my spine. Why was everyone, even this stranger, acting like I was dangerous?

Just what the hell was going on?

For the first time, I started to wonder if maybe there really was something supernatural about me. Maybe I wasn't just imagining things—maybe I *was* part Werewolf or part Vampire or whatever strange hybrid the man in the park claimed me to be. Or maybe the whole world, including myself, was just going crazy.

"Munks," Torito called, his voice stern but calm. "Can you wait for us in the house for a second?"

Munks raised an eyebrow, casting a quick glance between me and Torito. For a moment, I thought she might refuse, sensing something off. Then she smirked.

"Why, you wanna be alone with my friend here, huh? She's got a boyfriend!" she teased, nudging me playfully. I stared at her, my brain still reeling, wondering if she knew about this "mate" nonsense that my wolf Luz kept mentioning. I shot her a questioning look, not really in the mood for her jokes.

"Aren't you and Raybans together?" she asked with a sly grin, her green eyes twinkling with mischief. Munks had that natural beauty that came with her mixed heritage—like me, she was a blend of cultures, though her striking green eyes and bronze skin set her apart. It was easy to see why people gravitated towards her.

"Ugh, no. He was never my boyfriend," I muttered, rolling my eyes. "I'll be fine. I just need to get this thing off."

She gave me a cheeky smile, tossing back a teasing "Mmhmm" as she sauntered toward the house, leaving me alone with Torito.

followed him into the shed, and the moment we were inside, the air felt different—heavier. Clutter filled the space, tools and containers of silver and other metals were strewn about, with stones of all shapes and sizes scattered across the workbench. It was cramped and Torito's nervous energy only made it worse. He sat across from me, and I tried to stay alert, but exhaustion was creeping back in, thick and relentless. My eyelids fluttered shut for a moment before I snapped them open, catching him watching me, assessing.

"I'm single, but I'm also not looking," I said, my voice sharper than I intended. I wasn't here for any kind of weird vibe. "Can you get this thing off or not?"

He jumped up, shuffling around the shed as he moved boxes and metal containers outside away from us. When he finally sat back down, his eyes seemed more focused and less jittery. The weird tension in the air had eased, but I was still tired—exhausted, really. I missed Luz, her voice, her strength. I wanted to hear her reassuring me that everything would be all right.

It was hard to believe that not that long ago, I would have done anything to keep her quiet.

“Unbelievable,” he muttered, almost to himself. I stared at him, confused.

“You’re just like my aunt,” he said, his voice softening. “She used to send the animals scurrying too. She’s been missing for a long time now. When I heard the dogs barking, I thought for a second that you were her. Sorry.”

“What?!” I gasped, trying to process what he was saying. His aunt had been like me? What did he mean exactly?

“No, I’m sorry,” I said quickly, unsure of what else to say. “I hope you find her soon.”

He shrugged, his expression distant, as if remembering someone long gone. “Well, she wasn’t blood-related, but she was my aunt in every way that mattered.” He paused. “She had the same reaction to silver and other sacred stones, too. I didn’t think there was anyone else like her around here. She was from New Mexico.”

My heart skipped a beat. New Mexico. My mother was from there too, but I didn’t say anything. Could his aunt be connected to me in some way?

“Was?” I asked quietly, dreading the answer.

“It was too long ago,” he said, his voice hollow. “We had her declared dead after ten years.” His words hung in the air, heavy with loss. I felt a pang of sadness for him, even though I didn’t know what it was like to lose someone close. I’d never had anyone to lose. But imagining what it would feel like made my chest ache.

“I’m sorry,” I whispered.

"It's okay," he said, though his voice said otherwise. "Let's get this thing off of you." He leaned forward to inspect the bracelet, his fingers running over the intricate designs. "This isn't the kind of bracelet that's usually made to be worn like this. It should have slipped off, but . . . it doesn't look like it was designed to come off easily."

watched as Torito continued to examine the bracelet. He wore silver, too—small turquoise earrings and a delicate necklace with a bird charm. Even though he had removed most of the silver from the shed, those pieces remained.

"So, you just woke up with this on?" he asked, glancing up at me.

"Yeah," I replied, keeping my voice casual. "I went to prom, then to the beach with my friends. I can't remember much after that. I don't even remember getting home. Maybe I drank too much?" I lied, not ready to spill the truth about my Vampire father or the compulsion that had stolen my friends' memories.

Torito frowned. "That's strange. Whoever put this on you really didn't want it to come off." He turned the bracelet over in his hands. "It's not pure silver. The outside is, but the underbelly—the part touching your skin—is steel. If it were pure silver, I could try to flatten it and bend it open, but the steel makes that harder. Silver's a soft metal, but steel . . ." He attempted to squeeze the bracelet with his fingers, but it didn't budge.

"They were either very strong or used a special machine to close this around your wrist," he said with a soft laugh. "I don't have either."

"Just cut it off then," I snapped, my patience wearing thin. "I don't care."

He hesitated. "Are you sure? It's beautiful and looks really expensive. Handmade, for sure."

"Yes," I said, my voice firm. "I think you're right—I probably have your aunt's allergy to silver. I feel horrible. Just get it off please."

Torito shrugged, then pulled out a small soldering device. He carefully placed a piece of hardened leather over my wrist, followed by a flat piece of wood between my skin and the bracelet to protect me from the heat. As the saw began to hum, small sparks flew around us, and I found myself staring at his necklace, the bird charm catching the light. It wasn't an owl, but the image reminded me of the large white owl I had seen at the bonfire. I couldn't shake the feeling that the owl was important.

"Have you ever seen large owls around here?" I asked casually, trying to make conversation.

Torito stopped mid-cut, his eyes narrowing. "What kind of owl?" he asked, his tone suddenly serious.

"A white one. Like a barn owl," I replied.

He stared at me for a long moment, then abruptly stood up. "I'll be right back," he said, his face a mask of uncertainty as he disappeared out the door.

When Torito returned, he carried something in his hands that immediately caught my attention—a kachina doll, intricately carved from wood. The figure depicted was of a barn owl man, with real leather wrapped around it like ceremonial garments, and genuine feathers attached to its arms. The face was unmistakably that of a barn owl, but the legs were human, standing in a posture that exuded both power and grace.

blinked, taking in the doll's eerie beauty, but quickly reminded myself why I was there. "Well, I mean a real owl, just larger than usual, flying in the sky. I saw one the other night, above me," I said, choosing to keep any mention of the supernatural out of the conversation.

Torito laughed, a sound that didn't quite reach his eyes. "Well, either you saw La Lechuza or—wait. What kind of Native are you?" he asked, his tone suddenly serious.

"How do you know I'm Native?" I countered, my brows furrowing. "And who is La Lechuza?" I usually hated discussing my Native side with strangers because I never knew how they were gonna react to a 'halfling'.

He shrugged, a casual gesture that did little to hide his curiosity. "Everyone around here has at least some Native blood, it seems. And I was just joking about La Lechuza. She's an old legend," he explained, though there was a hint of something more in his voice.

"Well, I'm mixed, but I don't know much. My mother died a long time ago. She was from New Mexico, like your aunt. That's all I know."

Torito nodded, his eyes flickering with something I couldn't quite place. He smiled at the floor, his hands resting on his thighs as if he was about to stand, but hesitated. "So, you don't know any of the legends or stories?" he asked, still looking down, as if avoiding my gaze might soften the question.

"Owls? Nope," I replied, hoping this wouldn't turn into one of those annoying "I'm more Native than you" conversations. Thankfully, it didn't. I didn't want to dive into my past as a foster kid—it always shifted people's perceptions, turning me into someone they pitied. I hated that. But Torito was kind enough not to pry.

"In mothers my tribe," he began, finally meeting my eyes again. "Owls can either be good or bad messengers. Usually, a white owl is good, but only you can answer that. If the owl spirit is protecting or guiding you, then maybe you should keep this," he said, gesturing to the kachina doll he had placed beside me.

"Oh no, I couldn't," I protested, realizing I didn't have any money to offer him, not for the doll or the work on the bracelet. I had a card but no cash.

"No, you keep it. It's yours. My dad makes them. He has a whole bunch! Maybe it will pique your interest, and you'll start learning about your people and where you come from," he suggested. I nodded, appreciating the sentiment, though my mind was spinning with thoughts of my uncertain future, my possible supernatural lineage, and the danger lurking in the form of a Vampire father and a Vaewolf spirit.

Torito turned his attention back to my bracelet, chiseling away at it for a few more minutes, effectively ending the conversation. The kachina doll now belonged to me, a beautiful yet haunting artifact that I wasn't sure how to feel about. Maybe I'd place it in my room as decor, a silent sentinel watching over me.

"Is this a god of some sort?" I asked quietly.

"No," he laughed. "Not a god but a type of spirit, I guess. You can compare them to angels, but I don't pray to them like I do to the Creator. The spirits are messengers to the Creator and can bestow blessings," he said nonchalantly. "They are neat, though, aren't they?"

"Very neat," I said with a smile, looking over at my new gift. "Thank you." I wasn't used to receiving gifts from guys, and it felt nice.

He smiled at me. The saw whirred to a stop, and I looked down at my wrist just in time to see Torito finally prying the bracelet apart with a pair of strong pliers. It worked. The shackle was off, and I felt a wave of relief so intense that I couldn't help but giggle, a sound that surprised both of us.

Torito looked at me with that strange expression again. "I'm sorry, I don't have any way to pay you just yet," I said, still clutching my wrist. My skin felt cold, almost numb, where the metal had rested.

"Don't worry about it . . . unless," he hesitated, "I can keep this? I can repair it for you, and then you can sell it if you need the money. It's very expensive silver. And the turquoise is very pure as well. You can give me however much you want out of it after you sell it."

The idea that the bracelet might be worth something had never crossed my mind. All I had cared about was getting it off. Now, holding the cool, smooth silver in my hand, I felt a strange connection to it—a sense that there was more to this bracelet than I understood. It had scared me when it warmed to my touch, but something deep inside urged me not to let it go.

"Let me hold onto it," I said quickly. "I have to get to an atm, then I'll pay you. I need to find out where it came from."

"Smart," Torito replied, slipping the bracelet into a small pouch and handing it to me. I stuffed it into my pocket.

As I turned to leave, a painting on the wall caught my eye—a bird with wings spread wide, almost identical to the one on Torito's necklace.

"It's a Thunderbird," Torito explained, noticing my interest. "Have you seen one of those as well?" he asked, his tone half-joking but with a hint of curiosity.

"I don't think so," I replied with a scoff, though the idea intrigued me.

"Well, ask Munks," he said with a laugh. "She swears she's seen one."

"I'll make sure to do that," I said, smiling at the thought. It would be fun to tease her about it later.

"Hey, you should come to one of our powwows one day. I can introduce you to the elders and see if they can find out what tribe your mother was from."

"Really? They can do that?" I asked, surprised and a bit hopeful.

"They would have records," he said, scribbling his number on a piece of paper from his cluttered desk. I slipped it into my other pocket, the one not weighed down by the bracelet. "There were a lot of our kind who got dispersed during the colonization of this land. The records are mainly census records of the names of people who lived on the reservations. You should definitely have a look through it," he suggested. I wanted to tell him about my case manager and my involvement with the Bureau of Indian Affairs, but it felt like too much to share right then.

"Sure," I replied, though I hesitated. "I . . . can't give you my home number, though. We don't have one." It was a lie, but the truth was worse—my foster mom never let me use the phone. I didn't want to risk her wrath by having people call the house. I use it secretly when she's out of the house, like this morning.

"It's okay. Just call me from Val's, and I'll give you the details about the powwow. It's not for another month anyway."

A sudden pounding on the door interrupted us. It was Munks. "Are you guys making out in there or what?!" she called out, her voice dripping with playful sarcasm.

Torito and I both laughed as he opened the door for me. Munks stood there, tapping her little black rabbit moccasins on the cement porch, her arms crossed with mock impatience. She was the friend who had given me my own pair of moccasins, a gesture that had meant more to me than she knew.

"It's off!" I exclaimed, holding up my now bare wrist with a grin. The dogs and other animals were still hiding from me, but Munks didn't seem to notice.

"Well, it's getting hot. Let's go," she said, leading the way back to the car.

"Goodbye, cousin!" Torito called after me as I followed Munks back into the house. I turned back to look at him, surprised by the term of endearment. Cousin? Okay, I could live with that. I smiled and waved goodbye.

As we drove back, I felt a strange sense of happiness and contentment wash over me. Luz hadn't spoken to me yet, but I could feel her presence, like she was slowly waking up, stretching her limbs after a long sleep.

The rest of the morning passed in a blur of contentment. Munks and I sat in her room, listening to her favorite Metallica album, *Ride the Lightning.* As the heavy riffs filled the space around us, I leaned in closer, my curiosity piqued.

"Munks, tell me about the time you saw the Thunderbird," I asked, trying to sound casual but failing to hide my intrigue.

"Who told you that?!" she exclaimed, her eyes widening in mock surprise. "Oh, it must have been Torito. He's so full of it sometimes." Munks chuckled, shaking her head as she recalled the memory.

"Well, I saw something, but a true Thunderbird? I'm not sure. A Thunderbird is a sacred creature in Native legends, known for great power. They say it can make it rain and cause thunder and lightning with the beat of its wings. I never thought it was a true Thunderbird. It didn't have any feathers. The beak of this animal and the pictures of Thunderbirds were very similar, though." She paused to flip the cassette tape over to the next half of the album. I sat there on the floor, leaning against her bed, petting my new kachina doll.

"I was out in the canyons with my dad. We were riding our three-wheelers, just enjoying the desert, when this massive bird came out of nowhere. It soared up from the canyon, its wings spreading wide like a shadow over the sun. It was huge, like nothing I'd ever seen before."

My eyes widened even more. "What did it look like?"

"Well," Munks hesitated, "it didn't really look like a traditional Thunderbird, like I said. Its wings were leathery, more like a bat's, but still very colorful. Orange, yellow, blue, and green skin that changed like a lizard. Imagine wings so vast they blotted out the sky. The shadow flew over us, and we stopped riding just to stare at it. Its body was strong but sleek. Honestly, it looked more like a giant pterodactyl. But it was so majestic I couldn't think of anything else to call it. The air seemed to hum with electricity like a storm was brewing just from its presence, but there was no thunder or lightning."

"That's incredible!" I exclaimed. "Do you think it could really have been a pterodactyl? I've heard some people claim to still see them."

Munks shrugged. "Who knows? The desert is full of mysteries."

"Speaking of mysteries," I said, a smirk playing on my lips,

"who is La Lechuza?"

Munks frowned, shaking her head. "What's with all these questions?"

"I dunno. Torito told me I should look into my Native stories," I answered.

"We'll his dad is Mexican and his mom is from Arizona I think. So I'm not sure what kind of stories he has to tell. I've heard of the name, but I'm not sure. You might want to look it up at the library. The internet's got all sorts of info on folklore and legends."

I nodded, a determined look in my eyes. "I'll do that. Thanks, Munks."

As the music played on, I sat there, my mind swirling with thoughts of owls, Thunderbirds, and the strange and mysterious world I was just beginning to uncover. It felt like the start of something big—something that would change everything.

Before heading home, I decided to stop at the town's one and only library. It was a small city, and the library was a modest building, but to me, it was a sanctuary. I was grateful prom had been on a Friday, giving me the entire weekend to explore without worrying about school.

The library was one of my favorite places. Not only was it air-conditioned, a precious reprieve from the relentless desert heat, but it was also free. The computers here were a lifeline in a town where personal computers were a luxury few could afford. Today, if you wanted to know anything, you either needed a complete set of Britannica

Encyclopedias at home or a library card.

When I was younger, one of my former foster moms would drag me and four other foster kids to this very library, a sack lunch of bologna sandwiches in tow. During the long summer months when school was out, she would drop us off in the morning and leave us there all day. It wasn't the best situation, but I made the most of it, devouring book after book. It was here that I discovered my love for storytelling and writing. I used to scribble down short stories and give them to friends as gifts—little tokens of my imagination.

I also learned how to use the microfilm machine, spending hours poring over old newspaper clippings, searching for any mention of my mother. Her name was Aiyana, and all I knew was that she had lived on a reservation in New Mexico before she passed away. I found her name on a census once, but after that, it was as if she had vanished. Perhaps her family had moved off the reservation or changed their name. The trail had gone cold, but I never gave up hope.

This time, I had several things to research. I wanted to find out more about my father—a man I had never known. My case manager had mentioned that he was of European descent, but that was all I knew. The Vampire from last night had called himself Sebastian, and I couldn't shake the possibility that he might actually be my father. I also planned to look up La Lechuza and Thunderbirds, curious to see if I could find any information that might explain the giant owl I had seen flying above me.

I spent the entire day at the library, then returned the next day as well. Two days passed, and I found nothing about my father. Searching for someone based on a single name was frustrating, but I had hoped that cross-referencing his name with my mother's might yield something—a marriage record, a car title, anything. But there was nothing.

Feeling disheartened, I decided to satisfy my curiosity about La Lechuza. The stories I found were chilling. It was an old urban legend that had many variations, but the gist was the same: La Lechuza was a woman who lived alone near a small town in Texas. She was accused of witchcraft after a baby mysteriously died, and the townspeople burned her alive one night. But before she died, a large white owl appeared in the sky above her, and she cursed the townspeople, vowing to return as an owl and exact her revenge.

I shivered as I read the story, the vivid descriptions of her death and the vengeance she sought from beyond the grave sending chills down my spine. Could the owl I saw have been La Lechuza? I wasn't easily convinced, even if my life had taken a supernatural turn recently. Just because some things were real didn't mean every rumor or legend had truth to it.

Good thing we don't live in Texas, Luz said in my mind, her voice laced with humor. And yes, my Luz had returned to me not just yesterday. Quieter than usual, but still there.

I scoffed. "This story says she lived in Texas when she was human," I replied. "Doesn't mean she stayed there after dying."

Real or not, the story was fascinating. According to the legends, sightings of La Lechuza had been reported from Texas all the way to Southern California. The tales were meant to scare people, keep children from wandering too far and prevent them from petting strange animals that might be rabid. She was like the Mexican equivalent of Bigfoot or the Chupacabra—a cautionary figure used to instill fear.

Yeah, just like werewolves and Vampires. They aren't real either, right? Luz replied sarcastically.

"Touché," I muttered.

The stories painted her as a monster, a Witch who cannibalized people—mostly men who treated women badly. The avenging-woman angle didn't bother me as much as it probably should have. If anything, I found myself oddly sympathetic to her plight. But something inside me told me that the owl I saw wasn't La Lechuza. It didn't feel right. Besides, the owl I had seen was so white, and according to what I had read, male owls were whiter than the females, who had more brown in their feathers.

I thought of the kachina doll Torito had given me and his words about the owl spirit protecting me. It felt better to believe that the owl was a guardian rather than a vengeful Witch.

A strange sensation crept over me as I looked away from the microfilm machine. I glanced around the room, but it was quiet. The library was nearly empty, with only a few patrons scattered among the shelves. I turned toward the window on my right, and that's when I saw him.

Not the Vampire, but the man from the park—the one I had given up hope of ever seeing again. My heart skipped a beat as our eyes met, and in that instant, everything else faded away.

Though I was technically on the first floor, the library was built on a slight mound, so when I looked out, he was below me, staring up at me with a look that made my heart race.

He was wearing a hat, much like the one he had worn when I first saw him at the park. But this one looked brand new, it was clean and polished, a smooth suede that gleamed in the sunlight. The large brim reminded me of the hats the local Natives wore, except his had no feathers, only a silver hatband adorned with red turquoise and coral stones. Red coral had always been one of my favorite stones, but I could never afford it—it was too expensive, a luxury far out of reach.

His hair was longer than I remembered, now braided down his back, giving him an even more striking appearance. He looked . . . exquisite. There was no other word for it. And different, too—cleaned up, younger, not at all like the dark figure who had hypnotized me that night. Yet, despite the unease lingering in the back of my mind, I found myself utterly captivated by him.

When he smiled at me, the world faded away. The sudden rush of emotion was so overwhelming that I nearly fell back in my chair. I realized I was staring at him, and embarrassment flushed my cheeks. Instinctively, I moved away from the window, hiding from his gaze as if it were too much to bear. Why was I feeling so shy? Was it the intensity of his stare, the way it seemed to pierce through all my defenses? I wasn't used to being seen like this, laid bare without warning. Normally, I kept my guard up, choosing when and how to let people in. But now, with one smile, all my carefully built walls crumbled, leaving me vulnerable in a way that terrified me.

Then, out of nowhere, I felt a gust of wind, and before I could react, warm, strong arms were around me, steadying me. "Did you fall? Did you hurt yourself?" he asked, his voice filled with concern.

I turned to face him, my breath catching in my throat. Up close, he didn't have fangs, nor did his eyes glow with that eerie light. He just looked like a man—a breathtakingly handsome man who smelled absolutely divine. How had he reached me so quickly?

Luz stirred in my mind, purring like a contented kitten. It was so unlike her that I felt a twinge of confusion. She still hadn't told me what happened when we encountered my supposed father, the Vampire, the day before last. Her memory, she claimed, was blocked for some reason as well. Strange, considering we were two complete entities. But what puzzled me more was how uninterested she seemed in reliving that meeting with my father. You'd think encountering another supernatural being would have excited her, but no—only this man seemed to hold her attention.

"No," I finally managed to say, trying to regain my composure. I realized my mouth was hanging open, and I quickly shut it, hoping to hide my surprise and the growing attraction I felt.

He was standing so close to me, and the scent of him—whatever cologne he wore—was intoxicating. Without realizing it, I found myself leaning in closer, my face almost brushing against his shirt buttons. It was like being under a spell, as if I had been given a dose of the most potent catnip, and I couldn't help but be drawn to him. I could feel Luz's presence growing stronger, her eyes glowing with an ethereal red in my mind as he held me. We were only touching at the arms, yet there was something deeply sensual about his proximity.

When I looked up into his face, the connection I felt was undeniable, as if I had known him in another life. It sounds ridiculous, I know, but they say you recognize your soulmate when you meet them, and right now, staring into his dark hazel eyes that had a patch of a yellow sunflower around his irises, that's exactly what I felt. He was the one.

Luz's voice echoed in my mind, a single word repeating over and over: *Mate. Mate. Mate.*

She was relentless, urging me to say it out loud, to acknowledge what she already knew. "Mate?" I whispered, but my voice was uncertain, and I saw the flicker of hurt in his eyes as the word left my lips. His face turned cold.

I immediately regretted it, feeling a deep sadness welling up inside me, an emotion so strong it nearly brought me to tears. And it took a lot for me to cry. I stepped back, putting distance between us, and sank into my chair, burying my face in my hands as the tears came, unbidden and unwelcome.

"Stop it," I whispered, this time directing my words at Luz, willing her to stop howling in my mind, to stop amplifying the sorrow that was threatening to overwhelm me.

I felt him hesitate, his presence a comforting warmth nearby. He paused, probably unsure of what to do after hearing me speak. When I finally looked up, I saw the concern etched on his face, and I quickly shook my head, trying to reassure him.

"I didn't mean you," I said softly, hoping to alleviate the worry in his eyes.

He slowly walked over, pulling up a chair to sit across from me. He didn't touch me this time, but he was close—so close that I could feel the warmth radiating from him. We were sitting in the back of the library, a secluded spot that I was thankful for. I didn't like crying, especially not in public. And I usually never did.

"I'm sorry for how we met the first time, Magdalena," he whispered, his voice heavy with regret. "I swear to you that I am no monster." He paused, then continued in a louder voice, "I swear to you that I would never hurt you." His eyes pleaded with me to believe him, but I couldn't bring myself to meet his gaze.

"My friends call me Mags," I said, the only words I could mutter at the time.

"Ok, Mags it is. I do hope to be one of your friends, " he said, bending his neck to look into my eyes. My instinct told me he wanted to be more than friends, but he didn't want to admit that at this moment.

Despite my chaotic emotions, his words and the deep resonance of his voice soothed me. For some inexplicable reason, I felt safe with him—this stranger who seemed to know so much about me already.

I managed a small smile, trying to push past the turmoil inside. "Please wait," I said, my voice trembling. "I . . . I'll be right back." I hurried to the restroom, needing to wash my face and pull myself together. As I splashed cold water on my cheeks, I reached into my small purse and pulled out my bottle of Lithium. I hadn't taken my dose today—maybe that was the problem.

I swallowed two pills quickly and made my way back to him, hoping the medication would settle my erratic emotions. I know I have been through a lot these past few weeks but that was no reason to fall apart over a simple introduction.

To my surprise, he was still there, standing over the work I had left on the table, examining it with quiet curiosity. When he saw me return, he smiled, but it quickly turned into a frown as he walked over and grabbed my purse.

"Hey!" I protested as he reached in and pulled out the bottle of Lithium. He opened the cap, but the moment he sniffed the contents, he recoiled, coughing as he quickly recapped the bottle.

"What are you doing with Wolfsbane?" he demanded, his voice tinged with anger and worry. For a brief moment, his eyes seemed to glow, not with the eerie red I had seen before but with a deep, oceanic blue. His voice, too, had changed, growing deeper, more rugged, and distinctly animalistic.

I wasn't scared, but I was definitely startled. "Wolfsbane? What do you mean?" I asked, thoroughly confused. "Isn't that a plant? A poisonous plant?"

"Yes it's poison, my love. It could kill you," he said, tossing the bottle into the trash with a look of utter disdain. "Why are you taking that? Who gave it to you?" His sudden switch from "friend" to "my love" shocked me as well.

Before I could respond, a passing security guard approached us, his gaze suspiciously fixed on Andy—yes, his name was Andy. It had been so long since I last saw the man from Bucklin Park, but I never forgot the name he gave me. He looked so different now, cleaned up and respectable, yet still enough of a mystery to draw the guard's scrutiny.

"Is everything alright here, ma'am?" the guard asked, his tone laced with authority as he glanced at Andy.

"I'm fine," I replied quickly, but my eyes were locked on Andy, trying to understand what had just happened.

Andy, however, seemed on edge, his posture tense as he stared down the guard. "We were just leaving," he growled, his voice thick with impatience. He reached out his hand to me, and for a moment, I hesitated. But then I took it, feeling the warmth of his skin against mine, and the connection was electric. Goosebumps erupted along my arms, a visceral reaction to his touch.

As we left the library, I retrieved my bike from its stand and walked alongside him down the street. "Let's go back to the park?" I suggested, needing to be somewhere familiar, somewhere where I could try to process everything.

"Sure," he agreed with a smile, though there was an underlying tension in his voice.

The short walk to the park was anything but quiet. Andy spoke rapidly, as if he had a wealth of information to share and only a few moments to get it all out. He sounded very business-like. Or maybe he was just nervous—excited, even. I couldn't tell. All I knew was that I was too overwhelmed to respond. Lithium was poison? How could that be? And if Andy wasn't a Vampire, then what was he? Was he a Vaewolf, like me?

I felt like a kitten, both wary and mesmerized by his presence, wanting to flee at the first sign of danger but also drawn in, soothed by the sound of his voice. Despite my confusion, his words made me happy, though I barely understood half of what he was saying.

"I know it's been a long time since we've met—weeks—but I promise you, it was for good reason. I had to figure out the best way to help you," he explained, his tone earnest.

"Help me?" I echoed, trying to grasp the meaning behind his words.

"Yes, and help myself," he replied, and then launched into an explanation that left my head spinning.

He told me he was a Werewolf from a northern Siberian pack, cast out by his uncle and labeled a rogue for a long time. He said he had undergone a ceremony to cleanse himself of a curse. Then he explained that the pills in my purse weren't medicine at all, but Wolfsbane—a deadly poison to werewolves. He urged me never to take them again, saying they could kill me or my wolf. The security guard, he added, was a ghoul—a Vampire's servant, a reanimated corpse—and warned me to stay away from him.

He continued, saying that my wolf and I were not yet "one," which was why I couldn't sense the danger of wolfsbane. He apologized for not noticing it earlier, claiming he was too enthralled by my scent of jasmine and roses. His words were dizzying, a mix of fairy tales and reality, and I struggled to keep up.

Luz seemed totally engrossed in his story, understanding everything he said with ease. As for me, I was drowning in a sea of confusion, wondering how much more of this I could take. Maybe that's why I had cried in the library—maybe it was all just too much.

As we walked, his voice became a comforting background hum, and despite my fear and uncertainty, I found myself drawn closer to him. There was something about Andy—something I couldn't quite put my finger on—that made me feel safe, even as my world seemed to unravel around me.

We sat beneath the sprawling branches of an old oak tree, the evening shadows lengthening as the sun dipped below the horizon. The cool grass beneath us was a welcome relief from the day's heat, and the shade provided a quiet, secluded space where we could talk. Or at least, where he could talk. I had been listening intently at first, trying to absorb every word, but at some point, I found myself drifting. My focus shifted from his words to the way his expressions changed as he spoke.

I noticed how his fangs seemed to grow and shrink depending on his emotions, as if they were an extension of his mood, just like eyebrows arching in surprise or knitting in worry. It was otherworldly, mesmerizing, and I couldn't help but wonder how I appeared to him. Did he see me as ordinary, or was I something more in his eyes?

Normally, I despised seeing women who were completely infatuated with a guy, losing themselves in the process. Yet here I was, utterly spellbound, hanging on every word, not because of what he was saying, but because I was lost in the depth of his eyes. He could have been telling me the secrets of the universe, or confessing that he was an alien from another planet, and it wouldn't have mattered. All I could do was stare, entranced.

Eventually, I laid my head down on the grass, turning onto my side to face him, silently inviting him to do the same. He fell silent as we lay there, not a foot apart, our faces close enough that I could see every detail, every subtle shift in his expression. He seemed to take this quiet moment to study me as well, his gaze tracing the contours of my face.

Gently, he reached out with one arm and brushed a stray lock of hair from my face, his touch sending a shiver down my spine. "I forget that you're still so new to all this," he said softly, his voice calm and dreamy. "It's probably very overwhelming. Maybe you'd like to tell me something about yourself?" He smiled, his eyes warm. "Or maybe we can just sit here quietly and reflect for a bit?"

I returned his smile, glancing down at the grass as I considered his offer. There were so many things I wanted to ask him, so many questions that had been swirling in my mind since the night we first met. But he had already answered most of them, explaining in depth the mysteries that had plagued me.

Should I mention my father and the shackle he had placed on me? Should I tell him about the owl I had seen? Or maybe that I had recently come to understand and love my wolf, Luz? But something told me he already knew about Luz.

Of course he knows about me. I can sense his wolf too, even if I can't see or speak to him just yet, Luz admitted.

Why not? I asked her with my mind, curious about this new revelation.

I could sense Luz's frustration, but instead of howling in my mind, she sighed. *I don't know exactly why. I just know that I can feel him when Andy touches you. So please, touch him again. Maybe I can find out why.* Her plea was almost desperate, and instinctively, I reached out to take Andy's hand, holding it firmly as if that would somehow help Luz understand.

"My wolf is asking me to touch you," I said, filling in the silence.

Andy smirked and shook his head as he understood. I felt him circle his thumb around the top of my hand and the electricity jingles were back again.

We lay there in silence, and I couldn't decide if I liked it or if it made me uncomfortable. Only one question kept pressing at the back of my mind, demanding to be voiced. "Why do you look so different?" I finally asked, breaking the quiet. Andy ran his free hand nervously through his hair, a small, happy laugh escaping him. I could see he knew I was attracted to him, and for a moment, I thought I saw a blush on his cheeks.

"Well," he said, his smile turning flirtatious, "I don't know about how *I* look, but I'm looking at a beautiful raven-haired maiden right now."

His words made me blush, even at the corniness. You would think someone this fine would be use to speaking with women. I quickly clarified, "No, I mean, you mentioned something about no longer being a rogue? Is that it?"

His expression grew serious as he studied my eyes. "Yes," he said quietly, "I did it for you. For us."

I looked down at the buttons of his shirt, the same buttons I had buried my face into earlier at the library. "Is that why you smell different too?" I asked, trying to keep my voice steady. "Or is it a new cologne?"

His smile widened, revealing his pearly white teeth and those fangs that seemed to dance with his emotions, elongating suddenly to a menacing length. I couldn't help but wonder why I didn't have fangs like his if I was supposed to be supernatural, too.

A memory surfaced then, from when I was thirteen. I had an extra set of canine teeth growing above my regular adult incisors. The dentist called them supernumerary teeth, and he performed surgery to remove them so I could get braces.

He said my teeth were overcrowded, and the memory brought a tinge of sadness with it.

I reached out, fingers brushing over the soft cotton of his off-white shirt. The fabric contrasted beautifully with his golden-brown skin, making him look as if he had spent hours in the sun. I leaned in closer, inhaling his scent once again, letting it wash over me like a warm, comforting wave. I felt him breathe over my head, inhaling my scent as well.

"Werewolves don't wear cologne," he said, his voice low and intimate as he scooted closer to me on the grass. "We want to smell the real thing, not the chemicals or pheromones of another animal."

I looked up at him then, noticing how his lips parted slightly, and I felt an overwhelming urge to kiss him. I imagined tiny fangs extending from my gums, a thirst rising within me, a hunger that was both physical and emotional.

I want to smell him, too! Luz's voice echoed excitedly in my mind. *Let me get a whiff!*

"How do I do that?" I asked aloud, forgetting for a moment that Andy could hear me.

"Do what?" he asked, confusion flickering in his eyes. But then his expression changed, his eyes widening in sudden fear as he grabbed me by the arms.

"Don't!" he exclaimed, his voice urgent and filled with panic. "Don't let your wolf come out! You're not ready! You could die!" His eyes darted from my empty wrist to my face, and I could tell he knew about the bracelet, about what had happened before.

"What?!" I gasped, feeling his panic infecting me. My heart began to race, and I could hear it pounding loudly in my ears. My voice sounded different, deeper, and it was then that I realized what was happening to me.

A searing pain shot through my abdomen, so intense it took my breath away. I hunched over, clutching my stomach, unable to speak as the shock of it paralyzed me. The pain came in waves, each one more powerful than the last, as if my body was trying to push something out from deep within my soul.

Through my squinted eyes, I saw Andy's face, twisted in fear and helplessness, but he seemed so far away. His voice was muffled, drowned out by the pounding in my head.

But then, a sharp, high-pitched whistle cut through the chaos, a sound so piercing it commanded my attention. It wasn't just a whistle—it was an order, a command that reverberated through my entire being: *Stop!*

The pain eased almost immediately, and in my mind's eye, I saw Luz, no longer fighting to come out but instead curled up, her fluffy tail wrapped around herself as if the whistle had lulled her to sleep. She was out cold.

I gasped for breath, clutching Andy's shirt as if it were a lifeline, only now realizing that I had ripped off every button. His lips were slightly puckered, and I understood—it was he who had been whistling. But the sound had already faded, though his lips remained pursed for a moment longer.

He gently stood me up, holding me close as I cried into his chest, my tears soaking into the remnants of his shirt. His voice was soft and soothing as he whispered sweet words, calling me "baby." Normally, I hated that term, but coming from him at this particular time, felt right. I melted into his embrace, grateful for the comfort he provided.

So much for a smoother second meeting, I thought bitterly. I hoped I hadn't scared him away with my hysterics for good, though I wouldn't have blamed him if he wanted to run. We stood there for what felt like an eternity, and when I was finally calm, we walked over to another hill overlooking the pond, watching the ducks settle down for the night. They weren't afraid of us this time, quacking and honking as they nestled into the reeds by the water's edge.

We didn't speak for a long time, both lost in our thoughts. Finally, I broke the silence, looking up at him. "Maybe I should have kept the bracelet on," I said, my voice tinged with regret.

Andy looked at me, then gently lifted my arm where the silver bracelet had once rested. He cupped his hands around my wrist as if he could somehow bring it back. I could see the wheels turning in his mind, and I knew he was piecing together the last few days' events.

"Were you the one who put that bracelet on me?" I asked, remembering the look in his eyes earlier.

He hesitated, then looked down at the ground, his voice barely a whisper. "Yes."

"Why didn't you say anything?" I pressed, feeling a mix of confusion and anger. "I thought my dad had given it to me. I thought he was trying to harm me!"

Andy sighed, his expression pained. "I'm sorry," he said. "But I wasn't trying to trick you. I came to visit you in your room the night you returned from seeing your father. I couldn't wake you. You were enthralled." He paused, his jaw tightening as if the memory filled him with anger. "I followed you, you know. All the way up to his house and again when he brought you back down in a car driven by one of his ghouls. I had to keep an eye on you, had to make sure you were okay."

Suddenly, the memory of the big black wolf on the mountain flashed in my mind. The wolf had been him, watching over me just as he said. He had been telling the truth all along.

"Silver is more than just protection from Vampires," he explained, his voice gentle as he rubbed his thumb over my wrist. "It does many things. It repels Vampires and ghouls' compulsions and abilities, but most importantly, it suppresses our shapeshifting abilities. It can kill us, too, if taken internally by way of knives or bullets, but that's why I made you a bracelet—something pretty to grace your wrist and remember me by. I kind of half-thought your wolf would at least remember me and tell you when you woke up."

I pulled my arm away, frustration bubbling to the surface. "She doesn't remember anything about that night either! And even if she did, I couldn't hear her. It was hurting her!"

My voice trembled with emotion. "It weakened my wolf so much I couldn't hear her voice, only her whimpers! That's why I had it cut off!"

Andy's face fell, his expression filled with regret. "It wasn't the silver alone, my love," he said softly. "It was the combination of wolfsbane and silver. It was too much for you to handle together. I'm sorry I didn't realize it sooner. Someone is apparently poisoning your wolf with it. I think it may be your father trying to kill off your wolf so your Vampire abilities can grow. From what I can tell, you can only be one or the other. You cannot have both. If you lose your wolf, you will lose your connection to me, your mate. I cannot have that happen." His eyes pleaded with me, filled with an urgency that made my heart ache.

"I don't know why I didn't think about it before," Andy continued, his voice steady but filled with frustration. The man could talk, that much was clear. And while his words were meant to be reassuring, I needed him to listen to me—just once, to really listen.

"Usually, your wolf would have emerged when you were thirteen, but since you're a hybrid, it would have killed you," Andy explained, his eyes searching mine for understanding. "He's been trying to delay the shift for as long as possible, probably by feeding you wolfsbane in small doses ever since Luz awakened."

His words made my head spin. I couldn't take it anymore. I stood abruptly, needing space, needing air. The pounding in my head grew louder with every revelation. Why couldn't I have just had a normal father? Why did everything have to be so complicated? I thought about Carmen, my social worker. Was she one of those ghouls Andy had mentioned?

She was the one who brought me to the doctor and brought all my medicine. Luz had warned me not to trust her. Could she have been the one poisoning me all along?

My thoughts turned to my father—the man I had only just found. Andy seemed convinced he was evil, but how could I accept that? He was my link to the world, my only parent. Yes, he was a Vampire, but did that automatically make him a monster? I couldn't believe it. I didn't want to believe it.

"No, Andy!" I shouted, pacing along the hillside, my voice trembling with a mix of anger and confusion. "So you're telling me my father is trying to kill Luz?" I looked up at the sky, at the pale stars beginning to twinkle, at the trees swaying gently in the evening breeze—anywhere but at Andy's face. I couldn't let him distract me with his looks, not now.

I reached into my bag, which lay on the ground near my bike, and pulled out the silver bracelet. I stared at it, conflicted. Should I put it back on?

"He would have killed her earlier, don't you think?" I said, my voice rising. "If that were the case, he would have killed my wolf the moment she emerged." I was infuriated, but not necessarily with Andy—more with the world that had lied to me my entire life.

"Why are you able to wear silver?" I demanded, my frustration bubbling over. "You have silver on your hat. And silver necklaces and rings as well. Why can you wear it?" My whole life felt like one big lie. From my case manager to my foster mom, even down to my dentist—who else knew the truth about me?

"You know," I continued, not letting him speak, my voice shaky, "I had an extra set of fangs when I was thirteen, Andy. They were called supernumerary teeth. My case manager sent me to the dentist, and they were surgically removed! Was that my Vampire fangs, or were they my Werewolf fangs?" I was pacing now, a small path worn into the grass beneath my feet. "And the braces? Were they silver, too? Have I been secretly shackled my entire life?"

Andy gasped, running a hand over his chin as he shook his head. "I . . . I don't know. I'm not sure," he stammered, his voice filled with uncertainty. Then, in one swift movement, he was in front of me, his hands gently but firmly holding my jaw.

He slipped a finger into my mouth, feeling along my gums. The gesture was intimate, almost sensual, but I pushed the thought away, not wanting to believe he might compel me if werewolves had that power, too.

After a moment, he stepped back, his expression serious. "He had you defanged," he said, his voice heavy with the weight of the revelation.

"What do you mean?!" I demanded, my voice breaking. "What part of me was defanged? My Vampire self or my

Werewolf self?!"

"I don't have all the answers," Andy admitted, his eyes locked on mine. "But I think you have Vampire fangs. For Vampires, their teeth are everything—they can't grow them back. It's how they feed, how they survive. As wolves, we regenerate and heal, but Vampires . . . they can't." He paused, deep in thought. "That's why we don't age, at least not for centuries. We live long lives, but we're not immortal. We don't wear metal or get tattoos because our bodies just metabolize the ink and heal over. And the silver I'm wearing? It's not really silver; it's platinum with no silver. I have to blend in. The stones are real, but they don't harm us. Don't you see what this means?"

His voice softened as he reached out to me again. "This means you have to choose your wolf." There was a hint of happiness in his voice, as if this was the answer to everything, but I wasn't ready to accept it. It wasn't fair that my choices were being stripped away from me.

I stood there, arms crossed over my chest, staring at him as he continued talking. He spoke of how there had never been a hybrid like me who survived the shift. He told me about a boy he had met in the forest, left deformed and in agony after a failed transformation, and how he had ended his suffering. The story was too much for me to bear, and the emotions I had been holding back finally broke free.

Deep down, I knew I could never abandon Luz. She was a part of me now, even if she had almost killed me just moments ago. But I couldn't let anyone else make that decision for me.

"Maybe he tried to kill your wolf, but she was too strong," Andy suggested, his voice gentle as he tried to make sense of it all. "Maybe she went into hibernation to protect herself. Can you ask her? I don't know why he did this to you, but your Vampire scent is very faint, my love. I barely detected it the first time we met."

He's telling the truth, Luz murmured in my mind.

"Well, well, well, look who's finally woken up!" I snapped, my frustration spilling over. Luz just huffed and curled up in my mind, turning her back on me.

"Are you going to try to kill me again, Luz? Because that's all I need right now!" I shouted, my voice carrying across the hills. I didn't realize how loud I had gotten until I saw the ducks and geese scatter in a panic. I wanted to fly away with them.

I grabbed the bracelet from the grass and slid it on, ignoring the way the broken silver pinched my skin. The moment it was on, Luz went silent. I didn't want to talk to anyone right now, not even her.

I started to mount my bike, hesitating for a moment to look back at Andy, but I couldn't bring myself to meet his eyes. I knew I was being self-destructive, pushing away the one person who seemed to care about me. But every time I got close to someone, I sabotaged it. It was a defense mechanism—if I kept people at a distance, they couldn't hurt me when they inevitably left.

But this time, I wasn't sure if I could handle losing him. It wasn't his fault. He was trying to help me, and I respected him for telling the truth, even if it made me angry.

Reality had finally set in tonight, and it was harsh. I knew what I was now, and it wasn't a fairy tale. There was no denying it anymore.

The pain from nearly transforming into my hybrid form was a vivid memory etched into my brain. No amount of therapy would make me forget that. I needed to be alone to process everything. Andy had said I wasn't ready for my wolf to emerge, and he was probably right. But would I ever be ready? I needed him, in more ways than one, but I couldn't let him know how much. Not yet.

"Please don't disappear again," I said, my voice barely a whisper as I rode off. "I just need time to process."

As I pedaled away, I heard his soft reply. "I won't. I'll bring you a new bracelet tomorrow, my love."

His words hung in the air as I rode away, a bittersweet promise that left me wondering if I had made the right choice to leave him there standing alone.

Chapter 6

Change

Andy

I trailed her until she got home. After making sure Mags got home safe, I ran in a fury back to the abandoned mine and busted further down into the caverns using just my fists. Since having joined with my wolf, I was stronger than ever, and even in my human form, I could borrow his strength. I was angry. How did I mess up? I had told her the truth.

I was starting to doubt this whole mate arrangement again. She cried or sulked the whole night! Is this what I made her feel? Maybe I was better off alone. And Ash had nothing to say this time, he was rolled into a ball in the back of my mind.

As I pummeled the rocks, a small pile of black stones fell to the ground. I looked them over and realized they were not just stones but looked like black diamonds! Some were clear with black speckles, and a few were completely dark gray or black. They weren't normally found in this part of the world. I would have to show them to Tecos and Santana later. I placed them in my pocket for safekeeping.

I sniffed and searched out the mine for more silver. I found a fresh batch. Larger pieces. Usually, I would wear leather gloves, but I needed the ore to temper my rage. I would put them in the kiln tonight, just the way Tecos had taught me to purify the metal. Since finding my mate and my new life as a non-rogue, I finally needed money. I had already submitted and sold some pure silver bars and even a few gold ones to the precious metals stores in and around San Diego.

Tecos wasn't exactly happy about it, he didn't want me raping the earth, but we had come to an agreement that as long as I was using the leftovers to make it into jewelry for other Natives to use and not taking more than I needed for a home and basic necessities, he would be okay with it.

I used the money to buy new clothes for the first time in my life. I had taken the cue from her Vampire father to look nice for my new mate. I needed to change her impression of me if she was going to accept me. If she could accept a Vampire for a father, why would she not accept a wolf for a mate?

I still did not have a proper home to take her to but soon I would, after I completely gutted this corner of the old mine and a few others around the world I had found abandoned.

The owls come and go, preferring to travel back and forth from Texas to Mexico and then back again. Creatures like us don't have the same type of border systems as humans do. We have territories, yes, but the lines of these lands were laid down hundreds of thousands years before the Europeans came. Land was divided up by territories and whatever supernatural creature controlled the area became that land's caretaker, according to Tecos.

This whole desert, from the coast of Mexico, near Ensenada, to the East of Texas, laid a vast desert area that was mainly inhabited by rogues. So I was free basically from the clutches of other packs that might know who I was to venture to and fro. Having my true form allowed me to run back and forth with the speed of lightning to conduct all my business and errands.

I had ventured down south into Mexico one night to trade gold for a doctored birth certificate and all the necessary paperwork required to gain property. I had a new name, which isn't important enough to mention, but I had come far in my preparations to secure a place for my mate and I. I would have a home as soon as the paperwork was finished.

I just needed her to be on board. Together, I was positive that I could help her. She may have to wear my specialized jewelry all her life and never trigger her shift, but I was willing to accept that. It was daunting to realize that she may never be willing to accept that herself.

I quickly finished up with a new bracelet for my love. It also had steel on the inside to protect her skin from rubbing up on the silver. I made it with a gap this time to allow her to remove it whenever she needed to. This type of cuff bracelet was very popular for Native jewelry. I trusted that she was smart enough to realize it was for her own good. Once the Wolfsbane was completely out of her system she'd have her wolf to converse with in her mind again.

I would never allow any wolf to use wolfsbane; it was how my parents were killed. The plant left a bad feeling in my gut, even if the kind that killed my parents had been supernaturally laced with death magic, even regular wolfsbane was a no go for me.

With silver, she just wouldn't be able to shift. And, best of all, the ghouls and Vampires would stay away. Silver is all she needed.

Maybe her father was trying to protect her. Maybe he removed her fangs to delay shifting. Or maybe he removed them to allow her to have a chance at a semi-normal life. He used silver on her, too. But I could not take any chances. He will eventually find out that I was a vampire hunter and take her away from me.

What she told me gutted me. He used ghouls to make her wear a small silver retainer at night. The wolfsbane would have suppressed her wolf; the silver would not have burned her then. When Ash was hibernating, the silver did not affect me much either, come to think of it. Even now, after years of hunting Vampires, I have to admit that I didn't really know their kind as well as I thought.

I did try to wake her so I could explain the bracelet, but she was entranced. I half-hoped her wolf would be able to explain what happened, but her wolf was repressed. I did tell her the truth. I had bent the bracelet thin enough to let her tiny fingers in and then bent it back into a round form when it was over her wrist. Looking back, maybe I should have just made a cuff bracelet. I smashed at the wall again thinking about how I would not have liked to have woken up shackled that way either. Stupid!

All these years alone hadn't helped my social skills.

She was right for being mad. Did I like it? Nope. Did it turn me on? A smile gleamed across my face. Of course it did, a little bit. She had so much vitality! Something that made she-wolves irresistible.

Ash had been quiet. He moped in the back of my mind since leaving our mate so distressed tonight. He also didn't like when I worked with silver, so he would usually just nap anyway. But it seemed like something deeper was causing him to sulk.

I'm too heartbroken to nap, he said. I knew why, but I let him talk.

I can't mark her if she cannot shift, he said. He stood up and turned around two times before sitting back down again with his furry tail neatly tucked around him.

Marking was a sacred sacrament. By doing this, we imprinted the souls of our wolves together, becoming one.

"I know, buddy. I promise you, we will find a way," I said aloud.

We will never be able to mindlink or welcome her into our pack when we take over as alpha. She will grow to resent us. What's the point of making a house? It wasn't like him to be this down. He was usually the one bringing me out of my dark thoughts.

"Here wolf," I said as I undressed. "Let's go and deliver this gift to our mate. I know seeing her always brings you, us, much joy. We left on bad terms. Maybe a few hours break is all we needed." Instantly, I shifted and headed in the direction of our mate's home.

The caverns stretched before me, a labyrinth of darkness and echoes. Each step was a whisper against the stone, my breath misting in the damp, cool air. In the desert, the night was always refreshingly cool. In my muzzle, I carried a precious gift, a silver bracelet wrapped in a piece of buffalo leather. I had promised her this gift and surprised myself with how beautiful it came out.

The weight of the journey pressed upon me in my mind, a melancholy shadowed by the vast loneliness of the desert night.

Emerging from the caverns, the transition was abrupt, the dry desert air greeting me like a silent guardian. The moon cast its ethereal light on the sands, turning them into a sea of shimmering white waves. Each stride through the desert was a note in a symphony of solitude. The world around me was alive with the quiet hum of nocturnal creatures, but I felt the ache of distance and the cold edge of isolation.

Had I messed things up with her? Was she angry at me? I was angry at myself. No matter all the advances I had made, I still felt so inadequate.

As I neared her home, my heart pounded with a mix of anticipation and sorrow. The town was wrapped in the blanket of night, its inhabitants lost in dreams. I approached her sliding back glass door with the silence of a ghost, nudging it open with my muzzle before quickly swooping into her room to find her asleep, her presence a beacon of warmth in the stillness.

She lay on the bed, her breath a gentle cadence, her body curled into a serene posture of peace. Her scent always hypnotized me. Jasmine and Rose. Sweet but with a tinge of danger, roses have thorns. Her fangs . . . it saddened me that no matter how much I wanted her to lose her Vampire side, it made her sad to have that choice taken from her. I hoped for his sake that she was right about her father and that he was not trying to kill her wolf.

I placed the leather pouch gently beside her pillow, my movements careful and deliberate. I couldn't help myself. Soon, I found my wolf-self climbing into bed with her. Ash nestled close to her, our forms fitting together like pieces of a puzzle, the connection between us a balm to my weary soul. I would have shifted back to being human if I didn't think she'd be insulted by finding a naked man next to her. I was slowly starting to understand her human nature. She was raised around humans, so I had to expect and respect that part of her.

I kept our cuddle innocent. If we were going to have a chance, I would have to see her more often. We would have to bond another way if we could not mate bond.

As dawn began to whisper its arrival, the first rays of light filtered through the open window. Mags stirred. Her eyes opened slowly, taking in the world with a sense of newness and wonder. She breathed deeply, catching my scent, a blend of Eucalyptus and Alpine Lupine flowers, a reminder of the wild and tamed lands of both Siberia and the States. The desert here does not grow the Lupine flower, so naming my scent would be difficult for her, but nonetheless, she was drawn to it as my mate.

Her eyes grew for a second, then suddenly relaxed. She recognized me.

Her gaze fell upon the pouch, curiosity lighting up her features. She unwrapped it, revealing the silver bracelet within, its intricate designs dancing in the morning light.

The bracelet was a symphony of silver and rare stones, more beautiful than the one I had given her before, each etching a testament to my love. I had also placed more than just one stone. Ash had hinted that her favorite was red coral and black onyx. Red corral is a type of shell that the owls had plenty of. This was something he learned from Luz, her wolf. Though we were not bonded with mindlink, it seems when the wolves touched, they could receive vague images from each other.

I wanted to create a buffer to protect her skin if she accidentally rubbed it against herself.

Santana had explained to me that for the Skin Shifters, the silver and stones worked differently. They were protective, of course, against negative energies, but they also revitalized their supernatural abilities. Our wolves did that for us. We had no need for it, especially the silver because it was toxic to us otherwise, but if it kept Mags from turning into a twisted and deformed monster if her wolf ever tried to come out again, I was all for it.

In the center was a large circular piece of mother of pearl, which symbolized the full moon. Around the whole bracelet were other medium pieces of mother-of-pearl each symbolizing a different phase of the moon. Around the medium moon phases, I embedded the onyx stones to act as a backdrop for the night sky. I also placed white buffalo stones shaped like stars inside the curtain of black onyx. To border the rim I used red coral, her favorite color.

On the inside of the bracelet, the part that would be touching her skin, I covered the steel with turquoise. Turquoise was used to represent the sky, according to Santana. For me, it also represented the dual nature of werewolves. Human by day, wolf by night. The final touch was the onyx stones shaped like a howling wolf. That was me. I didn't want her to forget who made it for her. Call it my signature.

She slipped it onto her wrist, the metal and turquoise cool against her skin, a perfect fit. Tears of joy sparkled in her eyes as she looked at me, her face radiant with happiness.

"I love it," she whispered, her voice trembling with emotion.

"I can't thank you enough."

I nuzzled her gently, the sadness that had weighed upon me melting away in the warmth of joy. I prayed that one day I'd be able to gift her a ring to grace her finger as the people of this land do when getting married. She was part of this land. And I wanted to do right by her in every way.

Our bond was reaffirmed, stronger than ever, a beacon of light in the desert's vast expanse, and both Ash and I were content again. A simple smile and thank you was all I needed to forget my past anger. I was totally smitten by this woman, one thing was for sure.

"Please change back for a second," she whispered. "You're a little scary this way." My wolf laughed in my head. He enjoyed being big and scary. I grabbed her sheet from the bed and laid it at my feet. I then shifted before her eyes, grabbing the sheet simultaneously and letting it fall around me like a cape, then letting it fall down lower to cover my sex and expose my chest.

I could tell she was amazed even though she was trying her hardest not to show it. Something of that caliber would have sent normal humans running for the hills. I remember hearing her scream when she first got her wolf, Luz. But I think she was finally accepting what she and I were. She showed no more fear. Only curiosity.

"I'm glad you love it," I said while I removed the old, broken bracelet from her other arm. She gasped and looked up at me.

"That's mine!" she said, jesting with me. I laughed with her. She seemed so happy! I couldn't help but feel proud of my work, even of this first bracelet. It was plainer than the other but still nice.

"Of course!" I said. "I will fix it, then return it to you. As a cuff bracelet of course." She seemed content with that and didn't protest when I placed the silver bracelet into the leather sack for safe keeping.

"Now you can take it off if you need to heal for whatever reason or just take a break from it. It will deaden your wolf's senses a bit and keep her from trying to shift but it's only temporary until we can find out what our plan will be for her." I said, pointing at her chest with my eyes. She knew instantly I was talking about Luz.

She seemed to zone out for a second, I saw the change in her eyes as the pupils dilated. She was speaking to her wolf.

Then she looked at me with those same dark eyes that were still dilated. She was watching me. I have never been stuck up in my life, but I knew she was 'checking me out' as I've heard people around here say. I could feel the rush of blood making itself down to my loins.

"I'm just so surprised at how human you look now. Only a minute ago, you were a large wolf!" She said, averting her eyes as she realized I had caught her staring. Oh, she was trying to lie to me!

Nice try, Little Red; I can smell your desire.

I smiled and went to sit down next to her so I could bask in her pheromones. She was only wearing a large t-shirt for pajamas, and her legs were sprawled out on the bed beside me.

I wanted her right then and there. All I had to do was spread those inviting legs. I could feel myself reaching peak erection, and I realized it was a good thing I had sat down because I could kind of hide it this way. But this wasn't the place or the time. Her foster mom and siblings would soon be waking up and getting ready to go to school. She, too, would have to go to school soon. I didn't want to mess up our first time together like I had messed up her first impression of me. The vision of my wolf biting into her and killing her was still so real in my mind also. I had to be sure I would not lose control.

She reached out to me then and ran her fingers up and down my scalp, playing with my hair. Suddenly, I didn't think I could keep it together any longer. I leaned back and rested on her hips while she played with my hair. It was torture having to keep it together.

Just then, I heard her foster mom wake up and walk to the restroom to get into the shower. That shook me out of the mood real fast.

"I'm sorry, I have to go," I said as I stood, one hand still grasping the sheet.

"Can I watch you change?" she asked, looking up at me from the bed. "All of you?" That last part was a whisper, but I recognized her tone for what it was. She was more than curious about my shift. She wanted to see me, all of me.

I released the sheet from my single-handed grip and let it flow to the ground. I wasn't shy. I had never been shy about my nakedness. Shifters never usually were, but this time, even my soul felt totally exposed in front of her. My member was up in a high salute, showing her just how much I wanted her. I heard her gasp lightly and she could no longer remain stoic. She longed for me just as I longed for her. I could smell it, almost taste her scent, her desire. It made me dizzy with want.

Just as she was about to reach out and touch me, I shifted back into my wolf form. And she pulled her arm back. I had never felt pain after my first time shifting until today. It definitely was not fun shifting with a huge erection. But I quickly stifled the pain and licked her face with my big, sloppy wolf tongue before leaping out her window.

Mags

I didn't want him to leave, but I knew he had no choice. I could already hear my foster family stirring. *Fuck!* Why do I act so reckless when he's around? I barely even know him, and yet here I am, feeling like a harlot.

I lay in my bed a little longer, the emptiness gnawing at me, leaving me unsatisfied and craving more. I wasn't usually this sexual. Normally, my meds kept my mind calm and dulled the sharp edges of my thoughts and urges. But now that poison was out of my system, wasn't it? I started to wonder if I was ever really bipolar at all.

I don't think so, Mags, Luz's voice whispered in my mind, calm and confident. *I'm afraid I was the "bipolar." I have been trying to emerge since I first awakened when you turned thirteen. The Wolfsbane is completely out of your system now though, thanks to me and my fast metabolism. That's why I can speak now, even with the bracelet.* There was pride in her voice, a sense of accomplishment.

You don't need that retainer anymore either, she added, her tone laced with disgust as she glanced at the little plastic box on my nightstand. *You were right—it's also silver. But our handsome alpha's bracelet is enough to keep me from wanting to break free and accidentally hurt you.* In my mind, I pictured Luz stating that with her head hung low. Her big, soulful eyes tore at my heartstrings.

"Luz!" I said aloud, my voice trembling. "I'm so sorry I yelled at you last night. I love you. You're my only real and best friend. The only one who knows the real me. I didn't mean to."

I know, Luz replied softly. *I can feel what's in your heart. But, woman, if you ever talk to me like that again, I'll bite you!* Her playful threat broke the tension, and we both started laughing, the sound filling the room and pushing away the lingering darkness.

"Yeah, you probably would!" I said, our laughter helping to dissolve the heavy emotions that had been weighing me down.

I finally got up and headed for the shower, letting the cool water wash over me, hoping it would help quell the lingering desire that still clung to my skin. The thought of school loomed ahead—just one more day until graduation. And then what? Not that school had been particularly hard for me; I actually liked it. I was already taking college courses in English, biology, and chemistry. Math, though—math was still a pain in my ass.

Today, I was going to get my grade back for my paper from Mrs. Cervantes, or Mrs. C, as everyone called her. I was proud of it, more so because it felt like a piece of my soul had been poured into it. It was personal, and I wasn't used to sharing personal things with anyone. The paper was about the night that had changed my life forever, and I hoped Mrs. C wouldn't ask too many questions. For a moment, I wondered if it was too revealing.

Before leaving, I glanced at the kachina doll Torito had given me, gently petting its head for luck. Then, I grabbed my bike and headed to school. Nah, I thought, reassuring myself. It's cleverly disguised as fiction—she'll never know.

Today was too hot to wear black. I put on my sunscreen and white shirt with black long skirt with pleats. Okay, so it was too hot for a black shirt. I loved the way my skirts flowed in the wind. I wore my red and black combat boots today with my red puffy velvet hat. I hurriedly streaked on some black lipstick before heading out. I felt great!

But my confidence was shattered when I saw the big, red "F" scrawled across the top of my paper at the end of class. "An F!" I blurted out, disbelief and anger tightening my chest. Mrs. C had already returned our papers, and I sat there, staring at the grade like it was a slap in the face. There were only six of us in her class—most seniors had taken work credit and didn't have to attend anymore. Lucky them.

But here I was, stuck with a teacher who seemed determined to ruin my day.

As the bell rang, I marched up to her desk at the front of the class. She was scribbling something on a notepad, which she quickly tucked away as soon as she saw me approaching.

"Magdalena, how may I help you?" she asked, her tone indifferent, as if she already knew why I was there and was bracing for it.

"I don't understand why you gave me an F," I said, trying to keep the frustration out of my voice as I watched her shift uncomfortably in her seat. Mrs. C was in her fifties, a larger woman with gray hair and thick glasses. She kept her hair short and curled it daily to keep it off her face. There was a time, I imagined, when she had been quite beautiful, but now she seemed weighed down by something heavy, perhaps her own regrets. I almost felt sorry for her, but that didn't change the fact that I needed to know why she'd graded me so harshly.

"You didn't follow the directions," she replied, her voice flat. "You were supposed to write a nonfiction essay using visuals and emotions. You turned in a piece about werewolves and owls. I just don't get it. I thought you were better than that." She cleared some stuff off her desk into her drawers. "Or vampires and owls, whatever they were.".

"What? You never said anything about nonfiction," I argued, my frustration bubbling to the surface.

"It was listed on the assignment sheet I handed out," she said, pulling out a piece of paper and handing it to me. Sure enough, there it was in black and white: 'Nonfiction descriptive essay using visual and emotional writing.' Clear as day.

"So you wanted us to write an informative page using emotions and visuals?" I asked, still trying to wrap my head around the assignment.

"Yes," she said, her voice laced with disappointment. "And also, please be careful about what you turn in for others to read, Magdalena. It can give people the wrong impression of you. People might think you're a Witch or something, writing about such things."

To hell with what people thought!

"I'm not a Witch!" I exclaimed. "This is a creative writing class. I didn't think I had to censor myself here."

"You're right," she said, her tone softening slightly. "You don't have to censor anything. Just be careful! You know our people didn't have a form of written language for a reason." she added, letting her hand rest on my arm, her fingers brushing against the silver bracelet I wore. She left it there for a moment, her gaze meeting mine, and I couldn't help but notice that the silver didn't bother her the way it did me.

"It's not because we couldn't write, but we are a strong people, and our words, writings, and symbols all hold power," she continued.

I understood what she was saying but why then did she also call me a Witch? She wasn't like me. She wasn't a ghoul either. Didn't Andy say silver would burn them? So why was she looking at me like that? I glanced up at her short hair, wondering if I had ever even realized she was Native.

"I'm in mourning," she said quietly, almost as if she'd read my thoughts. "Please don't judge me."

Oh, like how she just judged me? Ridiculous. "I'm not judging you." I said. "I just didn't know you were Native."

"Words are powerful Magdalena. Just come back tomorrow and turn in a new assignment—a nonfiction essay—and I'll accept it. But as for that," she said, nodding toward my paper with her lips, "burn it, cousin."

Her words sent a chill down my spine. What did she know that I didn't? Why were people suddenly calling me cousin? I was going to have to call Torito soon. Maybe digging into my past wasn't such a bad idea after all.

As for my writing, I'd be more inclined to frame it rather than burn it after her accusation. Even with a big ol' fat "F"!

Andy

As the sun began its slow descent toward the horizon, painting the desert in hues of pink and gold, I stood at the entrance of the kiva, bracing myself for the most rigorous preparation for battle. I quietly sat and reflected while centering my thoughts before the real training began.

The oppressive heat of August clung to the air, suffocating and relentless, but it was nothing compared to the weight pressing down on my shoulders. This wasn't just another fight—it was a test, a final mission that would determine the fate of my people, and I could feel the gravity of it in every beat of my heart.

I had taken care of Magdalena, securing a silver band around her wrist to prevent her from shifting while I was away. The thought of being apart from her gnawed at me, especially after the few nights we had just shared. But knowing she was safe allowed me to focus, at least a little. Still, the distance between us was like a physical ache in my chest, and I couldn't shake the feeling that I was leaving a part of myself behind.

Today, I wasn't just a Werewolf. I was more than that—I was the last hope for my people. They needed a leader, and I needed them. This mission wasn't just about a new life, a new name, money, or property—those were all just surface details. This was about earning my warrior insignia, about claiming the most powerful relic of all: the dark diamond. But to do that, I would have to face an ancient and terrifying Uktena, a creature so formidable that the mere thought of it made my blood run cold.

"Brother, these are sacred leathers made a very, very long time ago," Tecos said as we stood inside the smoky kiva. Santana had flown off, promising to return with weapons for the night's battle. The air inside the kiva was thick with the scent of sage, and the ancient garments before me seemed to hum with a life of their own. I looked at the robe and the multicolored feathers, my breath catching in my throat as I took in the bird mask. It was unlike anything I had ever seen, otherworldly and powerful.

"There are not many Thunderbirds left in this world, Andrei," Tecos continued, his voice pulling me from my thoughts. He used my name deliberately, making sure he had my full attention. "So if anything happens to this skin, it would be lost forever."

"I understand," I said, my voice barely above a whisper. The weight of what lay ahead was almost suffocating. Before I could even lay a hand on the sacred garments, they had me bathe in the natural hot springs nearby and smudge myself dry with sage and cottonwood root, purifying my body and spirit for the task ahead.

"There are even some Thunderbirds who have given so much of themselves, plucking out their feathers to help our people, that they fly nearly naked through the skies, like ancient dinosaurs," Tecos added, his voice tinged with sorrow and admiration.

"Really?" I asked, trying to imagine such a thing. "Why would they sacrifice so much?"

"Because our people need them, now more than ever. But I believe a time will come when our strength will return," Tecos said, a flicker of hope in his eyes.

"I hope so," I replied, my heart heavy with the thought of all we had endured—rogues, evil uncles, sabotage, Vampires, colonization. How much more could we take? "How did you come by this?" I asked, glancing at Tecos, my brother in spirit.

"The same way I obtained the one I wear now. It was a gift," he said, reverence deep in his voice. I knew of Skin Shifters who could commune with multiple spirit animals who could shift into different forms, but those were the ancients. The allies of my pack had totems with two, sometimes even three spirit animals, but it had taken them centuries to attain such power. To wear the skin of a Thunderbird seemed impossible—unreal. Had he really hunted down a

Thunderbird?

"Not hunt," Tecos said, reading my thoughts as only an owl could. "A Thunderbird spirit offered its skin to me voluntarily. No man can hunt a Thunderbird."

As he spoke, my vision blurred, and I was pulled into a vivid, trance-like state, much like the one I had experienced the last time I was in this kiva. Shadows began to move around the walls, taking on the forms of countless spirits—Thunderbird, Owl, Eagle, Bear, and so many more. The kiva, which had seemed so vast moments ago, now felt tiny, suffocating under the weight of these magnificent beings. Drums and singing filled the air, growing louder and more insistent.

I was taken to a time when Tecos was young. I watched as the animals, no longer shadows but real entities, left the kiva one by one, standing outside to observe the humans who danced for them, leaving silent prayers at their feet. Some prayed for a good harvest, others for rain, and some for love. But Tecos—my brother—wanted none of that. His heart yearned for wisdom, and I could hear and understand his ancient language as he sang and chanted. He had worn eagle feathers in his hair back then, but in my vision, another creature answered his call.

The Thunderbird stood near him, its beak open to the sky, wings outstretched like a baby bird begging for food. Then, from within its beak, a head emerged, and its skin and leathers peeled away to reveal an ancient man, old beyond comprehension. He stepped out of the Thunderbird's skin, and as Tecos watched, the crowd around him chanted louder, their rhythm joyous and celebratory. The old man placed his hand on Tecos' chest before collapsing into his arms, passing away into dust that flew into the sky as he gifted Tecos the sacred skin.

I blinked, and suddenly, I was back in the kiva, the skins being placed over me, their weight pressing down on my shoulders.

"Wait," I said, my voice thick with emotion. "I'm not worthy."

Tecos laughed, his voice booming with warmth. "No, brother, my time is not yet, and you are a wolf . . . in Thunderbird's clothing." He laughed out loud at his words.

"You get that?! Thunderbird clothing, not sheep's clothing!" Then he laughed some more.

"Yes, yes, I get it." I responded in a slow scoff.

"You cannot do what we do, and we cannot do what you do. We each have our own calling in this world. Only Skin Shifters can truly become animal spirits using regalia. I am merely lending you this skin. But the Uktena won't know that. It is a serpent, driven by an insatiable hunger for Thunderbirds. These serpents can only be killed in one way—you must find its heart and pierce it."

"And where is its heart?" I asked, trying to visualize the anatomy of a snake.

Tecos chuckled, a sound that was both comforting and unsettling. "Oh, I'm sure a wolf with your keen senses can find it." I nodded, understanding the task ahead. Wolves always went straight for the heart in battle.

"The serpent emerges only once a year, at sunset, during the Perseid meteor shower. You will wake him with your dance; he will feel the vibrations in the ground and caverns where he sleeps. Once he surfaces, he will see you dancing and mistake you for a Thunderbird. You must strike quickly if you want his diamond, but you must do so while protecting my suit."

He placed a hand on my chest, his eyes locking with mine. "You must kill him fast. If he has time to charge his diamond under the night sky, the lightning strike will kill you."

"I promise," I said, my voice firm, though my heart pounded in my chest. I looked at Tecos, this majestic bird man, with a respect that bordered on reverence. I couldn't help but wonder what other powerful costumes he held, what other secrets he guarded.

"One more thing," Tecos said as he prepared to climb the ladder. "Don't fear change. Don't fear death. Don't fear. All things change. All things die. It is the circle of life." He pointed to the ground, where the circular indent of the kiva surrounded the fire. "Fire is life. Fire is also death. You must choose."

I nodded, the weight of his words settling over me like a shroud.

At that moment, Santana swooped down in her owl form, screeching as she alerted us to her return. In her talons, she carried my old weapons, dropping them near the entrance. She was fast—remarkably so. My weapons had been buried hundreds of miles apart, in places only I knew. I thanked her through the mindlink. Perhaps it was the owl spirit that had guided her to my treasures.

She screeched again, beckoning Tecos to join her. He climbed up the ladder with surprising ease, his earlier wisdom and gravity replaced by a childlike glee.

Santana's owl eyes reflected the vibrant Thunderbird feathers glowing in the firelight near me. I looked down at the feathers, examining their colors, and a chill ran through me. They were eerily similar to the feathers worn by the bald Witch who had once tried to kill me. There was a connection between these feathers and his—I could feel it. So many questions swirled in my mind, but I knew the answers waited for me in the caverns of the Valley.

My physical training was persistent. For the past two weeks, I have been using the rocks and boulders for weight to gain muscle mass. Ash trained for speed and agility by running through the tight ravines, careful to avoid noise and detection from other animals. Tecos brought along with him rogues from our Shadowland nation to spar with me. But now, with my training complete, tonight was the night. I was left alone to pray and gather my thoughts.

I sat down to stretch in the exact spot where Tecos had sat during my coming-of-age ceremony. The air was thick with the scent of sage and smoke, mingling with the lingering presence of the spirits that had filled the kiva moments ago.

Once I was loose enough, I took out the wooden pipe Tecos had given me and began packing it with the tobacco and other sacred herbs he had provided. My hands moved with a practiced familiarity that belied the turmoil in my heart.

The fire crackled softly in front of me, casting flickering shadows across the ancient walls. I reached into my pouch and pulled out a small batch of powdered aluminum collected from the remnants of my jewelry-making. With a steady hand, I tossed the powder into the flames, watching as the fire flared with a brilliant burst of light, the aluminum burning bright before settling back into its steady, comforting glow.

My thoughts turned to Magdalena, my mate, and the heavy weight of our unresolved dilemma. I had grown accustomed to being alone as a rogue by necessity. Now that I had her, and without her at my side, I was miserable.

We couldn't mark each other because of the strange nature of her hybrid animal. But we had bonded these past few weeks in other ways. I had bought her a car and brought her to my new home. Without her, I would never have made a home. Bonding with Luz though, was tricky for my wolf.

From the moment I first sensed Luz, I knew something was different. I had felt it that day in the park when she tried to shift, her wild energy spiraling out of control until I had calmed her with the animal whistle Santana had taught me.

A normal wolf wouldn't have responded to that—not a Werewolf from a pack with a strong alpha. But Luz had, and that had set off alarm bells in my mind.

I needed this diamond not just for myself and my pack but for her, too. She was going to be a part of my future pack. It wasn't just about power or status—it was about saving her life. Her wolf was more primal than I had realized, and that wildness bled into Magdalena as well. She wasn't just struggling with her dual nature—she was fighting something far deeper, something feral that threatened to consume her entirely. Mentally, she was like a rogue in a way, though I could never admit that to her.

The thought of her falling victim to a deformed shift, of her losing control and becoming something beyond saving, terrified me. And even more terrifying was the idea that one day, I might have to end her life, just as I had been forced to kill the other hybrid I encountered centuries ago in Romania.

Tears welled up, threatening to spill over, but I fought them back, refusing to give in to the despair that clawed at my heart. I didn't care about being a strong warrior or reclaiming my position as the alpha of my lost pack. None of that mattered anymore—not compared to the fierce, unwavering need to save my mate. She was my home now, my pack, and I couldn't imagine a world where she wasn't by my side.

Do not fear change. Do not fear death. Remember what Tecos said, Ash's voice echoed in my mind, steady and grounding. *I, too, rose from the grave. Don't you remember?*

It's why you call me Ash.

A sudden realization struck me like a lightning bolt, and I leaped to my feet, my heart pounding in my chest. Was that the answer? Had her father known all along? He hadn't been trying to kill her wolf—he had been trying to kill the Vampire inside her. That's why he removed her fangs. Vampires weren't Vampires because they lived—they were Vampires because they had died and been reborn.

The old question emerged. Did Magdalena have to die in order for her wolf to be transformed into something new, something whole? The thought sent a shiver down my spine, the implications terrifying yet strangely hopeful. But there was only one way to know for sure if my theory was true—without testing it on her directly.

Was this the meaning behind my vision during my coming-of-age ceremony?

I had to take the diamond. It was the key, the answer to everything. I could feel it in my bones, in the fire that burned in my chest. I had to succeed, not just for myself, but for her—for us.

I did as Tecos had done in my vision of his past. I prayed for the strength to save Magdalena.

I was ready to dance.

Chapter 7

The Uktena

Mags

Even though the heat was blistering, I went with Munks to the powwow that Torito had mentioned. I never got around to calling him, but Munks found me at the library and whisked me off to her house to get ready for the big event.

School was finally over, and the uncertainty of what lay ahead in life didn't bother me at that moment. All I wanted was to enjoy myself, to let loose and have fun. My birthday was also approaching—born in August, right when the Perseid meteor shower was at its peak. Every year, I would wish on those falling stars, praying that I'd find my parents, whether they were alive or dead. Never did I imagine that when I finally found my father, he would be undead.

Tonight's celebration was a gathering of multiple tribes, and although I didn't know my mother's tribe, I knew tribes from New Mexico were coming. They weren't from

California, but despite the distance, I felt an inexplicable connection to everyone here. This was the only place where I ever truly felt like I belonged, even as an orphan. But was I really an orphan? Not anymore.

I had a Vampire father and, perhaps somewhere out there, a Werewolf mother who might still be alive. It was the secret hope of every orphan. With this newfound knowledge, tonight felt different. I imagined my mother being here, hidden in the shadows, watching me from afar, just like my father. If they were here, I desperately hoped they would come and speak to me again.

I was happy to be out and feel normal again with my new bracelet, and overjoyed to have found a new best friend. I had known Munks for a few years, but we had only recently become close. My other friends—Cell, Manda, and Moniker—had drifted away. Cell went straight to work after high school, Manda moved to another state, and Moniker married into the military and was off with her husband.

Ever since my dad compelled them to forget my presence at prom, it felt like they had almost forgotten me entirely. I wasn't sure if it was because of what he did or if they simply didn't want to hang out with me anymore. I had a strong suspicion it was my dad's doing, of course. Either way, I figured a little time apart wouldn't hurt anyone. I didn't know if that Vampire mind trick could have a permanent effect on them, and I didn't want to risk exposing them any further.

I've been dying to tell Munks about my parents and Andy, but I wasn't sure how she'd react. She was always so confident, so carefree—why would I want to burden her with the dark secrets of my family? So, I kept it to myself.

Yet, I couldn't shake the feeling that Torito knew something. Even if he didn't say it outright, there was something in the way he looked at me, the way he called me "cousin," just like that teacher did. I often wondered if he was a Werewolf, too, like Andy. Maybe that's why I never called him back. Things felt too awkward between us.

Supposedly, I was Andy's mate. Whatever that meant. We had been spending a lot more time together recently, but there were moments when he seemed distant, like he was struggling to communicate with me. I didn't know if that was a Werewolf thing, but Torito and I never had any problems talking. If Torito was a Werewolf, how was it that he wasn't a rogue? Was there a pack here? I was probably wrong—he was nothing like Andy.

Andy was strong. He had a unique scent, different from everyone else, and there was something about him that made me feel at home, even when he retreated into his own thoughts. When we touched, it was like I could sense what was on his mind, and sometimes, his thoughts were just as dark as mine. And that was okay. We were both still processing dark memories from our past. Sometimes there was nothing one needed to say.

I think he knew this, but for some reason, he shied away from me that one night. The night I requested to see him shift into a wolf while naked. I didn't think he was shy. Serious, yes, but not shy. So, that night had left a hole in my heart. I needed a connection from him.

The last time we spoke, though, was completely different. He had gotten his own place and was going to bring me there in his new car.

"I want to get your approval," he said as he opened the door to his Jaguar, smiling softly. The dark green leather interior screamed luxury, and even though I never considered myself materialistic, something about the car made my eyes grow wide, and I said "yes" in my head. I slid into the seat, my leather Doc Martens clicking against the floor. The car smelled clean and well cared for.

"What do you need my approval for?" I asked, though what I really wanted to ask was if being his mate meant being his girlfriend. But I held back, afraid he might say no.

"You're my mate," he said matter-of-factly. There's that word again. I just rolled my eyes. "Whatever I have is yours, and I want to make sure you like it."

"Oh," I whispered, unsure how to process what he was saying. Did this mean he wanted to marry me? I didn't grow up calling people "mates." Did we only get one? Was it the same as being a girlfriend or boyfriend? I didn't want to start the night with a barrage of questions, though. We were barely just getting to know each other.

"I like the car," I said, looking up at him. His hair was loose tonight, and I noticed he had gotten it trimmed. A sharp pang of jealousy flashed through me—I didn't like the idea of someone else running their hands through his hair. I hadn't realized I was giving him a look until he asked, "What's wrong?" He paused before turning on the car, waiting for my response.

"Who cut your hair?" I asked. He smiled, the smug bastard, knew I was jealous. He looked at me again, his smile even more pronounced.

"I did," he said. "I needed to cut off some old ties to an old life." I scoffed, not entirely pleased with his answer. "You can inspect it if you want," he teased. "I have nothing to hide, baby." He invited me to sit closer, and I was glad the seats in his Jaguar were not bucket seats.

I started to play with his hair, and it was so soft, smelling nice and clean. I inched closer to catch another whiff, and that's when I felt his arms wrap around me, pulling me closer. Suddenly, I was on his lap, the seat reclined beneath us, and I could feel his hard member pressing against me through my straddled legs.

He began kissing my neck, his hands exploring my body, and I had to stop playing with his hair just to savor his touch. Then he started making these strange noises—almost growling or huffing—and for a moment, it startled me. I pulled back, only to see his glowing blue eyes staring into mine, his fangs elongated. He kept growling, his desire evident as he faced me.

To anyone else, he might have looked terrifying, but to me, he was beautiful. His broad shoulders and strong chest muscles were visible through a few open buttons on his shirt. I grabbed the buttons and popped them off one by one, exposing more of his chest to my eager lips. I kissed him there, feeling his hands grasp my hips, pulling me closer as he rocked us together, making me want to scream.

After a while, I pulled back and undid his pants, reaching for the hardened length I had been dreaming of since I first saw it before he teased me and left after shifting. He let out a stifled growl and moan as I touched him, feeling the blood surge toward my hands.

"You can pull blood to you?" he asked suddenly, just as I was about to take him into my mouth. I always knew I could do this—draw blood to the surface with just a touch. It was a trick I had always been able to do, though I never understood why. When I saw him shift for the first time, his member had engorged with blood on its own, and it fascinated me. Not that I hadn't seen one before, but this time was different. This was Andy, and it was as if his blood called out to me in ways I had never felt before. I wanted to put my lips on him, to kiss him, to make him mine in every possible way.

"Yeah," I whispered, my voice barely audible as I trailed my tongue along the length of his hardened member, savoring every inch like a kitten savoring milk.

"You're going to make me . . ." he began, his voice strained with the effort of holding back. But before he could finish, I took him fully into my mouth, letting his entire length fill me. As I did, I used my unique ability, drawing the blood to pulse rhythmically like a heartbeat, bringing it toward my lips and then releasing it, only to pull it back again. The sensation was electrifying, a teasing dance that sent shivers through my body. I reveled in the control, rubbing his full erection against my lips, moving my head back and forth as I relished the taste of him.

"Wait . . ." he suddenly gasped, his voice taking on an almost inhumane tone. Stopping seemed to physically pain him, and I couldn't understand why he wanted me to stop.

But then, without warning, he pushed me back down into the seat, away from him.

"What the fuck?!" I blurted out, confused and frustrated. What was wrong with him?

"We can't . . . not yet. Ash will . . . take you," he stammered, his voice still tinged with that unnatural edge. Before I could respond, he bolted out of the car and ran off into the night, leaving me alone and fuming. I was humiliated and burning with shame. What had come over me? Why couldn't I keep my hands off him? I sat there, feeling a mix of anger and embarrassment, wondering if I should just leave. Luz howled in the back of my mind.

But before I could decide, he returned, opening my door and scooping me up into his arms. He carried me off into the darkness. I didn't know where we were going, but relief washed over me as I pressed my tear-streaked face into his sleeve. Whether it was Ash, his wolf side, or Andy in control didn't matter—Luz and I just wanted to be near him.

When he finally stopped at an incredible speed, we were in a new house, isolated in the middle of the desert. We stood in a spacious bedroom, a massive king-size bed draped in luxurious white cotton before us. He gently laid me down on the bed.

His face was fully Andy again—human, calm, and composed. Slowly, he began to undress me, removing my clothes with deliberate care, and then he shed his own. I reached up to touch him, but he quickly grabbed my wrists and pinned them to the bed.

"Not this time, little Vampiress," he whispered, his voice filled with a fervent intensity. "It's my turn to show you what I can do with my tongue." A gasp escaped my lips as he lowered his head, taking my right nipple into his mouth. His tongue and lips worked together, teasing the sensitive peak into a firm salute. The sensation was overwhelming, and I tried to squirm away from the intensity of it, but he held me in place, his heat radiating into my cold, awakening body.

As he let my wrists go, his hand moved to ravage my other breast while his hips grinded up against me. The friction between us sent waves of desire pooling between my legs, soaking the bed beneath me.

Suddenly, with an effortless move, he flipped me over and lifted my hips, diving face-first into my bottom and pussy from behind. His tongue explored me in ways I had never experienced, and I felt a mix of embarrassment and pure, unadulterated pleasure.

"Your smell is driving me mad," he growled through muffled breaths, his voice thick with desire. I couldn't form words; the sensations were too overwhelming.

"Say my name, baby," he demanded, his hot breath against my skin sending a shiver through me. I tried to respond, but all that came out were whimpers.

"Say it," he insisted, punctuating his command with a sharp slap to my ass. The sting made me cry out, finally managing to mutter, "Andy."

As soon as I said his name, I felt his hand slide across the bridge of my clit, and another finger plunged deep into my vagina, and even my ass was not ignored. I felt him penetrate it with his thumb. The sudden intrusion made me yelp with shock initially, but eventually, my body accepted his intrusion. My hips started rocking in time with his movements until I was consumed by a whirlwind of emotions and ecstasy, calling out his name even louder until I felt the release exit my body and I was left panting.

I couldn't believe it. It was the first time I had ever come. Luz purred inside my head, and my once startled and wide eyes slowly shut and reveled peacefully in the aftermath of the climax.

"That's right," he growled, his voice dripping with satisfaction. "You're all mine, and don't you forget who licks your ass this good." He pulled me around to face him, and my cheeks flushed with embarrassment. How could this man make me feel both ashamed and utterly content at the same time? I wanted to reach out and touch him, but I hesitated, unsure if he would allow it or restrain my wrists again.

"I'm not done with you yet, my little Vampiress tease," he murmured, his eyes locking onto mine with an intensity that sent a thrill through me.

Something clicked inside me, and I smiled wide, giggling as my bare breasts bounced with his movement.

"I want more," I said, my voice laced with need. I knew my Vampire nature was coming in full force. I knew my eyes were shining red at these cocky words, daring me to show just how much of a freak I could be. How much of a freak I didn't I could be until now. But the wall had been torn down. And the wild fervor had come crashing out of me like a tidal wave.

"Here you go!" Munks suddenly chirped, snapping me out of my nostalgic memories from our first night together. We were together for three nights like this until he said he had some work to do. I didn't see him last night or today. I was already missing him.

I sighed. I didn't want to pull myself from my memories, but Munks' truck came to a stop in the parking lot. We both got out so she could hand me her gift.

"I got this for you!" she said, handing me a silver necklace with a turquoise pendant shaped like a 'pterodactyl', the nickname she had given the Thunderbird. Munks had her hair braided with ribbons, and she'd also done mine. We'd done each other's makeup before the powwow, and I had to admit, we both looked deadly.

I was shocked by the gift, not knowing what to say, especially as the metal began to heat up and sting my fingers. I pretended to trip and dropped the necklace, using the opportunity to quickly snap the chain.

"I'm so sorry!" I exclaimed, quickly picking up the pieces and tucking them into my hidden skirt pocket. I threaded a red ribbon through the charm and tied it around my neck, letting it rest above my shirt to muffle the burning sensation.

"I'll get it fixed as soon as I can, I promise," I added, thinking I might have my new jewelry maker fix it for me.

"Fiiiine," she said, trying not to sound disappointed. "Come on, let's go find a seat on the bleachers." We made our way through the growing crowd, quickly moving past the tents that were filling up with eager buyers and curious onlookers.

My heart was racing, and I wasn't sure why. I could feel it in my bones—something magical was going to happen tonight. It wasn't the same sharp, physical anticipation I felt the last time I visited the Pit; this felt more spiritual, like there was magic in the air. Or maybe I was just getting used to being free from the poison. What if this was how my life was meant to be experienced? My vision was sharper, my sense of smell more acute, and the energy—it was unreal, like a constant caffeine buzz that never wore off.

Vibrant, free, strong . . . and *bloody*. I stopped myself at that thought. Bloody? The craving was back. Maybe this was more like that night in the Pit than I realized.

I imagined myself with fangs and swished my tongue around my mouth, feeling both relieved and disappointed that they weren't there. The look of horror on Andy's face that night when he noticed my father had had them removed was like a punch in the gut. I know being in foster care can drive a person to imagine all sorts of things about their parents—alive, dead, coming to rescue them. If he really was my father, and he hadn't killed me or my wolf yet, then it just felt right that he wasn't evil. It was a sense I got, just a hunch. But what if I was wrong?

I just wished he hadn't erased my memories of our meeting. That a-hole is going to have to explain himself when—if—we meet again. If he's here tonight, I'll make sure to tell him just that.

Just then, we heard our names being called, and I saw a few familiar faces waving us over. Torito! I hoped he had forgotten that I was supposed to call him. He was up on the bleachers with some friends, waiting for us.

"Hey!" Munks called out, waving back. I smiled at them, trying to avoid direct eye contact in case my eyes were glowing. Munks and I quickly got situated one row below them.

I shoved the desire for blood deep down, focusing instead on my pretty little black moccasins. I needed to get Munks a gift soon—some turquoise earrings to match her green eyes would be perfect. Perhaps this powwow had an atm somewhere or maybe they took cards.

"Hi, Mags!" Torito greeted me as he slid into the empty seat next to me. His sudden presence made me tense up, my bloodlust flaring momentarily. But within seconds, it vanished, leaving me perplexed.

It's probably all the silver he wears, Luz whispered in my mind. Oh, right—Torito was a silversmith too. Even though I preferred Andy's jewelry, the thought of my new bracelet gracing my wrist brought a smile to my lips.

"Daaaaaang, look at that!" Torito exclaimed, grabbing my wrist to inspect the bracelet. He examined it closely, his expression shifting as if he was trying to figure out if I had somehow lost my aversion to silver.

"Who made this?" Torito asked, his tone filled with genuine admiration. "The craftsmanship is exquisite. Can you take it off so I can see it up close?"

"I better not," I replied, gently pulling my arm back. The moment felt awkward, a tension hanging in the air. "I just don't want to risk losing it," I added, turning to give him a small, apologetic smile.

"Okay, don't worry about it," Torito said, waving off my concern. Then, with a casual air that caught me off guard, he asked, "So, do you have a boyfriend?" His straightforwardness made my face flush with heat. He didn't waste any time, did he?

"No, she doesn't!" Munks interjected before I could even formulate a response. I stammered, caught off guard, but when I saw Torito's smile widen, something—or perhaps it was Luz's protective instinct—made me blurt out, "Yes."

"Yes?!" Munks exclaimed, her eyes narrowing in surprise. "Who?" she demanded, leaning in closer. I laughed nervously, feeling the pressure mount. I might as well tell them.

"Well, he's not exactly my boyfriend. We just hang out sometimes," I explained, trying to downplay the situation.

"Gheeeeheehe!" Torito laughed out loud. "Well, if I had a girlfriend, I'd claim her right away!" He shook his head, his voice turning more serious. "Not just 'hang out,'" he muttered, clearly disapproving. And he was right, but how could I possibly explain the complexities of my situation?

"His name is Andy, and he's new in town. I haven't told you yet, but I was planning on telling you tonight," I lied, trying to sound convincing.

"Well, why isn't he here with you?" Munks asked, clearly intrigued.

"He's working," I lied again, feeling a bit foolish. Honestly, he did say he was going to be busy tonight and that he'd accompany me to the next powwow. “I promise I’ll introduce you guys soon," I added, hoping to deflect any further questions.

"Well . . ." Torito said after a pause. "We better go in, guys.

We gotta get ready."

"You’re dancing?" Munks asked, her excitement evident.

"Yeah," Torito replied with a grin. "But you’re going to have to guess which one I am. I’ll be in full regalia." And with that, Torito and his two friends, whom I hadn’t been introduced to, climbed down the bleachers and headed off to prepare.

"Are you sure you two are cousins?" Munks teased, nudging me playfully. I didn’t know how to respond, so I just shrugged. "He likes you," she added, her tone suggesting more than she was saying.

I just shook my head. *I like him too, but not in that way.* He felt more like a brother to me.

And we have a mate, Luz interjected protectively. *I know! But I can’t tell her that!* I shot back, feeling the familiar tug of our inner dialogue. *But he’s also not my boyfriend . . .*I teased Luz, knowing it would drive her crazy. I couldn’t help it. I knew she’d go ballistic, even though she knew I wasn’t interested in Torito that way. Sometimes, it was nice to be the one causing her a little bit of stress instead of the other way around.

I burst out laughing, feeling Luz paw at me in the recesses of my mind.

"What?" Munks asked, puzzled by my sudden outburst. "He’s cute! And nice. If you don’t want him, I’ll take him, seeing that you’re ‘cousins’ and all."

For a while, the night returned to its usual rhythm. The excitement in the air remained, but it mellowed into something more peaceful. The sun began to set behind us, and the temperature finally started to drop. Speakers came and went, children danced in their little regalia, and we cheered for them as if they had just won the biggest game of the season.

The kachina dancers were up next, and we sat there, talking about life and the future while watching the crowd grow. I was grateful we had found good seats as the bleachers began to fill.

We bought drinks and fry bread tacos from a vendor who was making their rounds. I hadn't realized how hungry I was until I took that first bite, realizing I hadn't eaten all day. And then, the festival truly began. The kachina dancers emerged earlier than I expected, and I could barely contain my excitement—I had never seen kachina dancers before.

I had assumed the women would dance too, but when I asked Munks about it, she quickly hushed me, mentioning something about, "not at this one."

The dancers came out from the side of the football field, each one dressed as a different spiritual being. There must have been a hundred of them, all adorned in mystical regalia. I recognized a crow, a horse, even a lizard. There were others I didn't recognize, but I knew they represented various nature spirits as well. I spotted three owls—great horned owl spirits—but none were barn owls.

My heart ached as I saw about twenty wolves, none of them Andy. I searched the dancers for someone who might be Torito, but they were all so well camouflaged in their regalia.

Their dancing was vigorous and energetic, each performer surpassing the next in skill and balance.

Look with your nose, Mags, Luz suggested, making me cringe a bit. I wasn't used to relying on my wolf senses, and sniffing people still felt strange to me—invasive and too intimate—well, except for Andy. My nose was practically obsessed with him.

Ug! Luz groaned. *Just take a whiff. You know what he smells like!*

Fine, I sighed. I lowered my head and closed my eyes, bringing my bracelet—Torito had touched it—close to my nose. I took a moment to sift through the hundreds of scents coming from it. My own scent—jasmine and rose, just as Andy had mentioned. The lotion I wore, though technically unscented, had a faint coconut oil base. The spices from my fry bread taco were overpowering, so I had to take another whiff to get past the peppers and seasoning.

And then, yes—there he was. Torito smelled like coconuts and aluminum. No, that was his deodorant. He smelled like mint and chocolate. Chocolate mint!

I lifted my head, tracing the scent trail with my nose until I opened my eyes and spotted him. I should have known—he was a Thunderbird. A beautiful turquoise, yellow, white, and green bird. He didn't look anything like a pterodactyl, I thought to myself, smiling at the comparison. I watched him for a second, admiring his determination and concentration as he danced.

He turned, his feathered arms sweeping through the air as if flying gracefully. I saw him pound his feet with strength and rhythm to the drums echoing behind him.

And then, suddenly, I got a strange feeling in the pit of my stomach—like déjà vu. The sensation was unsettling, making me hunch over in pain as I scanned the crowd.

I started seeing things—strange faces among the crowd, staring at me with red eyes filled with hunger. What was wrong with me? As quickly as I noticed them, they shifted back into normal human faces.

I grabbed my new pendant and rubbed it with my fingers for luck. The burning sensation intensified, and before it became too painful, I let the charm fall, letting it dangle over my chest.

The music seemed to grow louder, rushing into my ears. I could hear a Native flute playing in the background, its haunting, serene melody both soothing and aggravating me at the same time. Tears welled up in the corners of my eyes, and I quickly wiped them away before Munks could notice.

I grabbed a plastic water bottle being passed around, grateful for the cool liquid against my throat. The water was partially frozen, a blessing against the blood hunger that was beginning to creep back. Maybe the sun had just been too much for me. It was almost nighttime; I just had to hold on a little while longer. Silently, I pleaded for the faint falling stars to hurry up and grace us with their presence.

A new rhythm of drums filled the air, a powerful symphony that resonated deep within my bones. Normally, I loved the sound of drums, their steady beat grounding me, but tonight, my head was already pounding with its own erratic rhythm, and the added noise was unbearable.

I closed my eyes, trying to steady my breathing, but when I opened them again, the world around me had shifted. My vision blurred and sharpened in strange ways, and I knew that Luz, my wolf, was near the surface.

Stop it, Luz, please, I begged her through the mindlink, as Andy had taught me. He said I had to take control of my wolf and I was trying.

I'm not doing anything, I swear! Luz's voice in my mind was frantic, and I saw her in my mind's eye, anxiously scanning the area. *There are other wolves around, but they're not themselves. They're under someone else's control.*

I peered back into the crowd, trying to see what Luz was seeing. The dancers' movements became ghostly and ethereal, their forms blurring as if caught between worlds. Among the living, I began to see figures that didn't belong—ghosts of ancient Natives, their eyes fixed intently on me. Their presence was both comforting and unnerving, a reminder of my roots and the struggle that weighed on my shoulders. But why were they watching me? I could hear the faint sound of their singing, the jingling of their skirts as they shook them at me. If these were my ancestors, where was my mother? Perhaps she really was alive.

Then, I noticed someone else watching me from across the bleachers on the other side of the field. It was a man, bald but with features that still held a Native resemblance even if pale. He wore regalia, but I couldn't identify what kind of kachina he was supposed to be. I didn't really think he was a kachina dancer. His eyes glowed a bright, unnatural red, and his face was pale and gaunt like a skull stitched together with scraps of rotten flesh. Why couldn't the people standing next to him see that? He mumbled something at me, and though my ears heard it, the words made no sense.

"Munks," I whispered, nudging my friend who stood beside me. "Do you see them?"

Munks followed my gaze, but her eyes remained focused on the dancers. "See what, Mags?"

"The ghosts," I insisted, my voice trembling. "They're watching us."

Munks shook her head, concern etched on her face. "I don't see anything. Are you feeling okay?"

I wasn't sure how to answer. My head spun, and the world seemed to tilt around me. I avoided making eye contact with her, afraid my eyes might be glowing red like that night in my bathroom. Why did I forget my glasses? I needed to buy some sunglasses, and soon.

I stared back at the creepy man, and the scent of decay filled my nostrils.

Rogue. Shifter. Evil, Luz whispered, her voice barely a murmur, as if it took all her strength to speak.

The drumming grew louder and more insistent, and I could feel my heart racing in time with the beat. My eyes felt dry, and a strange sensation gripped me, as if my very soul was being sucked away by the creature staring at me. I struggled to breathe, my chest heaving, but no air seemed to fill my lungs.

Then, out of the corner of my eye, I saw it—the owl. Its piercing screech cut through the air, a loud, aggressive sound, but it wasn't directed at me. It was aimed at the rogue.

This owl had appeared before, at the Pit. I was sure of it. Its large, unblinking eyes bore into mine as if looking past me and straight at Luz. A chill ran down my spine as I pointed up, my hand trembling.

"Munks, the owl. It's here," I said, my voice shaking as I pointed upward.

But Munks only saw the night sky, clear and star-filled. "There's no owl, Mags. You need to calm down. Did you take some shrooms? I didn't think you did stuff like that," she added, her tone tinged with annoyance.

"No!" I protested. "I don't do those things."

How could I explain to her the battle raging inside me? The ghosts, the owl—they weren't just symbols of my inner turmoil. They were real manifestations of the war within me. The Vampire in me craved to feed, to surrender to the primal urges, while my Werewolf side fought desperately to maintain control. I was a creature of two worlds, and tonight those worlds were colliding.

I stumbled back in my seat, desperate to find some clarity. The ghosts whispered to me, their words lost in the overwhelming noise of the powwow. I needed to regain control, to ground myself.

"I'm going to the restroom," I said abruptly.

"Uh," Munks scoffed, clearly irritated. "Mags, you're going to miss everything."

"That's the point!" I called back, walking away quickly and waving goodbye. I made my way to the parking lot and found a tree to hide under. I wished Andy were here—he would know how to help me, just like he had last time.

I focused on the earth beneath my feet. It was the only place where I didn't see ghostly faces. This was my heritage, my strength—but why did I seem allergic to it? To nature, to life?

It's not you . . . it's that man! Luz whispered to me.

Taking a deep breath, I centered myself, pushing back the Vampire urges with all my might. The ghosts faded, and the owl disappeared into the night. In the distance, the dancers came back into focus, their movements a beautiful blur of color and tradition. I was still Mags, still part of this world.

Just then, a dark car pulled up next to me. I gasped, staring at the tinted windows, trying to see who was inside. Andy? No, It was my father.

"Get her!" someone shouted from behind me. A sheet was suddenly thrown over my head, blinding me. I tried to scream, but strong hands clamped over my mouth. I struggled, but within moments, I was shoved into the car, speeding off into the night to some unknown destination.

Luz! I called out to her in a panic. *I'm sorry, please don't let my father take you away! You must stay strong!*

And then everything went black.

Andy

I stood at the entrance of the caverns, the cool air brushing against my skin as the setting sun cast long shadows behind me. The valley stretched out before me, vast and empty. This was the first time I had left the Shadowlands since meeting my mate, Magdalena, and the distance between us now felt unbearable. The memories of our precious moments together last weekend haunted me, making every step away from her that much harder.

Ash was restless that night, craving to claim her, to mark her as ours. But I kept reminding him of the vision I'd seen—*Not yet!* I had to tell him over and over again throughout the night, even as the temptation gnawed at me. Her allure was impossible to resist. My little Vampiress had her own tricks, and I hadn't expected her to seduce me so easily, so completely.

The sensations she invoked in me, the pulsations from her mouth, the way she pulled my blood toward her with that strange, ancient power—it drove me to the brink of madness. It wasn't just a sexual trick; it was primal, a survival instinct kicking in. I'd seen Vampires do this before, deep in their hibernation, lying entombed in the earth. They'd send out those compelling signals, drawing blood from their surroundings, feeding from whatever life that slithered near them, pulling them like a magnet, even in their sleep. It was a terrifying and dark thing to witness.

I'd encountered these hibernating Vampires before, their resting places marked by the heaps of bones, corpses, and body parts littering the ground above the earth. The faint heartbeat, slow and deliberate, would echo through the earth, a haunting reminder of their dormant power. These were the easiest to kill—when they were vulnerable. The earth around them was soft like quicksand. One could get sucked in if they weren't careful.

So when Magdalena performed the same act on me, drawing my blood in that tantalizing way, it both exhilarated and frightened me. For a moment, I panicked, the memories of those lifeless Vampires flashing before my eyes. But I knew she would never harm me. It was like watching a spider suck the blood out of a husk they've entombed in a web. For a second, I felt trapped with my vulnerable member in her mouth.

I had to come to terms with the fact that my mate was half

Vampire, half wolf. She was going to be different. And that was ok. It had to be. And yet, the strange, creepy feeling crossed my blood brain barrier alerting my senses to their core.

Are mates even our mates, though, if they didn't creep us out a little? Ash joked. It brought a smile to my face. Who would have thought this once Vampire-hunting rogue would be seduced by the very thing he once hunted?

It was Ash, not me, who made us return to her. He wanted to protect her, to keep her close. He could sense her disappointment. Under one condition, I said: that he would stay in the back of my mind, not pushing to mark her. And he agreed, surprisingly easily at that moment. But as the night wore on, he forgot about his promise.

"I want more," my little Vampiress whispered to me, her lips curling into a perfect cupid's bow, her hunger almost palpable after feeling her come from my own hands. I wanted more, too. She drew my blood closer to the surface of my lips, teasing me, pulling at my very essence until it nearly broke through the skin, only to have it heal instantly. Her bites were playful, testing the boundaries, but I wouldn't let her taste my blood—not yet. Not until I knew she wouldn't be in danger of turning too soon.

All night long, she kissed me, her lips traveling across my body, leaving behind hickeys and bruises that healed almost as quickly as she made them. Her passion was intoxicating, and eventually, I couldn't resist any longer.

I spread her legs wide and entered her, but not before getting an eyeful of her perfect southern lips parting for me. I felt her innocence give way as I tore through the gentle folds of her skin. She let out a soft cry, as a delicate mix of undulating waves instinctively caused her hips to rock back and forth.

Her nails dug deep into my arms and back, but being a wolf, my wounds closed up too quickly for any blood to spill. I wrapped my arms around her, lifting her hips off the bed, marveling at how her full breasts moved in rhythm with my thrusts. The need to be as deep inside her as possible consumed me; her body commanded my swollen member's full, undivided attention.

I felt her swell around me as a glaze fell over my eyes, being close to exploding. She suddenly got so tight I could barely move; it was as if her gash clung onto me like a vacuum, milking my hard shaft. The knot. She had it, too. As distant memories of schoolboys talking about what Werewolf women did when they were in the throes of passion slipped past me, I suddenly started thrusting harder and harder, driving myself forward until we both finally released with guttural moans that echoed in the stillness of the night.

I felt myself engorge fully after the release, trapping all my contents and my member into her embrace, leaving us in a tight cradle that both of us were helpless to escape from. The sacred knot.

We collapsed together, our bodies entwined, her body still slowly milked the remaining of my cum and I could not move a muscle in this contraction.

It took a good thirty minutes until I could move again and while kissing her quivering lips, I pulled out. We dozed off briefly before giving in to our desires once more.

I think the owls knew we were intimate, though, and thankfully, they didn't bring up the subject. Was this why I received such a stark cleansing of my body? Truthfully, it pained me to no longer smell her on me.

It's safe to say I didn't get much sleep before my fight with the Uktena, for I had spent my days preparing for my fight and my nights with Magdalena. In hindsight, it was probably not the most tactical thing to do. But when I'm near her, I can't help myself . . . we can't help ourselves. It's the primal wolf in us.

Do we have regrets? Ash boasted, his voice smug in the back of my mind.

Not at all, I replied, gazing out over the wide valley before me, the memories of our nights together still vivid, still lingering on my skin. The weight of the coming battle pressed against my shoulders, but in that moment, all I could think of was Magdalena—her touch, her taste, the way her body had responded to mine. And I knew, deep down, that nothing could keep us apart for long.

This was the great crevice, the great divide known as the Grand Canyon, home to the Uktena I was hunting.

Tecos had said the right one would come, that the ancestors would beckon him to seek me out once I took on the spirit of the Thunderbird, one of its ancient enemies.

The air was thick with anticipation and the scent of damp earth. I donned the Thunderbird regalia; its intricate designs and vibrant colors were a tribute to the powerful spirit I invoked. The feathers rustled softly, whispering secrets of the ancient battles between the Thunderbird and the Uktena. The regalia was more than just a costume; it was a living tool of power, a conduit to the spirit world.

As the final rays of moonlight filtered through the cavern entrance, I began the dance. My feet pounded the ground rhythmically but slowly at first, each step echoing through the vast chamber. The sound reverberated off the walls, creating a symphony of power and intent. The Thunderbird and Uktena had been ancient enemies and visions of their battles flooded my mind. My dance was a challenge, a call to the serpent to face me.

With each movement, I felt a transformation taking place. The power of the Thunderbird flowed through me, merging with my own Werewolf strength. The air crackled with energy as I danced, my body moving with a primal grace. The ground beneath me seemed to pulse in response, and I knew the Uktena could sense my presence.

Tecos had said I would not transform physically into the Thunderbird. But he never said anything about spiritually. I could feel the Thunderbird spirit with me.

It has always been with me; I realize that now, from my parent's death and losing my wolf temporarily to my first kill, to now. It was with me, signaling its presence as lightning in the sky, only I was too young to realize it. Just like the owl spirit that ran through me after Tecos gifted me his feather, the Thunderbird spirit was here too, with power reverberating in my bones.

And it made sense after the story Tecos had told me. All shifters have a piece of the Thunderbird feather in our souls, it is a part of us, entwined in our DNA.

Moments later, a deep rumble echoed through the cavern. The ground shook, and the air grew heavy with an oppressive force. The Uktena was coming. I could see its massive form slithering through the shadows, its scales glistening like obsidian. The diamond in its head, dark and vibrant, pulsed with a malevolent energy.

The creature was a colossal black serpent, its sleek scales glistening with a menacing sheen as it moved with the sinuous grace of a viper. Every motion was calculated, predatory, its body undulating with an eerie elegance that sent shivers down the spine. But what truly set this monstrous serpent apart was the magnificent wreath of purple feathers that encircled the base of its head, a vivid and regal contrast against its dark form. These feathers fluttered softly with each movement, creating a striking halo that hinted at some ancient, mystical power. Atop its head, towering above the fearsome diamond-shaped eyes that glowed with an unearthly light, was an enormous set of antlers. These antlers arched gracefully like a crown, circling the black diamond on its head in a protective measure. It added an air of majesty to the beast's terrifying presence. The creature was an awe-inspiring fusion of primal savagery and otherworldly beauty, a living embodiment of nature's most fearsome and exquisite creations.

The Uktena's eyes locked onto me. They were filled with an ancient hatred. It lunged, but I was ready. In an instant, I removed the regalia and let it flow away with the wind. It seemed to have been carried away by a spirit of its own, as I saw it flying away in the periphery of my sight as if it were alive.

I then shifted into my wolf form, my senses heightened, and my muscles coiled for action. The Uktena struck, but I dodged, moving with the agility of a predator. Ash's sharp howls permeated the air in response to the Uktena's squeaks and hisses. His roars were like thunder echoing off the ancient caverns. Our battle had begun.

I attacked, aiming for the spot just behind the diamond. I could hear the quickening of its beat reverberate against my eardrums. But the Uktena was swift and cunning. It twisted and turned, evading my strikes with ease. Each time I missed, the serpent's hiss grew louder, its rage more palpable. The cavern was a blur of movement and sound, our forms locked in a deadly dance.

Frustration began to seep into my mind. I had missed several times, and the Uktena showed no signs of weakening. I needed a new strategy, a way to outsmart the ancient beast. In a desperate move, I shifted back into human form. The Uktena paused, perhaps puzzled by my sudden change. Maybe the beast was shocked that I would fight him as a human. Nonetheless, this was my chance.

I whistled, a high-pitched sound that pierced the discord of battle. It was the same sound that I had lulled Mags' beast with. A sound that could hypnotize and that only shifters could make. The Uktena's movements slowed, its eyes glazing over as the whistle took effect. The serpent swayed, caught in the spell, and I seized the moment.

I ran in the direction of where my silver sword lay, the same sword I had taken from my first Vampire kill in Romania. It felt cold and familiar in my grip, a weapon of both legend and necessity. With a determined cry, I lunged forward and thrust the sword, aiming for the heart of the serpent. But even in a lulled state, he recoiled quickly and I missed again. His mouth was wide and his fangs folded outward. He was about to swallow me whole as I stood there looking up at him, vulnerable.

But I wasn't afraid of this monster. It had horns on its head that resembled antlers and a few feathers graced the periphery of its bald scalp. It was then that I made the connection. This monster was where the Witch had gotten his feathers from. Not from a Thunderbird. The feathers were alike but so different. They were waxier and thicker than the plumes of the Thunderbird. Perfect for swimming.

"Kill him fast!" the last words of Tecos rang in my ears like a distant echo. At the time, I was confident that I would succeed in just that, but as the battle dragged on, the certainty of my hubris began to erode. The Uktena was unlike any foe I had ever faced—its ancient power was a force that seemed to defy time itself. Every move we made was countered by the serpent's unyielding strength, and I started to question whether I could truly conquer this beast.

The terrain we traversed was unforgiving. We clashed across jagged cliffs that seemed to tear at the sky, over vast stretches of rocky ground, and through waterways so deep and dark they felt like the veins of the earth itself. The Uktena was cunning, attempting to lose me by diving into underwater caves, its sinuous body slipping through narrow crevices like a liquid shadow. Each time, I lunged after it, my muscles straining as I grabbed hold of its tail, using all my might to yank the creature back into the open air. But it was exhausting work, and the constant battle was wearing me down in ways I hadn't anticipated.

Ash was struggling, too. His power lay in speed and agility on land, but water was another matter entirely. The continuous need to shift, to partially transform and then revert, was taking a toll on both of us. My limbs ached from the effort, my mind straining to maintain control over the relentless shifts. The storm above us grew darker with each passing moment, the clouds swirling like a gathering tempest. Thunder rumbled ominously in the distance, a harbinger of the storm's fury.

We found ourselves in a narrow ravine, the walls closing in around us like the jaws of some great beast. The air was thick with the scent of ozone, sharp and biting, a warning that the Uktena's diamond had fully charged. My heart pounded in my chest, the realization hitting me like a blow. We were running out of time.

Without a second thought, I shifted fully into my wolf form, the transformation seamless and immediate. Ash's power surged through me, his speed and agility like a lifeline in the chaos of the fight. But even Ash, as powerful as he was, could feel the strain. Every muscle screamed with exertion, but there was no room for hesitation. *Crack!* The first bolt of lightning struck, and before I could fully register it, we had vanished from where we stood, reappearing several meters away. The movement was so swift that it felt like we had been ripped from one place and stitched into another in the blink of an eye.

The ground beneath our paws was still vibrating from the impact when another bolt followed. *Crack!* In an instant, we were behind the Uktena, our breath coming in sharp gasps, the air charged with electricity. The serpent's enormous, coiled body twisted violently, its scales glistening in the dim light.

But despite its terrifying presence, I could sense something shifting in the battle's tide. The Uktena was beginning to slow. Each strike it launched was less precise, its movements more labored. I could see it in the way its massive head dipped and how its tail thrashed with less force. It was growing tired, just as I was. The realization should have filled me with hope, but all I felt was a deep, gnawing fear. This wasn't just a fight—

it was a test of endurance, of who could outlast the other in this deadly game.

The storm overhead had reached its peak, the sky now a churning mass of black clouds and crackling energy. The wind howled through the ravine, tearing at my fur, stinging my eyes. Every instinct I had screamed that this was the moment, the point of no return. I couldn't afford to wait any longer.

Come on, Ash, I urged, the words a desperate plea in the silence of my mind. *We have to end this. Now.* I could feel Ash's agreement, his resolve hardening into something almost tangible. He was my partner in this, my other half, and together, we were going to bring this creature down. We had to—for my people, for Magdalena, for the future that hung in the balance.

The Uktena turned, its eyes blazing with a mixture of fury and fear, the realization of its own weakening dawning in those ancient, malevolent depths. It reared back, its head snapping forward in a final, desperate attempt to strike. But I was ready. My muscles coiled like springs, every fiber of my being focused on this one moment, this one chance.

With a burst of speed that defied the storm, that defied even the limitations of my own body, Ash and I lunged forward, forgoing the silver weapons I had previously used against him. The world around us blurred, reduced to a tunnel of sound and light; the only clear image was the gleaming diamond embedded in the Uktena's forehead. Time seemed to slow as I reached out, my claws extended, aiming for that one vulnerable spot.

Crack! The sky exploded in a blinding flash as the serpent unleashed its final attack, the diamond glowing with an otherworldly light. But I was faster. Ash was faster. In the split second before the lightning could strike, before the Uktena could unleash its deadly power, my claws found their mark.

With a roar that echoed through the ravine, I plunged my claws into the Uktena's head, piercing the flesh beneath the diamond—the creature's vulnerable heart. There was a moment of silence, a pause in the universe itself, and then the Uktena convulsed violently, its body writhing in agony. The energy from the diamond exploded outward, a shockwave that knocked me back, but I held on, refusing to let go.

The serpent's death throes were terrifying, its massive form thrashing and twisting as it tried to dislodge me. But it was too late. The light in its eyes dimmed, the power in its body drained away, and with one final shudder, we closed in on the beast's heart with our muzzle. Tearing through its flesh, we lept in the air covered in the blood of the Uktena. The beast was dead. We landed on the desert floor with a light thud. The Uktena collapsed to the ground, lifeless.

I took a moment to gather my senses while letting Ash continue to have full control. Ash tore at the heart in his muzzle as if it were still alive. He gulped it down in one clean swallow. It tasted like metal and death, but it went down smooth.

My body trembled with exhaustion and adrenaline. I stared at the deformed snake and revoled in my victory for a while longer. Its blood was in my mouth, its taste a hard reminder of a certain little Vaewolf who was probably wondering where I was.

The storm above began to dissipate, the clouds parting as if the heavens themselves had been waiting for this moment. The air was heavy with the scent of rain and ozone, but there was something else—a sense of peace, of completion.

I looked down at the Uktena, its once-mighty form now still and silent. The diamond, no longer glowing, was embedded in its head, a trophy of the battle we had just fought. Carefully, reverently, I reached out and took it, feeling its cool weight in my hand. This was what I had risked everything for. But it wasn't just about the power it held—it was about the promise it represented, the future I could now secure for my people, for Magdalena.

As I stood there in the aftermath of the battle, the world seemed to come back into focus, the colors more vibrant, the sounds clearer. The fight was over, but the journey was just beginning. There was still so much to do, so many challenges ahead. But for now, I allowed myself a moment of relief, of triumph. I had done it. We had done it.

Suddenly, my body collapsed as I surrendered to my exhaustion and sat on the hard and jagged earth. I was exhausted and sticky with sweat and the blood of the

Uktena.

I reached for my hat that lay nearby and placed it on my head. I then reached down and plucked a feather from the Uktena and placed it into the brim nonchalantly, on the right side of my hat. How I wished I had some of Tecos famous tobacco to smoke.

Then I gathered the diamond from its place on my lap, its dark surface still pulsing with residual energy. It was a black diamond, vibrant and strong, a symbol of the Uktena's power. It was not like the other diamonds I had heard about Uktenas having. As my fingers closed around it, the diamond began to melt, its essence absorbing into my body.

A surge of energy coursed through me, energizing my once war-torn muscles—a mingling of my own power with that of the fallen serpent. Its power was mine. Instinctively, I leaned back with my arms out as the power of the diamond coursed through my veins, communing with my own spirit.

I gazed up at the night sky, the darkness above mirrored the storm that brewed within me. Lightning crackled in my eyes, a fierce and untamed energy that surged through every fiber of my being. As the final surge of power coursed into me, I could feel it building, an unstoppable force demanding release. With a primal instinct, I threw my head back further and unleashed a deafening, thunderous howl that echoed through the night, shaking the very air around me. In that moment, I felt my fangs elongate as my eyes burned with a piercing light, glowing like twin beacons in the darkness. I was no longer just a being—I was a force of nature, wild and unstoppable, a predator ready to claim the night.

The transformation was complete. I could feel the strength of the Uktena within me, a dark power tempered by my own will. The battle had been won, but the journey was far from over.

I would always carry the essence of the Uktena with me, a reminder of the ancient battles fought and the ones still to come. The next step would be to defeat my uncle and his Witch. With the spirit of the Thunderbird and the essence of the Uktena within me, I was ready to face whatever lay ahead.

As I stood, the last rays of the setting sun painted the sky in hues of red and gold. The world felt different, charged with a new energy. The battle had been fierce, and the victory hard-won. I had triumphed.

We triumphed, inserted Ash. I couldn't help but let out a momentous laugh.

"Yes, we triumphed, old friend," I said aloud. "I guess I didn't need those swords after all. You're my greatest weapon."

I was naked and dirty, so I shifted and looked for the owl's Thunderbird regalia. Something told me it wasn't here, though; it was back at the kiva. I could suddenly see it in my mind's eye, primed and pressed, sitting on a wooden rack inside the sacred kiva.

I gasped at the realization that the dark diamond had granted me powers of farsight. I couldn't wait to see what else it could do.

Wait. Mags. I saw her tied to a table and blindfolded. She was in trouble. I could see her father's blond hair as he spoke to one of his ghouls. Damn that man!

I knew it was too good to be true, growled Ash.

Let's go get our mate! I growled back with the mindlink. Another loud howl escaped my muzzle and power surged through my veins. Thunder shook the night skies as if it were returning my call to action. It started to rain, and I felt the droplets cleanse my coat of most of the serpent's blood as I ran like lightning in the direction of her father's house, towards our mate.

Chapter 8

The Wendigo

Sebastian

I had always known about the Wendigo. My ability to read minds and see memories when I drank blood from unsuspecting people revealed its presence to me way before I met Aiyana. The images I received from the local Natives of the new land were monstrous.

I had just crossed from Romania to the New Lands with my small coven of blood drinkers. The year was 1549.

The Wendigo's appearance was a grotesque perversion of nature. I had heard stories about these creatures but never witnessed one personally. It piqued my curiosity and I set off in search of the crazed creature who appeared as half deer and half man.

Its hooves, which should be sturdy and whole, were deformed, adding a grotesque clumsiness to its gait. The flesh that once covered its bones had rotted away, leaving a ghastly sight of exposed bone and decaying sinew. This decay did not end at its limbs; the entirety of the Wendigo's body was a testament to its suffering and unnatural existence.

The creature's face was perhaps the most haunting aspect of its visage. It was nothing but a deer skull. No flesh, no signs of life. Hollow and gaunt, it is a visage of eternal hunger and despair. Its eyes, or rather the empty sockets where eyes once might have been, were sunken deeply into its skull. Within these dark voids, a faint red hue barely flickered, a sinister glow that spoke of the malevolent force animating this cursed being. This dim light served as a beacon of dread, a warning of the malevolent presence lurking within the creature.

I caught its disgusting scent and raced the night in search of the creature. I had come too late. It had reared its ugly head in a fishing village and was taking out the last of the Werewolves that lived there. This land I speak of is now called Canada.

I, with my royal entourage of fellow Vampires, was about to spring into motion to capture the Wendigo, but it had vanished into thin air. You see, my father was a monster collector. He wanted it for his collection.

"Impossible," I said aloud.

Suddenly, the night was pierced by the sickening sound of bones snapping and flesh tearing. My senses homed in on the direction of the disturbance, and that's when I first saw her—Aiyana. She moved like a shadow, her scent masked so thoroughly that even I, with my heightened senses, could not detect her. Her kind was not unknown to me; we also had

Werewolves in Romania, but she was different somehow... feral and yet graceful at the same time. It would be a lie to say I hadn't fallen in love with her the moment I saw her.

She was clearly running from the devastation that had claimed her village. But how had she survived?

This particular Wendigo was no ordinary beast. It craved Werewolf blood with a hunger that mirrored my own thirst for human blood. The twisted desires lurking in its dark thoughts were disturbingly familiar to me. Though it appeared as a grotesque, undead deer, it retained enough humanity for me to catch glimpses of its thoughts—deranged, ravenous thoughts that spoke of an insatiable hunger. One word dominated its mind: *Want.*

I saw her wolf form before I saw her true self. She had fully shifted by the time I found her—a magnificent creature with thick, luxurious fur, a blend of brown, black, and silver that could only have come from surviving the harshest of climates. She was a sight to behold, her colors allowing her to blend seamlessly with both the night and the day.

For months, I tracked her, driven by a curiosity that I could not fully explain. How had she escaped a monster that had killed an entire village? The Wendigo would return periodically, always managing to find her despite her attempts to remain hidden. How he tracked her, I had no idea. Whenever it came close, I would intervene, leading it away, chasing it off to give her time to escape. It seemed to have no interest in my undead flesh; it simply wanted to avoid me.

I still don't know why I got involved, but I didn't introduce myself to her until weeks later. Looking back, I can only assume that even then, I was beginning to fall in love with her—but I knew that by doing so, I was putting her in even bigger danger. A royal Vampire like me, with a Werewolf, was taboo. It was a death sentence for us both.

Regardless, night after night, I pursued her. She evaded me each day while I was forced to rest, but then I would hunt her down again by nightfall. My father had sent me to explore this new world and its creatures, but my interest had shifted from mere exploration to desire. I wanted to know more about *her*. Wolves were nothing new to us, but she might as well have been an entirely new creature to me.

It took many nights before I finally managed to speak to her. Aiyana radiated a magic that I had never encountered in any other wolf. She knew I was watching her; she was a

Werewolf, after all. She could sense my presence, sense that I meant her no harm. Perhaps that's why she didn't flee that fateful night we met, even when she knew I was near.

She sat by her fire, singing softly as she cleansed herself with herbs, masking her scent from both predators and prey alike. She looked around, waiting for me to make my move, but I never did. She was the first one to make contact.

She was a medicine woman, wise in ways I could only begin to understand. One night, she covered herself in mud mixed with herbs, and then her wolf would dig a hole in the ground to sleep, curling up inside. She draped her leather dress and shawl over the hole, concealing herself completely. If I hadn't seen her enter, I would never have known she was there. I was enthralled. The Vampires in Romania also buried themselves in the earth. It gave us renewed strength and great healing after a type of hibernation. Yet she did not hibernate. I realized then that we were alike in some ways.

I remember trying to get near her sacred mound, but it was as if a giant, invisible bubble of power surrounded her, so I watched over her from afar.

Later, she confessed that she had been communing with the earth around her. Praying for the Butterfly Maiden to cover her and protect her. We had no Gods or spirits to protect us. Our kind lived for so long that we were our own ancestors. But there were rumors that once there were Gods of sorts. A type of bat shifter.

I found myself falling for her, drawn not only to her beauty but to the strength and mystery she embodied. When she would shift from wolf to woman, she moved with an effortless grace, her bare skin covered in salves she made herself. I caught myself wanting her in ways that had nothing to do with bloodlust. I desired her—not her blood, but *her*.

But I was not her fated mate. I had learned about fated mates from the Werewolves back home. Vampires did not have these sorts of mates. I realized eventually that the Wendigo was her fated—and she had rejected him. He had attacked her village because of her, and now she was destined to run from him forever. Her thoughts, when I touched them, were full of despair. She knew he would never stop chasing her. He needed her to complete himself, to lift the curse that had twisted him into a monster.

He was a rogue, cursed and cast out, but she was not. Even with her clan dead, she had never been cursed like he was.

He didn't love her; he only loved what she could do for him. He wanted to mark her as his, to claim her power and free himself from his fate.

One night, the Wendigo returned after a long absence. Together, Aiyana and I fought him, tearing into his decaying flesh. I managed to rip the antlers from his head with my bare hands, but instead of weakening him, it only enraged him further. He cursed us both before retreating back into the shadows.

I was a prince of darkness, an undead royal. In my homeland of Romania, I had killed many to sustain this cursed existence, but nothing had prepared me for what I found in this new world. Something about Aiyana softened me, made me feel alive in ways I had forgotten. A rush of vigor, of life, pulsed through my veins when we were together.

I knew what happened to those who crossbred, especially those of royal blood. The consequences for me would be even more severe. When we finally met, I tried to warn her of this. She understood, even though we spoke no common language. Her body language, her scent—she understood. She had simply extended her hand to me. In it were herbs, a mixture of dried flowers and crushed leaves. I had seen her collecting them throughout her journey, but I hadn't realized until that moment that they were for me.

Our fates were now intertwined, bound by a destiny neither of us could escape. She had given me a chance to see the sun. Something I had never seen in all my years. These herbs, when covered with mud, protected me from the sun's rays. It was its own sort of Vampire sunscreen. The red earth also gave me a type of flush to my skin I've never had, a tan so to speak. No one had ever done anything like that for me. Nobody had ever treated me so kindly, or rubbed my body with fragrances humming a sacred song under the moonlight. It was then that I knew she was the one. Although we were not mates, I vowed to be by her side, living as one.

Before I could fully embrace this new chapter, I knew there were steps I had to take. My path had to be cleared of all past ties, and that meant severing the darkest connections I had left. So, I slaughtered the remainder of my coven, the echoes of their screams fading into the night as I cut the final threads tethering me to my father. I hoped he would believe I was dead, extinguished by the sun or some other misfortune, rather than imagine that I had fallen for a wolf.

Vampires don't share the same mind-linking abilities as wolves, but we do have something more sinister—a blood bond. My father, being my maker, could sense whether I was alive or not. It was only after I met Aiyana, and locked eyes with her as she shared with me the secrets I needed to dampen my Vampire nature. And sever the blood ties to my father back home.

The herbs she gave me did more than ease my hunger; they tamed the very essence of my darkness. With time, she prepared me with silver charms and protection symbols, strengthening my resistance to the sun's harsh rays and dulling my relentless thirst for blood. Silver had once been my greatest fear, but now, as I watched the sun rise for the first time in centuries, I welcomed its cold embrace like a knight donning his armor.

For a while, the Wendigo vanished from our lives, allowing us to settle in what is now New Mexico. We found refuge on the outskirts of a Skin Shifter tribe, a place where I kept the rogues and new colonizers at bay in exchange for their alliance. I was tolerated, if not welcomed, but Aiyana—she became one of them. Her skills as a medicine woman earned their respect, and she was accepted into their fold.

It wasn't long before Aiyana conceived, a miracle in its own right. Her medicine was so potent that it had nearly turned me human again. To create life instead of taking it felt like a gift, a redemption I didn't think I deserved. But the tribe didn't see it that way. Our child was the final straw. They turned on us, forced us to leave the place we had come to call home. We harbored no ill will toward them. They were being smart. They knew if they harbored us, their tribe would be like a beacon for all sorts of supernatural hunters. They would rather risk the colonizers and occasional rogue Vampires on their own. One Vampire would not be enough to fend them off, especially one that was now more human than Vampire.

Years passed, and with them came the return of the

Wendigo. His relentless pursuit brought devastation, and in the chaos, we lost our first baby. We buried her in the red earth of New Mexico—the grief heavy in our hearts. For over three hundred years, we evaded him. Each time he attacked, he grew weaker until one day, he simply disappeared.

A hundred years later, another miracle came—Aiyana was pregnant again. This time, we had settled in rogue territory, where I had built an empire of ghouls fortified by the herb magic Aiyana had taught me and my own knowledge of alchemy. I was determined to be ready for the Wendigo if he ever returned.

We were accepted into the rogue nation as allies to the owl and, in exchange for Vampire sunscreen, the rogue Vampire colony in the city of what is now called San Diego.

Magdalena was born via C-section, delivered by my own hands, and given the name Twinkling Star by her mother. She came into the world in the early hours before dawn, just as Aiyana had requested, after she saw a large white owl that night. Tecos had come for a visit and agreed to be Star's protector. It had to be that night, she insisted. Born early, Magdalena did not harm her mother as most Vaewolves were known to do. We raised her for five years until the Wendigo found us again.

For her protection, I entrusted her to the ghouls under a new name: Magdalena. I had strategically placed ghouls everywhere in the deepest part of the Valley where the Ancestors' shadow shielding was strongest—instructing them daily on how to care for her. Sadly, Aiyana and I stayed behind, knowing it was the only way to keep her safe.

I compelled Magdalena to forget our faces, watching over her from afar. It wasn't an easy life for her in rogue land, but it kept the Wendigo at bay. It was never her he wanted anyway.

"My little twinkling Star, my child, a gift from the sky. I need you to listen to me baby." Aiyanna stayed quiet, unable to speak at this time. She only teared up and held onto our child tightly and for a while I did not think she was going to let go.

"You are going to have to go with Tecos. He will take you and protect you from the monster." Her gleaming black eyes, a backdrop to her pearly white skin gleamed up at me.

"No!" She said. And it made me smile. She always had such a fire. "I go with you dada!"

It was tearing me up. But I vowed that one day I would save these memories and return everything to her one day.

Aiyana kissed her soft black waves on top of her head as I held onto her little hand. "Come here baby." I said beckoning her will and memories to come forth and stored them in my own blood.

I told myself it was for her own good. That we were doing the best thing for her. That we were keeping the monster away from her but it killed her mother and I to let her go.

Aiyana suffered the most. She was never quite the same after we left our daughter. Each morning, she would pray to the Creator to bring down the cursed monster. She never missed a prayer, her voice filled with a desperate hope.

We were on the verge of creating a concoction to keep Magdalena from shifting for the rest of her life, to make her practically human, when that Werewolf—her mate—ruined everything.

I wasn't about to let another monster take another one of my daughters away.

With a trembling hand, I pulled down the bandana I had used to blind my now adult daughter. If the Wendigo had found her once, he could find her again. I had to cover her eyes to prevent her from revealing the location of my lair.

She looked at me with fear in her eyes, and I gently brushed my hand over her forehead. My ghouls alerted me to a wolf's approach. I knew her mate was coming for her. Through my connection with the ghouls, I saw his massive black wolf barreling toward us.

That fool is going to lead the demon back to us! I thought, but when I saw the fear in Magdalena's eyes, I relented. If his presence could calm her, then so be it. The Wendigo already had what he wanted.

"Dad! What are you doing?" Magdalena's voice broke through my thoughts, desperate for answers. I remained silent. She would know everything in a few moments. I only had a few minutes left to restore her lost memories of Aiyana and me before her mate arrived.

As I placed my hand over her forehead, she closed her eyes. Her breathing slowed, and I could see the rapid movement of her eyes as she fell into a deep, dream-like state. The memories poured out like water from a dam, flooding her mind—her birth, her mother feeding her for the first time, her first birthday. I watched as she remembered the dress Aiyana had made for her, a beautiful regalia of deer leather with jingle tassels, crafted with love and care. She had been as white as a lily, with hair black as night, her smile contagious like her mother's.

I unraveled all the lost memories right up to our last meeting. She saw the night of her prom when I brought her home, her mother's embrace, the tears they shared. I had hated concealing that memory, but I had suspected the Wendigo's return. I had no choice but to keep her past hidden. I knew Wendigos weren't psychic, but this one had been some kind of shaman. He had powers unknown to me.

Aiyana had told me who he was—a cast-out shaman from a northern tribe banished for his dark magic and cannibalism. He had the power to see through the eyes of animals or even unprotected humans, and he had used that dark magic to find us.

I showed Magdalena why I had kept her friends away from her. It was for their protection, and for hers. Even if she had forgotten, her instincts would guide her to those who shared the Thunderbird feather in their blood.

As I opened her mind to all these memories, I shared a few of my own. She knew about me, her mother, her people, and the monster that had torn our lives apart. She knew her mother had been taken by the Wendigo that morning, aided by wolves who had betrayed their own kind.

I could hear her wolf howling in the depths of her mind as I passed this knowledge to her through our sacred blood connection. It only took a few minutes, but a lifetime of memories had been restored, like a torrent of data flooding into her consciousness.

She was going to need all this information now but it was going to take time to process it all.

Suddenly, the door to the brick cellar was kicked open and shattered. Andy, her mate, stood before us, unapologetically naked, staring at me with fury in his eyes.

"Take your hands off her!" he shouted, his voice filled with raw power. There was something different about him this time. My ghouls were right—he was no longer a rogue. But there was something else. He had been empowered by something, something dangerous.

He lunged at me, slamming me against the wall. Without Aiyana's herbs and the protection of the silver, I would have overpowered him, but he was also stronger than before. My ghouls were ready to intervene, but I blood-linked them to stay back.

Then, a soft voice cut through the tension.

"Andy, don't!" Magdalena called out. I sent another command to my ghouls to untie her. She reached out, her small hand resting on Andy's bloodied back. He flinched, lost in thought, but her touch brought him back. After a few moments, he released me.

I ordered my ghouls to bring him clothes, and he quickly dressed, covering himself in one of my trousers. He sat beside Magdalena, embracing her. I sent my ghouls away, prepared to leave them alone to talk, but Magdalena surprised me.

"Dad!" she called, stopping me in my tracks. "Where are you going?"

My eyes shifted downward. My daughter wanted me. Did my memories start to show her just how much I loved her?

"My little Star!" I said while embracing her.

"We have to find Mom, now!" she said urgently.

I turned and addressed everyone in the room. "Meet me in the cellar in ten minutes! And I mean everyone." I gestured toward Andy, knowing he would call for his shifter friends. We were going to need all the help we could get.

As I left the room, I slid off my silver jewelry, letting the pieces clank discordantly onto the floor. It was time.

Chapter 9

La Lechuza

Tecos

Upon rising in the early evening, the scent of Wendigo and foreign Werewolves filled our nostrils. Santana looked at me, and instantly, we knew that the monster had returned. He was nowhere near us as we were visiting Santana's hometown out of state, but we sensed him passing through. The cold, unnatural chill in the air gave him away.

The thing had returned in search of its mate. It was always ravenous, not just with physical hunger but a deep ache for chaos and destruction. It left him crazed and irrational. Seeking his mate as a type of refuge from his despair, he never stopped seeking her out, even after she had refused him thousands of times. This time, though, he was not alone. "Oh, he's back, off schedule this time," Santana said, looking up at the coming stars as if they held the answers to her questions. The beast, being a type of frost giant, never came to the desert during the hottest summer months. This was very unusual for him.

I nodded at Santana's observations, feeling a shift in the wind and realizing that it would be different this time.

"And he's brought an army," I said, sniffing a strand of my wind-tousled hair that flew, electrified, wildly in the air. No matter how beautiful and soft the wispy owl feathers were, I had missed my hair.

We had been watching this tale unfold since finding ourselves stranded in the desert. With no way to fight in our past shape, we simply observed. Occasionally, I would fly over him, screeching his brain to oblivion, and then he would finally take his leave, annoyed with me.

He was never allowed here for very long, though. The Shadowlands, an underground and unseen world among humans, remains a home to rogues who followed the neutral laws of these lands created by ancient ancestors many years ago.

In the mysterious and often perilous desert lies the heart of the shadowlands, where the veil between light and darkness is thin. A rogue may find a path to redemption—if that is what they seek. This land, hidden from the eyes of the uninitiated and shielded by ancient magic, offers sanctuary to those who have been cast out or have chosen a life of solitude. It is a place where second chances are granted, but not without cost or commitment. Here, the rogues—whether they are shifters, Vampires, or other supernatural beings—must adhere to a strict code of conduct if they wish to remain.

The pull for vagrant souls was so strong here that even some humans with remnant and untouched magic in their systems could feel it. It was a place to start over. A refuge.

The rules of the Shadowlands are unwavering, designed to maintain a fragile peace among its inhabitants. Rogues are forbidden from feeding on or attacking humans, for such actions would disrupt the delicate balance that protects this realm from the outside world. They are also prohibited from turning on one another, ensuring that the Shadowlands do not become a battleground for personal vendettas. Furthermore, the creation of fledglings—whether by bite, curse, or dark magic—is strictly regulated. No new life may be brought into existence without prior authorization from the Shadowlands' enigmatic guardians, a group of ancient beings who oversee the laws of this domain. Myself being one of them.

Many rogues who enter the Shadowlands eventually find their way back to their original tribes or clans. The prospect of redemption and reintegration often outweighs the allure of continued isolation. For them, the Shadowlands serve as a temporary refuge, a place to reflect and atone before returning to the world they once knew.

Yet, there are those who choose to remain in the

Shadowlands indefinitely. These individuals, each with their own unique reasons, prefer the solitude and the shadows over the complexities of tribal life.

Some may stay out of fear of rejection, knowing that their past actions have left deep scars. Others might relish the freedom that comes with life on the fringe, unbound by the strict hierarchies and expectations of their former lives. And there are those who simply cannot forgive themselves, finding life in the Shadowlands a fitting penance for their sins.

For these rogues, the Shadowlands is not just a place of refuge but a permanent home, where they live out their days in the twilight, bound by the rules but free from the judgment and hunters of the supernatural from the outside world.

Wendigos, Witches or evil shifters never followed the rules and, therefore, were run off by the Guardians of the Shadowlands and our fellow allies. The ancestors protected this land, and they were once giants, not to be confused with the cannibalistic, red-haired giants of the past but giant animal spirits that ruled over each of their kind. Their very shadow hovers over these valleys, lending their ethereal silhouettes as a form of camouflage from people, hunters and anyone who wishes to disturb our peace.

Allies in tune with these ancient guardian spirits can blend in with the shadows, hence the name Shadowlands.

The Wendigo always returned despite being chased off. He was always only here for her. Aiyana.

When Aiyana came to me, her presence was heavy with a desperation I hadn't seen in many moons. She approached with reverence, her voice trembling as she spoke, "Great owl spirit, I come with love, seeking asylum and communion with your tribe, for the great Wendigo is hunting my pack, in search of me."

My feathers ruffled at her words, and I asked, "Why is he searching for you?"

She hesitated for just a moment before locking eyes with me. "Because I am his mate."

The weight of her admission hung in the air between us, and a cold realization crept over me. This was no ordinary Wendigo; if it still retained any shred of its human self, it would be a force far more formidable than the maddened beasts I'd encountered before. The thought alone made me screech, a sound that echoed through the valley.

"And what else?" I pressed. I could sense there was more to her story. The smell of it clung to her like the scent of a distant storm. "There's a Vampire involved, isn't there?"

Her shoulders sagged slightly as she answered, "The Vampire is Sebastian, my chosen mate, but he is also a rogue. He left his family, and now it is just us." She motioned her hand towards the distant mountain. He did not dare to come near me, which was a wise decision. Though rogues are welcome here, Vampires were not welcome in my particular corner of the shadowlands. I sent them west or south.

"I made him stay back," she said, eyeing me respectfully.

My screech came again, sharper this time, as visions of the past flooded my mind—visions of the trouble Vampires had brought me long ago. "I do not contend with the undead," I stated firmly, the memories still fresh in my mind.

Aiyana sighed and I felt her countenance give away to despair. Seeing this softened my heart.

I couldn't deny the need for compassion, even in the face of my old wounds.

"Nonetheless, as a rogue, you are granted asylum, but not here." I pointed toward the distant mountains with my wing stretched out, their peaks barely visible through the mist. "Vampires stay over the mountains near the coast. He is not allowed here. There is a small colony of rogue Vampires that have formed their own pact and he must be accepted there, or you two can go south, with the allies of the Were-jaguars, serpent and Vampire alliance."

I watched as Aiyana processed my words, knowing that this was the best I could offer her without compromising the safety and sanctity of my domain. It was a difficult balance, but one that had to be maintained, even as the winds of change began to stir. I was a Guardian and though at the time I was tempted to ask for help from them to open the Ancient Kachina, the ancestors held me back. They had whispered to me that the kachina would not yield until "he" entered these lands. They never told me who "he" was, but when I felt Andrei enter the realm a few hundred years later, I knew he was the one.

I never knew then why I even accepted the challenge of protecting their daughter years and years later, but I did. And I also allowed a few ghouls into my lands for that reason. I guess I have a soft spot for lovers and babies.

The Vampires protected the cities in the West of the Shadowlands. The Skin Shifters protected the cities in the East. The wolves protected the north, and the south belonged to a different alliance made between Skin Shifters, Weres and Vampires. The Shadowlands comprise most of what they call Central and Southern California, parts of New Mexico and Arizona.

"Thank you, owl spirit. I dare not go to another 'Were' place. That is where he will search for me. I do not want to cause them trouble," she said with big round eyes. "Wendigos are repelled by Vampires, being undead and not consumable."

"He may still search for you here," I said, looking at her with curiosity. "Wendigos are formidable hunters and when they seek you out, they never stop. Continue to protect yourself as long as needed," I said before she turned to leave for the mountains.

He showed up at least once a year, near the winter solstice, in search of her. Even if it was to catch her scent and feel confident that she was still alive, then it was off again. He would leave the Shadowlands to retreat to some faraway place. I had my suspicions of where he went, but even I, ordained with an owl's spirit, had no idea just what exactly he was up to when he was gone.

He was somewhere very cold, somewhere North, my visions told me but once I caught wind of the wolves he traveled with, I realized exactly where. Those wolves were Andrei's wolves. His old pack, or a small piece of his pack. Were they all that were left? But I did not know at the time how this story would unfold until Andrei set foot into the shadowlands. I knew he was the warrior we were waiting for to rid us of Aiyana's Wendigo mate.

"It's come full circle," Santana said, eyeing me.

I nodded again at her wise understanding.

Santana is the beautiful woman who captured my heart and for whom I risked everything for. Rescuing her was no simple task—it was a battle that left scars deeper than any physical wound. The fight to save her cost us both dearly, damaging our skins in ways I hadn't anticipated, leaving us trapped in our owl forms for centuries.

I have no regrets, though. The choice was mine, and I would make it again if given the chance. It was my fault, after all—I was never a great warrior, not in the traditional sense. I am a medicine man—a spiritual and prayer warrior but not one strong in battle. I should have trained as both.

When it came to Santana, I was forced to put up a fight, not out of duty or pride but because my soul demanded it. I fought for her because she was worth every sacrifice and every moment of pain that followed. She is my mate, after all. My other half.

I had grown too confident in my abilities as a Skin Shifter, a dangerous hubris that nearly cost me my left talon. The memory of that moment still burns in my mind, the searing pain, the smell of scorched feathers—a reminder of my own fallibility. The Creator saw fit to humble me, and in my pain, I understood the lesson. I accepted it without bitterness, knowing that perhaps this was why He had sent the barn owl to be my final teacher. Humility is a hard-won virtue, and one I was forced to embrace. Or at least that is what I have come to understand.

The barn owl is not a spirit many of my people revere. They are solitary, silent hunters, their wisdom shrouded in the night. Unlike the eagle or the falcon, who are seen as noble and fierce, the owl is often feared, its nocturnal nature and haunting call are associated with death and the unknown. I soon realized I could not rely on my people for support while on this new path. So I had become a wanderer. The owl's lessons were mine alone to bear.

They had good reason to fear me. There was already so much fear during that time of war with the colonizers and we are often seen as harbingers of doom. So naturally they avoided me. Our presence is unsettling, for we tend to appear before death, like a shadow before the storm. There was so much death back then when the first settlers came, like aliens they took over and abused our people's generosity.

But the tug of death is a constant pull on our owl souls, guiding us to those who are soon to depart from this world.

We are not death itself but merely its messengers, the silent couriers who announce its arrival. It was a very dreary path in the beginning for me.

It was through this path that I met my mate, though, so there is a silver lining to this dark cloud.

When I saw her, the Spanish had begun to spread across the Southwestern land, their arrival marking the beginning of profound changes. I had done my best to heal my fellow people, but I admit the diseases and injuries of the foreigners were not a match for my medicine. I was not accustomed to their level of disease and darkness, and being a young owl didn't help anything. If I had known then what I know now, things would have been different.

They redrew borders, imposing new names and identities on the land and people as if it were theirs to claim. I did not yet dwell in the Shadowlands during that time; back then, I lived near what they call the Grand Canyon, but I had felt a tug to enter the southwest land now known as Texas, sensing something in the air.

The Spanish, with their hunger for gold and land, brought with them a wave of bloodshed. They took the land by force, spilling the blood of many of our kind. Chaos and confusion spread like wildfire, and our people, once proud and strong, began to forget who they were. They were forced to blend in, to abandon the old ways and customs. Many of the shifter clans were lost to a spiritual sickness—a sickness born of despair and hopelessness.

But it wasn't just the Spanish who brought death and destruction. Following in their wake came the Eastern monsters—Vampires. These bloodsuckers, disguised as human Europeans, were different from those we knew in the southern jungles. In the deep forests, we had Vampires who lived in peaceful alliances with jaguar and serpent shifters. But these new Vampires were rogues, cut off from any kinship or allegiance. They refused to ally with anyone but themselves, and their presence brought a new darkness to our lands. Even our own wolf brothers were not spared; many were captured and enslaved, forced to serve these creatures of the night.

Santana had managed to escape and blend in as a so-called Spanish family living in a homestead. Her family had fled the wars in their native New Mexico, traveling to Texas under the guise of a new Spanish name and identity. They had learned the language, adopting the customs of the invaders because they had no choice. The new Vampires did not tolerate other supernatural beings in their domain. If they caught the scent of a shifter's blood, they would hunt down and annihilate the entire family.

So Santana's family abandoned their medicine and rituals and disguised their scent with great care under layers of European clothing and the use of certain herbs used as a type of perfume as a disguise. They had bought some land with the money from melting down all their silver jewelry in a small town near a lake. Shifters always had access to silver jewelry, even if they didn't make it themselves. We didn't always require jewelry for we could pull power from deep in the earth via the caves or kiva's from the silver embedded in the earth. It wasn't until they moved us off our lands into barren wastelands that we devised a way to make silver ourselves using the scraps we could find. This is why at the time when Andrei found us, neither I nor Santana had silver jewelry.

Silver is what makes Skin Shifters strong. We never had a need to buy or trade for land before, but desperation took hold of her family to hold onto sacred grounds, and they did what they had to do to secure their land.

Unfortunately, this was their downfall, for a certain band of Vampires wanted this land. Nearby, deep in the ground, lay a large reservoir of oil. The Vampires at the time had great insight into how to make money and knew oil and land would somehow make them rich another hundred years or so later, so they came to take it in whatever way possible.

Humans, twisted by the Vampires' dark influence, became their spies and playthings, leaving Santana's family with no one to trust. These are the half-turned humans and were called ghouls.

"I still remember this little house," Santana said softly, her voice tinged with the bittersweet memory. She gazed at the remnants of her childhood home, a small smile playing on her lips. I wrapped my arm around her shoulder, offering silent comfort.

We were standing in the ruins of what had once been her family's refuge, a place built with love and care. Part of the house still stood, though much of it had decayed by time. We had returned here after preparing Andrei for his mission, to pay homage to her past, to the life that had been taken from her.

The last time we were here, the air had been thick with the smell of burning wood and flesh. Humans, whipped into a frenzy by the Vampires, were preparing to burn Santana at the stake for witchcraft. The Vampires had already slaughtered the remaining shifters who had refused to flee.

When they discovered her family's true nature, they did not kill her immediately. Instead, they had the humans confiscate whatever was left of their silver and then compelled her to sign away her land, forcing her to relinquish everything her family had worked for. Only then did they throw her to the ghouls they had created.

Sick, twisted creatures who fed on the living. They tied her to a stake, intending to burn her alive after they drained her of almost all her blood. They wanted to make an example out of her to warn the rest of the Skin Shifters who dared try to hide from them.

I sat down beside Santana as she silently wept, her eyes tracing the ruins of her home. The walls that had once sheltered her, built with the strong hands of shifters from brick and adobe, were now nothing more than the bare bones of a foundation. The ghosts of her past lingered here, a testament to the life she had lost, the family that had been taken from her.

"A change is coming," I said, my voice gentle as I tried to soothe her. I knew she could feel it too—the shift in the winds, the gathering storm on the horizon. "You're right; that monster is not on schedule. A new war is coming. We each have our role to play, and our people are not forgotten. We will rise up, as if from sleep, for I hear a death toll for this era."

Santana nodded, her tears falling silently into the dusty ground.

"It's been so long," she said, looking up at me with gratitude in her eyes as she lifted her left arm. She was thankful for having her wing restored and the ability to be a human again. "I am ready for this change you speak of."

I had thought about so many ways to bring her back here. Over the years, there had been so many changes, trains and even planes, but they were all too dangerous for her to take as a wounded owl, and I could never leave her alone in her condition. Transportation was never the true problem, though; it was what the Vampires had done to her image that kept us from returning. We were safe in the Shadowlands, from Vampires, from everything, because of the Ancestors, but we were also in our own type of prison.

Imprisoned in a fancy gilded cage as beautiful birds of prey.

"Not anymore," Santana said as she reached up for the sky, beckoning the winds to caress her human skin.

"Not anymore," I said, doing the same as her and letting the wind take all our worries. Her black hair flew loose in the wind and wrapped around my arm—a tingle of electricity shot down through me. Over the years by her side, I had loved her, even as an owl woman. I won't lie, though, and say this human form of hers wasn't even more enticing. She was right about it being too long. My human body, unashamedly, craved to know her.

The night I found her, she had already made her first regalia.

It was a rushed and quick job because she knew the Vampires were coming for her. They put her up on that fire, wearing her regalia and attempted to burn her alive in front of the whole village of settlers, condemning her as a Witch to the villagers for the regalia she had made out of owl skins.

I came, feeling death nearby and circled my mate up in the heavens. But death soon made his plan apparent, for it was not my mate who was destined to die that night. But the Vampires I killed and the dozens of ghouls that followed afterward. The memory is still etched in my mind like no other.

The night sky stretched wide and deep as I flew over the desolate clearing, my silent wings gliding effortlessly through the cool air. Below, the flickering glow of a fire caught my keen eyes. A woman stood at its center, her white leather garb stark against the dark backdrop. Barn owl feathers adorned her hair, and a small leather pouch filled with herbs hung from her neck, signifying her connection to ancient magic.

Vampires, disguised as priests from their European lands, surrounded her, their malicious laughter piercing the night as they prepared to burn her at the stake for being a so-called Witch. Being called a Witch was an insult to our kind. And yet they somehow knew this and used it against her. Despite being satiated, the Vampires toyed with her like cruel vipers, relishing the torment of their prey merely for the thrill of the kill, savoring the power they held over her shifter form.

They used sticks and poked at her with the charred ends. A few others hurled stones at her head, causing her to bleed and they even erupted in cheer as if it were a game. Their preternatural voices were thick with blood, and so I knew they had just eaten; they were not starving creatures awaiting a meal, they were simply enjoying tormenting her.

The sight ignited a fury within me. Even before I knew she was my mate, the sight of a sacred woman being treated like trash threw me into a heated madness I had never known.

I had always served as a mediator, a healer bridging the gap between two dark forces, calling upon the light to bring peace between them. Yet, for the first time, I could feel what death must feel right before he takes a soul. I could not let this atrocity unfold. It was a protective instinct that awoke inside me. There was no plan, just time for action.

Diving swiftly and silently, I transformed mid-flight, my feathers giving way to human skin and muscle. My form was now that of an owl-man, powerful and determined.

With a fierce cry, I descended upon the Vampires, talons extended. My first strike was swift and lethal, my claws ripping through the cold, undead flesh. The Vampires' snarls turned to shrieks of agony as I tore through them with a vengeance. But amid the chaos, one managed to evade my attack and, with brutal force, kicked me into the fire. Agony seared through my left talon and leg as the flames licked my flesh.

My pain was mirrored by who I realized at that exact moment, was my mate. In her own desperation, I heard her call out.

"You will not kill me! I will return as an owl and I will avenge my family's deaths!" A loud, shrill call to the wild shrieked from her lips, her warrior call. In my mind, I swore I saw the harbinger of death cast a shadow over the whole village, causing the night sky to darken even further and a cold chill to run through everyone's veins.

Yet, in her eyes, I saw a fierce resolve. As the fire singed my feathers, it also singed and weakened the rope. She drew upon her own shapeshifting powers. With a burst of energy, she broke free, her form shifting into that of a formidable owl-woman. Her eyes, once full of fear, now blazed with determination. Had I helped ignite that fearlessness in her, seeing her own kind? I hoped so.

Together, we turned the tide. Despite her burned arm, singed by the updraft created when my body and wings hit the bonfire with such force, and my injured leg, we remained a formidable pair.

I swooped upon the remaining Vampires, and she fought from the front, pecking at their eyes, her beak and talons as deadly as mine. We fought side by side, a whirlwind of feathers and fury. When the last remaining Vampire fell before us, his screams echoing into the night, we finally stopped to look around at the chaos that had ensued.

Those few who survived the initial onslaught fled, their cowardice leading them to hide in the shadows. One of them, come to find out later, compelled the whole town to think of Santana as an evil Witch who took babies' lives in their sleep. Soon, everyone was hunting down owls. The rumors spread far into New Mexico, Oklahoma and Nevada.

It was a scorned Vampire's last attempt to ruin Santana's victory and any chance of a normal life in her ancestral lands.

Silence reclaimed the clearing when all was done. In my half-shifted form, I grabbed hold of Santana as best I could, being careful not to injure her further. I quickly flew us to the rogue desert I had heard about. It was a difficult shift. I barely managed to gain lift-off as the leathers were badly injured. I shifted into the full owl form that has remained with me for hundreds of years. She had done the same and shifted into her full owl form during lift off.

"That was the most awful ride of my life. I think you hit my head on a boulder," joked Santana in the background, shaking me out of my nostalgia. I laughed back with her, taking a deep breath afterward and feeling happy that she was becoming her normal cheerful self.

"Well, that's what eating the White man's food will do to us. I couldn't carry us both very well." I clapped back at my woman, who knew better than to take me seriously. I looked her in the eyes, though, and smiled, just in case she wanted to bop me on my head for saying that. I tried my best to look cute so she'd kiss me instead. She did.

Then she just laughed some more. She has the most beautiful laugh I have ever heard.

I claimed her as my mate when we reached the Shadowlands desert. But we had not physically known each other with our human bodies until these past few weeks. Seeing her laugh and smile made me want her again but I held back, knowing this land was sacred to her.

All shifters knew about this neutral land called Shadowlands, but I had never been there. I had not planned on us to hide out here for so long, maybe a few years at best. But when we got there, we realized the toll that night had taken on us. We were unable to shift back due to our partly destroyed leathers. The Shadowlands became our home, knowing that owls were unwanted back in her hometown, where the rumors of the Witch infiltrated the whole area. Her beautiful face, once regal and admired, was now brought to shame by the lies of a Vampire who compelled everyone he crossed with tarnished images and nightmares of my beautiful Santana.

We had our conversations in mindlink for about four hundred years until Andrei helped us recover. She named me Tecos because of my gimpy leg. She retained her new identity as Santana.

"Yeah, you look like a drunk when you waddle around." Santana teased back at me with a laugh.

The name Tecos is a derivative of the Spanish word 'teco' for drunk. Then we both couldn't stop laughing. She was right. I did!

"You mean it wasn't for Tecolote?! The word for owl?!" I said half seriously.

"No, it never was old man!" Santa laughed again.

I sighed knowing this fun wasn't going to last long.

"Ah, but honey, we gotta be serious for this new war is coming," I said, not wanting to dim the mood, but I knew that we had to leave soon. We needed to get back to the Shadowlands. The Wendigo was on his warpath, and we needed to get ready, despite my urges to show her my love by the lake she once called home.

The Shadowlands was once an ocean, many years ago when the first territorial borders were established by the animal guardians for supernatural creatures. Later, when humans came about, they created their own borders over and around the guardian's borders, but our borders never changed. Water has always been a neutral ground, even for most humans. When the waters pulled away and left the land, the exposed new earth remained a neutral territory, just as if it were still water.

The water would come and go over the years, flooding and pooling and then becoming a desert again. So the rogues flocked to it in the hundreds when it was dry. For a while, a large lake remained, and a few Uktena made their homes there, having swam down the Colorado River from the Grand Canyon, but soon that lake shriveled up as well, and thanks to people's interventions, diverted the river, leaving only a salty reservoir in its wake.

This drying up lent even more land for the rogues to call home. During this time, the Shadowlands was not the peaceful place it was now, despite its neutrality. And that was when the Guardians appointed the council to maintain peace.

Only one known Uktena had dared to enter the salty waters of the tiny reservoir. It traveled through underground cisterns from the great caverns of the Grand Canyon and back in search of its next meal. It was a large black serpent with a few ringlets of feathers that lay like a crest around its head, and on its crown was a diamond like no other. A rare black Uktena diamond that appeared to be made out of the shadows itself— the perfect diamond for a rogue black wolf. That was the monster we sent Andrei to kill.

If he wanted to rule the Thunder wolf clan, that was the only way to do it. He had to kill the strongest one to become strong enough to reclaim his pack. He was, after all, born and bred for monster killing.

There are people and tribes there now living in the desert, but to the supernatural, it will always remain the Shadowlands and neutral rogue territory. A hidden gem in the desert that gave those like us refuge.

The invisible borders are obvious. Sandy and barren beaches remain, where the Natives hunt for shells to use in their jewelry. The kiva, built long after the ocean receded, stands as an ancient structure below sea level, as all the land in the Imperial Valley remains below sea level to this day. Therefore, it was built to remain airtight by the first ancient peoples, the guardian animal giants and ancestors of Skin Shifters. One never knew when the Creator would bring the water back.

As a child, I had heard about the ancient kiva from my elders, but it wasn't until I came to live in the heart of the Shadowlands that I decided to help protect it and become one of the Guardians of the rogue territory. It was rumored that all old regalias from the original kachinas resided there, guided there by the spirit itself. I was only half surprised that the rumors were true. There are only a handful of great kiva like this one.

The entrance to the kiva once resembled a turtle head and the body of the turtle was considered the sacred room. But the winds and floods have since washed it smooth to resemble a large stone on top of a mountain. The ancestors kept this area hidden, and only I knew of its whereabouts until it was opened.

As a guardian, I can commune with the ancient guardians before me, and they let me know if any creature needs dealing with. I usually assign a few eager and bored rogues to this task, a feat they all jump to do, for it is the only time they are allowed to hunt monsters here in this neutral land.

Many Skin Shifters call it home, yes, but only a few actual werewolves call the Shadowlands home for long. After achieving an alliance, they usually wander up north to find a pack—all except Andrei. He had his reasons for remaining hidden.

We flew back with ease, bending our sense of smell to the salty and arid winds of the desert. Then, without warning, a stench hit our senses. Its breath was stale and acidic as if it had digested its own entrails with a roaring hunger. The exhalant of this monster made the sky just a bit darker with an eerie green mist that exited its mouth with each expiration.

We flew up, high and screeching with a warning to all the denizens. As our screeches returned to us like echolocation, visions returned to our minds. The visions were like a painting unfolding. We finally captured the image of the old shaman turned Wendigo. It had grown stronger since we last saw him. And he had discovered how to use the skins of humans to mask his real ghastly image, although not quite well. The Wendigo spirit could not grow human hair, only fur and not even fur very well. He was as bald as an old man.

Then we saw the werewolves. These were the

Thunderwolves. They followed his every command, but they were covered by dark magic. They were disillusioned, or dare I say compelled? It could not have been the Wendigo who compelled them. A Vampire was behind this. And I knew exactly who it was.

They were being controlled by a Vampire who was giving orders by mindlink. We saw the spirits of the dead shamans in the background. He had eaten all the shamans that had remained on his land, absorbing their power, and now was coming for more.

It made sense why he searched out Aiyana so relentlessly. In order for his transformation to be complete, he needed to bond with a sacred oath with his mate, Aiyana. But there was more to it.

Could it really be? How could he bend the laws of the Creator that way? Sanatana mind-linked me, concerned.

He is seeking out the help of the serpent, his last and final form The Thunderbirds' enemy. He doesn't care about the Creator or laws or traditions. Some people are only in this world to disturb the peace. They don't realize they also inadvertently create great new warriors to fight them off. This is one of those times. I thought of Andrei, our prince yet to be crowned. He doesn't know it, but that uncle of his was wolfless. That was why he could not rule and took his current place as Alpha by force.

Do you think Magdalena's father is aiding them?

I smiled and asked her to look through the visions for me as I kept my focus on the Wendigo.

When we finally caught sight of him, he was no longer monstrous-looking but like a simple man, a bald and extremely thin man. We knew, though, that under those skins, he was just as vile as ever. He was dressed like a Native man, only without feathers or silver. He was cursed. He could not wear either unless it was from another cursed animal, even though silver usually strengthened Skin Shifters' power. For cursed ones, it repelled our powers.

Skin shifters who were Witches and dressed as humans could not attach hair, the essence of our soul. Some scalpers tried in the past but were unsuccessful, for they had no soul to attach it to. Shifting into other humans is considered taboo, for it required the death and feasting of humans. And when they do such a horrible deed, they are considered cursed, for it goes against the Thunderbirds' blessing.

And he was dangerously close to Magdalena. We circled the powwow where she sat on the bleachers with her friend. We recognized a few latent Skin Shifters in the crowd but they were young and had never fully shifted. I was not sure if they were ready to be called.

I wasn't ready. Santana was onto something. *But I answered the call anyway.*

You're right. We might have to pull them into this war as they are. We will have to make them ready, I said.

Using the Ancient Ancestors' gift to the Shadowlands, we cloaked ourselves in shadow, rendering us invisible. This was why we called this place the Land of Shadows. It was a way for rogues to hide even from the cameras and thermal tracking in today's modern world.

We kept ourselves hidden from everyone but Magdalena. It was good that she wore the silver we taught Andrei to make. That was helping her more than she knew. The silver will weaken the monster's powers. So, what exactly was he doing here with her?

With a sense of urgency, Santana's voice echoed in my mind: *He's trying to make her shift!* Her words came with a piercing supernatural screech that reverberated through the night, a tone designed to reset the frenzied wolf spirit within Magdalena. The air thrummed with tension as the Witch, consumed by a fevered intensity, chanted ancient curses that swirled around the distressed Magdalena. From above, I watched her skin turn ghostly pale, her heart racing as if trying to escape her chest. But why did he care so much whether she shifted or not?

I released a sharp cry, my voice slicing through the night like a blade, and twisted my neck with the flexibility of an owl to meet Santana's gaze. "*Stay focused*," I urged her through our mindlink, sensing the undercurrent of fear in her thoughts.

He's using dark magic, Santana warned, her mental voice edged with a chilling certainty. *He can control a shift—either force it or prevent it. That's how he kept Andrei's wolf suppressed for so long. We need to stop his words from poisoning the air.* With that, she unleashed another shriek, her call resonating with mine as we attempted to drown out the malevolent incantations.

Questions swirled in my mind. Why was he even here? What interest did he have in Magdalena? Could it be jealousy, born of the fact that she was the forbidden love child of his mate and a Vampire from the mountain? No, it had to be more than that. He could have come for her at any time, yet he chose this moment. Why?

My gaze drifted downward, catching sight of a young boy in Thunderbird regalia, dancing with a precision that triggered memories of Andrei. I knew he was battling the Uktena as we fought this new threat. The realization struck like a thunderclap: Magdalena was just a distraction. The Witch was stalling us while the real battle raged elsewhere. Was he distracting Andrei on purpose?

Moments passed, the air crackling with the raw power of the Uktena. I felt its energy surge toward Andrei, saw him in a vision, crackling with electricity and radiating unmatched strength. He reached for the diamond embedded in the beast's head, claiming it as his own. He absorbed the diamond, a perfect relic. The Uktena's lifeless body lay behind him, but Andrei's face twisted in concern, sensing danger still ahead.

A piercing screech from Santana jolted me back to the present. Below, Magdalena clawed at her throat, her breaths coming in shallow gasps. The Witch had failed to trigger her shift, and now he was simply trying to kill her.

Santana's voice cut through the chaos again, frantic. *He's gone—moved with the wolves.* I scanned the scene, but the Witch had vanished into the shadows, his minions moving with eerie precision.

Then, from the edge of the powwow, I saw her—Magdalena's mother, sprinting from the parking lot, desperate to reach her daughter. But before she could get close to her or any human spectators, the wolves struck, dragging her off into the night. One of the largest wolves had her in its jaws, alive but unconscious.

I'm going to help her, Santana declared, her voice steely with resolve and gesturing towards Magdalena.

Santana moved with a predator's grace, her eyes fixed on Magdalena, who had bolted towards the parking lot where her mother had just been taken from. I watched as Magdalena, her breath ragged and her hands trembling, sought refuge beneath a gnarled tree. She leaned against its rough bark, trying to steady her nerves, completely unaware that my mate was perched above her. Santana had partially shifted, her form blending seamlessly into the shadows of the branches, remaining cloaked from sight.

With deliberate calm, Santana reached for the medicine bag hanging from her neck, her fingers brushing against its worn leather. *Corn pollen,* she murmured, her voice like a soft breeze in my mind. *And some herbs to help calm her.* She sprinkled the sacred powder, letting it drift down toward Magdalena, who began to breathe more evenly.

I tilted my head, absorbing the scene with quiet admiration. *You are brilliant, my love,* I sent back through our link, feeling the warmth of pride bloom in my chest.

But as my gaze shifted, the rage within me began to stir, driven by a primal need to protect. The Witch—now a twisted shadow of his former self—was a disgrace to all shifters. The anger simmered, a familiar fire that had been stoked time and again. I had never been a warrior, but sometimes evil creates them out of need. The memory of barely saving Santana, both of us escaping by the skin of our teeth, still haunted me. But now, once again, I had no choice. The time for hesitation had passed.

Creator, I prayed silently, knowing my plea would be heard. *If this is what you ask of me, so be it. I'll become the spirit warrior needed to save my people. They have suffered for far too long. My time for idly watching is over. But I cannot do it alone. I ask for your blessing and your strength, Creator, and I thank you.*

The prayer was followed by a fierce screech that tore through the evening, this time without the concealment of stealth. I spread my wings wide, letting the full moonlight catch their span, making sure everyone below could see. The reaction was immediate—gasps and startled cries came from those who saw me. The people feared owls, but this cry was not for their deaths; it was a battle call, a demand for the Wendigo's head. Those who understood answered my call, their spirits merging with mine as they howled or screeched back in their animal forms.

Even as the echoes faded, I sensed him—moving swiftly, a blur of dark intent, weaving through the night to reach the body of the Uktena. Magdalena had been a mere diversion, a ploy to lure Andrei away from the corpse. But Andrei, driven by his new foresight from the Uktena, would not leave the body unguarded unless his mate was in danger and that is why he attacked. This Wendigo was much more formidable an enemy than previously perceived. The Wendigo's plan was clear now—he intended to steal the Uktena's hide and horns, to transform into something even darker and more powerful. That, I could not allow.

Before Andrei could reach Magdalena, her father appeared. With a swift motion, he took Magdalena to his realm, her form glowing with a radiant, golden aura I had never seen before—a brilliance that was both otherworldly and pure. Death had no hold on her; she shone with a life force so strong it outshone the sun. Was this all due to the corn pollen? It seemed like so much more. A hint at the future, perhaps. My smile returned.

Below, those who had heard my call gathered near the tree where Santana had watched over Magdalena. She, too, had uncloaked, her form partially shifted but ready to strike if needed. Meanwhile, the powwow continued in the distance, the drumming and chants growing louder as the attendees danced, singing to cleanse the air of evil spirits. It was an ancient tradition, one I had always respected. We needed all the help we could get—from the ancestors, from the Creator, and from each other.

Ten young warriors stepped forward, each adorned in the regalia of a different kachina. Their faces were set with determination, their eyes reflecting the firelight. I could feel the power in the air as I descended, shifting into my human form.

"Warriors!" I called out, my voice ringing with authority. "There is much to learn, and little time to do so."

The teaching would begin now, as the battle loomed ever closer.

Chapter 10

Taken

Sebastian

"It's war!" I growled at my reflection in the mirror. My eyes were tinged with blood fury, and my appetite for blood had returned since removing the silver cuffs that kept it in check. I could feel the familiar tingles in my extremities ignite as empowered vampiric blood circulated throughout my system, awakening dead, numbed cells. I had forgotten what it felt like to be unrestrained by herb magic and silver ions.

Silver was exactly why I became a scientist. I had been studying it since I was a young fledgling in Romania with my father. It was a flimsy element that often oxidized and needed constant cleaning and care to keep it up to standard, yet it managed to single-handedly destroy the lives of countless Vampire victims.

When I restored Magdalena's memories, I bestowed a handful of my own. They were locked deep inside her mind and would emerge over time once her mind had a chance to categorically release them. My studies, all the knowledge that I had gathered over the centuries starting in a crude makeshift laboratory in a tower of one of my father's castles in Romania, all belonged to her now.

I smile now, thinking back to how I must have looked to the rest of the undead royals. I was almost mad with my obsession, and I was often teased for inspiring Mary Shelley's Frankenstein. It wasn't until I came up with my first elixir to ease the blood hunger that they finally took me seriously. When I had found a way to ease the pain of hunger and still keep our energy and vitality at full force, well I was respected. But when I devised an elixir to keep our ions in a stable state under the sun, then I became something of a celebrity.

If it weren't for me, the royals would still be required to sleep in a death-like slumber, a type of hibernation, if they went longer than a few nights without a drop of blood. The answer was an absurd amount of magnesium supplementation, let to steep in a silver flask for twenty-four hours. This new oxidized substance, when ingested by the Vampire, would cause an enzyme I named NosKinase007 to be released by the Vampire's body. The body would feed on it as if it were blood and keep the machine running smoothly for a while, so to speak. It is a fairly simple elixir that I take to this day.

The elixir for internal sun protection was even easier to replicate. It was simply a mixture of broken-down copper ions, calcium and potassium. Coupled and coated over a few leather outfits, it worked for a short time.

As the years progressed, so did my concoctions. Together with my Aiyana's blend of herbs that aid in my phosphorus ignitability, I can usually walk around almost human with small exposures to sunlight if needed, even without a large coat, hat and cloak. If only it didn't make me weaker in the process, I could have reached Aiyana in time and saved her from being taken. If I had my full Vampire powers, that would not have happened. This realization brought out a fury in me like none I've ever felt before.

Not only did I appear more human due to the less luminant skin, but if I kept my fangs retracted, I could pass for one. But my strength was also about the same as a typical human. Something that was utterly detestable next to a strong Werewolf wife like Aiyana, but she never seemed to mind my frailness.

I walked out of the bed chambers that Aiyana and I shared. There were too many memories of her here. It had only been a few hours, but a deep panic had started to stir up inside my body, and I felt my head was about to bust. I could not sense her nearby anymore. They had to have taken her hundreds and hundreds of miles away for me to lose her sense of presence from my blood memory.

We had avoided the Wendigo, my love's so-called mate, for years. And now he has finally succeeded in taking her. I knew her life was not in danger; he needed her too much. But the thought of him sinking his teeth into her and claiming her was beyond abandon.

Claiming her was something I had always wanted to do, something she had wanted me to do. But neither she nor her wolf would ever be able to claim me. I am a Vampire, an undead; one bite, and I risk the chance of turning her, taking her wolf from her. I could never allow that.

It was true that only certain, very ancient Vampires acquired a true form. I'd only seen my father do it once. It took a lot of fury and a lot of blood to acquire the energy required for the transformation. What my love did not know was that I was working on an elixir to do just that. To give me the ability to turn into my true form. A cross between a gargoyle and a bat is the only way I could describe it. I had envisioned it once in a type of dream after electrocuting myself one night in my lab.

I yearned for a body that could fly and attack from both the sky and the ground with unmeasured power. I wanted to ensure my love's protection and that of my daughter, and this was one way I knew I could.

It was a form that didn't even require a sense of smell, for its other senses were just that great. And the greatest thing of all? Having a form so meticulously ghastly that not even an army of Wendigos would dare go head-to-head with.

It wasn't ready, though. I had not yet tested the many samples nor logged the side effects. What if it failed or worse, it was a success, but I was unable to change back? Then my appetite for blood could go unchecked and I'd be a danger to all, even my own family.

I was in no mood to be scientific, though. And this was not the time to be second guessing anything. Every second that passed was a second wasted.

In one powerful and swift move, I grabbed the mirror off its hinges and threw it out the open window onto the cliffs overlooking the sea below. Quickly, I shadow-stepped out of the room and entered my lab.

We were also on the verge of creating the greatest elixir—an elixir that could completely reverse Vampire nature. Initially, it was for my Magdalena, but I also considered using it on myself. I even dreamed about being turned into a wolf like Aiyana. I dreamed of living with my whole family as a pack of wolves once. Now, those dreams seemed like child's play.

"What a waste of time!" I yelled out into the lab, my voice reverberating off the stone walls. What good would it be to be human if it would make me weak and unable to help my family? I smashed some vials of blood I had prepared for my ghouls onto the tiled ground. They were pointless now, even if I did have the world's most powerful ghouls. What did I think I would do with them if I ever abandoned my vampire nature? Would I abandon them as well? Or worse, kill them just because they were of no use to me?

These ghouls were my family, my new family. *My* pack.

What did I truly think I'd accomplish?

I grabbed some empty flasks from one of the tables and tossed them to the ground. I grabbed some notebooks and tore the binders in half. I didn't need these anymore. Every juicy detail was now safely locked in my daughter's brain. I did not dare risk them falling into the wrong hands.

I was in such a fury and rage that I didn't even hear Magdalena stumble down the stairs and into my lab. She was followed by that wolf of hers. I had never lost it before like this. I am not the emotional type. Something had shattered inside me.

"Are you ok, Dad?" called Magdalena softly. I had always made sure to place her in human homes that would make her tough. Make her fight because life for shifters was especially tough. She was not going to grow up coddled with empty riches like I was. She had to learn to be strong. I questioned that action for a while seeing that she had grown up too tough and required an emotional shield. But right now all I saw was a kind and caring soul, devoid of shields and barriers. For a second, she reminded me of her mother. Tough and wild but with a tenderness of a soft flower.

"We will find her, don't worry," she said.

I turned to say something to the fact that we might not, but she ran into me. The rational one, the cold one with thoughts and ideas, that is who I was, but I knew better. I was never without emotions, I merely lacked the capability or talent to show them. I was vulnerable now, as if my skin had been ripped off and left exposed to the elements. Like a snake who had just sloughed off its skin.

Magdalena wrapped her arms around me and buried her face in my sweater. Did she just shadow step? In a slightly disorganized movement she leapt towards me and almost instantly she was in my arms.

Her Vampire nature was not being subdued.

"She's no longer taking your medicine," Andy said, remaining back against the wall, his arms across his chest. His body was still, too still. Almost as dead and lifeless as a Vampire's. Where did he learn that trick of ours? I remained staring at him for a while, even when I returned my daughter's embrace.

This was a defensive stance. This rogue-turned-alpha stood before me, and I finally took a good look at him. His hair was dark, long and straight, and his face was carved similarly to that of the Natives that belonged to Aiyana's tribe. However, he was lighter skinned like the northern Natives. I had seen those eyes before, back in Romania. All Vampires have a photographic memory.

"Well, isn't this a small world?" I said, still looking at Andy right in the eyes. I was prepared to compel him to tell me the truth if I had to.

"Tell me, did you ever spend time in Romania?" I knew the answer. I just wanted to see how he would deliver it.

Andy remained lifeless and unreadable. His eyes glowed with a blue hue that resembled ice, but I had seen those same eyes glow red once. When I was just over a couple centuries of being a fledgling, I was due to embark on my Western mission of exploring the new lands. He never had a chance to see me, though. Vampire vision was better than a Werewolf's, and I focused on him as if my eyes were a telescope. He was only a child and wolfless at the time from what I gathered, but a rogue nonetheless.

I spied on him about fifty miles down the river from a brand new steamboat, a first of its kind, having just been invented. It was to transport us onto the main ship that awaited us on the Mediterranean. He was upriver and scrambled out of a tiny canoe. I took notice of how frail and near-death he was. A storm had started to brew, and lightning lit up the sky. It acted like a beacon for both him and I. It showed just how frail he really was. And at that moment, I felt for sure he would surely perish in the wilds of Romania. Just a scrawny pile of bones and nearly naked, he made his way across a field and then disappeared into the forest.

I was positioned further than even he could see or smell. I would have taken his life, as my father detested rogue werewolves, but I was already running late for the ship that was going to take us to the new world. So I simply retreated into my private chambers on the steamboat, engrossed my mind in a new book, and forgot about him.

But look at him now. A man with a formidable wolf, a warrior and mate to my own daughter. A lethal and self-taught Vampire hunter.

While abroad, I heard rumors about what had become of the wolfless vampire hunter who traveled throughout Romania.

I heard that he had even managed to kill off a royal named Roland who had a herd of young Strigoi under his command. Strigoi were different from ghouls. And most royals had one or two in their families. They were half human half vampire children and treated like pets, but I honestly detested them. When I questioned my father about the rumors, he merely laughed and joked about how the hunter was doing him a favor, displacing the perils of Romania.

He told me he was planning to get rid of him soon, but I suppose he never got that chance.

If anything Aiyana has taught me it was that these shifters and wolves were protected by the spirits of very ancient shifters. The Ancient People, Aiyana had called them.

"Yes," Andy said. "I was escaping my uncle, who had taken over my pack. They cast me out thinking I was dead but I

survived."

I eyed him for a second before responding. I recalled the lightning again and how it seemed to light his path. It was the last thing I saw before he stumbled into the Carpathian Mountains, and everything went black again.

"You are protected by the Thunderbird," I said to him, recalling the story my love had taught me about their origin as shifters with allied clans. She even taught me a few other stories about one of the Thunderbird's enemies, the Uktena. I had thought them only stories at the time, something I would never admit to her, but now I realized there were truths to those stories.

"And you have taken down its enemy and wear the diamond of the Uktena," I continued while still eyeing him. Another thing about Vampire eyesight is that we can hyperfocus and use our eyes like microscopes. We use it to read people and compel them. We Vampires may not have a strong sense of smell, but I could feel myself drawn toward the blood essence that he was still bathed in, even if the rain had washed most of it away. I was drawn to it like a shark. And it was a type of blood I had never sensed before. It had to belong to the Uktena that he just slaughtered.

He moved then, taking a low, deep breath that would have been invisible to humans, but I know that he knew I understood the reasoning for his defensive stance. He must have seen the blood hunger in my eyes.

Magdalena let me go and turned to look at Andy and then back at me.

"What are you guys talking about?" she said with big brown eyes so dark they were almost black, just like her mother's. They glittered like obsidian and trapped you in their vortex type pull.

I squeezed her arms and whispered, "Don't worry, the memories are still unfolding inside you. You will understand ..." I waved my arms across the destroyed laboratory. "all of this soon."

Then I walked up to Andy and watched him attempt to petrify himself again like a gargoyle.

He nodded "yes" then in response to my question. He still didn't trust me. Well after tonight, I would hope that he wouldn't, for I didn't even trust myself.

"Good," I said while clasping my hands. Then, I brought my right arm out and held it out for him to shake. "We will need you," I said.

Shocked, he let out the rest of the breath he was holding. And I then took both of his hands and shook them both as one.

I shadow-stepped to the refrigerated locked unit where I kept all my elixirs. I broke the lock easily and carefully opened the door. I moved some other bottles around until I found exactly what I wanted: my unlabeled flasks I had hidden in the back. There was no turning back now.

I reached first for the dark red vial, a reversing agent for the herb medicine Aiyana kept me stocked on. It felt cool and refreshing as it went down my throat. Almost instantly, I felt my head spinning and I had to lean against the wall.

"Dad!" Magdalena said. She came up next to me, but I held my arm out.

"Don't come near me," I groaned. Andy ran up and was by Magdalena's side then, and they both watched as the blood power surged through my veins. I opened my mouth large like a viper, and a pair of large, sharp fangs erupted from my mouth.

Quickly, before I changed my mind, I leaped forward and grabbed hold of the larger, green flask in the fridge and took that too.

"What are you doing?" Magdalena panted and jumped towards me, taking away the empty green flask from my lips. "What are you taking?"

"Let him do what he needs to do, Mags. Just wait. I'm sure he knows what he's doing," Andy said while looking around, taking in the room as if he had just noticed it was a laboratory.

I nodded at him as I could not muster a sound. Even my throat was changing, and he knew to take that as a sign to get her away from me. Hastily, he took a hesitant Magdalena to stand back against the wall to give me space. He held onto her tightly.

Suddenly my voice called out in a guttural scream I had no control over. A wave of pain shot through the core of my body that deployed my body down to kneel on the ground. I grunted as the waves of pain grew and I could feel myself grow bigger, taller, and stronger. My muscles broke through the very clothes I wore and I gasped as I looked at my hands. Long black claws had replaced my perfectly manicured nails and my skin, once bright and white like the moon, had turned a pitchy dark gray. It was working!

My eyes pulsed with power and I knew I was close to my primordial Vampire true form. I glanced up to peek at the two standing there watching me. Suddenly my vision was muddled and they were no longer Andy and Magdalena but just two red heat patches directing my hunger to their heat source, blood.

Beautiful, enchanting blood. My body ached for it like the thirst of a thousand deserts. It had been too long!

Then, another wave of excruciating pain surged through me, and I felt a tremendous force explode outward from my upper back. Wings. The iconic wings I had always longed for escaped from my form like a pair of caged lions. I was moments from full transformation and the uncontrollable blood thirst was a threat looming in the atmosphere. In a desperate, split-second decision, I summoned every ounce of strength I had left and launched myself through the ceiling of my laboratory, hurtling into the sky. I couldn't risk putting my daughter in between myself and the bloodlust.

The last thing I heard before the burst of fury caused me to break through the ceiling was Andy hunching down and whispering something into Magdalena's ears.

"We need to get you out of here!" he said to her, but my daughter had the most peculiar look on her face. She was not frightened of me, so foolish, she was not even frightened for herself. She looked rather happy, her face shining in amazement as if I were some majestic being. Ugh, teenagers.

I hovered over the night, floating in midair, looming over my mansion. I let out a loud preternatural screech much like that of a bat but deeper and more intense. To my surprise, the sound reverberated intensely as if it sent out sonar. The end of my screech ended in a high pitch ring I knew was too high for mortal ears to hear.

Vampires were once part bat. We, too, have echolocation, much like the owls use with their screeching. Only our sonar did not return visions. It pointed the way towards blood in a type of magnetic intensity that drew us towards it, or vice versa.

I looked down at the crowd gathering below me on the balcony's steppes. All watching me, the war party was forming, but I could sense hesitation on their part. Was I considered friend or foe in this form? Just then, I felt the hum of my power start to fade slightly and slowly. I began a ghostly descent to the ground that awaited me. My true form was out of fuel. Without blood, the power was draining.

Mags

"He is so badass," I said to Andy as I watched my father hover in the sky like a gothic Superman.

His hair was long and black-the complete opposite of his normal platinum- and acted like a shroud to cover his naked body. He had matching large black leathery wings that casually fluttered in the wind. And his face was different, more angular but still very beautiful. Out of the side of his head were long, pointy ears like an elf, but they were different; they widened out like a fan at the base, much like a bat. His skin was a dark charcoal color like a gargoyle on a gothic mansion, and like his hair, his very eyes had changed from blue to black and glowed a bright fiery red when the light hit them at a certain angle, like how Andys used to glow.

But besides all this, he hardly looked human. He was bigger, almost ten feet tall, I reckon and had more muscles than the Hulk. I had never seen anything like that in any of the movies I had ever seen about Vampires, except maybe Nosferatu, but he wasn't bald, nor ugly. He looked like he had been carved out of dark marble. A true creature of shadow and night.

It dawned on me that my freaking Vampire dad was the coolest thing I had ever seen. For the first time since meeting Luz, I considered living a life of the undead. I wanted to be up there flying with him, feeling what he was feeling. A howl escaped from Luz in my mind and I realized my mistake.

No, Luz, I could never give you up, I said to soothe my wolf.

Don't worry.

"Hey, you!" said a happy familiar voice from behind me. "You got a naked Vampire up there in the sky."

I turned around and there was the Thunderbird from the powwow.

"Torito!" I said happily. He then removed the headdress from the regalia and smiled at me. I knew I had been right.

"You guessed correctly!" he said, returning my smile. I ran to him, hugging him, happy to see another familiar face in the void of confusion.

Was he a Werewolf, too? I was so happy that I wasn't the only younger person alone with a bunch of ancient but glorious people. Not that Andy was ancient . . . well, he didn't look it, at least. He might not understand my slang, but he was still the hottest guy to look at. I was growing accustomed to being called Andy's mate, even if it wasn't official yet.

Just then, I felt an arm go around my shoulder. It was Andy. He slid his arm down around my waist and kept it there. I could sense something odd in the air. Was he jealous? Of what?

I side-eyed him and just shook my head. He has yet to even ask me to be his boyfriend, let alone his lifelong mate, so as far as I'm concerned, he could just relax. I didn't understand how a guy I liked could also annoy me so much. Is this how love is?

I think Torito could see what was happening, so he nodded and waved at Andy, and also took a few steps back. Why are guys so weird? Torito was just my friend. They were both making it awkward.

"Okay, so look, " I said, trying to ignore the tension in the air. My mother is missing, and we need to find her. I raised my voice so that everyone could hear. "I haven't met many of you. And I don't know what you all are. But I'm tired of being kept in the dark. My father has recovered my lost memories, so I know who my parents are, but you guys?" I paused for a second to look at the owls and the rest of the kachina dancers dressed as different animals.

"You guys were dancing at the powwow. Are you werewolves, too?" I asked, trying to make eye contact with as many people as I could.

Just then, I heard a faint tap on the ground from behind us, and I knew my father had come down from the sky. I saw his ghouls run to him and cover him in a type of makeshift loincloth so he wouldn't be naked. I quickly turned my head away when I realized what they were doing. Ew.

"Magdalena . . ." my dad spoke.

"No, no, Dad," I said, turning back to look at him when I heard the ghouls scatter. They had also brought him vials of what looked like blood to drink that he was gulping down.

At this moment, his memories of Mom and their love for each other were starting to focus, and I just couldn't face him right now. Their love and intimacy was too much for me to handle at that moment.

Andy reached up his arm as if to say something, but I stopped him before he could.

"And not you, Andy." I could never focus seriously when Andy was around. "Just give me a moment." The pull from the mate business just made me feel like I was in heat. I gently released myself from his grip and looked for the eyes I had seen gleam over me earlier.

"I would like you," I said, reaching out my hand at the owl woman, the one I suspected was La Lechuza, "to please explain what is going on here. I could use a woman's

perspective here, please."

She smiled and nodded. "Let us go away and talk a few things over privately, and let the men plan the best attack while we speak." She placed an arm around my shoulders and led me back into the mansion for privacy.

Once inside I turned to her, recognizing her for what she was. Luz had whispered her name to me when our eyes connected the first time I saw her.

"I don't mean to pry, but I have to ask . . . are you La

Chuza?" I asked kindly, trying hard not to insult her or bring shame to her if she had, in fact, killed people in the past. I didn't want her to be angry at me.

She looked back at me with big, sad eyes. I knew I had somehow cut her with my words, so I hugged her to apologize.

"It doesn't matter . . . whatever you did or didn't do. I know you are good. If you did, it was for a good reason and . . ." I was pulled away from her, and she looked me right into my eyes.

"Yes and no," she said with a soft and gentle expression. She wasn't angry. She brought me to the couch in the middle of the living room and sat down with me, holding my hand.

"I will tell you everything you want to know about me when the time is right. Right now, let's focus on getting you caught up on the important things." She paused and looked at me softly.

She let out a big sigh before continuing. "I know you have memories unfolding inside your mind right now. I can almost see them in a vision, blossoming like a rose. As each memory unfolds like a petal, another petal is revealed. I do not want to bombard your mind with too much more

information at this delicate time, but I will tell you this."

She scooted closer to me on the couch, and I took this time to examine her very beautiful jewelry of beads and turquoise. She barely looked a year older than twenty, but I knew that was deceptive because when she walked or talked, she moved gracefully like a queen, not a princess. Her eyes held a wisdom I wasn't yet familiar with. They looked almost amber in this light.

Deep-set and oval, her brows were high, as were her cheekbones. They made her face appear long and in the shape of a heart, a very feminine contour, much like that of the barn owl she could transform into. Her black hair fell in two thick braids, entwined with red cloth. And on top of her head, she wore one large barn owl feather. She was the most regal-looking woman I had ever seen. If there were anyone to aspire to be like, it would be her and my mother, for sure.

With her this close, I could almost detect the scent of vanilla. Do I have that correct? Luz has been very quiet lately. Not that she was much of a chatterbox, but something seemed different about her, and though I didn't sense anything wrong, her vibe was just off.

Yes, Mags, Vanilla and Maize. She has a very clean, earthy and sweet scent, Luz said in the back of my mind. *Now, please excuse me; I have a lot of memories to organize.*

Oh yes, that's right. My memories are her memories. Andy had told me once that wolves didn't like to delve into the past. I left her alone to gather her thoughts. When this was over and my mother returned home safe and sound, we all were going to need a vacation!

"Andy told you about our people and the Thunderbird and how we obtained our shifting abilities, correct?"

"Yes, the first day we met. I admit it was a lot of information, but I think I understand most of it," I answered truthfully.

"Well, those people out there, the kachina dancers, they are your people, they are my people, Tecos' people and very distantly, Andy's people. We may not all be from the same tribe, but we are related. We all share the same shifter gene and we all swore an oath to help our brothers and sisters—those born under the wolf or physical nature and those born under the skins or spirit nature. Together as allies and brothers, we have body and soul. He told you this, yes?"

It was all coming back to me. Even all the things he said when I thought I wasn't listening. "Yes, and Werewolves were once cousins to Skin Shifters, but after taking an oath, they become brothers and sisters," I said, happy to be remembering this story. This information was from the night at the park. The second time we met. I guess I was paying more attention than I thought. Or, maybe Luz really is helping me organize my memories.

That's your vampire nature Magdalena. You vampires have great memory. Luz chimed in.

"Yes, my little mariposa," she said with a smile. Mariposa means butterfly in Spanish. Being so close to the border, many Natives here also spoke Spanish and had Spanish names from when they were colonized by Spaniards. Even I knew some Spanish. Terms of endearment were common among the people here. I didn't cringe, though, when she did it, only when Carmen, my stepmother, would use those types of words.

Carmen! It's been a few days since I've been home. I wonder if she has even tried looking for me.

"Yes, that's exactly right, Magdalena. It means butterfly. My name is Santana. It was one of the names given to me by my mother, who was forced to give me a colonizer name. I was born before the great revolt. I have no hate towards the name, even though my family was slaughtered during the revolt. I keep it because it was still one of the names my mother called me by. Names are very important; remember that," she said, looking very motherly herself. So she was older, I knew it!

"But you can call me Aunty if you'd like as we are family. It is very nice to meet you, niece," she smiled.

I returned her gracious smile and gave her a quick hug. "It is very nice to meet you too, Aunty, and I'm sorry you had to endure that." The tears I had been holding back came rushing forward again. I had a family. That was something I had never expected. And they were beautiful and strong people who had endured many hardships. I, too, would have to make them proud, as they had made me.

"I'll leave you with this before we return to the roosters outside," she said, pointing to the window. I couldn't help but let out a small laugh. It was quite funny, actually; they did look like a bunch of roosters, especially the way they argued with each other.

"Your time for swearing the oath will come very soon. Make sure you find a way to join us at the war party. You will have to prove yourself to your ancestors first and then you will be called forth as a woman. Being a woman is more than just your age. It's about giving life, creating and multiplying blessings for those around you. Just like the corn pollen that gives life everywhere it flows. If you can do that, then you will be considered a woman. You will know you have given yourself to the spirit and accepted the oath when you find your way out of darkness and take your first breath afterward. You will be reborn as your ancestors out of the ground and like a corn seed." She paused for a second to process the images that came to my mind.

Then she took my hand. "Your very breath hums the name of God, our Creator, out of your lungs and through your lips. He is like a spirit that flows through everything. If you do not take the oath, you will die," she said seriously, looking at me with those big, beautiful eyes of hers.

There was something surreal about an owl telling you that there was a chance you could die. Owls are harbingers of death. I knew she spoke the truth, even if I had no idea how I knew it, but I felt it in my bones.

"Don't worry," she said. "Take this and don't be afraid." She handed me a medicine bag she had carried around her neck. It was a little pouch.

"My family is so giving," I said, feeling tears well up in me. But I haven't anything to give you back," I said, remembering all the times all my people had given me gifts, and I had turned up empty-handed.

"Don't worry! Your time will come. Right now, receive as a child receives. For when you become a woman, you will have plenty and more to give back."

"Okay!" I said, giggling and wiping a tear away. "What's inside?" I put it over my head and let it rest on my chest. It felt pretty full.

"It's a mixture of herbs but, most importantly, corn pollen," she said with a happy smile. "Let it guide your feet."

I nodded, and by now, my tears had dried. I was ready to go back outside and see what those roosters were talking about.

I took a breath and said, "Let's go then." As we walked back out into the night with a new goal, I realized something. I was going to find a way to meet the war party. Nothing was going to keep me from rescuing my mother.

Andy

"What the hell are you?" I said out loud to Sebastian, a little too roughly even for my own liking. But I think I spoke for everyone here. We all wanted to know what he was. I'm sure Magdalena wanted to know, too. He was her father, after all, and she was half of him.

Sebastian looked at me with a stoic gaze. But behind that face of stone shone two sparkling eyeballs that hinted at danger.

"I'm a Vampire," he said with a deeper voice than I was used to hearing him speak in. "Apparently, the Vampire hunter still has a lot to learn about our kind. I don't blame you, though, for your ignorance. We are a rather secretive type," he said with red eyes still blaring into me. Did red eyes for Vampires mean rogue, too?

"I only needed to know how to kill them," I said confidently. Sebastian scoffed.

"This is my true form," Sebastian said. You all are shifters; what did you think I was? I am a shifter as well. We don't usually undergo such transformations unless time has done its perfect work to age and refine us, like a fine wine. We achieve our true form much later than the age of thirteen."

"Are you good or bad medicine?" yelled out one of the kachina dancers dressed like a badger. "That's all we need to know!" he added. He was an old medicine man, much like Santana in directness from what I could gather.

"And why are you naked?" yelled out another dancer from the shadows. I think it was coyote.

"I am like you," Sebastian said with a roar, annoyed with all of us. "I can be both good and bad. But none of this matters right now. We need to find Aiyana now!"

Even Ash was confused by the commotion of the night. He could not stay focused on what Sebastian was saying, too concerned about Torito. *Does she not love us anymore?* he asked. *It's that pigeon over there isn't it? He's younger than us and she thinks he's nice! I'll tear his throat out!*

Soon, there was more commotion, and nay sayings and mutterings were heard all around us. It was at this moment that I saw Sebastian lose his calm and stoic nature.

"Enough!" Sebastian piped up with a loud and booming voice. "Are the Skin Shifters up to date and ready?" He was looking at Tecos. Did they know each other somehow? Well, Sebastian must have at least known that Tecos and Santana had protected our Mags from the Wendigo. They didn't seem too friendly with each other, though, at this time.

Tecos stood there silently for a few seconds completely unfazed. He then casually walked up to him while pulling a quill from his feathered regalia headdress. He took the quill of the feather and poked his hand with it, causing himself to bleed. Blood pulled up into the stem of the quill like an old-fashioned pen with osmosis.

Tecos placed the quill in his mouth and shifted. His owl carried the feather to Sebastian who had managed to once again fly up into the air and regain his stone form after drinking goblets of blood. I could tell Sebastian was hungering to taste his blood. He took the quill quickly and leaned his tongue into the small reservoir in the feather and let his eyes roll back.

Sebastian stood in mid-air like a spector for what seemed like an eternity. He was absorbing information.

He suddenly pulled the feather back and placed it back into Tecos awaiting beak. Tecos nodded and flew back to us and shifted back. I didn't know exactly what he saw when he tasted Tecos blood, but it was apparently enough to realize who the real ancient was. It wasn't surprise that ran across Sebastian's face, though, but respect.

"I'm glad those Vampires who injured you two are disposed of," Sebastian said to Tecos. "They weren't any of my people. I took all my people down shortly after I met Aiyana. But unfortunately, many more broods were making their way to the new world during those times."

I glanced at Tecos. Vampires? Was it the Vampires who had injured them? This Vampire knew before me? I just shook my head at Tecos. He was going to have to give me the details later. They may be "taken care of," as Sebastian said, but I might have to find out for myself just how well.

I'm a Vampire hunter, for God's sake! If any of the Vampires from Romania had followed me here in search of me but instead attacked other innocent shifters, I don't know how I could deal with that. I would have to make sure no threat like that ever came to them again.

Just then, Mags came back out with Santana. She was up to date, her face told me. She was looking at the kachina dancers again. Ash couldn't help himself and let out a low growl, warning the shifters about getting any ideas.

We are going to have to talk soon too, Santana mind-linked me. *About the ways of women and how to treat a lady!*

What did I do? She was not happy with me for some reason. As she passed by, she looked down at my midsection and then looked back up at me with a displeased look. It was then that I realized she knew about what Mags and I had been up to intimately, and my face went beat red. Oh great, now I was in trouble with the owl lady. But just how do these owls know everything?

I rolled my eyes and sighed at the floor, my hands on my waist. There really are no secrets among us, are there?

No! Santana screeched at me via mind link. *You wild and unrestrained child! Could you not have waited until you two were properly bonded?*

I tried to mind link her back that Magdalena was my mate, but she blocked me. These were the ways of the wolf. Ash would have taken her and marked her already if he could. We did nothing wrong. We did what our instincts told us to do. Both Mags and I were wolves. There was no shame in that!

She brought Mags to stand next to her and wrapped her arms across her chest and just stared me down with her big black eyes. She was partially shifted. I know Mags would not have told her.

I went to stand next to Torito, first to escape my auntie's gaze and then to keep an eye on him. He reached out his fist, and I accepted his modern handshake despite Ash's protest. "Nice regalia," I said as I realized he was wearing the same one I had used to lull the Uktena from the waters at the base of the Grand Canyon. I don't know why I felt a tinge of possessiveness towards the regalia I had only meant to borrow. I wasn't even a Skin Shifter. I had no use for it, but seeing it on him made Ash sneer and growl.

"Yeah, it's mine now, a gift from Tecos," he said, smiling, taunting me.

"Oh!" I said while nodding. I was so quickly replaced. Another knife in my back from an owl. Had I done something to offend Tecos now? No wonder he wanted it back in good shape.

"Well, I hope I didn't get any Uktena blood on it for you," I said. I knew for sure the Uktena would have had him for breakfast.

"Oh yes! You slayed the Uktena! Yes, I was told!" Torito answered with a small laugh. I scoffed.

"I'm impressed, such a great warrior!" he said while petting the top of my head as if I were some common dog.

"Yeah, and an even better silversmith," I said while removing his hand from my head and pointing at Mags' bracelets. "I made those for my mate."

He just laughed. I never wanted to punch anyone so much in my life.

Just then we all were silenced by Santana when she turned her head in a complete 180 degrees to stare at us. Her eyes were even larger than before; she stared at us like a mother having to keep her children in line. The sight was enough to shake the pants off of us, not that we would admit it.

She shushed us both with a shriek and everyone, including the kachina dancers and me, hid our eyes from her glare.

Well, she didn't need to tell us twice to be quiet.

Tecos

As the night stilled and the voices from our war party finally muffled down, I let the last of the sage, sweetgrass and willow cleanse the air. Our minds were all out of focus. Our spirits confused and tangled with emotions but we had to gather our thoughts so we could remember the real reason for this gathering.

"Listen up! This is what the spirit of the trickster Wendigo does," I said loudly so that everyone could hear.

"He confuses us, makes us focus on things that do not matter. Right now, the life of a sister is in danger, and we, the allies of wolves, must come to her rescue. We must work together." I said while looking at Santana, who had moved her hard, disapproving stare from the two young squabbling men towards that of Sebastian, the gargoyle Vampire. She didn't trust him because of what he was, a Vampire, but he was also our missing sister's chosen mate. And for that reason alone, I gave him the benefit of the doubt.

"We must think with our rational minds and detach from negative emotions that will only cause us to fumble and make bad decisions," I said, this time looking at Sebastian. Sebastian looked down and shifted back into his human form.

I was not utterly convinced it was his choice to shift back; his potions were unstable. It was unnatural to play with nature's gifts that way. Alchemy bordered on witchcraft! But he was not on the same path as me in this lifetime, so I remained silent and did not offer my wisdom.

Once he was back in human form, I could once again hear his heartbeat. Interesting how the undead are truly dead and yet truly alive at the same time. For an owl, one could become transfixed in this seemingly deluge of death but even owls do not come for these types. Their ends are invisible to us-unless of course it is we who are taking that life, remembering our war in Texas.

I digress. Seems like the confusion is even spreading to me.

"We must pray to the Creator for strength and wisdom, for in doing so, that is the only way we will escape the tricks of the Wendigo. He is a great manipulator! Able to hide just about anywhere, even hide from the great foresight of the Uktena," I said while nodding towards Andrei. "He has taken on its skin and, therefore, is invisible to even you, Andrei."

Andrei sighed. I knew he had attempted to search for him and had come up with nothing. He can't use the diamond to see the Uktena; it was the Uktena's diamond and therefore rendering it useless upon itself.

"As long as he remains in the skin, he can hide himself and anyone near him from our sight," I said aloud for the others.

I took a moment to pause and think through some of my plans for the night. I stared into the low rumbling fire I had started on the Vampire's stone balcony. All my herbs were near extinguished but the air remained clean.

"We must fly higher than eagles so that we can see the big picture," I paused and looked at Chris, the eagle kachina. He was older than the others and a late bloomer when he realized just what kind of powers he had as a Skin Shifter. He was the first to answer my call, but he was also the quietest. I hope he could lend us some insight.

"Tell me great Eagle, what is he doing with the Werewolf pack that once belonged to Andrei?" The tall, quiet one came from the back of the gathering. He stood there for a second, looking unsure as to what was being asked of him.

Then, finally, he looked up and spread his wings. We all stood and stared at the majestic bald eagle that went out and swarmed the periphery of the mansion. He quickly came back down to stand as a human as he landed. Eagles had great vision—not farsight but actually great eyes. He could pierce the landscape between us with no problems.

"I see the wolves unable to shift back into their human bodies. I see them being held down by nearly invisible silver chains enchanted by the Wendigo in a cave. They are not in their normal home. But a cold and distant, dark land full of blood and death." He then walked back to where he had originally stood.

"Wonderful. Thank you, brother Eagle, for your insight. Your vision is stronger than us all," I said. "And what is he doing with Aiyana? What can she give him? What does he want?" I asked out loud already knowing the answer. Sebastian, the Vampire, came forth and answered to inform the others.

"She is his true mate. And I also saw him, with my own two eyes, run and steal the skin of the dead Uktena moments after he kidnapped her. He placed its horns on his head like a trophy, but the feathers he could not absorb," he uttered with pain in his voice as he thought about Aiyana being mated to that monster.

"Your eyesight truly is great! Not as great as brother Eagle's but no less useful," I said. For him to see like that was ironic to me. Strange because bats usually had poor eyesight-atleast during the day.

My suspicions were true. I knew she was mated to that monster, but I was not sure he had indeed taken the Uktena skin.

He nodded and looked down at the ground, lost in thought, pining for the wolf he called "his love."

"He took the skin? That's why he attacked Mags! To lure Aiyana and distract me away from getting rid of the body after I killed it!" Andrei said, visually upset. "I had plans to dispose of it in the fire but I was stopped when the diamond gave me the vision!"

"And he needs to mark her wolf," answered Santana. "To remove the curse the Manitou placed on him for eating a fellow shifter. He needs the mark of the Thunderbird in his system again so he can start absorbing the spirit feather. The only way now to regain the Thunderbird blessing would be to join in her blessing."

"Yes, mates share everything once they are marked," I added. "DNA, thoughts, spirit, everything. They are one. Skin Shifters are only temporarily marked for a given animal spirit's lifetime, that is, until another spirit animal comes to take its place. If a Skin Shifter has a wolf as a mate. He will gain the ability to keep all four spirit animals with him at all times. It looks like he is attempting to commune with four of our darkest monsters. Deer being the first, Human Wendigo the second, Uktena third. After the mate bond he will be part Wolf. And how will we stop him?" I asked out loud to anyone who would know the answer. It was so much fun having this conversation. As dreary as the situation was, puzzles and mysteries were where I reveled. Santana and I had not conversed like this with others for far too long.

"Beating him at his own game!" It was Coyote. He came out already transformed as he hung his head low to the ground as if he didn't like exposing himself but knew he needed to introduce himself. "It takes a trickster to understand a trickster." He said in a barely comprehensible growl type of way. A coy, wolfish smile came out of his angular face as he looked up at us. He then yipped several times into the air while transforming back into this tall and thin human figure. He looked an awful lot like me as a kid. Lanky, dark and with thin straight long hair that he kept slightly unkempt down his back like a feral adult. Wait . . .

"Nice try, Coyote," I said. "You are not related to me that much."

He laughed and then moved himself in a way that exposed his true features. Coyote was not a human-to-human shifter. That would be bad. But he is an expert at tricks and can use light and shadows to almost manipulate how he looks. It was a very canny but also very effective trick on humans, not so much other shifters. He then headed back to the rear of the crowd.

Coyotes were always trying to blend in. It's a funny joke to them. "Wait," I said to the coyote. "You are saying he is blending in with one of us." Coyote turned back to look at me and gave me a simple nod. "If not him, then his accomplice," he replied before disappearing in the shadows.

"I know the Witch and the Wendigo are the same people now. I had my suspicions, but having used the diamond to see him attack Mags cemented this hunch," Andy said, addressing the crowd. "He is working with my uncle Regis. Why he allowed me to live is beyond me. Could Regis be the accomplice?"

"Perhaps there is more than one accomplice," I said. But who would be aiding a Wendigo, let alone two people? Another Wendigo? Seems absurd to me. Wendigos were territorial and would never share their meals or accomplishments so to speak. Well, nothing but another owl would know "who".

I had decided earlier that I was going to start training a new owl. A medicine man owl, a great horned owl. He would be my successor once my owl spirit left me. I could feel the shift in the air, but I already had four forms. What lay ahead for me, the Creator has kept it hidden, but I suspect I will no longer be on this earth like I am now. Perhaps I would die in this battle. A fate I have accepted. What troubles me now is leaving Santana alone.

I called out to Takoda just then. He walked forward, unsure as to why I called him out.

"You are a medicine man, same as me. What do you see that this old owl does not?" I asked him.

He reached out and took a puff from a rolled up cigar he had obviously made himself. He then offered some to me. I took it gladly then handed it back. He too was older when he heard his calling. He was already working in the clinic in the laboratory where Magdalena received her treatments and knew what she was before she even did.

"Hey I know you!" Magdalena piped up. "You work in the lab where they draw my blood."

He looked at her and nodded.

"Yes, I am a recorder." He said out loud. "I keep track of all the people who have shifting abilities." He said while pointing to his head. "So yes, I knew of you."

"Oh." Magdalena said, eager to listen to what he had to say.

He did well concealing what he knew because he also knew about the ghouls that ran the clinic. He kept track of all of them, learning their ways and also kept tabs on all the other shifters who had yet to know who or what they were.

Unbeknownst to the ghouls, he was testing everyone's blood for the trait. He was like a scribe, just dotting down information in his mind, learning constantly. A good owl.

"I think the Vampire's history is going to come full circle now," he said, motioning towards Sebastian. "It is not so much one of us but of yours, Sebastian. Your father is in cahoots with the Wendigo. They made some sort of

agreement."

"My father?" said Sebastian as if he had forgotten that his father even existed. He took a moment to digest the information.

"My father had never known about Aiyana as far as I was concerned. I tried to make it seem like I was dead. I guess it's possible he found us out. He would never approve of our relationship or of Magdalena," he said with near tears in his eyes. "Wendigos are not known to wander into my homeland. Vampires and other creatures deranged with want usually don't get along. They have similar feeding habits and neither can feed or destroy the other. I suppose he found a reason to ally with him." He said, his face darkening.

I saw Magdalena run to her father and hug him. Santana was right. She was a volcano of emotions and memories erupting right before our eyes. A beautiful and young woman to be proud of. If Andrei had not been a rogue for so long, he would have known how to talk to her better from the beginning.

Her heart was somewhat closed off to him; the only thing that kept her even slightly interested in him was their mate bond. A physical connection, but what she needed right now was a rock. An emotional connection. He's trying now but he took too long.

I knew she resented him for disappearing after he told her what she was. He has made many changes since then, but he needs a little more time to blossom as well. He had to learn how to be a man, not a rogue. Santana helped him find a new wardrobe. She gave him a new look with the money he earned working in the mines, trading in silver and gold at various trade facilities. She taught him how to make beautiful jewelry.

I taught him to be patient and to learn how to speak with words and not just body language and grunts and animal sounds. He may not have thought he was initially in such bad shape, but others noticed, and he definitely realizes it now. I made him recite the history of his people and our creation stories until they were all memorized. Ingrained in his soul, so to speak. Which is why I hardly mind-link him. I needed to lure him away from his shell. He had gone too many years being just a wolf and man. I would have told him about the Vampires who had injured us many years ago during the revolt. I was just waiting for him to ask with words.

I guess, as a fellow man, I gave him more credit than the women. He is a good kid. Both those kids, Magdalena and Andrei, were clueless about their history. They were so alike and so different at the same time, each having their own strengths and weaknesses that complement each other. The creator did well pairing the two, even if they don't see it right now.

"Where is Aiyana from?" asked Andrei.

Good, see, he is already learning to ask questions.

"From the land now called Canada," said Sebastian.

"But her ancestors are from my lands. The land they now call Siberia," Andrei followed. "That is what Ash, my wolf says when he communicates with Mags' wolf. He can smell that."

I turned my gaze towards Mags. She was eyeing Andrei closely.

"That is why Mags and I are mates even though we are many years apart and partially from the same tribe, many, many, many cousins removed," Andrei said. "The Creator brought us together for this reason. To save our tribe!"

She smiled at Andrei, seemingly no longer annoyed with him and it made my heart swell to see young love like that.

"Yes, and that is why the Creator made my love his mate. Because she would never willingly give herself to a curse," Sebastian said.

"So a mate is someone that you're destined to be with by the Creator?" asked Mags.

"Yes," Andrei responded softly, his gaze deep and unwavering, as if he hadn't realized the weight of his words might be lost on her. His eyes held a mixture of tenderness and something unspoken, as though he expected her to understand something so profound, so innate. But the confusion in her eyes pulled him back to the present, making him pause before he spoke again.

"It means . . ." he began, his voice lower now, almost reverent, "when two fated beings—mates—are joined, we don't just come together. We become one." His words carried a sense of awe, as if he were speaking of something sacred. "Bound in spirit and soul. Forever."

His expression softened further as he watched her, as though he were both explaining and confessing something he hadn't fully allowed himself to feel until this moment. "It's not just a bond," he continued, his voice barely above a whisper, "it's an eternal connection. No matter what happens . . .

we're tied. Always."

There was a flicker of vulnerability in his eyes, something raw and intimate, as if he was offering her not just an explanation but a glimpse into his own guarded heart.

I saw her smile then look down at the ground as if feeling a little shy. What a hoot that child was. I have seen her whole life and watched her grow up, and I have never seen her blush.

Andrei moved to stand next to Magdalena. He reached down to hold her hand, and she did not fight it.

"Her family was nomadic but settled in those lands before the rest of the pack continued on their journey. Years before that monster came into view, they had created their own pack. He is from the shaman shifter clan of your lands, Andy, a traitor and cursed, she had told me. When he came to her village and found out who she was, he attempted to steal her away, but she knew how to hide herself.

Unfortunately, her whole family and village," he said while holding Magdalena's shoulder, "perished under his rage the night she escaped," Sebastian said while nodding at Magdalena.

"Yes, I remember everything you showed me about your life together," Magdalena answered, looking up at her father. Now, the three of them huddled together. It was nice seeing the lingering effects of the Wendigo's presence finally gone.

Minds were being made clear and a plan was starting to form. I just had to throw it into action.

"You are right that she would not willingly give herself to him," I said. "Unless she was compelled by a certain Vampire with strong memory manipulations." I said while looking accusingly at Sebastian.

Everyone followed suit and looked at Sebastian then. There was enough mistrust regarding Vampires for the Skin Shifters that I had to make it clear to everyone just whose side Sebastian was really on. It was my final test to see if the confusion had finally left us.

I saw his face turn sour and anger seemed to return to his face. If I didn't know any better his heart almost seemed to slow just enough to make me wonder if his true form would return. But it did not.

"Not my father!" Mags yelled out. "It is another Vampire! I have my father's memories now, and his love is true! It has to be my grandfather, my own fucking grandfather, who hates me enough to want the Wendigo to kill me!" she said with blood tears streaming down her cheeks. Her Vampire nature was growing stronger and stronger every minute and I knew it was close to time for her to choose her true nature, whatever it was she chose. Wolf or Vampire.

Soon enough, I thought to myself. Soon enough.

"You're right," Santana responded. Your father is a . . ." she paused for a bit and then continued, "honorable Vampire. He cared for Aiyana and you for many years. He is not behind this, but his father is. He is trying to tear up this family." Her admission of his innocence made me happy. The confusion was finally gone. That meant the Wendigo was far away from here, and we had to get going soon now that our minds were reset.

Her eyes glazed over for a second. I recognized that look. Death was speaking to her in visions, like he did for many animals but especially the owl.

"Valerian turned Regis. The wolfless bastard is now a turned Vampire and working along with the Wendigo," she said, her eyes becoming clear again.

"Oh, this is fucked up!" Magdalena said. Letting her shoulders fall in a slump. "This is so Jerry Springer." "Who is Jerry Springer? Another Vampire?" I asked.

The young girl who I had protected with my life all these years, laughed at me.

"No, it's just a saying, Tecos. Sorry," she said, quieting herself. Young people are so weird.

I saw Andrei's gears starting to turn as he looked at me. His uncle was wolfless. He finally knows. Regis was powerless. That is the only reason behind his taking over the pact. Andrei was next in line for the throne—not him. I sensed an anger burning inside him that I had not seen for quite some time.

"Then it's time," Sebastian said. "I have been hiding from him long enough. It's time we had a heart-to-heart." And with that, he leaped up into the sky again, this time as his normal Vampire self, fully detoxed from any suppressing herb. So, his potion had unlocked his true form and made him stronger. Interesting.

"I know where she is," said a booming voice from the Vampire hovering like a ghost in the sky. His concoctions were unstable! He must have shifted back and forth now like five times! "She's in the last place I would ever search for her. Romania. He is making me come to him. So be it!

Let's go!"

The dancers cheered and gave off their battle cries. And in an instant, everyone had shifted.

Everyone except for Andrei and, of course, Mags.

"I'll stay with you," Andrei said.

"I'm going!" Mags said. "She's my mother too!"

"It's not safe for you there, Mags!" rumbled her father from the sky.

"No!" she said firmly. "The time has come for me to stop being protected. I need to get out of these chains too!" She pulled her silver cuffs off and threw them to the ground in a loud clunk. But already, the ghouls were coming to compel her into a calming sleep and sneak her inside the mansion.

Vampire compulsion was so different from our whistles. Our whistles were not so much soothing but rather an instinctual ping to reset the animal mind. Compulsion was hypnotic in nature and emitted a type of ionic energy, usually repelled by silver ions like magnetic energy. But her "shackles" were on the floor now, and she was vulnerable to her father's and his ghouls' compulsion.

"I have to go! For mom!" she called back, fighting it until the end, until she was fast asleep in Andrei's arms.

"She will be safe here. I will leave my ghouls here to watch over her," called down Sebastian. "Andy, you're in charge!"

I saw Andrei stand there, panic-stricken. He didn't want to go against her wishes. And I didn't blame him.

"Come and meet us later when she has had time to calm down," I said. "Your skills will not be needed for another couple of days anyway."

He nodded and carried his mate into the stone mansion.

I took a final glance at Sebastian, who was the last one left hovering in the sky. Everyone else had taken off, waiting for us to catch up. His long black coat flapped in the wind like a cape. He nodded and looked satisfied.

"Look after her," he said to Andrei and his ghouls before darting off like a shadow through the sky. I reached my arms up to the sky and joined the war party.

Chapter 11

War

Sebastian

The moon hung high in the Carpathian sky, casting an eerie glow over the darkened land of Romania. This was my homeland, a place I once knew well, but now it felt foreign and hostile. As I stood at the edge of the forest, the shadows of my companions—the two barn owls, the badger, the bull, the Thunderbird, and other animal shifters—moved silently around me. We had come a long way in such a short time, driven by a shared purpose: to confront my father, King Valerian, and retrieve the most precious thing to me, my love.

Truthfully and sadly, I would have left that madman of a Wendigo alone to do his evil upon the world as long as my life was left alone. But it was becoming very apparent to me that this world was very small and my thinking was even smaller. I could not raise a child in a world where I allowed evil to trample. I could no longer hide like a bat in a cave and pretend that evil would never find me.

My father was a legend, but not the kind that inspired tales of heroism. His was a legacy of fear and domination. Under his rule, the

Werewolves were nothing more than slaves, their spirits broken by his relentless cruelty. His ghoul army patrolled the kingdom, ensuring that no one dared to challenge his authority. Although, I have to say, his ghouls were nothing like mine.

As for me, I always turned a blind eye to my father's folly until I met the woman who changed me forever. In my years of exploring the new world for my father, I found something my father never understood—loyalty born of respect, not fear. My companions, the ghouls I made, were my family now, bound by a common cause and unwavering loyalty. He treated his ghouls like slaves and, therefore, were beaten down and died or killed off quickly. Mine were a different breed of strong. They were almost as strong as Vampires, but they could walk in the daylight. I also could mind-link with them. Something my father never cared to do. Communicating with those he considered beneath him except to command them was all he knew.

The same went for my mother and myself—his only true child. Royal Vampires are born, not turned. Descended from a long-ago type of bat shifter, we carried the capabilities of reproduction, but only once every millennia or so.

When Aiyana managed to have not one but two of my children it was deemed a miracle. After the first one did not survive, I made it my duty to make sure the second one would, even if I had to do things I was not proud of, like defanging my own daughter. I knew I had to rescue her mother, but I feared what going to war with my father would look like to her. Would she also see me as a monster? Would she pull away from me like I pulled away from my father?

These thoughts plagued me as we made our descent into my old and blood-soaked land.

Our journey to Romania was fraught with opposition. We traversed treacherous landscapes, faced hostile creatures, and dealt with the ever-present threat of my father's spies. The closer we got to our destination, the heavier the air seemed to grow, thick with the weight of anticipation and fear. Our resolve never wavered. We knew the risks, but we also knew the stakes. Yet these fights were easy. Not with fresh young new warriors but we made it work. It wasn't until we neared the castle, my family home, that we came across a true opposing force.

As we crossed into the heart of my father's kingdom, the signs of his reign were everywhere. The land, once vibrant, was now shrouded in shadow. The enslaved Werewolves lived in constant fear, their eyes hollow and defeated. The ghoul army patrolled the streets, a constant reminder of my father's iron grip. The citizens, both human and Werewolf, were broken, their spirits crushed by years of oppression.

We took great joy in releasing the wolves from slavery. And they followed us in our fight. They had no alpha, and they were all either rogues or from different packs but they joined as one with us. No words were said. It was a silent alliance.

We arrived under the cover of darkness, our presence concealed by the thick forest. The initial confrontations with my father's forces were swift and brutal. We moved like shadows, striking with precision and retreating before the enemy could regroup. Each skirmish brought us closer to the heart of Valerian's castle, but with every step, the weight of the inevitable confrontation grew heavier.

The Vampires we took down had no idea just how quickly we would be able to do it. It almost seemed like a joke until the moment I saw new wolves descend. These were not rogues or vagabond random pack members. These were Andrei's wolves. About fifty of them.

Andrei's army. He should be here. I know he wouldn't want us to harm any of them. Aiyana wouldn't want me to harm any of them. The few dozen wolves we had rescued cowered under their howls and left us, scattering off into the night like roaches to light. So be it. We were not their alpha.

Tecos flew out in front of us and shrieked at the wolves with his preternatural scream. The wolves halted and looked up, confused. I took this small moment to wave my hand in their direction to remove their compulsion—a blood trick only strong Vampires could do. There was no leader of their pack now. I had dismantled their connection.

No one wolf seemed to stand out more than the others. They were like toy soldiers being led by a single leader, but for wolves, that leader was usually an alpha wolf, not a Vampire. Whoever was controlling them split quickly after I erased his command.

One by one, the Skin Shifters revealed themselves to the wolves, and slowly, we could see true independent thought coming from a few wolves as if awakening from a dream. Some of them shook their heads, and some whined and looked about as if they had no idea where they were. Some of them remained growling like us, or me in particular, because of what I am but not engaging.

The wolves stood still on the foggy forest floor, watching as each kachina shifter presented itself. Instinct had awoken. The Thunderbird inside them recognized itself in the Skin Shifters, and I knew then that the wolves were no longer a threat to us. And that is when I saw him.

My father was off in the far distance, running away from the pack he once controlled. He stopped the moment he noticed my eye on him. His form was magnified by the eyesight he bestowed upon me, and I could see him turn and transform into his true form.

For a short moment my heart called out to him. He was my father after all. I was his son. I wanted a relationship with him. Then Aiyana's face came into my memory and all those thoughts of reconciliation were cast away.

He was no stranger to wolf slavery, a practice he had used to control and manipulate, but as I have stated earlier, he wasn't a leader. There he stood, a large bat form, a ghastly figure haunted by years of regret and war. If a picture could tell a thousand words, his vision was a stark reminder of his ruthless nature and long history of brutality.

My father never tolerated competition; he kept his ghouls weak and only allowed fledgling Vampires to survive if they served to protect his castle. He couldn't bear the idea of anyone becoming strong enough to challenge him.

I held back, not revealing that I, too, had embraced my true form. I needed to be strategic, to bait him into a vulnerable position. As I watched him, I could see the burden of his past weighing heavily on him, yet he walked toward me with a slow, deliberate gait. It was a human walk, a curious choice given the circumstances, but I knew he was confident, perhaps too confident.

The wolves that had surrounded him moments earlier had suddenly fled, scattering into the forest that led to the back of the castle. I wasn't sure why they had left at first, but I sensed a familiar presence nearby—Andrei. The thunder that had rumbled through the sky earlier confirmed it. It was the same thunderous sound I had heard the first time I saw him, back when he was a wolfless boy, struggling to find his place in a new land full of Vampires.

The memory of that moment flashed in my mind. It was a time when the thunder seemed to herald the beginning of something new, something powerful. Now, it served as a reminder of the Werewolf spirit, an unwavering presence I had grown to love. It was the storm that followed them, the thunder spirit my Aiyana loved and adored. She was not my true mate, but that never stopped us from choosing each other.

Aiyana. I knew she was close, and her presence bolstered my resolve. My father might have been a master of control and fear, but this time, things were different. I was no longer the same person I had been under his thumb. I felt a surge of confidence and determination fill me like fuel for our impending confrontation.

As my father continued his slow approach through the forest, I remained calm, keeping my true nature hidden. I was ready to confront him, to stand my ground and protect those I cared about. The old dynamics of power and fear would no longer define our relationship. This time, I was prepared to face him, not as a submissive child but as an equal, ready to challenge him for control and, perhaps, for redemption.

I let out my fangs and geared myself to strike.

Mags

The moon hung high in the sky, casting a silvery glow over the sprawling gardens of the mansion. From my window, I could see the city lights twinkling in the distance, a world away from the prison I suddenly felt myself in. The estate, with its Gothic architecture and iron gates, was my father's way of keeping me safe. But to me, it was nothing more than a gilded cage. Another shackle like my beautiful bracelets that hindered my wolf and Vampire nature. More poison disguised as fake drugs to keep me "less feral". When was it going to end?

My heart yearned to run free, like a wild animal, unrestrained and driven by pure instinct, with no destination or goal in mind other than just allowing life to move me. Yet, my mind did hold a purpose. I needed to rescue my mother.

I paced the length of the room, my heart heavy with frustration and longing to join the fight. In the corner of the room, I saw a pile of neatly folded clothes that I had not noticed until now. Then suddenly, I realized those clothes belonged to me. Someone had packed up all my belongings from my foster house and brought them here. Even my beautiful owl kachina doll was there. I picked it up and hugged it.

Who had moved all this stuff here?

Just then, there was a tap on the door. And a woman I knew instantly came strutting in.

"Mrs Galindo?" I gasped in disbelief, surprised to see her here.

"Yes, Mags. I'm so sorry," she said, putting down one last thing in my pile of belongings.

"You're a ghoul," I said, looking at her, remembering the past—both mine and my father's. I remembered the night I first heard Luz speak to me. Galindo had climbed through my window and soothed me with compulsion. I remembered my father's instructions to her were to guard me with her life. I also remembered Carmen's slaps when I had lost it, and a tinge of anger flushed my face.

Other memories and times of her doing something similar came to mind as well, but I didn't say anything. She stood there looking at me sheepishly, fully aware that I had my memories returned. I decided to use this opportunity to help me escape.

"Again, I'm sorry I had to keep you away. Your father knows what he is doing. And so does your mate," she motioned towards the closed door as if he was right outside. "He just finished showering because the blood of the Uktena was too strong for my hunger. I . . . might have tried to bite him."

"You bit him?!" I asked, shocked. Was that a tinge of jealousy I felt? I didn't like the thought of her mouth on my mate.

"No, but I tried. I'm sorry," She said. "I wasn't going to kill him. I'm not strong enough anyway, but I couldn't help myself."

I gasped. I couldn't believe it. I tried to conceal my anger so she wouldn't get defensive. I needed her on my side. If these Vampires and ghouls had taught me anything, it was how to play chess with people's minds and actions. And I didn't need to know how to compel them to do that.

"So Carmen," I asked. "Is she a ghoul too?" I already knew the answer but I was trying to get her to open up. I knew she wasn't a fucking ghoul. She was just a greedy woman who enjoyed taking my father's money. Why he had me live with her is beyond me. But I asked because I needed to make her feel safe to answer me when I eventually asked for her help to escape.

"No, but she is compelled to believe you moved out. Which is why I brought you your things," said the ghoul.

"You have to get me out of here, Galindo," I said, reaching for my Docs and a new outfit for colder weather. I was really glad she brought my things. "I need to go find my mom," I told her again, reinforcing my ideas.

"I can't," said the ghoul. "And you cannot compel me to go against a stern order from my master. I cannot go against your father or mate. Sebastian put him in charge."

I gasped and looked up at her, forgetting about being half-naked in front of her. Was I really using compulsion just now? I didn't even know I could. And why did she have to call my father 'Master'? Seemed strange; he's not

Dracula.

Just then, Andy came in as I was dressing.

"Excuse me!" I said. His eyes widened before turning around and walking right out again. I was very angry at him. How could he just let me be imprisoned like this? My mother was in danger and Santana had given me a message earlier. I couldn't be here right now!

"Please, Mags, let me in. We have to talk, " he yelled through the closed door. I finished putting on my shirt and then a sweater. Great! All I had were Levis and a sweater to wear to Romania. It was summer, though, so I should be war-ready enough. I was ready to smash heads!

As I sat on the bed, applying my thick red lipstick, Andy had the nerve to walk in again. I rolled my eyes at him.

"What are you doing?" He said watching me put on make-up.

"I'm putting war paint on, FYI. I'm going to find my mother, and neither of you is going to stop me," I said, looking at Andy, who had just frozen and looked like he was off in la la land.

I stared at him a while longer, challenging him to say no to me. Galindo had walked out then, which I was happy about. The fewer people holding me back, the better. I stood up then and was about to walk out, too, when Andy grabbed my hand.

"Stop, you cannot keep me prisoner!" I said.

"You're right; I don't want to keep you prisoner," he said, and he turned to face me. His face looked different—paler as if he had seen a ghost.

"What's wrong with you?" I asked. He was still my mate. I was very angry, but he looked strange. We had not had the proper time to get to know each other as I would have liked, yet I still always felt right when he was around. Even when he was a rogue and gave me the creeps, something about me ached for him when he left me so quickly that night.

I know he cares about me. I can see all the things he has been doing to change, but right now, all I needed him to do was trust me. I had a mission!

The air was electric with tension. I placed my hand on his chest. I could feel his heart beating. It was strong.

"Trust me, Andy," I said into his embrace. "Don't be scared. If nothing else, just trust me."

He grabbed my hand then and said, "You're right. I do trust you."

Just then, Galindo returned to the room carrying a little black box. She gave it to Andy and then motioned towards me.

"These are hers," she said. If you're going to take her, then take all of her." She shrugged and walked out, mumbling, "You're in charge now. You'll have to answer to Sebastian, not me."

Galindo turned towards me then and said, "This is my apology to you. I don't know when or if your father was ever planning on returning these to you but if you're going to go into your homeland, you will need these." I nodded at her in understanding.

Curiously, Andy opened the small jewelry box. Inside were a pair of really long fangs. And as I looked at them, my body hungered for them as if I were staring at blood. A feeling that waxed and waned inside me these past couple of days.

"My fangs," I whispered, barely audible. Andy reached down and took them out, handling them with a reverence that matched the gravity of the moment. It was almost as if I could read his mind; the anticipation in the air was palpable. I opened my mouth, and as he pushed each fang back into my gums, a surge of power coursed through me. It was as if a long-lost piece of my soul had been returned, completing a part of me that had been missing.

The sensation was overwhelming—a heady mix of euphoria and an electrifying rush. I gasped with a really goofy smile but didn't care how I looked.

My senses sharpened instantly, and I felt more alive than I had even in the last few days after gaining my wolf. Every sound, scent, and flicker of light became intensely vivid, and a profound sense of strength and belonging washed over me.

This was more than just a physical restoration; it was a reclamation of my identity, a reawakening of the ancient force within me. As the final fang settled into place, I knew that I was whole again. I felt stronger than I ever had.

The world around me seemed to hum with a newfound energy, and I couldn't help but laugh, feeling an intoxicating blend of invincibility and purpose.

Andy kissed me then and the spark between our mate bond held us both captive to passion. Words could not explain how much I wanted to become part of him. To join him.

I looked at Andy again. I saw his fangs elongate and his face contorted into a wolf-like version of himself. "Are you ready?" he asked as his fangs glided along the crest of my neck.

"Yes," I answered back wholeheartedly.

He lifted me in his strong arms, his scent whirling around me like a cloud, and I felt at peace. I wanted him then more than I ever had, but we had work to do. He seemed to know this and looked into my eyes as he kissed me once more.

He walked us out onto the patio where the war party had initially gathered. He carried me like a bride under the night sky, and I felt the promise of freedom. The bonfire was completely out now, but I was warm in his embrace. With that, Andy leaped into the sky and with the quickness of shooting stars, we flew off to join the rest of the war party.

Andy

If the vision granted to me by the diamond hadn't come to me just then, I would have made the worst decision of my life.

The connection I felt with Magdalena was unlike anything I'd ever experienced. It was as if the boundaries between us blurred, the line between Werewolf and Vaewolf almost meaningless. But I couldn't ignore the nagging sense of caution that lingered in the back of my mind. Ash had warned me once before, but at that moment, while our bodies were crushed together, I wasn't thinking of anything else but her.

The Uktena's diamond had granted me a vision and a warning when I entered Magdalenas room for the second time. It shook me to my core. And its visual was one I could not ignore.

In the vision, I found myself walking through an ancient, mist-filled forest. The air was thick with the scent of jasmine and rose, and a soft glow emanated from the ground, illuminating a pattern of roots that seemed to pulse with life. As I moved deeper into the forest, the trees around me grew taller and more imposing, their branches intertwining above to form a dense canopy. Suddenly, an ethereal wolf appeared before me, its eyes shining like stars. Its white fur shimmered in the moonlight, and its presence exuded a sense of wisdom and power. I knew instantly that this was a spirit guide, a manifestation of ancient knowledge.

The wolf's gaze locked onto mine, and in that moment, a flood of images overwhelmed me. I saw Magdalena, caught in a state of flux, her form shimmering as if trapped between two worlds. She reached out to me, and as her fingers touched my skin, a sharp, searing pain radiated through my chest. I looked down to see a dark mark forming where she had touched me, spreading like a shadow across my body. My heartbeat slowed, my breath became shallow, and an icy fear gripped me. In the vision, I saw myself changing—my eyes losing their vibrant color, my wolf spirit fading away, replaced by the cold, lifeless pallor of a hollow Vampire.

The spirit wolf growled a deep, resonant sound that seemed to echo through the forest. It stepped protectively between Magdalena and me, its message unmistakable. If Magdalena marked me before she achieved her true form, it would spell disaster. I would lose my wolf nature and forever change into something else, something not entirely a wolf or a Vampire. The thought was unbearable, the potential consequences too severe to ignore.

Then, the vision shifted. I saw Magdalena and me standing on a battlefield, the tension of impending conflict thick in the air. There was no mark, no painful transformation—only an understanding, a mutual respect for the boundaries that needed to be maintained. The spirit wolf was still there, watching over us, its eyes softer now, almost approving.

As the vision faded, I snapped back into reality, my heart pounding in my chest. The warning was clear, and the weight of the responsibility settled heavily on my shoulders. Despite my deep feelings for Magdalena, I knew I had to resist the temptation to mark her—at least until she had received her true form. If she ever did. Her parents suffered the same fate, unable to mark each other because of his Vampire nature. Ash howled in my mind, a sad and longing howl. The risk was simply too great. I couldn't lose my wolf, nor could I allow her to make a decision that would seal her fate before she fully understood her own nature.

I knew what I had to do. Without hesitation, I whisked us away to the war front in Romania. The chaos and urgency of the battlefield would serve as a distraction, keeping our minds focused on the task at hand and away from the dangerous temptation of marking each other.

To my surprise, though, she wasn't feeling the same way about marking me. At least she didn't seem to be bothered by the interruption at all. She was ready to leave for Romania. Maybe I confused her euphoria for something else? Her new fangs?

As I carried her in my arms, her gorgeous thick black hair wisped around my face, and her scent was all over me. I did not shift this time to travel. Since no longer being a rogue, I could borrow Ash's speed anytime I needed in human form. I was able to keep her closer to me this way. Maybe I was more in love with her than she was with me, but it didn't really matter. She was here with me now, smiling up at me, so excited to be part of the fight.

I know that a Vampire could never turn my wolf away from me, no matter how much it bit me. It was only the sacred act of a mate bond that could do such a thing. It had to be consensual. I would have to be willing to expose my wolf's soul in order to do such a thing. So fighting against other

Vampires would not put me in danger. The Skin Shifters, though, were vulnerable, but they had their silver to protect them. Just like I could not turn a Vampire into a Werewolf with my bite. But something inside me told me that Magdalena would soon have her true form, and I would perform the sacred act of the mate bond with her soon.

I could smell it on her. Her body was changing. What I didn't know was if she'd be able to handle the transformation. I hugged her closer to my body. She kissed my cheeks and neck as we flew in the night together.

She seemed to understand everything I was thinking even though we could not mind-link.

Did you forget I could speak to her wolf when you two touch? Ash said, his voice bringing me out of my reverie. *She knows what you're thinking. She knows we will pick the right time to make her ours.* That last part, he growled out, barely making it audible. He and Luz were lost in their own conversations.

As we arrived in Romania, the air was thick with the scent of impending conflict. The distant sounds of battle and the occasional howl of Werewolf echoed through the night. My wolves. I knew we had little time to waste. These wolves were my people. Tricked into fighting against us by compulsion. I hoped that Sebastian realized just how much I did not want them harmed. Instinctively, I let my fangs out at the thought and howled into the night air.

With Magdalena by my side, I closed my eyes and tapped into my farsight ability, reaching out with my mind to locate our comrades. The process was always a bit disorienting, like peering through a foggy window into a world beyond.

Images and sensations flickered in my vision, a chaotic jumble of sights and sounds.

After a moment of concentration, the vision started to sharpen. I saw the river where I had once made a desperate escape, its waters dark and swift. The memory of that night came rushing back—the fear, the adrenaline, the narrow escape from a pack of relentless Vampires. The river's course was still the same, winding its way through the landscape like a serpentine guardian. I followed its flow with my mind, tracing it to the ancient catacombs hidden beneath a crumbling fortress. These catacombs were a maze of tunnels and chambers, long forgotten by most but still holding echoes of the past. It was a place steeped in history, shadowed by secrets and dark energies.

I knew these catacombs well. They lead to the back of Valerian's castle.

The vision of the catacombs solidified, and I knew it was the perfect place to regroup and strategize. It was hidden, out of reach of the prying eyes of both Vampires and humans. But more importantly, it offered a sanctuary where we could plan our next move without interference. I opened my eyes and turned to Magdalena, the urgency clear in my expression.

"We need to go to the catacombs," I said, my voice steady. "It's safe, and we can pick up some supplies there."

Magdalena nodded, her eyes filled with a mix of determination and concern. We moved quickly, making our way to a hidden cache where I had stored some old belongings—relics of a time when I hunted Vampires without mercy. The wardrobe I pulled out was a set of old leathers, worn and scarred from countless battles. They were infused with the scent of Vampire blood, a scent that could cloak us from detection, masking our true nature.

Incidentally they belonged to the first vampire I killed with the strange child ghouls.

I handed Magdalena the long, dark coat, the fabric still heavy with the faint, metallic tang of dried blood. "Put this on," I instructed. "It'll help hide your scent and give you some protection."

She squinted her nose at it. "Is this . . . blood?"

“Yes, Vampire blood. It will cover your scent. Put it on, please,” I emphasized again, feeling protective of her even more so now that we had arrived.

As she donned the coat, I quickly replaced my own clothing with my old hunting leathers. The familiar weight of the gear was both comforting and sobering, a reminder of the harsh realities we faced. I had brought my old trusty hat with me. Complete with a Uktena feather plume.

Once dressed, we looked at each other, a silent understanding passing between us. The disguises were more than just a practical necessity; they were a link to my past, a nod to the Vampire hunter I had once been.

“So my father was right. You were a Vampire hunter in Romania,” she said, unsure as to what to think about it.

“Yes, but it was a very long time ago when I was just trying to survive,” I said, hoping I wouldn’t scare her off.

“When you were a rogue. You were wearing this type of clothing when I first met you. Were you going to kill me?” I gasped as I looked up at her solemn face.

“Never,” I answered truthfully. I didn’t even know you were part Vampire until I was close. I truthfully thought you were a wolf, a type of rogue yourself until Ash smelled our mate bond.” I stayed silent for a moment. Unsure how to

continue. “I was scared, I guess.”

“Scared of what?” she asked, looking surprised. “Me?”

“No, I was afraid you would reject me,” I admitted. “I was a rogue, unworthy of you. One of the reasons I left so quick.”

She hugged me again. A long and tight squeeze. "You were right."

I blinked, unsure as to what she meant.

"I was also a type of rogue. I still am, just different because I'm also part Vampire. I need to go through what you went through. That is why I had to come."

Then, the vision from the mansion made even more sense to me.

She loves us! Howled Ash in my head and I smiled as I returned her hug.

I smiled then. "Yes, I suppose you have your mission as well. Do I frighten you in these clothes?"

"Not at all," she answered. "I like the way they look on you, actually."

She better be careful how she talks to me right now or else I'd have to take her in the forest. Standing so close to her, her scent filling my nostrils, it was driving Ash crazy.

"Doesn't it anger you?" I asked. "Knowing I have killed some of your people?" I hoped she wouldn't see me differently, having hunted her father's family, but I desperately needed to change the subject.

"No, but I was wondering if we could try that trick that Tecos did with my father so I could see and understand," she said, sounding unsure.

I stopped fidgeting with my swords and gear then and looked at her again.

"I am willing to give it a try," I said. What could be the harm? She had her fangs now, I thought to myself. "Let me do it," I said. "Don't want you to be tempted to take more." I said with a grin.

Quickly, I reached out and with a prick from my teeth, I drew blood on my wrist. Carefully, I picked up a few drops with my other hand as I watched my wound instantly close up and heal. I placed my bloody thumb in her mouth and wiped it across her fangs.

Her eyes slowly blinked closed and then opened, and I watched as her pupils dilated, expanding until they filled the entirety of both her eyes. She stood there like a perfect Greek statue, her expression serene yet unnervingly vacant. I wondered for a second if that is how I looked when I used the diamond for farsight. Her empty stare seemed to pierce through the walls of the catacombs, gazing into a supernatural realm that only she could see. In that moment, she appeared otherworldly, an ethereal presence caught between the spirit and the physical. Blood was her conduit into the spirit world. The sight sent a shiver down my spine, a reminder of the vast, mysterious powers within her, which were still unfolding and yet to be fully understood.

It dawned on me that I was probably her first real taste of blood. And it was probably a little too strong for her to handle being a Werewolf and all. But before I had a chance to worry, she snapped out of her statue-like presence.

"I want more," she said with a new hunger in her eyes.

"You will get more on the battlefield," I said quickly, fumbling with my swords again.

"Of course," she stated, realizing the severity of our situation.

Just then, she reached for a silver sword, swirled it above her head, and quickly brought it down to land on an empty tomb next to us. It was quicker than I had ever seen her move before. Exactly what memory did she pluck out of my blood to warrant her becoming an instant expert with a sword, I wonder?

"Why don't you carry this one as well?" I said, handing her a small dagger. "There is an inside pocket right here." I opened her coat and exposed her just enough to show her the pocket. I nervously ran my hand through my hair, realizing just how intimate a gesture that was.

Focus! said Ash.

"Oh, you're one to talk!" I replied back.

"Hm?" muttered Mags, not paying me any mind. She adjusted the dagger in her pocket, then buckled the jacket again.

"Nothing. I was just wondering why you had one of Santana's medicine bags around your neck," I said, hoping she wouldn't notice my shenanigans.

She looked up at me with the sweetest smile as she tucked the bag into the coat as well. She noticed. Vampires can sense blood and pulsations, arousal.

"It was a gift from Santana. Are you ready?" Now, she was hiding something from me. I thought I noticed a change of scent on her, nervousness, rebellion, but I shooed the thoughts away. We didn't have time.

With our preparations complete, we made our way through the shadowed streets and toward the entrance to the catacombs that would eventually lead us into the castle. The air grew cooler as we descended into the ancient tunnels, the walls lined with the bones of the long-dead. It was a haunting place, but it was safe. Here, surrounded by the echoes of history and the scent of old blood, we could plan our next move: finding her mother.

As we settled into the catacombs, I felt a strange sense of calm. My wolves were near, my family. My mate is by my side. What else could a wolf ask for?

"I can smell my mother!" she said as we neared the back entrance to the castle where Sebastian's father ruled for centuries.

"Andy, she's calling to me!" I turned my head, but I couldn't hear anything. When I looked back at Mags, she was gone. She had taken off in a shadow sprint.

I searched with farsight and found nothing. As much as I had her scent memorized, with that coat on, her scent diminished by the second. When I came back from searching with farsightedness, it was barely a faint whisper.

"Mags! Come back! It's the Wendigo!" I yelled, but she didn't answer me.

She was already too far. She was so fast now. To the east, I could hear Sebastian confronting Valerian, his father. My family's wolves were so near, less than a mile away and they needed a ruler. I was their alpha! Not that coward and traitor Rufis or Valerian! Without an alpha, the wolves were confused about what to do. Their scents gave off confusion and hesitation. And I knew they could not smell me because my scent was disguised.

But I knew they could feel me, as I felt them. I was their alpha, their guard. It was a type of ethereal aura they could sense, but they didn't know where I was.

Confusion was afoot. And what was it that Tecos said? Confusion is what the Wendigo wanted.

I couldn't leave Magdalena, though. Her scent was faint but still traceable, lingering like a thread leading me into the depths of the castle. Just as I was about to descend, a loud and boisterous thunderclap resonated through the sky above me. The sound was powerful, almost primal, and sent a tremor through the ground beneath my feet. A few seconds later, an intense light erupted from my eyes, as if I had become a conductor for the lightning that split the heavens above.

It took me a moment to comprehend what had happened. The Uktena's diamond, the ancient artifact I carried, had been the conduit once again. The gem was known for its mystical properties, rumored to connect the earthly realm with the spirit world, and it had now channeled the energy of the storm directly through me. My vision cleared, and I heard them—long-lost howls and yips, the unmistakable sounds of my old pack. They echoed through the night, growing louder, more distinct as if the storm had summoned them from the very edges of the universe back towards me.

I paused, turning around to see them emerge from the shadows. My wolves—strong, fierce, and loyal as always—came rushing toward me, their eyes reflecting the same loyalty and recognition that they always had for my father. They had found me, after all, without my scent; after all this time, we were suddenly face to face again. The bond we shared was unbroken, transcending time and distance. As they approached, I felt a surge of pride and responsibility. They looked to me, their alpha, for guidance, and I knew that I couldn't let them down.

For a brief moment, I stood there, watching them approach, their howls mingling with the rolling thunder. The power of the storm, the mystical energy of the Uktena's diamond, and the return of my pack all felt like a powerful blessing. My wolves had instantly accepted me as their alpha just as they had accepted my father many years before, reaffirming the bond that was stronger than any other force in my life. With them by my side, I felt invincible, ready to face whatever challenges lay ahead.

I turned back toward the castle, determination hardening my resolve. I had a mission to complete, a duty to protect Magdalena and my pack. With the loyalty of my wolves at my back, I descended into the darkness.

The air was thick with an eerie silence as I wandered through the desolate landscape. Suddenly, within the periphery of my vision, I caught the fluid movement of a familiar type of enemy: Vampires. An old cemetery blocked the back entrance to the castle, and they were breaking themselves out of hibernation. I had never fought ancient Vampires like these in all my years as a wolfless child Werewolf hiding out in Romania as a Vampire hunter. These were not the common variety.

These were true ancients, having slumbered and hibernated in the ground for an unknown number of years. Their presence felt like a heavy weight pressing down on the atmosphere. The ground where they rose was left barren and scorched, an indication of the dormant power they possessed. Each movement they made was deliberate and filled with the wisdom of countless centuries.

Their pale, almost translucent skin had a ghostly blue hue, a testament to their unique biology, making them appear both otherworldly and dangerously volatile. I knew that any spark of lightning could ignite them in a fiery blaze, but their ancient knowledge made them cautious, calculating each step they took.

Their eyes locked onto me with an intensity that sent shivers down my spine. These ancient beings were not just predators; they were living chronicles of a bygone era, carrying with them the secrets and shadows of the past.

"Vampire hunter!" shrieked one particularly ghastly undead Vampire woman from nearby.

"Wolf! You are no match for us!" sputtered another, black blood spilling from its mouth, congealing as he spoke. They spoke in an ancient tongue I had no knowledge of, but the translation was made imminent to my soul.

Then, one form stood above them all, a shadow overlooking the balcony from the castle, peered down at us with an arrogant grin. Regis. The coward refused to join the fight even with hundreds of ancient Vampires by his side. He was trying to compel my wolves, MY pack, again, but from the looks of it, not one of my wolves was having any of it.

As the ancient Vampires surrounded my wolves, I realized that this encounter was not just a battle for survival. It was a confrontation with history itself, with entities that had seen the rise and fall of empires and whose existence was a testament to the enduring nature of darkness. Vampires never liked Werewolves. Perhaps because, as these realize now, deep inside, they knew they were no real match for us as a pack. They took rogues as pets and enslaved them. They couldn't control this many pack members though, not with their alpha by their side.

And this time, though, I was no longer a boy. No longer wolfless or a rogue. I had my own ancients with me, too. My pack was older than time and some of my fearless fighters were even older than I. I recognized some of them. And they recognized me: their prince, their missing alpha.

Wolves never backed down from a fight; in fact, when backed up against a wall, we were even more ruthless. I felt the power of the diamond start to churn inside me, a deep, pulsating energy that surged through my veins like molten lava. My vision began to blur and then it went completely white, a blinding light that signaled the awakening of an ancient force within me. This was it, the ultimate battle for which I had been preparing my entire life.

As I stood there, bathed in the radiant glow of the diamond's power, I could sense my wolves close in. Their growls echoed in the silence, low and threatening, resonating with the anticipation that hung heavy in the air. Each one of them was ready to leap into action at my command.

The ancient Vampires, with their ghostly blue skin and eyes that held the weight of centuries, paused momentarily as if recognizing the power I now wielded. Their hesitation was brief, but it was enough to remind me that even the oldest of beings could still fear death.

I threw down the silver swords I once used as a child and let them pierce the ground, waves of electricity traveling up and down the bars like natural conductors.

Drawing on the diamond's energy, I felt a surge of strength and clarity. My mind sharpened, focusing on the task ahead. In a communal strike, I sent out licks of lightning from my eyes, hitting each of my wolves within the vicinity and igniting them with power. Within seconds, each wolf had communed with the diamond, and soon, they, too, harbored the ancient power of the diamond. Only it wasn't the diamond causing this transformation. It was the power of the Thunderbird.

In the sky, I witnessed an ancient bird soaring through clouds, its wingspan unmatchable by any earthly bird. Its call was a deafening roar that commanded attention.

Torito. Only it wasn't him. It truly was the spirit of the Thunderbird.

We were ancient people with ancient customs and traditions that had not been taught to me, but they remained ingrained in the very fabric of my being. These memories, buried deep within me like DNA, began to unravel, revealing the true power of the Thunderbird within me. The diamond did not simply work because it had once belonged to the Uktena. It was the power of the Thunderbird that I drew from it like a concertmaster directing with fierce precision with a chorus of death howls. And now my wolves shared in this power too.

As the energy flowed from the diamond to my wolves, I could see the transformation in their eyes. They gleamed with a newfound power, a bright, electric blue that mirrored the lightning now coursing through them. The few ancients that had been standing a little too close to my wolves also tasted the power and were obliterated by it. The bond between my pack and I strengthened, forged anew by the shared power. A ferocious howl escaped my mouth as I shredded the old Vampire hunting gear, and I went on all fours to my wolf form.

The ancient Vampires, sensing the shift in power, recoiled slightly, their ghostly blue skin almost blending with the pale moonlight. They recognized the ancient force that now stood against them, a power as old as they were, if not older. The air crackled with tension, the scent of ozone sharp and biting.

My wolves and I moved as one, a synchronized force of nature, ready to confront the darkness that had risen from the ground. The memories of my ancestors guided my movements, and each strike was imbued with the wisdom and strength of those who had come before me.

I tore through them limb by limb like a wild animal, without thought and without hesitation. The ones that tried to run were instantly shot down by lightning and obliterated. The hunt. It was all Ash and I set our minds on.

That is until I heard the piercing cry from Magdalena in the background. Regis.

With my hackles up and fangs blaring, I swept past the sea of Vampire blood spray that now surrounded the vicinity like rain.

Once inside the castle, the scene before me was both heart-wrenching and infuriating. Regis tightly gripped Magdalena, his hold on her a display of cruel dominance.

"Coward!" I growled hoarsely in my wolf form, my voice trembling with a rage unlike no other.

"Wendigo told me why he kept you alive," said the traitor.

Tecos

Everything had converged to this fateful juncture. While Sebastian remained ensnared in the sinister clutches of his power-hungry father, I pursued the Wendigo—an ancient entity imbued with magic as formidable as my own. Our prior encounters were mere skirmishes, trivial compared to the storm brewing now. The origins of the Wendigo's curse were cloaked in enigma—some murmured it was the Creator's wrath, others spoke of a vengeful shaman, or perhaps it was the result of their own tragic descent. A sacred law had been shattered, darkness had seeped into their core, igniting a hunger that surpassed even a Vampire's insatiable thirst for blood.

Tonight, the Wendigo wore the guise of the Uktena. An old skin-shifter like myself. Completely human, yet graced by the feather of the Thunderbird. The Uktena were a tribe of Skin Shifters that had run away from the Thunderbirds' teachings. They were a type of cursed rogue Skin Shifter. And now it was an even greater curse as a Wendigo possessed it—two dark, powerful beings in one. I would make sure I took it down now before it got even stronger.

The unsettling thought that he had already entangled Aiyana in a mate bond gnawed at me, but I had to focus. As I readied myself for the confrontation, Torito, the young Thunderbird spirit, appeared beside me.

"I'm with you, brother," he said, his voice vibrant with youthful resolve. Though new to battles of this magnitude, his bravery shone through. He was prepared to risk everything to summon the Uktena spirit and lure its skin away from the Wendigo. He jumped into the air and shifted into the mighty predator bird—a sight to behold. Our roles were clear—I as the medicine man, and he as the guardian.

A blast of thunder and lightning hit the skies like no other I had ever seen, commanding respect and attention.

I summoned my power, conjuring a roaring fire at the center of the clearing, where I suspected the Wendigo awaited. Santana soared above as well, her cries piercing the night as she called upon the ancestors for their guidance. I channeled every ounce of my magic into the flames, using words of power to ignite a towering inferno of raw elemental force. In went copper shavings from the sacred caverns to keep the fire going strong. It turned the flames into a haunting greenish glow. Then went the cornmeal to seal the spirit of the Wendigo in the fire. Corn was the Creators food and because Wendigo detested it, it was what subdued it. Then went the cleansing agents of sage, cedar and sweetgrass. Tonight, one of us would fall—either I or the Wendigo.

As the fire blazed, I chanted in an ancient tongue, the words flowing from my soul as if they had been carved into me. I invoked the winds, metals, earth, and flowing water, casting these elements into the searing blaze. Torito danced beside me, his movements a delicate rhythm meant to call out the Uktena spirit within the Wendigo. His role was crucial, but the true battle was mine to fight. This was not merely a physical struggle but a spiritual duel that only a shaman with centuries of wisdom could hope to win.

This was my destiny, the very purpose for which the Creator had extended my life. It was the reason I had recently been forged into a spiritual warrior. This revelation I felt in my soul. As these thoughts crystallized my resolve, a chilling whisper slithered through the air, unsettling my confidence. The Wendigo was near.

"I see you, owl," a haunting voice neither male nor female, slithered from the shadows.

"Leave now!" I commanded Torito, whose spirit was still high in the night sky, but his body was still dancing beside me. Yet as he turned to leave, a vile green fog erupted from the beast's maw, ensnaring him and dragging him back, tossing him against a nearby tree with a sickening thud. The Wendigo's breath was a toxic miasma, suffocating and malevolent. Above, Santana's piercing screech cut through the night. She had also been hit, but not as badly. She came crashing down to Toritos' side and attempted to whisk him away but could not.

Before the Wendigo could turn its deadly breath toward them again, I bellowed its true name—a sacred, resonant word infused with ancient magic. Santana had mind-linked it to me just in time before she passed out.

"Uhu-Tal!" I yelled into the night air.

The Wendigo recoiled, its monstrous form faltering as the utterance of its true name shattered its dark power. Santana's screech had revealed the name to her before crashing, a crucial fragment of knowledge that exposed the beast. The name held immense power, binding the Wendigo to the laws it had once transgressed. For a fleeting, critical moment, the creature was vulnerable, its defenses weakened by the truth of its identity.

"Uhu-Tal, little bird on the mountain, I banish you from the physical realm. Your leathers are no longer yours, and I tear the crown of antlers from your head," I proclaimed, offering thanks to the ancestors who had revealed his name to Santana for us. It was his own ancestors—the ones he had mercilessly consumed to steal their magic—who had exposed him.

In that moment, the Wendigo was trapped by an invisible prison, its garments stripped away. The spirit of the Uktena, having already met its physical demise, drifted from the Wendigo as if its spirit were concealed within its discarded clothes. The Wendigo growled and shrieked, pulling an arm free and hurling curses in an ancient tongue at the robes and antler crown tethered to the Uktena spirit, halting its descent into the fire.

Suddenly, the robes turned and noticed the injured Thunderbird on the ground next to a weakened female owl. It began its procession toward them, threatening doom and malice.

At that instant, Coyote arrived and transformed itself into a type of Thunderbird as well. Flashing its vibrant feathers near the fire, the Uktena took notice and changed its course to the new Thunderbird.

Suddenly, the bear kachina arrived, guiding both Santana and Torito from the fight on its back. I wasn't sure of Torito's survival, but I nodded to the remaining kachinas who stood by to assist him.

The Uktena spirit shrieked as it entered the ethereal spirit flames, sending clouds of black smoke into the air.

Suddenly, darkness enveloped me, and I found myself in a familiar dimension—a type of spirit world—just the Wendigo and me. Somehow, he had transported us here. His presence surrounded me from all directions, his voice echoing as if he were everywhere all at once.

"I know your name too, little drunk owl," he sneered, opening his mouth to pronounce my name. How he knew it was a mystery, but I would not allow him to complete his incantation. Suddenly, something caught my keen owl ears—his location.

He had overlooked one critical aspect of owl powers: our mastery of echolocation—the greatest of hunters even in complete darkness. I extended my claws and grasped his bony ribs. He yelled and I shrieked back at him, as we were expelled from the spirit world. We both fell back into the living world, and I rushed to carry his bony carcass to the heart of the funeral pyre.

I was almost there when I felt a piercing at my side. The Wendigo had a hold of me with his toothy snout. We descended together into the fire.

We burned together, but I clung to him, unwilling to release him or let him speak my name. I shrieked until my breath was spent and my feathers were consumed by the flames. Our bodies burned as one as I fought to keep him from escaping. When my strength faltered, I used the remnants of my beak to tear out his tongue and eyes from his lifeless form. When its tongue was shredded, and its eyes were nothing but sand and dust, I went for its heart. I tore through it like a sword using my beak, severing it from the rest of its body and rendering it obsolete.

I would not allow this creature a chance to return. Wendigos are a type of deranged frost spirit. I knew the fire would kill him, but I didn't know that my time would come at the same time as his. And now that it has, I accept my fate, sacrificing myself for the others. That's what medicine men do. We take care of our people.

The Creator had granted me this opportunity, and I would not waste it. The night was still young, but I hoped I had managed to turn the tide for the rest of those I leave behind. With the advantage now on our side, I braced myself for the final resolution. One of us was supposed to meet our end in the fire, but now it looked as if both of us would. It did not dishearten me, I was determined to see this ancient foe fall.

I continued to peck at him until the world around me turned black, and I heard Santana's final cry before I left this world—my Santana. I had never really had a chance to live a good, full life with her as a human. I wanted to give her a home, a real home. Better than the one she lost and mourned over after it burned down. Not an empty nest. Or a temporary cave.

Looking back at our time together, I can tell there were many instances where she missed being a human woman.

She wanted to dance, make beautiful clothes for herself, wear silver jewelry, sing with her heart and not just shriek, have children, and live in the sun, yet we were confined to the shadows for centuries. What good is it to know all about death and the unknown valleys of shadows if one does not know the light?

The owl was her first form and my fourth. There were no other animal forms for me to take now. My totem is complete. I wanted to see her fly, not just as an owl but as a true woman who had so much taken from her and yet never let her spirit die. My heart smiles now, thinking about what other wonderful forms Santana would take after I am gone. Perhaps an eagle or a beautiful deer—something graceful and beautiful.

I never regretted saving her. Not once, even when we were trapped in our skins. I only regret not being able to fulfill her wants and desires. Perhaps another man, greater than I, will come and give her those things for me. That is all I ask of the Creator. Is for someone good to enter her life.

A spirit appeared then as if being called. A human-looking spirit appeared to me in a golden light, and he spoke to me, urging me to leave the flames. He was beautiful and radiated love and light. Had my Creator come for me at last to take me home? The Great Spirit who is in all of us. I noticed he appeared to be tossing something else into the fire—something that glittered like gold, pollen.

"Is the Wendigo dead?" I asked, eyes tightly closed, though still being able to see him in my mind like a vision. I wouldn't leave unless I knew he was gone.

"It is done," the spirit assured. As I slowly emerged from the fire, the spirit revealed itself fully, and a beautiful white light enveloped us. We had entered a different spirit world—a realm of love and serenity, unlike the oppressive darkness of the one prior. The pain of the fire vanished, and I could breathe again as if I had never been burned.

This spirit was unlike anything I had ever seen—neither the Owl, Thunderbird, Caribou or Raven spirits in my past had ever glowed this vibrantly with a golden hue when they came to me. It felt very human and regal. Yet when it spoke or moved, I saw remnants of my four past animal shapes come through as if they were a fusion of all my previous forms, with an additional presence—man.

"Am I getting a new creature?" I asked, gazing up at its majestic form. The form moved, and suddenly, it was a collaboration of all my forms all at once. It was my totem, revealed. Tears welled in my eyes as I marveled at its beauty. Like an angelic cherub, it carried the presence of the Creator and his creations all in one body.

"Not new," the spirit replied. "But new for you. You have reached completion for this world and will enter your final form. You will no longer need leather to shift; those are obsolete for you. I am replacing the skins with my essence. As an Elder and Holy man, you will guide your people into the coming new phase of the world, ushering them into the world's final phase. Do you accept this form?"

The being spoke, and my whole spirit lit up at his news. So I am not leaving—not yet. I have more things to do for the Creator. I was ready.

"Yes," I cried out. "A hundred times, yes."

"Medicine man," the Golden Man spoke, his voice rumbling like distant thunder, steady and powerful. His eyes, golden and eternal, pierced through me. "It is then time to leave the old mountain. The place you have clung to is no longer your home. That mountain is death and destruction now, teaming with fire and lightning. It will destroy anything that comes too close, and if you stay, it will consume you too."

His words struck deep, my heart trembling under their weight. I had lived on that mountain for what felt like lifetimes, enduring its storms, its rage, thinking that was the path I had to walk. But now, he was telling me to leave it behind.

"You must journey to a new mountain before your transformation can take place," the Golden Man continued, his voice softening though the power in it remained. "This new mountain is sacred and holy. It will not burn you but give you life. It will not destroy but heal. You must go there, for it is where your true self awaits."

I stood frozen, my breath caught in my chest. Could I really leave everything behind? I did not know if he meant a spiritual mountain or a physical one, but instinctively, I felt as if it might be both. The old mountain was the place of my trials and battles, the site of all the pain and anger I had ever known, and it was sacred to me. It had shaped me, forged me in its unforgiving fires. And yet, deep down, I knew he was right. The old mountain no longer gave me strength; it drained me, broke me. It was time.

"Medicine man, there is one last thing to do while we walk," the Golden Man said, his voice pulling me back into the present. "If you can accept this, then I will grant you your final form."

My body tensed, my heart pounding as I nodded. "Okay, I'll do it," I gasped, eager yet terrified. I would do anything, *everything*, for my Creator.

"You must become as pure as silver," the Golden Man explained, his voice unwavering. "Pure and refined, without blemish. To become a Holy man, you must be tried by fire first on this mountain, by kiln. If you can remove the impurities from your heart, then—only then—you will be able to travel with me to the new mountain and be granted your new form."

His words weighed heavy in the air, as if they were sacred and tangible, not just spoken sounds. The fire in his eyes seemed to burn through me into the depths of my soul, where all my secrets lay hidden.

"Yes," I whispered, barely able to breathe. "Anything." I leaned forward, desperate to know what the task was. Eager to move, to change.

"You must conquer anger and master forgiveness," he said, and the ground beneath me seemed to tilt. "Forgive your enemies."

"Forgive them?" I repeated, my voice trembling with disbelief. Forgive them? Did he mean the Vampires? The colonizers? After everything they had done, what did this have to do with me?

"You must let go of your anger and old resentments," he said, his tone as steady as ever, but there was something more—something compassionate in his gaze. "Forgive your enemies and yourself as your ancestors forgave each other after the Thunderbird I sent. You will then have your glory. You cannot carry the fire of hatred and expect love to bloom in its place. For love to grow in your heart, the anger must go."

Suddenly, as if some floodgate had opened, memories surged to the surface—memories I had buried deep within, the ones I thought I had forgotten. But they had only been sleeping, waiting for a moment like this to rise up and drown me. I saw the faces of my people, their agony as they were destroyed by the enemies I could never forgive. I saw the villages burned, the innocence stolen, the lives shattered. I saw Santana, and her family tortured and murdered before her eyes, not just by people but by Vampires, and her soul was left broken. I saw the countless innocents who had fallen to the brutality of those who did not deserve forgiveness.

"But why, Creator?" I asked, my voice cracking with the weight of sorrow and fury. "Why should I forgive them? They are not my people. They are not holy or good. They don't deserve forgiveness. My people deserve justice."

The Golden Man's gaze held mine, unflinching. "They are all my people and your people too. All my creations. From the lowly crawling things to humans and the birds in the sky," he said softly, and the gentleness in his tone felt like a balm, even as it stung. "An eagle flies high during the day because that is who he is. An owl flies stealthily at night, hiding from the world because that is who he is. But a Holy man does good and harbors no ill will—not because others are good, but because *he* is good. To rise to the next level, to reach the new mountain, you must become like the Creator. Pure and holy."

Tears welled up in my eyes, hot and burning as they spilled down my face. The pain was unbearable, like a jagged knife tearing through my soul. How could I let go of this anger, this need for righteous vengeance? It was easier said than done. It had fueled me for so long. It had been my companion through the dark nights, my reason for standing tall after everything was taken from me.

"Let me show you what your owl could not show you." said the Golden Man, his voice like a low rumble of thunder. He raised his hand above my head and moved it clockwise over me, and the world shifted.

In an instant, everything went black, and my soul was yanked through a suffocating, narrow tunnel of swirling shadows. Red. All I could see was red. Blood stained the earth of my homeland, seeping into the soil that once thrived with life. My people, the ones I had sworn to protect, lay broken, scattered like fallen leaves in the wind. I felt a sudden hollowness in my chest as the memories flooded back, the ones I had buried deep within me, forgotten by choice or by curse.

The owl had called to me then—its wings cutting through the silence, its cry piercing the night as it circled above the ruins. It knew my thirst for revenge, sensed the rage simmering within me, and I welcomed it. I could see it now, clearer than ever. I had embraced the owl's spirit and called on its ancient magic, the power that had been forbidden to me. My hands, trembling and bloodied, performed the rites, and I whispered to *Gitche Manitou*, pleading for death, not just for the invaders who had torn through my people, but for all of them. The hunger for vengeance swallowed me whole.

Images of a crazed owl man, demonic in nature, raged through the lands, killing anything and everything in its wake. In its blood rage, it did not differentiate between the people and the colonizers. Did not judge or weigh a conscience once. It simply killed anyone and everyone in its path.

This was me.

I had forgotten . . . *How* had I forgotten? My mind raced as I watched this version of myself, this twisted reflection, perform the dark rituals. It was like staring at a stranger who wore my face. I had cursed myself with death. The owl had carried me then, consumed me. I had abandoned everything I once was—my vows, my soul—becoming something monstrous, something unrecognizable. No longer a shaman, but what these modern people now call, a skinwalker.

The memories, vivid and sharp, pierced through the fog of my mind. *Now you remember,* the owl spirit whispered, its voice cold and heavy with judgment. *"You became like a rogue. That is why you left your people; they rejected you even though you had come to avenge them. They knew the right way. So you wandered alone for years on your dark mission as a rogue. Cut off from me and Gitche Manitou. Until you found Santana and consumed the blessing in your bond, then, and only then did your bloodshed end. But it wasn't redemption, Tecos. It was hate. You used me. Used my powers for evil and I was your prisoner.*

I had never spoken to my owl spirit through a mind link, as if I were a Werewolf like Andrei. Skin Shifters did not have the same type of attachment.

My chest tightened, and a screech, loud and anguished, echoed in the air. Not mine, but the owl's. The owl spirit stood beside me, watching as my past unraveled like a nightmare on the horizon. The scenes unfolded with cruel clarity: the carnage, the destruction, the madness. My hands, my heart, drenched in blood. Night after night, I hunted, killed, and revoled in the chaos. I had become what I swore I never would.

"Stop!" I cried, my voice hoarse with the weight of my sins. "Please! I can't . . . I can't watch any more." My body trembled, though I knew I was in spirit form, but it felt too real—too much like that part of me still lived.

I collapsed to my knees in the vision, broken and hollow, ashamed to lift up my face and look into the eyes of the owl spirit in front of me, my guide. Then, as swiftly as it had begun, I was pulled back. The present washed over me like a wave, and I found myself face-to-face with the Golden Man once more, the fire flickering between us once again, though its flames did not burn.

My breath came in ragged gasps. "Please," I whispered, my voice trembling. "I see it now. I see what I've done. But it

was wartime, what can I do if it was war?"

The Golden Man, my Creator, stood silent, his face bathed in the glow of the fire. His eyes were full of something I had never seen before—an ancient sorrow, a wisdom so vast that it crushed me with its weight. He didn't need to speak for me to feel his disappointment, his pain. Yet there was grace in his stillness.

"How can you forgive me?" My voice cracked, tears filling my eyes. "After everything . . . how?"

His gaze softened, and he spoke with a gentleness that broke through the storm of guilt raging within me. "If you can forgive the invaders, forgive yourself and let go of this anger, of this darkness, then you shall find my forgiveness too."

The words hung in the air between us, heavy with truth.

Could I forgive myself for becoming the monster I feared? Could I ever let go of the rage that once consumed me?

Tears streamed down my face as I bowed my head. I had no answers. Not yet. But I knew the path forward would begin with those words—if.

But even as I wrestled with the thought, I could feel something else—something lighter, softer. I saw remnants of what this anger left in its wake. I saw a people with no hope and desolation. I saw my rogues wandering in the desert. My vision also flickered into the minds of those rogues who changed their ways and became a part of the people again. After hundreds of years of circling that desert, I finally wanted out.

The weight of my anger began to shift, slowly loosening its grip on me. The fire of the Golden Man's presence was not here to destroy me but to purify me, just as silver is purified in the kiln. Just as the fire that killed the Wendigo, it had made me stronger, this fire was refining me, cleansing me.

I took a deep breath and, with it, a final look at the memories that had haunted me for so long—the memories of blood, loss, and betrayal. And then, I let them go.

"I forgive and may their souls be blessed," I whispered through my tears, my voice trembling as I released the weight I had carried for so long. "I forgive, Creator." And in that moment, as the words passed my lips, something inside me broke free. Love—pure, boundless, and overwhelming—rushed into the space that had once been filled with anger. It cradled me, surrounded me, held me like the arms of a mother, like the protective embrace of a father.

"Let go of pride, arise now as a Holy warrior," the Golden Man whispered, his voice like the gentle rustle of leaves in the wind. I nodded, closing my eyes as I let that last vestige of myself fall away. I felt humility wash over me, a gentleness that was not mine but came from the Creator himself. The Golden Man, humble and kind, was as soft as a rabbit and yet stronger than anything I had ever known.

And then I saw his face—his beautiful, kind eyes. I understood. This was not a man before me. This truly was the Creator who created us all. I recognized his eyes like a child recognizes his father's eyes.

We stood together in the sacred fire, and I stood in its light, unburned and untouched. The pain was gone. The burns no longer hurt like when I first fell into it.

In a vision, I found myself standing on the desolate shores of the old mountain, watching the fire and lightning tear through its jagged peaks. The sky above was thick with storm clouds, and the earth beneath my feet trembled with the violence of the mountain's destruction. Flames licked at the air, devouring anything in their path, while bolts of lightning cracked through the sky, as if the heavens themselves were at war.

I turned my back to it and took my first steps forward, away from the chaos and toward the new mountain that rose on the horizon. It stood tall and holy, a sanctuary of life and light. Between the two mountains lay a vast valley, empty and desolate, a wasteland of shadows and sorrow. It stretched endlessly before me, a place where no life grew, where darkness clung to the earth like a curse.

But I was not afraid. The Golden Man was with me, his presence steady and guiding. His light showed me the way, illuminating each step as I crossed the valley, leaving behind the mountain of death and destruction. I could feel the weight of my old life lifting, the shadows retreating as I walked toward the sacred mountain, toward my new home, in a symbolic sense.

And I knew, without doubt, that I would reach it. I had been refined in the fire. I was no longer bound by the past. Now, I was ready to rise.

Sebastian

"My sole heir, I give you one final opportunity to forsake that wretched wolf woman and resume your duties as the Prince of Romania!" My father's voice thundered across the dimming fields, his figure stark against the twilight. His presence was distant yet overwhelming, piercing the veil of the spiritual tempest where Tecos and the Wendigo unleashed their ancient powers nearby.

"Abandon these imbeciles and join me. We shall rule the new world together. All is in readiness for our reign," he roared once more, his voice slicing through the chilly air like a knife. I stood resolute, my fangs bared, and my muscles tensed like a cobra poised to strike. His words, however tempting, were but echoes to my defiant spirit. He may be my father but I could never live without my Aiyana.

I knew better than to trust anything he said. All he ever sold me were dreams.

Suddenly, from the shadows, a silver sword spun through the twilight, glinting under the crescent moon. I caught it deftly, my eyes immediately drawn to a small vial of blood tied to the hilt. It was unmistakably his—a silent summons from a father who favored deeds over dialogue.

"Just take it and see," he whispered from the shadows, his voice a soft yet insidious invitation.

Cradling the vial between my fingers, I observed the dark blood within swirling as if possessed by its own malevolent spirit. It bubbled and surged forcefully, the cap bursting open as it spilled over the top of the vial into my palm. The scent was foul, an odorous bloom that spoke of deep corruption, as if it mirrored the decay of his very soul.

As the cacophony of the nearby battle crescendoed, voices seemed to whisper from the vial, a chorus of temptation: "Drink the blood." "Just taste it." "It's exquisite."

I recognized the Wendigo spirit nearby. It permeated the air around us. A trickster spirit Tecos had called it.

Raising my eyes, I saw my father had edged closer, his face a tapestry of anticipation and dark hope, waiting for me to yield. His blood promised enhanced strength, a tantalizing surge in vampiric power. Yet, as I felt my abilities stir within, thoughts of Aiyana and Magdalena anchored my resolve.

I did enjoy my powers as a Vampire. Yet I enjoyed the peace I received from not killing and spending time with my love and family even more. That was something he could never give me. I wasn't a fool.

"They make you weak, Sebastian!" he bellowed, his voice tinged with venom.

Our gazes locked, and in his eyes, I glimpsed the ancient power that roiled within him—but also an emptiness, a hollow void where joy should dwell. Once, as a child, I might have been a source of pride for him, a living testament to his power, paraded before other Vampires like a trophy. But it wasn't love he had for me, he simply loved what I brought to him. Ego.

What had twisted his heart so? Had he ever known simple happiness?

He roared and within seconds he was in his true form. He was dark and furry. An old and ancient connection to our bat spirit ancestors turned his true form into something Dracula himself would be proud of. He sent squeals and shrieks out, coordinating my exact location with echolocation. But I did not move. I stood still, awaiting the attack.

My true form was different from his. Stronger, the next generation and tweaked somehow by the elixirs I made and more importantly, my time in my old laboratory. He didn't know what I had done.

Long ago, when I was still a young fledgling, attempting to learn about our kind, I purposely electrocuted myself during a storm. I had built a silver and copper lightning rod onto the roof of my laboratory.

After calculating the exact amount of voltage I would receive as it channeled through various metals and alloys, I injected myself with the strange light. The aftermath was amazing. It had burned me, but not my insides. It passed over me and down into the ground. Only my skin seemed to have been affected. As a result, since then, my hair has grown only stark white, and my skin toughened up with a type of scar tissue, impermeable to needles or weapons. Vampires do not normally scar. The voltage had activated a dormant part of my Vampire DNA, changing me somehow while enhancing other vampiric traits. It was after this that my father, probably ashamed of how I looked, sent me away on the ship to "explore the new world" for him.

In a flash, he lunged, desperation fueling his advance as he aimed for my throat. Instantly, moments before impact, I transformed into my true form—a formidable, gargoyle-like bat, my skin hard as stone, impervious to any Vampire's bite. His teeth clashed against my armored body, one fang snapping off in a futile attempt to penetrate and the other crushed entirely into the sand below.

A smirk spread across my features as I examined his shocked expression. With a swift motion, I hurled the vial to the ground, watching it shatter. The soil of the castle grounds—rich with the dark legacy of our bloodline—hungrily absorbed the spilled blood below his feet. Once the earth, having tasted his power, ethereal bony arms reached up, craving his blood and grounded him like a haunted tree, snagging its prey in its roots. This haunted earth was trying to take him down into the ground with them.

Ah, my old haunted land. The scientist in me couldn't help but marvel at its miracles. The land where my ancestors had been buried and burned over countless millennia might hold secrets, perhaps even a cure for our cursed existence. I must remember to take some home with me to my laboratory.

I gave the bat a few rounds of my stone fists to help his descent into the void go by faster.

My father let out a giant squeak and then met my attack with shadow form. As he morphed into a giant shadow, his attacks became a frenzied blur, pounding against my gargoyle form. Shadow form is not a true form but a mixture of fast and repeated movements that are too fast for a mind to comprehend. The mind sees only rat-tails and a black blur.

Initially his attacks were harmless, then the light taps turned into a dizzying onslaught. The punches reverberated just enough within me like a drum causing a ruckus within my stone heart. Just as I felt my defenses might give way, a chorus of ethereal howls cut through the night.

The rogue and enslaved wolves had returned. They were also accompanied by Andy's wolves. Andy's wolves were different, larger and more fierce than earlier. They carried lightning in their eyes and a hunger for the hunt that sent shivers down my spine. I thought initially they were compelled by my father to do his bidding, so I braced myself for their descent. But to my surprise, the wolves were not after me. Prostrate and wounded, I could only watch as they descended upon him with otherworldly ferocity. His formidable powers were no match for their relentless assault. They were like a well-oiled machine with one simple command behind their actions. KILL.

"Wolves! Stop!" he commanded uselessly. "I command you!"

Only no actions came from the wolves in response to his commands, only grunts and growls as they pierced into him at every angle.

They tore into him, his true form dissolving under their wrathful maws, his cries lost in their savage symphony. As they dismantled him, I lay amidst the tumult, reflecting on the twisted dance of fate that had led us to this desolate end.

I must get to Aiyana now!

Andy

Regis, the coward. He still wore the furs from our lands, but his hair, once straight and long, was now cut short like a modern man. He reeked of Vampire and blood, freshly ingested. I sniffed the air as my wolf paced back and forth, unable to stay still due to the power of the lightning inside me making me restless. I could not attack him and risk Magdalena getting hurt, too. She was half Vampire. Her blood would ignite.

But I sensed she was still intact. It was not her blood I smelled on him, which pacified Ash just a tiny bit.

In the background, the eerie green glow of a spectral fire flickered in a large hearth. Beside the fire sat Aiyana, Magdalena's mother, bound in silver chains that glinted malevolently in the ghostly light. She was a shadow of her former self, barely lifting her head to acknowledge us. Her lips moved in a constant stream of incomprehensible mutterings, her spirit seemingly broken.

Magdalena—my beloved, my mate—had finally found her mother, but the reunion was twisted into a grim tableau.

Regis turned to me, a sneer twisting his features.

"I cursed that stupid Wendigo for letting you live until he explained why, " he said. I growled in the air. I did not want to hear his yapping, but I had to formulate a plan, so I let him speak.

“He wanted the Uktena's skin. Never was able to get it himself because of that stupid diamond,” he said in a looming voice as if his words held power.

“He had a vision. You would take the Uktena for its diamond, and he would have its skin, " he said.

“Well, now he’s dead,” I said in a low rumble, ready to leap and tear him apart if the situation allowed.

“Well, I didn’t care for him much, but now that I see how much that diamond has helped you, I know you’re going to give it to me. Or else I will feed this mixed bitch to her mother!" His words dripped with venom as he spat them out, his eyes gleaming with malice.

"You're one to call her mixed, Regis. You forsook your wolf for vampirism!" I sputtered, my voice filled with disgust.

Then, Ash's voice cut through the tension, saying something peculiar that made me pause. *He is wolfless, and from the smell of him, he was always wolfless. It is true what the owls said. Can't you smell it?*

I didn't want to waste another minute inspecting this despicable man, but curiosity compelled me to follow Ash's suggestion. I took one whiff, and the truth hit me like a punch to the gut.

"You killed my family because you were wolfless?" I said with even more disgust.

For a moment, Regis's eyes twinkled and shifted as if I had dealt him an ethereal blow. He seemed to waver, his bravado faltering. "Not everyone gets a wolf, you stupid boy. Yet I am no less a wolf in spirit!" His voice was defiant, but there was a crack in his façade.

"You are a coward!" I retorted, my voice ringing with conviction. "You rejected our ways, and that is the only reason your wolf never came to you." My words were sharp, cutting through the air as I spat on the ground, the disdain palpable in my every action.

And he is all Vampire. No wolf. Give him the diamond, Ash said

But Mags! I protested.

She knows what to do. Luz knows, too. They will be all right, Ash insisted.

The room seemed to hold its breath, the spectral fire casting flickering shadows on the walls. Aiyana's mutterings were a haunting backdrop to the confrontation, her suffering a silent testament to Regis's cruelty. The air was thick with tension, the weight of unspoken truths and ancient grievances hanging heavy between us.

You're crazy, I said to Ash. This was eerily similar to the vision I had experienced in the kiva—Ash was going to kill Mags. Why? Was this another attempt, like when he tried to kill the Fae seal?

What? Hell no! This is not the same! Trust me! Ash insisted, his eyes alight with a fierce intensity typical of his battle-ready demeanor. His focus reminded me of the moment right before he jumped through the Uktena and bit through its heart. I was not going to let him do that to Mags.

I had entrusted him with my life before, but this? I had seen this very scenario play out in my nightmares: Magdalena dying in my arms because of my actions. I couldn't let it happen.

Just then, a slight breeze whispered past, and I felt the presence of the owl spirit beside me. Tecos. Was he dead? Why was he here in spirit form? Only I could apparently see him as Regis ignored him. Tecos was a being of light, golden light and he stood before me as he spoke.

Trust your wolf, he mind-linked me, then vanished as quickly as he had appeared.

My wolf, dazed by the encounter, shook its big furry head.

Was that a deception from the Wendigo spirit who entrapped Aiyana, or was it truly Tecos? Did he fall in battle? My mind raced, but I couldn't delay any longer.

"Well?" asked Regis.

I looked at Mags, and she appeared calm. She still wore all the Vampire hunting clothes I had given her. I felt for sure she would go up in flames, but her peace calmed me. She nodded at me. She did have a plan.

"It's okay, Andy. Do what you must do. I don't want to lose you or my mother again," she said, and then I realized just how smart she was. I inched closer. Below her feet were the remnants of an old silver and copper lightning rod that had broken. Without making it obvious, I took a moment to inspect the room. This was her father's old laboratory. Ancient glass vials and flasks laid around, reminding me of his mansion back home. She must know something from one of her father's memories.

Trust me, she mouthed silently towards me.

"Any day now, Andrei! What will it be? Your mate or my diamond?" said the coward.

"Fine," I said, my head low in confusion and hesitation. Just then, I saw her mother stand, still shackled to the ground but with a hunger that appeared in her vacant eyes. Her wolf was growing weaker by the second, and the Wendigo spirit would take full force once her wolf was dead. It was frightful to behold.

NOW! yelled Ash into my mind.

Without hesitation, I shifted into my human form. Reaching inside myself, I withdrew the large, beautiful diamond that had granted me my power. It flickered with electricity and energy as I held it in one hand. As I reached my hand out towards Regis, a swift and small hand armed with a tiny silver dagger shadow-stepped faster than I could react and pierced the diamond with a small silver dagger.

The silver acted as a strong conductor, unleashing the power of the diamond throughout the entire castle in one swift, static motion. An explosion of full force erupted from the diamond, shooting out in all directions. The entire room lit up in a roar of electric blue and green flames, the intensity blinding and overwhelming.

At the moment of impact, the ghastly image of Aiyana had reached out with a mouth full of fangs and latched onto Magdalena's ribs. When the light subsided, the devastation became clear. Aiyana has been tossed to the corner of the room on impact. Regis had attempted to reach for the diamond before impact but was not fast enough as a new Vampire. He was dead, reduced to nothing but a pile of dust, scattered where he once stood. I retracted my hand with the diamond and placed it back inside me.

Magdalena's leather outfit had caught fire, but I quickly covered her with my body, smothering the flames. Amazingly, the leather acted as a buffer keeping her from being too badly burned. I carefully examined her, relieved to find she was still breathing. I carried her in my arms, the same way I had done when I brought her here.

Aiyana awoke with a start, her eyes wide with realization. The Wendigo spirit that had plagued her was gone. The silver lightning had burned off the remnants of its influence, and her inner wolf had shielded her from its full effects.

Though it appeared her wolf was dead, from what I could sense, Aiyana herself was alive and free from the curse that had bound her. Her eyes, now clear and determined, met mine.

Magdalena, however, remained unconscious. Her breathing was steady, but she showed no signs of waking. I gently cradled her in my arms, feeling the weight of the battle and the urgency to ensure her safety.

The room was a scene of chaos and transformation. The spectral fire in the hearth had dimmed, casting a softer, more natural light that illuminated the aftermath of our fierce confrontation. The air was thick with the smell of ozone and scorched earth, a testament to the raw power that had been unleashed.

"We need to get Magdalena out of here," I said, my voice steady but laced with urgency. "This place is too unstable."

Aiyana, now free from her chains, which lay broken and useless on the floor, nodded in agreement. "She'll recover," she assured me, her voice firm and resolute. "But we must leave now."

I carefully lifted Magdalena over my shoulder. Her body was limp, and her breathing was starting to slow. Aiyana stood beside me, her strength returning with every passing moment. Together, we made our way out of the castle, the echoes of our confrontation fading behind us.

As we stepped into the cool night air, the weight of the night's events settled upon us. The castle loomed behind us, a dark silhouette against the starry sky. The power of the diamond remained within me, a constant reminder of the responsibilities and challenges that lay ahead.

In my arms, my mate had suddenly stopped breathing and I could no longer hear her heartbeat. I fell down to my knees, still cradling her, and let out a long and lonely howl calling to my pack and whoever was still left alive. I needed help.

Mags was dead.

Chapter 12

The Medicine Wheel

Sebastian

"She's part Vampire," I said, observing the concern etched on Andy's face. "She is not dead yet. Like I said, you still have a lot to learn about our kind."

My words seemed to ignite a flicker of hope within him. He sniffed the air, trying to detect any sign of life, but there was none. I knew there would be none. She is undead.

"She was breathing just a second ago!" he yelled out.

He couldn't hear her heartbeat no matter how hard he tried but Ash, his wolf, came out and spoke to me as well. I had never met his wolf, but I knew by the deepened and crude vowel sounds that it was him. Andy was half-shifted and delirious with emotional pain, barely holding it together. I had to do something before he did anything rash.

"She's not really dead?" asked Ash. A wolf would normally be able to tell if someone was dead or not, so my words only confused him.

"Vampires aren't really living creatures. We are undead and she is my daughter. I know what she has undertaken. She is in the 'sleep,'" I said, but I couldn't be exactly sure. She was part wolf, too.

"Maybe if I give her my blood, it will sustain her during her sleep. She had never had the drink before," I said more to myself than anyone listening.

"She already had mine!" Andrei yelled out. Madness lurked in his eyes, and I knew I had to take her from him before he took us all out with his lightning.

"I can't feel her wolf," Ash responded, his voice tinged with uncertainty. Just then, Aiyana appeared behind him, and she very gently touched him on his mid-back. The touch was simple and soft, but I could see Andrei's breathing start to slow.

"Aiyana!" I said, reaching out for her, but she seemed different somehow, too—a shell of her former self. She waved me away, not wanting to touch me. The action stung me to the core, and I wondered if she would ever want me again after forcibly joining mate bonds with the Wendigo. And as much as it hurt me, I stepped back and gave her the space she needed.

Instead, with eyes averted, she quickly covered Magdalena in a material adorned with butterfly emblems and tassels that jingled a cheery tune. It was the skirt she was wearing the night she fled from me in the car, hoping to rescue her daughter from the Wendigo at the powwow.

Another Werewolf who stood beside her, one of Andy's pack, lent Aiyana cover by moving to stand in front of her with its wolf. Even though Aiyana was never shy with her body, the action was more protective in nature and not for mere modesty. What had happened to my beautiful Aiyana? Through tears, she spoke then, her voice trembling with maternal fear.

"Save her, Sebastian! Place her in the soil!" She then locked eyes with me for the first time, emphasizing her urgent demand.

I glanced around at the area Andy and Aiyana had come from and realized the earth was soaked in Vampire blood. A massive battle had just taken place here.

"Yes! You're right, my dear! Our lands are special to us," I said. "Soaked in all our blood, it heals us." My mother had always said so, but she never explained why or how. Looking at Carpathia now with fresh eyes, having been away for many years, it made sense now as to why.

I attempted to take Magdalena from Andy's arms but to no avail. He would not let her go.

"Go dig a kiva for her," I told Ash. Andy's wolf did not want to part with his mate. My impatience was becoming palpable. I saw his teeth begin to elongate, and a desperation hit his countenance.

"No," I said, knowing full well that he wanted to claim her bond. I knew he thought it would help her, but she wasn't ready. His eyes began to gloss over and the wolves from Andy's pack began to howl a sad and longing turn. Aiyana's skirt peeled back away from her chest, and there we saw Magdalena's chest and neck covered in golden dust that appeared to be some type of pollen. It stopped the beast in its tracks.

"Kiva?" he questioned as if he was unfamiliar with the term. It was Andy's expression and voice that answered.

“Yes, in the ground there, where her ancestors on my side lie. They will help mend her wounds.” Aiyana poked at him from behind and he finally let me take Magdalena from his arms.

Without hesitation, Andy selected a spot under an old tree. As they dug, the ground seemed to yield to them, recognizing the urgency and sanctity of their task. The earth felt alive, imbued with a magical essence that cradled her gently as they laid her down. Covering her, he anxiously stated, “Will she be okay buried like this? How will she breathe?”

“She will breathe when she decides to breathe,” I assured him, my voice steady with faith. I knew full well that oxygen was not needed during our sleep; in fact, oxygenation just made it worse. We had to remain in a state of complete deactivation.

Santana came forward. In both her hands, she carried earth that appeared to glow with a golden hue. Once she was in the makeshift kiva, she the tossed earth on top of Mags.

“This is the earth where we lost Tecos to the fire,” Santana muttered, visibly upset. “She is also a wolf, a family member to us. Our ancestors also rose from the ground and were given corn pollen to help them rise from it like a sprout.” The kachina dancers yipped around her, a unison of cries of both lamentation for the lost Tecos and a prayer of hope for the Creator above.

“His sacrifice will cleanse the death that is in this land, " she said, looking down at Mags as she slept.

I nodded at her in reverence. I carefully returned the earth to the hole that was dug and covered my dear, sweet daughter in both the earth and my blood tears.

Once she was entombed, the wolves and her mother cried and howled, summoning their ancestors for comfort. The other shifters, the kachina dancers, murmured prayers in each of their prospective languages. Even a weakened Torito began a solemn dance beside her grave. He had survived the onslaught of the Wendigo, but barely.

Andy lay next to the fresh mound, his body pressed against the earth that now enveloped her, vowing never to leave her side.

The night was filled with the mournful yet hopeful howls of the wolves and the rhythmic chants of the Kachinas. I could not bear to stand so close to Aiyana and be unable to console her, so I walked away to watch from a place I knew they could not see me and collapsed.

This was why I did not want to bring her here. Why didn't Galindo keep her home? With a stone hand that I had summoned from a partial shift, I smashed a large granite boulder in half. I had never felt as much of a failure in my whole life as I did now. Not only did I lose my wife. I may have lost my daughter as well.

I stood guard from afar, feeling the weight of the moment, knowing that this sacred ritual was a bridge between life and death, and hoping that Magdalena would find her way back to us through it all. I said a silent prayer to the Creator that my wife has always cherished. To be honest, I never thought he cared for me. He didn't make Aiyana my mate. He didn't give her to me. He probably hates me. But I prayed anyway, hoping that he'd hear the prayer of a Vampire.

Mags

Tonight, something profound shifted within the depths of my soul. I've always known I wasn't like others—far from it—but this transformation transcended the mere return of hidden memories or the shocking revelations about my parents' supernatural origins. It was more than realizing my own supernatural heritage. For the first time, I experienced an unshakeable calm, erasing the turbulent years of misdiagnosis as a bipolar teenager and replacing them with a profound serenity I had never known. I was loved. I was wanted.

From the beginning, I explored my life with true intentions this time, not just partially erased memories that never gave me the full picture.

My father. Though I had gained wisdom through his memories, it was not my life, but because I somehow fused with the memories, I explored those as well.

My father had lived for many years, studying the ways of vampirism and running from his fate. He approached his work like a mad scientist, absorbed and fully focused on his aim. To find a cure for vampirism, even if he didn't realize at first what he was doing. He had his parents all his life, but he went through the same feelings of being unloved as I did.

He was a trophy, made for showing off and for his younger years, the importance seemed to satisfy his need for connection. He had riches and a castle but devoid of emotional attachment.

Way before he even met my mother, he craved a normal life. He would spy on humans and watch them celebrate their yearly traditions. He saw children grow up and celebrate birthdays when his own family couldn't care less about his birthday. He was an aquarius, and very much like one if you ask me.

His own mother, my grandmother, was also a royal and distant cousin to my grandfather, Valerian. She did not show him love nor his father any love either. Their marriage was simply a contract. An attempt to raise both of their prestige in the Vampire realm by showing off their royalty and producing my father. A born Vampire. And it worked for many years.

Until it didn't, when my father abandoned his royal throne to explore the Americas. I felt his rebellion against a pragmatic system, and it mirrored my own as a goth punk living in a small desert town. I guess I got that fire from him.

After he left, my grandmother was ruthlessly killed by my grandfather for producing a "bad egg." Upon hearing the news, my father decided to take the life of the last remaining Vampires he had as an entourage. Determined to start over on a new land.

My father was a scientist and is still a scientist, and with his memories, I absorbed his knowledge as well. He had been working like Dr. Frankenstein with electricity and Vampire blood/flesh for many nights, conducting his experiments.

He figured out how our bodies made energy by a strange ADP loop that relied on two precious metallic ions, phosphorus and magnesium. And silver was a catalyst. Silver was also the perfect conductor for his lightning. Many nights, my father used a silver and copper lightning rod to explore its effects on his own Vampire blood. One night, he dared to use it on himself. And though he did not die, it changed him. More than he knew. It changed his true form, giving him a gargoyle skin impermeable to anything, even lightning. Perhaps that is why his skin reminded me of sharks. It was thick, even in human form. And I knew then, as his daughter, what that meant. I carried his changed DNA, and even though I did not have my true form, I had the instructions for one inside me.

Silver was a pure metal capable of cleansing the darkest tarnish from a soul. Even a Wendigo was susceptible to it, but so were wolves. Silver made Skin Shifters stronger but Werewolves weaker. Vampires and Werewolves were both shifters that didn't require leather. But I used the idea of my Vampire leather armor as a buffer. It was covered in the blood of my father's people. It was also covered in the salve my father had given to the vampire who initially owned it. That salve was a protective element and protected the vampire from extreme heat.

This coat had made me invincible to lightning, the thing that Andy's diamond created. The idea would not normally work if it weren't for my mother's DNA as well.

I knew my mother's wolf would defend her. Without question she would sacrifice herself for her. And in that split decision, Luz and I knew it was the only way to save her.

So I took her bite. It pierced my leathers, allowing the lightning to pass through her fangs and into her body, but I had faith the leathers would protect me like that of a Skin

Shifter.

Her wolf also carried the Thunderbird regalia. Not all Werewolves carried the activated gene, but many from her pack did. It was Luz who informed me of this after meeting my mother for the first time. The memory had returned to me just recently. My mother was a Werewolf, a medicine woman who lived a calm, normal life that called to my father when they first met. But during that harsh environment where she grew up, she was also a warrior.

My father had told me about her adventures of escaping the Wendigo through his memories. Told me about the other shifters she encountered and how she took many rogue lives. My father didn't start following her nightly until she had claimed her third victim. A large bear shifter who was trying to rape her along the waters of a river in the northern plains.

She had very large claws, and she half-shifted, tearing off his junk before stabbing and dislodging his eyeballs. If that bear survived, it wasn't for long. She had the thunderbird gene.

If both my parents could survive lightning then I was safe, I had thought to myself then. And I was right.

I'm still here, floating around in the darkness looking for a way out. Santana had told me I had to find the path that would lead me to the light. And after several failed attempts, I think I finally found the light.

It started as a tiny spot in the corner of the dark prison that held me. I kept my eyes on it, not wanting it to disappear. Sometimes, it would grow and then shrink back again. I had to stay focused on it and keep it near me.

I also thought about all the Native friends I'd made recently through the subtle guidance of my father. Though I loved all my friends, I felt most at home with them. I had heard them once speak on the concept of a two-spirit person—those carrying dual spirits, making them distinct yet equally revered. This idea resonated with me, yet not in the way that it did for them.

I literally had three spirits inside me! A wolf, a bat and me. If they only knew how my triple natures added up, they'd understand my struggles. Inside me, a relentless battle raged between my wolf and Vampire natures, each vying for dominion over my human side in a way that stretched beyond the two-spirit narratives. They didn't work together. In fact, they pulled apart from each other constantly like the same sides of a magnet.

I had seen Luz once, inside my head, portraying herself as what she'd look like as a Vampire/Werewolf unit. It wasn't pretty, and in fact, it frightened me. It reminded me of those paintings of Dante's Inferno, where body parts congealed into one, but in a gross and distorted manner. It was chaos in physical form.

Even before I fully grasped my true essence, I felt trapped in an unending conflict between opposing forces. I was always cocooned in layers of protection, fed half-truths about my identity, never allowed to explore the depth of my being. Trapped.

Yet, tonight, as I delved into the visions of my father's passionate memories, I glimpsed his Vampire nature in full force. I witnessed the sharpness of his mind and his rapid ascent in strength as he shed silver cuffs similar to mine, cuffs that had bound him as they had bound me, to come to war for their love.

His transformation was monumental, not merely a shift from human to Vampire but something as profound as the transition from human to wolf. I felt the echo of his thirst, a primal urge I understood as part of the natural cycle, akin to eating meat for survival, yet devoid of any desire to prey upon humans. The horrific visage of the Wendigo had quenched any lingering curiosity about indulging in blood.

Observing my father's near abstinence from blood after meeting my mother filled me with immense respect and love for him. He had chosen to halt the dance with death, to embrace life—a path that suddenly seemed possible for me as well.

My Vampire ancestors, their souls buried in the ground around me, did not know what to think about me. The blood in my native soil was healing the wounds of the Wendigo bite, yes, but I knew since the moment of being encased in here that I, too, would reject blood drinking as my father had. Instead, I let the blood absorb inside me, fuse with me and heal me in a type of osmosis like a blood transfusion.

Then, suddenly, my thoughts shifted into emotion. I felt my mother's love wash over me anew as I recalled her songs from my childhood, songs sung in adoration of the Creator. I had forgotten her songs, but thanks to my father, I had my memories back. At that moment, her essence enveloped me, a radiant holiness illuminating her, bringing tears to my eyes. Through her, I learned of the Creator—an artist, storyteller, savior, comforter, protector—imbuing us all with a spark of His creative spirit. The little light at the corner of the dark embrace started to grow.

Lying in a self-crafted cocoon, buried deep like a dormant seed in the dark soil, I felt a physical change pulsing through me. It urged me upward like a tree's first leaves and stems reaching up for the warmth of sunlight.

Andrei had once likened his wolf, Ash, to a phoenix rising from deep slumber when he reemerged. The Witch/ Wendigo had put Ash into a state of temporary suspended animation; he was, for all intents and purposes, dead until time had healed his soul. The situation mirrored the introspective state I now found myself in. And I, too, wanted to be reborn and have a new name, not like the elder

Vampires that crawled out of the ground to kill but like something beautiful emerging from a cocoon. What was it Santana had called me? A mariposa.

As Luz, my inner wolf, lay dormant alongside the hunger for blood, I heard the echoes of my ancestors mingling with my mother's gentle calls. Like my first steps, her voice beckoned me. Lulled me forward like the sun coaxes the rooster's crow or a flower's nectar invites the butterfly.

I was that butterfly, encased in a transformative cocoon, on the brink of a new existence. I sensed the imminent whisper of my Creator urging me forward, pushing me toward emergence and the light started to grow again with an inviting warmth.

With teeth that magically elongated and sharpened, I began to gnaw through my confines. As I broke through, fresh air kissed the damp skin of my fingers, and the rush of lifeblood invigorated me, forgetting parts of my being that had once been dead and lifeless.

Luz had told me it would work. I didn't know if I could follow suit until I saw the state my mother was in. She still recognized me, even as the Wendigo spirit took hold of her. It was then that all fear was gone from me and I knew I had to help her. The light grew even bigger. I was so close.

The sounds of music, singing, and celebratory cheers filtered down, drawing me further out of the darkness. Waves of joy, love, and gratitude surged within me, no longer just emotions but palpable presences, each a distinct entity within my soul. I was craving to leave this place, to abandon the darkness and enter the light.

My people were waiting for me up there, cheering for me. I could not hear Andrei, but I felt the mate bond pull me up towards him stronger than I had ever felt it. It broke me, or broke my stubbornness, making me forget who I was and what I was. I only needed to be with him. He was waiting for me, I could hear the bond say without words.

Struggling against the earthen barrier, I finally felt air on my face and pushed myself up. Then, unexpectedly, wings unfurled at my back. They fluttered, still damp yet rapidly drying. Hovering just above the ground, a mysterious force guided me through the air in all four cardinal directions in a twirl. My eyes were still closed, but I saw nothing but pure light. The little light grown so large, it had obliterated all the darkness.

This was my metamorphosis, not just of body but of spirit. As my eyes fluttered open, a majestic golden spirit appeared, chippering with joy at my transformation. He urged me to come forth and "Choose a form," the spirit said. Was he the Creator? Suddenly, as they had appeared, my wings vanished, and I was on all fours.

I had chosen—for me, for us, Andrei, my destined mate.

I locked eyes with Andy. As I stared into his longing eyes, I caught a glimpse of my new wolf form in their reflection. She was a large arctic wolf, with a black bed of wool supporting an outer layer of guard fur that was a shimmery silver. As I moved, the fur moved like waves in the ocean, and it caught the light of the moon in its depth, causing an ethereal glow, not unlike the wings of a butterfly, shimmering and bright.

"Butterfly Maiden," Andy whispered softly, a tender sound that felt like a caress. Upon hearing his voice, I shifted back to my human side. My father was quick to cover me with a shawl using shadow form quickness.

"Andy!" I gasped, inhaling and exhaling for the first time. I felt the solidity of the ground beneath me as I descended from the air, my eyes opening to a new world. We embraced under the tree, and though it was day, the sun didn't seem to bother me anymore. I searched around for my father, and there he was, under the shade of the tree, standing close.

"I knew you'd find your way back, my little Star." He then waved an empty bottle of one of his elixirs. I guess he had taken one of the remaining elixirs from his once abandoned laboratory—an elixir to protect him from the sun. I was happy about that and gave him a hug, too. I was glad he joined us.

My mother stood beside him with a look of sadness and shame. I knew it wasn't her fault that the Wendigo had gotten to her. I knew she was compelled to perform the mating bond with the monster, so it wasn't her fault. She had lost her wolf, and the empathy that came forward for her almost made me tumble into her, to protect her. I engulfed her scent in a long hug and to show her how much I loved her. Unfortunately, there was only one scent that I could smell—hers and not her wolf.

"It's not your fault," I said to her. She just waved the thought away. She didn't want me to apologize or feel sorry for her. I respected that.

"It's going to take some time for me to recover from what that monster made me do," she said, tears in the corner of her beautiful, large, acorn-shaped eyes. "The worst part is not just that I was forced to give the monster my sacred bond or wolf. It's that it corrupted me and made me . . ." And she couldn't complete her sentence. She rubbed the part of my ribs where she had once taken a bite from.

She leaned her head down on my chest. After that, her calm resolve left her.

"Can you ever forgive me, daughter? For leaving you as a child, for having strangers raise you, for . . ." Her words were broken and coming out between sobs, but I understood every word.

"Shh, it's ok, Momma." It was strange saying the word but as much as I needed to hear myself recognize my mother, she needed to hear it and recognize the love and respect in my tone that I had for her. I did not harbor any bad thoughts against her. In fact, she was the sole reason I was able to find the light and crawl out of the darkness. How did she not see this?

Just then, a man came walking towards us; he had a human form but appeared to be a being made out of pure golden light. It was the same spirit that had urged me to make a decision. As he walked closer, his form materialized, and I recognized him as the owl, my protector. The one they called Tecos. He was changed somehow. Just like I had changed but different. I heard Santana gasp in the background as she ran towards him, her jingle skirt alive with bells and music as she ran.

The wolves that were Andy's pack bowed to him as he passed them by in reverence. They shifted into human form. They were beautiful people. The Skin Shifters looked away, realizing they were naked, but the wolves didn't seem to mind their natural skin. They were innocent. The men and women alike and they seemed to understand that Andy was their alpha somehow. It was in their body language. Andy, too, held himself differently. Oh, how much did I miss being down in the ground?

I got an ethereal feeling from the way they looked at him. The way I looked at him, there was a silent impulse of authority that hung in the air and emanated off him that I had never witnessed until now.

The Skin Shifters gathered close to Tecos, the kachina dancers as I knew them, and they also nodded at him in approval. They removed their masks, and the few that were in their animal forms shifted back into their human forms just as the wolves had, except they were the only ones who remained fully dressed.

Torito was among them, clutching his side as if he had been injured and my eyes grew wide. What had happened to him?

Tecos paused and nodded to him in reverence, then looked back at me. He and Santana stood before us, a radiant and happy couple. I was going to have to ask Torito what happened to him later. It was then that Tecos spoke.

"Oh, so you finally picked a form, ay?" Tecos said in a happy voice. I only nodded back. I had no idea what to say. Once upon a time, he was my guardian, my owl kachina, and now he stood before me, a man of light. Wisdom still flowed through his eyes like that of the owl, but this time, he looked sharper, stronger and more confident. Was he even human at all now?

“What happened to you? We thought you had passed on with the Wendigo,” Andy asked, looking curious but also filled with a deep happiness for both of our safe return to the living.

“Oh no, I guess it’s not my time!” Tecos said. “I, too, have gotten my true form,” he said while nodding at Sebastian and me. “I am a true Elder now. Someone has to keep all of you guys in line!” His light faded, and I could hear a faint vibration shake over him as he shifted back into his normal human form.

“And you!” he motioned towards Andy. “You finally got your pack back. It’s about time. I didn’t realize I had to die first before you finally made it happen.” Then everyone, including the Werewolf people, started laughing.

Andy just laughed back and looked at the ground, slightly embarrassed at suddenly being the center of attention. I guess old rogue habits die hard. He probably wanted to go hide under a rock right about now. I tightened my grip on him. I didn't notice how cute his smile was when he was embarrassed. He was normally so serious.

Then Tecos got more serious and looked at both me and my mother.

He nodded sagely at us both. "You are a woman now, a young butterfly maiden. You are free to take your choice among the men and choose a mate." We all laughed except Andy and his once-happy smile curved into a frown again.

"Hey!" he said. Well, maybe all his expressions were cute.

"I've already chosen!" I said, seeing Andy's smile return as I looked at him.

"And you, Aiyana, medicine woman of the north, you should be proud of the work you did here. You came out strong like a warrior and took care of her the way she needed to be taken care of. We all make sacrifices for the greater good. The Creator sees that, and you will be blessed soon! Your wolf knows this. So don't dwell on the past," Tecos said, looking confident.

My mother nodded, echoing his wisdom in her eyes. I could tell by her sudden change of composure that she took his words to heart. Does this mean her wolf would be returning? Whatever it meant, it made her happy, and I couldn't wait for her blessing either. He was a golden being of light now. His words were like the words of the Creator. And I had a feeling she understood this even more than I did.

"Well, you are meant to choose an animal to bite," Tecos indicated to me, looking around for a suitable candidate. But my choice was clear—I had Andrei right beside me, his broad smile welcoming me to this new life.

"I've already got my animal!" I declared with a joyous laugh, shaking Andy's chest as if to show him off. Everyone cheered except Andy.

"Wait," Andy said as he took on his serious and stoic expression once again. He moved my hands away from him and placed them at my sides. Then, he reached into his pocket.

"What is it?" I asked, slightly concerned.

"This needs to be made official first, the way you expect and want it to be," he said with a coy smile as he knelt down on one knee while holding onto my hand.

The crowd around us erupted in cheers and awe, and I could feel a rush of blood flow to my face. Was he really doing this? And in public? I gasped. I wasn't expecting this at all. The guy who never even asked me if I wanted to be his mate or girlfriend, for that matter, was going to ask me to marry him?

"I had a lot of time to think about us while you were in your cocoon," he said while looking up at me. "In my mind, you were never an option. True, in the beginning, I tried to pretend that you were too different from me. But in actuality, I was too different for you, being banished and a rogue. I used to hunt your kind, your father's kind and I was too concerned with seeking vengeance for my people to think seriously about a mate. But I was wrong." He paused for a second before continuing.

"I wandered around like a rogue for centuries, wandered in circles, lost until I met the young punk girl in a black and red ribbon skirt whose very feral nature reminded me of my wild and uncharted homelands. You rode that bike in the middle of the night, alone, unafraid of everything, even me.

You made me want to be better," he said, looking up at me with a slight blush on his cheeks.

I smiled down at him, remembering the first night we met in the park. He was a rogue then with bright glowing red eyes. I remembered initially being scared of him but still yearning for his presence. I know now that was the mate pull. He was the one who started me on the journey to find out my true self, too.

"You make me stronger. You make me better and you give me a reason to keep doing so," he continued.

He looked like he was on the verge of tears and I had never seen him like that. I was the one always losing my shit—the emotional one. Today, we switched roles. I was thinking rationally and calmly and he was the one with waterfalls. I didn't know how long exactly I laid comatose in the ground, but judging by his emotions, it was probably a little too long.

"So that being said, you were never an option. You are my mate. My true mate. My other half. There is no way I can make it more official than to mark you. I have been waiting for this moment for a long time now. So, in true fashion, I'd like to offer you a piece of myself. A true diamond unlike any other. If it weren't for you, I never would have found it."

Everyone gasped at this moment.

"Wait," I said. Was he giving me the Uktena diamond? That was his. He earned it, not me.

"You are my diamond. My dark diamond and I could never . . ." He then opened the jewelry box in his hands and brought out a large black diamond engagement ring, encased in a silver looking band. Had he carried this with him the whole time?!

"It's platinum," he said to my relief. "I find bending this metal easier and more enjoyable than silver. I found this diamond the night I went searching for new silver for you. It was rough and undefined, like myself. You made it shine, gave it potential. Just like you did for me," he said, holding it out for me to see.

"Oh!" Then we all laughed as I swatted him jokingly. "I thought you were giving me the Uktena diamond. I don't want that; I've already shocked myself with it once!" The guests and everyone around us laughed and some of them breathed after having held their breath for so long.

"Well, once we join in our mate bond, you will get half of that diamond, too." He slipped the ring on my finger. "Whether you want it or not, so you better learn how to ride that lightning." He said with a wicked little smile. My face flushed even more than his and I was starting to get visuals in my head of what lay ahead.

"U'hem!" Sebastian cleared his throat in the background and Andy quickly wiped the grin off his face and got serious again.

"So, do you accept me, Magdalena?" he asked, looking up at me with his beautiful brown/hazel eyes that hinted at gold undertones. His dark hair flowed in the slight breeze.

"Yes," was all I could mutter. I was starting to feel the emotional lump in my throat start to form, and I couldn't say anything else.

Then I witnessed Andy go on all fours as if in preparation to shift. I could see the lightning in his eyes start to stir, and soon, lightning was in the air, booming as a backdrop among the Carpathian mountains.

"Now we run!" Tecos bellowed, his voice thundering through the stillness, shattering the serene moment like a storm breaking over calm waters. His command wasn't just words; it was a spark, igniting a flame that roared to life within each of us. "Run, discard the old, and step boldly into the new. Lead the way, Magdalena! Go and find your place!"

In an instant, as if his very voice had summoned the change, we transformed. One by one, we shed our human skins and shifted into our true forms. A wild surge of energy coursed through my veins, and without hesitation, I led the charge.

I raced through the rat tails of the Carpathian mountains which is considered east, raced until I found myself eventually running in all directions. To the north where Siberia and the wolves from the Thunderpack were. Then, to my mother's ancient home in lands now called Canada. I continued running in wolf form to the south, where cousins of my Vampire nature greeted us as we "flew on by" the pyramids. I did not own a compass, nor did I need a map. I ran to where my wolf took me. And my family followed me.

Lastly, we came home to the Western United States.

My paws hit the familiar earth of the desert, the Shadowlands—a place I had known all my life as home. The moon cast silver beams across the sands as we raced toward it.

It was bittersweet. A knot twisted deep in my chest, an unsettling premonition. This might be one of the last times we ran through these lands as shadows. The wind carried whispers of change, and I felt it everywhere. New warriors were awakening, rising from their slumber, and with them, new monsters were stirring. The old balance was shifting, and I could feel the weight of it pressing down on my shoulders.

I stopped short, my breath catching as I came upon the house Andy had built for us. Nestled at the base of the mountains between the valley and San Diego, it was a refuge, a sanctuary. The Cottonwood trees swayed in the breeze, and the lake nearby, Lake Morena, shimmered in the moonlight. The manzanita shrubs and trees soothed my soul, even in this moment of uncertainty. There was a magic here I could not pinpoint. Andy did well in choosing this area for our home.

Here, in front of our new home, we would continue the ceremony. The air was thick with purpose, every movement carrying the weight of what was to come. The future was unclear, but I knew one thing: we would not remain in the shadows much longer.

Amidst the rumbling crescendo of thunder, Luz my wolf came forward first to greet Ash with a deliberate and reverent touch. Two spectral wolves meeting outside of our bodies for the first time. Though Luz and I were one, my spirit stayed back in our body and witnessed as the two spectral wolves greeted one another with sniffs and casual ethereal licks. The air was electric, charged with the raw energy of the storm, mirroring the intensity of the moment.

Ash's gaze was unwavering, his eyes reflecting the flickering lightning above as he reciprocated the gesture, his hands steady and sure. Then, the two ethereal wolves moved back into the furrows of our mind and made way for us to continue the ceremony.

Andy leaned forward then and marked me, cutting open the delicate piece of skin above my chest, over my heart, with his sharp canines. He was gentle yet firm and a feeling of surrender came rushing over me. The sensation was profound, as if the very essence of our souls intertwined, forging an unbreakable connection. He then began to lap at the wound and I felt it close almost instantly, healed and now unbreakable.

It was my turn now. I leaned forward, with love and adoration guiding me. I nipped at his chest and felt him surrender his soul to me. I felt the power of the diamond surge through me, and it lit up my eyes the moment he surrendered. Then, slowly, the hum of the electricity started to pacify as the exchange of energy and spirit was complete.

For a second, I wondered if my Vampire nature was still within me. When I tasted his blood, it gave off a similar type of passion, but it gave me none of the same type of hunger. I didn't feel famished and desperate for more. In fact, my cup was so full it felt like it was gushing over.

The sacred bond was sealed, a powerful fusion of our spirit. Just then, a white canopy of pollen started to fall from the sky, carried by the wind all around us.

We all looked around, and it appeared that the trees and wildflowers were rejoicing with us, blessing us with their gifts of life and power. Soon, it appeared as if it was snowing in August! But it was not snow. It was white pollen. Or perhaps a type of mana from the heavens? I could not understand it, nor did I try. August was not typically a time when plants sent off pollen.

Soon, we were all covered in white and yellow pollen. I and the other wolves who had shifted back into humans were no longer naked but enshrouded in nature's clothing.

It was a blessing and I was thankful.

The ceremony had reached its climax, and a palpable wave of emotion swept over the gathered assembly. I looked at the wolves—Andy's wolves—and they bowed their heads to me in reverence, a curious gesture.

They are bowing at their Luna, Andy mind-linked me. And I looked back at him shocked because I had forgotten learning about that trick. A smile swept across my face. I loved the idea of being able to speak to him anytime I wanted. But a Luna? I wouldn't know what to do, or what that even meant.

Oh, don't worry, little Butterfly, you've got me to help you, said Tecos. My eyes opened wide.

Tecos! You can mind-link us? I answered back.

And don't forget about me! Santana filled in.

Or any of the rest of our pack and allies, Andy said. *Don't worry; you can shut them out temporarily if it becomes too much. Just will us out. Imagine a door closing.*

I scoffed. "Well, okay!" I said, accepting them as my pack and allies.

"I have a feeling this little tribe of ours is going to suddenly get a lot larger soon!" announced Tecos meeting eyes with my mother and father. "And I don't just mean babies!" he said with a giggle. Then he suddenly looked at Santana as if he forgot she was standing right next to him. "Ok, maybe a few babies," he added. Oh, could the moment be even cuter?

In unison, they raised their voices, calling out in the unique sounds of their animal spirits—a symphony of howls, roars, chirps, and growls filled the air. The resonance of these primal calls was a testament to the communal joy and acceptance of our union.

It felt as though the entire universe was rejoicing with us, the natural world acknowledging and celebrating the new life we had embraced.

As the fog began to cumulate from all the ozone in the air, it moved like a spirit around each and every one of us. It drenched our skin, cementing the pollen even more onto it. Tecos stood there, his staff of eagle feathers and leather slowly fanning the fog within our circle.

He fanned the fog and the pollen around me and soon, like a fairytale, it seemed a type of long white dress was being formed and glued onto me, created by nature itself. I was covered and adorned with pollen, plant fibers, seeds and small leaves. I felt like a goddess.

"Now that you are a woman, you have been graced with blessings. You are free to hand out those blessings at your leisure." Said the beautiful Santana who stood beside Tecos.

The ground beneath our feet seemed to pulse with life, the earth itself resonating with the powerful energy of the bond we had forged. In that sacred moment, under a mixed canopy of fog and pollen, the ending rays of sunlight permeated the remaining fog, causing light crystals and rainbows to form between us. Something was lifted from me spiritually, like a curse had been lifted, and the earth was bending its will to us in homage.

Surrounded by the calls of our spirit kin, I felt an overwhelming sense of belonging and purpose, as if I had finally found my true place, with my family and friends, in the world.